Reaper's Property

Joanna Wylde

ELLORA'S CAVE
ROMANTICA®
ELLORASCAVE.COM

An Ellora's Cave Publication

www.ellorascave.com

Reaper's Property

ISBN 9781419970290
ALL RIGHTS RESERVED.
Reaper's Property Copyright © 2013 Joanna Wylde
Edited by Raelene Gorlinsky.
Cover design by Syneca.
Cover photography by Konstantynov/Shutterstock.com.

Electronic book publication January 2013
Trade paperback publication 2013

Dedication

ɷ

I want to express my appreciation to Raelene Gorlinsky, the editor and publisher who wouldn't give up on me, and my test readers, Mary and Alicia. Thanks also to my husband who is endlessly supportive of all my creative efforts. Finally, a special thanks to my first editor, Martha Punches, who has continually encouraged me to keep writing even though I took so many years off. Martha, you were right about past progressive tense verbs, and I was wrong...

Chapter One
Eastern Washington, Yakima Valley
Sept. 17 — Present Day

∞

Marie

Crap, there were bikes outside the trailer.

Three Harleys and a big maroon truck I didn't recognize.

Good thing I'd stopped by the grocery store on the way home. It had already been a long day and the last thing I wanted to do was to run out and buy even more food, but the guys always wanted to eat. Jeff hadn't given me any extra beer money and I didn't want to ask him—not with his money troubles. It wasn't like I paid rent. For a guy whose entire mission in life was to smoke pot and play video games, my brother Jeff had done a lot for me over the past three months. I owed him and I knew it.

I'd already grabbed some beer and ground beef that'd been on sale. I'd planned on burgers, buns and chips for the two of us, but I always made extra, for leftovers. Gabby had given me a watermelon she'd picked up in Hermiston that weekend. I even had a big potato salad all made up for the potluck after work tomorrow. I'd have to stay up late making another one but I could handle that.

I smiled, thankful something in my life was going right. Less than a minute to plan and I'd figured out a meal—might not be gourmet, but it wouldn't embarrass Jeff either.

I pulled up next to the bikes, careful to leave them plenty of room. I'd been terrified of the Reapers the first time they'd come over. Anyone would be. They looked like criminals, all tattooed and wearing black leather vests covered in patches. They cussed and drank and could be rude and demanding, but they'd never stolen or broken anything. Jeff had warned me about them lots of times but he also considered them friends. I'd decided he was exaggerating about the danger, for the most part. I mean Horse was dangerous enough, but not because of any criminal activity...

Anyway, I think Jeff did some web design for them or something. Some kind of business. Why a motorcycle club needed a website I had no idea, and the one time I'd asked him about it he told me not to ask.

Then he'd scuttled off to the casino for two days.

I got out of the car and went around back to grab the groceries, almost scared to see whether Horse's bike was in the lineup. I wanted to see him so bad it hurt but wasn't sure what I'd say if I did. It's not like he'd answered my text messages. But I couldn't help myself, I had to check for him, so I grabbed my groceries and walked over to the bikes to scope them out before going inside.

I don't know much about bikes, but I knew enough to recognize his. It's big and sleek and black. Not all bright and decorated the way you sometimes see bikes on the freeway. Just big and fast, with giant, fat tailpipes off the back and more testosterone than should be legal.

The motorcycle was almost as beautiful as the man who rode it. Almost.

My heart stopped when I saw that bike, right on the end. I wanted to touch it, see if the leather of the seat was as smooth as I remembered, but I wasn't stupid enough to do that. I didn't have the right. I really shouldn't even be excited to see him, but I felt a rush knowing he was right inside my trailer. Things weren't smooth between us and I honestly didn't know if he'd even acknowledge me. For a while he'd seemed almost like my boyfriend. The last time I'd seen him, he'd scared the crap out of me.

Even scary, the man made my panties wet.

Tall, built, with shoulder-length hair he kept pulled back in a ponytail, and thick black stubble on his face. Stark, tribal cuffs ringed his wrists and upper arms. And what a face... Horse was handsome, like movie star handsome. I'd bet he had women coming out his ears, and the fact that he'd spent more than one night in my bed made me all too aware that his beauty wasn't just above the belt. The thought of his below-belt assets led to a brief but intense fantasy about him, me, my bed and some chocolate syrup.

Yum.

Shit. Dessert. I needed dessert for tonight. Horse loved sweets. Were there any chocolate chips? I could do cookies, so long as there was enough butter. *Please don't let him be pissed at me,* I prayed silently, even though I was pretty sure God wasn't interested in prayers where the promise of fornication played such a prominent role. I reached the door and juggled the bags, sliding most of them onto my right arm so I could turn the handle. I walked in and looked around the living room.

Then I screamed.

My baby brother knelt in the center of the room, beaten raw and dripping blood all over the carpet. Four men wearing Reapers' cuts stood around him. Picnic, Horse and two I didn't know—a big, built hunk of a man with a mohawk, tattoos on his skull and about a thousand piercings, and another who was tall and cut, with light-blond hair in short spikes. Horse studied me with the same cool, almost blank expression he wore when we first met. Detached.

Picnic studied me too. He was tall with short, dark hair that looked far too stylish to be on a biker and bright blue eyes that pierced right through a girl—I'd met him at least five times. He was the club president. He had a great sense of humor, carried pictures of his two teenage girls to flash whenever he got the slightest opportunity and had helped me shuck corn the last time he'd come to visit.

Oh, and he also stood right behind my brother with a gun pointed at the back of his head.

June 16 — Twelve weeks earlier

"Marie, you did the right thing," Jeff said, holding an ice pack to my cheek. "That cocksucker deserves to die. You will never, ever regret leaving him."

"I know," I replied, miserable. He was right—why hadn't I left Gary earlier? We'd been high school sweethearts, married at nineteen and by the time I hit twenty I already knew I'd made a terrible mistake. It took until now, five years later, to realize just how terrible.

Today he'd backhanded me right across the face.

After that, it only took another ten minutes to do what I hadn't managed in all our time together. I threw my clothes in my suitcase and left his abusive, cheating ass.

"I'm kind of glad he did it," I said, looking down at the scarred formica table in my mom's trailer. She was taking a little vacation at the moment in jail. Mom's life is complicated.

"What the fuck, Marie?" Jeff asked, shaking his head. "You're fucked in the head, talking like that."

My brother loved me, but he wasn't exactly a poet. I offered him a wan smile.

"I stayed with him for way too long, just taking it. I think I might have stayed forever. But when he hit me, it's like it woke me up. I went from being terrified of leaving to just not caring anymore. Honestly, I don't care, Jeff. He can keep everything—the furniture, the stereo, all that shit. I'm just glad to get out."

"Well, you can stay here as long as you need to," he said, gesturing around the singlewide. It was small and dank and smelled kind of like pot and dirty laundry, but I felt safe here. This had been my home for most of my life, and while it might not have been a picture-perfect childhood, it hadn't been too bad for a couple of white-trash kids whose dad took off before they hit grade school.

Well, good until Mom blew out her back and started drinking. Things went downhill after that. I looked around the singlewide, trying to think. How was this going to work?

"I don't have any money," I said. "I can't pay you rent. Not until I get a job. Gary never put my name on the bank account."

"What the fuck, Marie? Rent?" Jeff asked again, shaking his head. "This is your house too. I mean, it's a shithole, but it's *our* shithole. You don't pay rent here."

I smiled at him, a real smile this time. Jeff might be a stoner who spent ninety percent of his life playing video games, but he had a heart. Suddenly I felt such incredible love for him that I couldn't keep it in. I dropped the ice and launched myself at him, giving him a fierce hug. He wrapped his arms around me awkwardly, returning it even though I could tell it confused and frightened him a little.

We've never been a touchy-feely kind of family.

"I love you, Jeff," I said.

"Um, yeah," he muttered, pulling away from me nervously, but he wore a little smile. He walked over to the counter, opened a drawer and pulled out a little glass pipe and a baggie of weed.

"You want some?" he asked. Yup, Jeff loved me. He didn't share with just anyone. I laughed and shook my head.

"Pass. I've gotta start job hunting tomorrow morning. Don't want to flunk a drug test."

He shrugged and walked into the living room—which was also the dining room, the entryway and the hallway—to sit on the couch. A second later his ginormous big-screen TV flickered to life. He clicked through the channels until he hit wrestling, not the sport but the kind where they wear funny costumes and it's like a soap opera. Gary was probably watching the same thing back at our house. Jeff took a couple hits and then set down the pipe and his favorite death's-head Zippo on the coffee table. Then he grabbed his laptop and flipped it open.

I grinned.

Jeff'd always been the shit when it came to computers. I had no idea what he did to earn money — although I suspected he did as little of it as he could get away with and not starve. Most people, Gary included, thought he was a loser. Maybe he was. But I didn't care, because whenever I'd needed him, he'd been there for me. *And I'll always be here for him,* I promised myself. Starting by getting the place cleaned up and buying some real food. So far as I could tell, the man lived on pizza, Cheetos and peanut butter.

Some things never changed.

It took a lot of work to get the trailer clean but I enjoyed every minute of it. I missed Mom, of course, but I have to admit (if only to myself) that the place was a lot more comfortable without her around. She's a terrible cook, she keeps the shades closed and she never flushes the toilet.

Oh, and everything she touches turns to utter chaos and drama.

Jeff doesn't flush the toilet either, but for some reason it didn't bother me as much. Probably because he'd not only given me the bigger bedroom, he'd also shoved a surprisingly large wad of bills into my purse that first morning and kissed me on the forehead for luck when I went out job hunting. I needed to find work despite sporting a nasty bruise on my face from Gary's little love tap.

"You're gonna kick ass, sis," Jeff said, rubbing his eyes. I was touched he'd gotten out of bed to see me off. He wasn't exactly a morning person. "Buy me some beer on the way home? And some of those coffee filter thingies... I ran out, and now I'm outta paper towels too. I don't know if TP will cut it and I need my caffeine."

I winced.

"I'll take care of the shopping," I said quickly. "And the cooking," I added, glancing toward the kitchen sink, which was piled high with dishes. And pots. And something green that might just hold the cure for cancer...

"Great," he muttered, then turned and stumbled back toward his room.

Now it was two weeks later and things were looking up. For one, I'd made enough progress in the house that I wasn't afraid to sit on the toilet any longer, or use the shower. My next project was the yard, which hadn't been mowed in at least two years. I'd also gotten a job at the Little Britches Daycare, which was run by my old friend Cara's mom, Denise. Cara and I had fallen out of touch when she'd gone to college, but I'd seen her mom around occasionally and always asked after her. Cara'd worked her way through law school and had a job in New York at some hot-shit firm. Her mom showed me pictures sometimes and Cara looked like a TV lawyer to me, all designer suits and fancy shoes.

Not me though. I'd had grades as good as hers, but I'd been in looooove with Gary, so I blew off college. Great thinking.

Anyway, Denise asked cautiously if I was still with Gary, eyeing the foundation I'd spackled over my bruise. I told her about my new living arrangements and that was that.

So I had a job now and while it didn't pay much, I liked working with the kids and had even started doing some babysitting in the evenings for different families who brought their children to Little Britches during the day. Jeff loved having me around because I cooked and cleaned and did the laundry. I'd done all that for Gary too, but he never said thanks.

Nope, he just bitched about how I'd done it wrong.

Then he'd gone off and fucked his whore.

I got off work at three that day, so I came home and made bread. Over the years I've perfected my technique—I start with a basic French bread recipe, but I add a ton of garlic, Italian herbs, five different kinds of cheeses and an egg-white glaze. The recipe makes two big loaves and I planned to serve it with spaghetti topped with fresh tomatoes from Denise's garden and my signature spinach salad. Of course we couldn't even come close to eating that much bread, but I planned to take the second loaf to work tomorrow for the girls.

Denise had a huge garden behind the center, and she'd told me to help myself. I planned to take advantage of it as much as I could before the season turned. I had this fantasy that I'd do some canning but it probably wasn't realistic. I'd left all my equipment at Gary's place, and I wasn't ready to go back there. He hadn't gotten in touch with me since I left (which made me happy), and I'd heard around town that he'd already moved Misty Carpenter into our bed (which made me want to puke).

I liked to think of Misty as THE WHORE, which I wrote in all caps for all emphasis whenever I texted someone.

I set the bread out to rise on a tray on our old picnic table outside and decided to get going on the weeds around the porch. It was hot, so I popped on a bikini top (which I must say, I filled out nicely, despite my smallish cup size). I grabbed some old work gloves I'd found in the shed and poured myself some iced tea, rolling down the windows on my car so could I blast the radio. Then I set out to commit some serious acts of violence against all weed-kind.

Half an hour later the weeds seemed to be winning so I decided to take a break. I climbed up on top of the picnic table, resting my feet on the bench seat on one side and lying back with my arms over my head, dangling off the far side. It felt fantastic to be so relaxed and free in my own yard without a care in the world.

Naturally, that's when all the bikers showed up.

I heard them coming, of course, although not as early as you'd think—I had the music cranked pretty high. I didn't realize we had company until they were about halfway down our long driveway, which wound through our landlord's orchard. I sat up and leaned back on my hands as they pulled closer, dumbfounded. Usually I liked the fact that we lived in the middle of nowhere without neighbors. Now I felt very alone.

Who were these guys?

It didn't occur to me that I was glistening with sweat and wearing a bikini top until they turned off the bikes, pulled off their helmets and turned to scope me out. To make my own personal cliché perfect, Def Leppard's *Pour Some Sugar on Me* blasted through the radio. I winced—I must look like a white-trash princess from hell, basking outside my trailer in a bikini to outdated butt rock. I actually felt their eyes crawling over me, and while all three seemed to appreciate the view, it was the one in the middle who really caught my attention. The man was big. I don't just mean tall (which he was—he had to be nearly six and a half feet compared to my petite five foot four) but large. Broad shoulders, muscular arms with tattooed tribal cuffs around his wrists and biceps. I'd bet I couldn't put my two hands around those arms, and thick thighs I wanted to squeeze...and maybe lick.

He got off his bike and walked toward me, eyes holding mine hostage. I felt a startling flush of warmth between my legs. I'd gone a long time without feeling sexual at all, to be honest. The last few years with Gary had been frustrating at best and painful at worst. But something about the way this biker swaggered, taking up space and the very air around him with his presence, caught me off guard and knocked me right in the...

Well, you know.

My nipples hardened and I swayed a little as he stopped, reaching out with one finger to trace my collarbone from my shoulder inward, then running it down between my breasts, grazing the sides. He raised it to his mouth, tasting my sweat. He smelled like motor oil and sex.

Holy shit.

"Hey, sweet butt," he said. That broke the spell. Sweet butt? What the hell kind of guy called a girl he'd never met something like that? "Your man here? We need to talk."

I scrambled backward off the table, away from him, nearly falling off in the process. The music stopped abruptly, and I glanced away from him to see that one of his buddies had reached into my car and pulled out my car keys. He put them in his pocket. *Uh oh.*

"You mean Jeff? He's in town," I replied, trying to compose myself. Shit, should I have admitted I was alone? I really didn't have a choice. I mean, I could have said I needed to go get Jeff from inside and then locked the door, but the trailer was thirty years old. The deadbolt had been rusted shut since I was a kid. Not to mention that they had my keys. "Why don't you wait out here while I call him?"

The big man studied me, his face cold and expressionless. I couldn't be entirely sure he was human, I decided. More like a Terminator. Unwilling to hold his gaze, I let my eyes drop to his vest. Beat to hell, black leather, lots of patches. One of them caught my attention in particular, a bright red diamond that had a number one with a percent sign next to it. I didn't know what it meant, but I was pretty sure I wanted to get into the house and put on some more clothing.

Maybe a burkha.

"Sure thing, babe," he said, straddling the table's bench and taking a seat. His friends sauntered over to join him.

"How about a drink, girl?" one of them asked, a tall man with short dark hair and startling blue eyes. I nodded and walked quickly toward the trailer, using every bit of my self-control not to break into a run. I heard them laughing behind me. Not a friendly laugh.

Thankfully, Jeff actually answered his phone on the first try.

"There are some guys here to see you," I said, peeking out through the kitchen window, careful to keep the faded curtains decorated with pictures of little flying vegetables closed. "They're bikers. I think they might be dangerous. They look like murderers to me, but I'd like to think I'm crazy on this one. Tell me I'm being paranoid, please."

"Fuck..." Jeff replied. "That's the Reapers MC, Marie, and they don't fuck around. Do what they say, but don't get too close to them. Whatever you do, don't touch them or talk to them unless they talk to you first. Don't even look at them. Just stay the hell out of their way. I'll be home in twenty minutes."

"What's an MC?"

"Motorcycle club. Stay calm, okay?"

Jeff hung up on me.

Now I was really scared. I'd expected him to laugh at me and tell me they were just harmless guys who liked to ride their bikes and play badass. I guess this was the real thing. I ran into my room and pulled on a baggy t-shirt I liked to sleep in. I dropped my shorts and put on a pair of capris, pulling my long, dark-brown hair back into a messy bun. A quick look in the mirror was enough to convince me that I was worrying too much — they might have been crude and suggestive toward me, but I was no man's dream girl. I had dirt smudges on my face, my nose had burned bright red and I'd somehow gotten a giant scratch across my cheek. It contrasted nicely with the fading yellow and purple of the bruise Gary'd given me.

My hands trembled as I poured three big plastic tumblers of iced tea, wondering if I should put sugar in them. I decided to bring some sugar in a cup and stuck a spoon in it. Then I wedged two of the tumblers between my right arm and my torso, grabbing the third with my hand. I snagged the sugar with my left and managed to get through the door with some careful maneuvering. They were talking to each other in low voices when I came out, watching me as I walked to the table. I pasted a bright smile on my face, just like I used to wear when I waitressed back in high school. I could do this.

"You call your man?" the big one asked. I glanced at him, forgetting I was supposed to avoid his gaze because his eyes were so deep and rich and green.

"My man?" I asked.

"Jensen."

Shit, I forgot about that. They thought I was Jeff's girlfriend. Should I tell them? I couldn't decide. I studied the biker, trying to figure out the safest answer. He met my gaze without giving anything away. His hair was pulled back in a rough ponytail and his chin was covered with thick, dark stubble. My stupid body came alert again as I wondered what that stubble would feel like if I rubbed my lips against it slowly.

Probably pretty damned good.

"Girlie, answer the fuckin' question," said the blue-eyed man. I jumped, splashing some of the tea against the front of my shirt. It drenched my right boob, of course, and my nipple came to instant attention when the icy drink hit it. The big guy's eyes followed it, his eyes darkening.

"Jeff's coming," I said, managing not to stutter. "He said he'd be here in twenty minutes. I've got tea for you," I added inanely. Big Guy reached out and took the cup from my hand. That left me in a bind because I couldn't unload the other two glasses without my other hand free. I could either give him the sugar or I could lean past him and put it on the table. I was pretty sure I didn't want to do that.

He solved the problem for me, reaching out again and wrapping his fingers around one of the cups I held clasped against my body. I felt all sorts of tingles as they slid between the cold plastic and my skin, standing frozen as he repeated the gesture. Then he took the sugar. He caught my hand and pulled me up against his thigh, until my stomach almost touched his face.

I couldn't breathe.

He reached up to take my chin, turning my face so he could study the bruise. I held my breath, willing him not to ask me about it. He didn't. Instead, he dropped his hand to my waist, rubbing down and up slowly along the curve of my hip. It took everything I had not to lean in and push my breasts into his face.

"Jensen do that to you?"

Dammit. I had to tell them, I couldn't let it look like Jeff hurt me. He didn't deserve that.

"No, he'd never do that. Jeff's my brother," I said quickly, jerking away, blushing. Then I turned and ran into the house.

They sat at the table drinking their tea and talking until Jeff got home. It felt like he took hours, even though he made it in record time. At one point the big guy reached over and peeked under the towel covering the bread dough, which was in danger of rising way too high if I didn't get it into the oven soon.

Crap.

I wasn't going out there though. Not until they were gone.

Unfortunately, they didn't seem to be in the mood to leave. When Jeff rolled up in his aging Firebird they all stood around and talked for a while. Then they got up and walked toward our front door. Big Guy glanced toward my window and even though I knew he couldn't possibly see me, his eyes seemed to lock on mine.

As they came inside, Jeff was smiling and looking relaxed. The others were too. Everything was friendly and I frowned, wondering if I'd imagined just how serious he'd been with me on the phone.

"Sis, my associates are going to stay for dinner," he announced grandly. "You better go get your bread, I think it's done rising. You guys are gonna love this, Marie's bread is amazing. She'll fix you a fuckin' great dinner."

I smiled at him a little shakily, cussing him out in my head. What the hell? Sure, I cooked for him, but I didn't want to cook for this group. They scared me, which combined oddly with my disobedient body's desire to jump Big Guy's bones. I couldn't think of a way out of it though, not without breaking our little pretense that there was nothing weird about three scary biker dudes showing up out of nowhere.

Not only that, the bread would be ruined if I didn't cook it soon. I had spaghetti sauce simmering on the stove and it smelled amazing. I couldn't even claim it was too hot to use the oven because we had a couple of those little window air conditioners chugging along like the Little Engine That Could, so the interior was pretty comfortable. The men settled themselves in the living room, except for Big Guy, who pulled out one of the stools at the kitchen bar, which was also our table. He sat down, leaning back against the wall comfortably, arms crossed in front of him.

He'd be able to watch me cook the whole time while still following the action in the living room.

I ran out to get the bread while Jeff turned on the TV. When I got back there was some kind of fighting on. Not wrestling this time, but real fighting in some sort of cage.

"Grab us some beers, sweet butt," said the third guy, a dark-haired man with slightly pock-marked cheeks. I bit my lip. I really didn't like being called that. Not only was it degrading, there was some sort of nasty implication in the way he said it. But Jeff glanced up at me and mouthed "please", so I set down the bread, went to the fridge and pulled out four beers. They ignored me for the most part while I fixed dinner, except for my Big Guy. Every few minutes I'd look up to find him watching me, pensive. He didn't smile, he didn't talk to me, nothing. Just studied me, with special attention for my boobs (smaller than some but perkier than most) and ass (slightly larger than I'd like).

I grabbed a beer for myself, relaxing after a while and rolling with it. I supposed I should be indignant that he just sat there, blatantly checking me out, but it felt kind of good to have a man appreciate me.

It'd been a long time.

By the time I pulled the bread out of the oven the fight on TV had ended. I set out some hot pads for the pasta and sauce and grabbed the salad. The guys fell on the food like a bunch of starving animals.

"This is amazing," the man with blue eyes said, as if seeing me as a person for the first time. He had strong, sculpted features and I decided he was pretty hot for an old guy. "You can really cook. My old lady used to cook like this."

"Thanks," I said, hoping I wasn't blushing. This might go down as the oddest dinner party of my life, but I loved to cook for people who appreciated good food. In fact, during high school I'd planned on going to culinary school.

Thanks for nothing, Gary.

Big Guy didn't say anything, but I noticed he took seconds and then thirds of everything. While they finished, I started cleaning up, but he reached across the bar and grabbed my arm.

"You might want to go for a drive," he said, jerking his chin toward the door. "We've got business."

I glanced over at Jeff, who offered me a placating smile.

"Do you mind, sis?" he asked. I shook my head, although I felt a twinge at leaving without even learning their names. Somehow over the course of dinner they'd stopped scaring me, turning alarmingly human. I knew when I wasn't wanted though, and I owed it to Jeff not to cause trouble. I smiled brightly at everyone and went to the door, grabbing my purse off the rack next to it.

"Well, nice to meet all of you, um…"

Mr. Blue Eyes, who I noticed had the word "President" written on his vest, grinned.

"I'm Picnic, and these are my brothers, Horse and Max," he said.

I glanced over at Big Guy. *Horse?* What kind of name was that? And they really didn't look like brothers...

"Nice to meet you, Mr. Picnic," I said, holding back my questions.

"Just Picnic. Thanks again for the food."

Horse stood.

"I'll walk you out to your car," he said, his voice low and rumbly. Jeff's eyes opened wide, and he jerked his head, then stilled. Picnic smirked at me knowingly.

"Take your time, we can wait," he said to Horse, reaching down and pulling my keys out of his pocket, tossing them to me. I walked out into the warm sun of the late-summer evening, Horse following me. He snagged my hand, leading me to the table. My heart raced with every step. I had no idea what was about to happen, but part of me really wanted him to touch me.

Maybe.

Probably not.

Shit.

Horse tucked his hands under my arms, popping me up onto the table. Then he slid them down my sides, wedging them between my legs and pushing my knees gently apart. He stepped between them and leaned into me.

I'm pretty sure I came close to stroking out.

"I don't think this is a good idea," I said, glancing back at the house, heart hammering. Jeff wouldn't like it. Horse was dangerous. I could smell it on him. Seriously. Under the delicious scent of leather, light sweat and man was a pungent strain of pure trouble. "I mean, everyone is waiting for you, right? I can just go, let's just forget this, okay?"

He didn't say anything, just studying me with that cool, expressionless face of his.

"That how you gonna play it, sweet butt?"

"I'm not your sweet butt," I snapped, narrowing my eyes. I hated getting called things like that. Gary did it all the time. Why did they keep calling me that?

To hell with him and to hell with Gary too.

Men.

"Fuck off," I said, glaring at him.

Horse gave a bark of laughter, the sound sudden and loud in the silence, which pulled me back to reality. His hands tucked around my waist, jerking me into his body where my crotch immediately came up against what had to be a pretty healthy erection.

He swiveled his hips into mine, slowly dragging it up and across my clit. I'm ashamed to admit that I creamed my pants right then and there instead of kicking him in the nuts like a sensible girl. He leaned over and I held my breath, waiting for him to kiss me. Instead he whispered in my ear.

"Nice ass. Sweet. Butt."

I didn't like his tone, so I bit his ear. Hard.

He jumped back, and I wondered if he was going to kill me. Instead he started laughing so hard I thought he might pull a muscle. I scowled, and he held up his arms to each side in pointed surrender.

"I get it, hands off," he said, shaking his head, bemused. "Play it the way you like. And you're right, we've got business. Go drive for an hour, that should be enough time."

I slid off the table and darted around him. He trailed me as I went to my car. I opened the door and almost got in, then the same stupid streak of curiosity that'd caused me trouble all my life drowned out my sense of self-preservation. I stopped in the doorway, looking at him across the roof.

"Horse isn't your real name, is it?"

He smiled at me, his teeth white in the darkness, like a wolf's.

"Road name," he replied, leaning against the roof of my car. "That's the way things work in my world. Citizens have names. We have road names."

"What does that mean?"

"People give them to you when you start riding," he said casually. "They can mean all kinds of things. Picnic got his name because he went all out planning some pansy-assed picnic for a bitch who had him twisted up in knots. She ate his food and drank his booze, then called her fuckwad boyfriend to come and pick her up while he took a leak."

I grimaced at his crudity, trying to understand.

"That seems...unpleasant. Why would he want to remember that?"

"Because when the fuckwad showed up, Picnic shoved his head through a picnic table."

I caught my breath. That didn't sound good. I wanted to ask if the guy had been all right but decided I probably didn't want to know the answer.

"And Max?"

"When he gets drunk, sometimes his eyes go all wide and he looks fuckin' crazy, like Mad Max."

"I see," I replied, thinking about the man. I guess he did look sort of like Mad Max... I decided I didn't want to see him drunk.

Silence hung heavy between us.

"So aren't you gonna ask?"

I studied him, narrowing my eyes. I had a bad feeling about this. But the words came out of my mouth, completely beyond my control.

"So why are you called Horse?"

"'Cause I'm hung like one," he replied, smirking.

I dropped down into my car and slammed the door shut. I heard him laughing through the open window as I peeled out of the driveway.

Chapter Two
Sept. 17 – Present Day

∞

"I'm so sorry, sis," Jeff said, the words muffled from his bloody, swollen lips. *Was he missing a tooth?* I looked around the room, unable to believe that these men—two of whom I'd cooked for, one of whom I'd done a lot more than cooking for—were actually threatening to kill my brother. Could this really be happening?

Picnic looked right at me and winked.

"Little brother's been a bad boy," he said. "He's been stealing from us. You know anything about that?"

I shook my head quickly. A bag fell off my arm, apples bouncing out and rolling across the floor. One of them hit Horse's foot. He didn't glance down, just maintained that cool, thoughtful expression I'd seen on his face so many times. It frustrated me—I wanted to scream at him to show some fucking emotions. I knew he had them. Unless that had been a lie too.

Oh. My. God.

My brother knelt in the middle of our crappy living room, bleeding and awaiting execution, and all I could think about was me and Horse. What the hell was wrong with me?

"I don't understand," I said quickly, looking at Jeff's puffy, bruising face, silently pleading with him to burst out laughing at the big joke they were playing on me.

Jeff didn't start laughing. In fact, his breath rattled through the room like a movie sound effect. *How badly was he hurt?*

"He's supposed to be working for us," Picnic said. "He's pretty good with that little laptop of his. But instead of working he's been playing at the casino with our fucking money. Now he has the balls to tell me that he's lost the money and *can't pay us back.*"

He punctuated the last four words with jabs of his pistol's thick, round barrel into the back of Jeff's neck.

"You got fifty grand on you?" Horse asked me, his voice cool and casual. I shook my head, feeling dizzy. Oh, shit, this was why Jeff had tried to get me to ask Gary for money... But fifty grand? *Fifty grand?* I couldn't believe it.

"He stole fifty thousand dollars?"

"Yup," Horse said. "And if it doesn't get paid back right now, his options are limited."

"I thought you were friends," I whispered, looking from him to Jeff.

"You're a sweet kid," Picnic said. "But you don't get who we are. There's the club and everyone else, and this stupid fucker is *not* part of the club. You fuck with us, we will fuck you back. Harder. Always."

Jeff's mouth trembled and I saw tears well up in his eyes. Then he wet his pants, a dark stain spreading between his legs pitifully.

"Shit," said the guy with the mohawk and skull tats. "I fucking hate it when they piss themselves."

He looked down at Jeff and shook his head.

"You don't see your sister pissing herself, do you? What a little bitch," he said, disgusted.

"Are you going to kill us?" I asked Picnic, trying to think. I needed to make him see me as human, they said that on all the TV shows about serial killers. He had two girls, I'd even seen their pictures. I needed to remind him of his family, of the fact that he was human and not some kind of Reaper monster. "I mean, would you really kill people you shared pictures of your daughters with? One of them is about my age, isn't she?

Can't we work something out? Maybe we can make payments or something."

Horse snorted and shook his head.

"You don't get it, sweetie, this isn't just about money," he said. "We could give a shit about the money. This is about respect and stealing from the club. We let this pissant fuck get away with it, they'll all start doing it. We don't let stuff like this slide. Ever. He pays with blood."

I closed my eyes, feeling my own tears well up.

"Jeff, why?" I whispered, shivering.

"I wasn't planning to lose it," he replied, his voice cracked and hopeless. "I thought I could win it back, make it up somehow. Or that maybe I could hide it in the wire transfers..."

"Shut the fuck up," Picnic said, smacking the side of his head with his free hand. "You don't talk club business. Even when you're about to die."

I whimpered, feeling myself start to tremble.

"There's another way," Horse said to me, still casual. "Paying in blood can mean different things."

"He doesn't need to die for that to happen," I said, thinking quickly. "Maybe you could burn down our trailer!"

I smiled at him encouragingly. Fuck the trailer, I wanted Jeff safe. And me. Oh shit, if they killed Jeff they'd have to kill me too.

I was a witness. *Fuckity fuck fuck fuck!*

"Oh, we're gonna do that no matter what," he drawled. "But that's not blood. I can think of something that is though."

"What?" Jeff asked, his voice full of desperate hope. "I'll do anything, I swear. If you give me a chance I'll crack so many accounts for you, you won't believe what we can accomplish. I'll stop smoking, that'll clear my head, I'll do a better job..."

His voice trailed off as Horse laughed, and the mohawk guy shook his head and grinned at Picnic.

"You believe this asshole?" he asked. "Seriously, douche, you aren't making a very good case for yourself, telling us just how much you been slacking."

Jeff whimpered. I wanted to go to him, to hold him and comfort him, but I was too scared.

Horse stretched his neck, dipping his head to each side, and then cracked his knuckles like he was warming up for a fight. Kind of made me think of an episode of *The Sopranos*, which would have been funny as hell if I didn't happen to know how that episode ended.

"Let's get a couple of things clear," Horse said after a pause that lasted approximately ten years. "We're not going to hurt you, Marie."

"You aren't?" I asked, not sure if I believed him. Jeff listened anxiously, blinking rapidly against the moisture in his eyes. I watched as a trickle of sweat rolled down his forehead, making a track through the still-oozing blood.

"Nope," Horse said. "You didn't do anything wrong, we aren't pissed at you. This isn't about you. You'll keep your mouth shut about this if you want to survive, and you're smart enough to know that. That's not why you're here."

"Why am I here?"

"So you can see just how seriously fucked your brother is," he replied. "Because we're going to kill him if he doesn't find a way to pay us back. I think he might be able to pull it off with the proper motivation."

"I will," Jeff babbled. "I'll pay you back all of it, thank you so much—"

"No, you'll pay us back twice as much, fuckwad," Picnic said, kicking him viciously in the side with his heavy leather boot. Jeff pitched to the floor, keening in pain, and I flinched. "That's if we let you live, which is entirely up to your sister. If it weren't for her you'd be dead already."

My eyes flew to Picnic's face. I had no idea what he was talking about, but I'd do anything to save Jeff. Anything at all. He was the only real family I had left, and while he was a dumbass, he was also a sweetheart who truly loved me.

"I'll do it," I said quickly.

Horse snorted, his eyes wandering down my body, lingering on my boobs, then trailing back up to my face. I realized the rest of the groceries had fallen to the floor and my fists were clenched tightly.

"Don't you want to ask what it is first?" he said dryly.

"Um, sure," I said, studying him. How could such a beautiful man be so cruel? I'd felt how gentle his hands could be, where was this coming from? Real people, people who laughed and shared meals together, didn't act this way. Not in my world. "What do I have to do?"

"It seems Horse here wants a house mouse," Picnic said. I looked at him blankly. He shot an annoyed look at Horse. "She's clueless, you sure about this? Seems like work to me."

Mohawk guy smirked as Horse narrowed his eyes at Picnic. Tension filled the room and I realized that contrary to what I would have thought, things could probably get a lot worse pretty fast. What if they turned on each other? Then Picnic shrugged.

"This is your option," Horse said to me abruptly. "You want to keep dumbass alive, pack a bag and climb on my bike when we leave. You do what I tell you, when I tell you, no questions and no bitching."

"Why?" I asked blankly.

"So you can cook dessert for me," he snapped. Mohawk man burst out laughing. My mouth dropped open—all this for dessert? I knew he liked sweets, but I didn't get it. Horse shook his head at me, wearing that frustrated look he got around me sometimes, like he thought I was a crazy woman.

"Why the hell do you think?" he said, voice strained. "So I can fuck you."

Chapter Three
July 8 – Nine weeks earlier

ຂ໑

My phone buzzed. I grabbed it to find a message from Jeff.

Krissys 2nite. Dont wait up

If a text could give a shit-eating grin, this one would do it. I shook my head and laughed silently, shoving my phone back into my pocket. Jeff was getting laid tonight and feeling pretty pleased about it.

That worked out nicely for me too.

It was the end of the day and only three kids were left on the playground. Gabby had started cleaning already so closing would be easy, and now I would have the trailer to myself. I decided I'd stop and get a Redbox video on the way home, and maybe some ice cream. Life was a lot better now that I'd gotten my first paycheck. When the last kid left, I checked with Gabby and discovered the cleaning was all done, as I'd suspected. We waved goodbye to each other and I went out to my car. The Redbox was outside of Walmart, which was busy this time of night but not busy enough for me to give up on the ice cream. I settled on slow-churned French silk, which I assumed was practically a health food because the package said it had half the fat and one-third fewer calories than the regular kind. This, combined with the Johnny Depp flick in my purse, almost guaranteed an orgasmic evening.

My mood just kept improving as I drove home.

One of my favorite dance songs came on the radio, which kicked ass because I didn't have a plug for an iPod or even a CD player in my little junker (thus the Def Leppard incident when the Reapers had come to call). I almost got caught behind a slow-moving farm truck, but they pulled off to let me by. I car-danced my way down our long driveway through the orchard to find a single low-slung, black motorcycle parked outside the house.

Not part of the plan.

I got out of the car and looked around cautiously but didn't see anyone. Nobody near the table, nobody in the folding chairs I'd set out in the newly cleared lawn area (I couldn't call it a lawn in good conscience). *What the hell?*

I walked cautiously to the front door, clutching my cell phone like a weapon. What I planned to do with it I wasn't sure, because if a murderer was waiting inside I wouldn't exactly have time to call for help. I debated getting back in my car and driving away, but part of me wondered if Horse had come back. You know which part—that little nub between my legs, the bitch. The door swung open at a touch and I found Horse sitting at my counter, texting, all muscular and tattooed and incredibly hot.

I opened my mouth then snapped it shut.

"You need to get better locks," Horse said casually. "It took me about ten seconds to get in here."

I shook my head, looking around the room, although I had no idea what I was looking for. Some kind of magical leprechaun to jump out and explain what the hell was going on?

"I'm here to see Jeff," he said, setting down his phone. "He's got something for me. Where is he?"

"He's off with some girl," I replied, still dazed. "Her name is Krissy, he said he'd be late. I'll try calling him."

He watched as I dialed Jeff. Straight to voicemail. I sent a text, hoping he was just busy and didn't want to answer. More nothing. I looked at Horse and shrugged.

"I don't think his phone is on," I said. "I can let him know you came by though."

Horse gave a short, harsh laugh that had nothing to do with humor.

"I rode three and a half hours to see him," he replied. "He knew I was coming."

I smiled weakly.

"Um, you know he's a great guy, but he smokes out a lot and can be kind of forgetful..."

Horse narrowed his eyes.

"I'll wait."

I didn't know how to deal with that, so I decided to put away the ice cream. Then my stomach growled audibly. I'd planned on eating a sandwich, but it felt weird not to offer him something.

"You want an omelet?" I asked, figuring everyone loves breakfast for dinner.

"Sounds good," he replied. "Beer?"

"Um, yeah," I said, opening the fridge. I was kind of surprised he hadn't just helped himself, considering he'd already broken into the place. I handed him a bottle and started on the omelet. I'd made some cinnamon rolls last week and froze half of them, so I pulled those out too, along with a frozen thing of orange juice concentrate.

I glanced up to watch him taking a long pull on his bottle, eyes following me, throat muscles working as he swallowed. I could lick right from that little dip at the base of his throat up to his jawline...

Maybe not juice, I decided. Now *I* needed a beer.

Horse just watched me as I cooked, not saying anything, which creeped me out and turned me on at the same time.

"What kind of work are you guys doing with Jeff?" I asked.

"That's club business," he replied. "Don't ask questions like that, you'll get yourself in trouble."

Noted. So much for conversation.

The omelet was done and I'd microwaved the rolls, so I dished up for both of us, thinking of my movie wistfully. I didn't get to watch movies very often and it wasn't like I'd invited Horse over. But I had the feeling he might not be quite as into Johnny Depp as me. Should I bring it up? He decided for me, sitting down on the couch and grabbing the remote.

"You coming?"

"Um, yeah," I replied, following him into the living room. I planned on taking the armchair, but he patted the couch next to him with an air of challenge.

Never could resist a challenge.

He clicked through channels, stopping on another one of those fights with the big cage. I sighed and decided I wouldn't share my ice cream with him.

"You don't like MMA?" he asked, taking a bite of his cinnamon roll.

"Not really," I replied, leaning back into the cushions.

He nodded.

"Lotta chicks don't," he replied. "But a lot do. All those sweaty bodies, you know?"

He glanced over at me, the slightest trace of humor in his eyes, and I couldn't tell if he was teasing me or not. I decided to just go to my room and eat there, but he reached out a hand to catch my arm, stopping me.

"What's the problem?"

"I'm tired," I said. "And I know you have business with Jeff and I'm really sorry he flaked on you, but I don't have the energy for this."

"This?"

I waved a hand around, encompassing him, the TV, etcetera.

"This," I said. "I don't understand if you're teasing me or not and it's confusing. And you took the remote."

He shrugged.

"So you pick what we watch," he replied lightly. "It's not that big a deal, Marie."

He handed over the clicker, giving me a smile that actually reached his eyes. I studied him—this was a new side to Horse and I liked it. He was still a big, tough bad guy (or at least not a good guy, I was pretty sure of that) but he honestly seemed relaxed and ready to let me out of whatever little mind game he was playing.

"Actually, I got a Redbox movie," I said after a pause. "It's the new Johnny Depp."

He smirked but gestured magnanimously toward the screen.

"Pop it in."

Unexpectedly, watching the movie with him was fun. During a fight scene he told me why it wouldn't have worked in real life (sort of scary that he knew so much about hand-to-hand combat), but he didn't tease me or anything during the sex scenes. When it ended we ordered another one on PPV. This time I let him pick, and to his credit he went for a thriller with a touch of romance that looked good to both of us without even pausing to scope out the porn. About halfway through I started getting a little cold, so I got up and grabbed a blanket. I figured I might as well share my ice cream too, so I filled bowls for both of us. When he finished he grabbed the bowls, set them on the table and pulled me across his lap, then sort of rolled over until he could lie back on the couch with me and my blanket on top of him.

I didn't protest. He felt good, and while one hand rubbed up and down my back slowly, he didn't cop a feel, which made me feel safe. In fact, I really didn't want to get up or even acknowledge how much I was enjoying being held.

A man's arms around me felt good.

In fact, they felt so good I fell asleep.

I woke up in my room, confused. I was in bed with Gary. Why was Gary here? Then I realized the body cradling mine was far too big to be Gary's and the arm across my stomach had more muscles than my future ex had in his whole body. It also had a black tribal tattoo around the wrist.

That woke me right up.

Horse lay in bed with me. I didn't have any pants on, just my shirt and panties. No bra. I brushed my leg against his to discover he didn't have pants either, and I felt his giant, erect penis poking my ass.

"Horse" indeed.

It's just morning wood, I told myself. *He's probably not even awake.*

"Good morning, sweet butt," he whispered in my ear, the warmth of his breath sending blood straight to my naughty bits. His words annoyed me though. Opting for the safer emotion, annoyance, I tried wrenching away from him. He hardly noticed my attempt, which bugged me even more.

"Don't call me that," I muttered sulkily. "Who calls a woman that?"

He laughed, the sound low and warm in my ear.

"You don't really want to know," he replied, kissing the back of my neck and reaching down with one hand to press against my stomach. My panties went moist, and I wiggled against his big tool, wondering if I'd lost my mind.

Body and brain fighting for control, winner take all.

"Wait," I said, brain pulling ahead for the moment. "What do you mean I don't want to know? I want to know."

"You don't want to know," he repeated. "It doesn't matter."

"If it doesn't matter, why won't you tell me?"

In answer, he slid his hand lower, catching the hem of my shirt and pulling it up, running the tips of his rough, calloused fingers across my belly. Oh very nice... My brain decided we could talk about the sweet butt thing another time. I squirmed my rear and he flexed his hips, rubbing his now-epic erection against the crack of my ass. His hand moved north, cupping my breast, plucking at the nipple as he kissed the back of my neck.

"Oh shit..." I murmured. "That feels amazing, Horse."

"Just getting started, babe," he murmured. He sucked my earlobe into his mouth and I moaned. My brain switched off entirely, ceding control to my body, which wanted him inside me.

Immediately.

I turned and slid down so my back lay flat on the bed, wrapping my hand around his neck and pulling his mouth down to mine. He'd been tender so far, so I didn't exactly expect what happened next.

He took my mouth hard and fast, rolling on top of me and wedging between my legs. I opened for him and he thrust his tongue in forcefully, plunging it in and out as his hips started grinding against mine. Just two layers of thin fabric separated us as his cock smashed against my clit, almost brutal in intensity. I shivered, lust and desire bursting through me, trying to see if I could lift my hips and move with him. In the process I accidentally pushed against his chest, which he apparently interpreted as me trying to push him away.

Horse pulled away from my mouth and growled, eyes dark with desire and a need so strong I froze. He looked like an animal in heat, a point his hard prick seemed to be determined to impress in its own way.

"I'm in charge here, don't forget it," he stated.

I nodded, mesmerized. I didn't complain as he reared up just enough to rip my shirt up and over my head, taking my arms with it. Instead of pulling it off all the way, he tangled it around my wrists, holding them captive with one strong hand above my head as he slid lower, mouth taking my nipple and sucking it in deep. Sensation exploded through me and I moaned. Loud. Aching emptiness grew between my legs and I imagined him thrusting into my body, stretching me open wide as he took his pleasure.

Horse fumbled at his waist with his free hand, sliding down his boxers. Then he thrust his hips between mine again. Oh shit, that felt so good. Now his cock head pressed right against my slit through my panties instead of stroking the length along my clit. This created a whole new sensation as the thin fabric stretched against the unbearable pressure, actually pushing into my body with the tip of his cock before the fabric stopped up.

I bucked against him, desperate for more.

He pulled his head up from my breast and leaned up and over me, still holding my hands captive. I twisted, aching and raw.

"Fuck me, you're a hot piece of ass," he muttered. I closed my eyes, trying to catch him with my hips, whimpering for him to take me.

"Hold your hands over your head or you'll pay," he ordered, pinning me with his intense, green gaze.

"Okay," I said, more than willing to do anything he asked. I hadn't felt this turned-on in forever, hovering within spitting distance of the Big O in less than five minutes.

It had never been like this with Gary.

Horse let my hands go, sliding lower, rubbing his nose along my belly as I twisted, then his hands caught the sides of my panties and tugged them down. I kicked one foot free, spreading my legs wide. He didn't hesitate, latching on to my clit with his mouth as he thrust two fingers into me hard. No warning, no preparation, just the rough pads of his fingers attacking my G-spot.

Goddamn. This was better than my special pink vibrator, the one with two heads and the wiggly thing. My body stiffened and I grunted, toes curling. It was right there, just out of reach.

He pulled his mouth away and laughed.

"Knew it'd be like this," he said. "I can't wait to get inside, you're tight as fuck so it might hurt the first time. But I'll stretch you out a little and then holy fuck, it's gonna be good. Time to come."

His mouth came over me again, sucking deep. His fingers starting thrusting in and out and I grunted, muscles trembling as I stiffened. So close. He paused again, but I didn't open my eyes to see what he was doing. Maybe I should have, it would have given me some warning. When he started fucking me with his fingers again, he found my ass with his other hand. I screamed as he thrust a finger in my back entrance, exploding into his mouth as my back arched off the bed.

It took me a couple minutes to come back to myself.

I opened my eyes to find him beside me, up on one elbow, studying me not with satisfaction but brooding, determined need. I blinked at him, dazed.

"Gonna fuck you now."

"Sure," I whispered, dazed. "Not sure I'm gonna be able to participate too much, think you blew a circuit or something."

He smiled, a look of grim satisfaction. Then he carefully positioned himself over me, reaching down between us to position his wide cock head against the lips of my slit. I came to my senses.

"Condom!" I gasped, pushing at his chest. "Stop! We need a condom."

"Want you bareback," he muttered, narrowing his eyes. "I'm clean."

I shuddered, closing my eyes.

"Maybe you are, but I might not be. Gary was cheating on me."

That caught his attention, and his eyes softened. He reached up and brushed his thumb against my cheek, where the bruise had been.

"He gave you that mark, yeah?" he asked. I nodded. "Your brother said he's history. That right?"

I nodded again, looking anywhere but his face, which wasn't easy with him right on top of me.

"I don't want to talk about Gary. Do you have a condom?"

"Yeah, out in my saddlebags," he said. "Believe it or not, I didn't entirely plan on this."

I laughed.

"Neither did I."

"I know," he said, rolling off me and flopping on his back. I turned on my side and looked down to see his cock for the first time.

"Oh my god…"

It was huge. I mean, huge. Not just long, but thick and hard and flushed bright red so it looked almost angry. It curved up, wider in the center of the shaft before narrowing under the ridge of his head.

I couldn't help myself. I reached down and traced the length, mesmerized by the heat of his soft skin over something so hard and formidable.

"Told you why they call me Horse," he said. I dragged my eyes away to look at his face, reading satisfaction mixed with his desire.

"They make condoms that big?" I asked, halfway serious.

"You'd be surprised," he muttered. "Saying this goes against everything I believe in, but you'd better let go of my dick."

He rolled off the bed, reaching down to grab his jeans, pulling them on over his length with some effort.

"Goin' outside to my bike. Don't move."

That wouldn't be a problem.

He opened the door, then stopped in the doorway.

"Fuck," he said, sounding resigned.

"The sweet butt's a screamer, I like that," I heard a man's voice say from the living room, right outside my door. *Oh shit.* I grabbed the sheet, jerking it up and around me. I couldn't believe we'd had an audience. The walls in this place were paper thin, they must've heard everything.

I turned and moaned into my pillow.

"Sounds like a hot little bitch," said another voice. "She ready for another round? I'll take a piece."

Oh my god.

Horse walked out, slamming my door behind him. I heard him snarl something. Then laughter, followed by a thudding noise and a grunt. More laughter. The front door opened and slammed shut. A minute later Horse opened my door and came back in the room, carrying a leather bag. He sat down on the bed, digging in it and pulling out a handful of condoms, tossing them toward me.

"No way," I said through gritted teeth.

Horse stood and pulled off his jeans, climbed up and over me on the bed on his knees, cock thrusting aggressively. He narrowed his eyes and I shook my head quickly, feeling frantic.

He reached down, fisting himself and a droplet of pre-come beaded on his slit.

"I know you want this."

I did, but not with an audience. I shook my head again.

"No, I mean it," I said. "I'm not doing this with a bunch of guys in my living room. When did they get here? I didn't hear any bikes."

"Came in a cage," he replied, squeezing himself hard, sliding his hand up and down. I'd never seen anything sexier in my life. He sucked in a ragged breath and I saw the pulse in his neck beating fast. "Doesn't matter. Open the fucking condom. I want to feel you slide it on me."

"No."

Horse stilled, and something dark and heavy rolled into the room with us.

"No?"

"No," I repeated, my voice small. "I heard what they said. I didn't like it and I don't want to have sex with them around."

Slowly and deliberately, Horse let go of his cock and leaned down over me, bracing his hands on either side of my face as he got real close. He held my gaze, eyes cold and hard.

"I fuck when I want and how I want," he said. I shivered. This was the intimidating man I'd met that first day. I'd forgotten how much he terrified me. "So do my brothers. It's my job to worry about them, not yours. You worry about taking care of me."

"No," I said again, scared but determined. "What we did earlier was incredible, and I'm sorry you didn't get your turn. But I'm not having sex with an audience. Period. Get off my bed."

"This is a mistake," he told me.

"Get off the bed," I repeated, holding my ground. I reached up and pushed at his chest. He exploded off me at the touch, spinning around to punch the wall. Then he grabbed his jeans, pulling them over his raging cock commando-style. His cut came next, sliding over his bare torso. He grabbed the saddlebag and stalked out the door, slamming it so hard behind him I heard something crack.

Then I was alone in bed, stunned and covered in unopened condoms.

An hour later, Jeff knocked cautiously at my door.

"Marie, you okay?" he asked, voice quavering a little. "Um, did you know your door is cracked down the middle?"

"Yeah," I replied softly, sitting in the middle of my bed, knees pulled up to my chest. I'd already gotten dressed and texted Denise, telling her I felt too sick for work. I'd heard Horse's bike leave, heard Jeff and the guys arguing about something. Heard a truck peel out of the driveway. Now I just sat, trying to process what had happened.

I'd never been with anyone but Gary.

Horse had blown me away, first with his gentleness and then his skill. But he'd followed it up by scaring the crap out of me, not to mention doing some serious damage to the room. Which one was the real man? Would I ever see him again?

Did I *want* to see him again?

"Marie, can I come in?"

"No," I said, looking around the room. Horse's black t-shirt, emblazoned with the Reaper's symbol, lay crumpled on the floor next to his boxers.

A neat pile of condoms sat on the bedside table.

Jeff didn't need to see any of it.

"I'm going back to sleep for a while," I told him after a long pause. "Let's just leave it at that."

Chapter Four
Sept. 17 – Present Day

∞

I gaped at Horse.

"You're threatening to kill my brother just so you can sleep with me?"

Mohawk man walked casually over to Horse, draping an arm around his shoulders.

"She's cute, but not real bright, brother," he said, glancing toward me with a smirk. "Why don't you let me take her for a ride, get her trained up for you?"

He gyrated his hips suggestively and the rest of the guys snickered. Horse turned fast, punching him in the stomach. Mohawk man doubled over but managed to stay standing as Horse grabbed my arm and jerked me out the door. He marched me away from the trailer into the orchard until we'd gone a pretty good distance, then pushed me back against one of the trees, leaning into my face and grabbing my shoulders.

"I don't want to *sleep* with you," he said, saying every word slowly and carefully, shaking me a little for emphasis. "I want to *fuck* you. Sleeping, cuddling, all that other shit is for girlfriends and old ladies. You've made it pretty goddamn clear you aren't interested in any of that, so let's get this straight. I'm threatening your brother because he stole from the club, which had nothing to do with you. You steal from the club, you pay in blood. You're his blood. We take you, he pays. Fucking you is just a bonus."

"So you're taking me to show that people shouldn't steal from the club?"

"It's a fuckin' miracle, she gets it," he muttered to no one, throwing up his hands. "Your brother's lucky, because I wanna stick my dick in you more than I wanna kill him. Otherwise this wouldn't be worth the trouble. If Jeff-hole gets his shit together and pays back the club I might let you go— *after* I'm done with you. If he doesn't, then I'll find some other use for you. Got it?"

I nodded again.

"No games, no bullshit," he said. Then he stepped back, running his hand through his hair roughly, pacing away from me. I started to follow him but he turned back around toward me. "You do this, it's your choice. I'm not raping you. You're making a decision to pay for your brother's mistake on your back. You get me?"

Not exactly much of a choice, considering the gun pointed at my brother's head. I didn't say it out loud though. If the Reapers were willing to give us an out, I'd take it and call it whatever he wanted.

"I'm serious," Horse said, glaring at me. "You call it off any time you want. I'm not gonna lock you up and watch you every minute. You make this deal, it's up to you to keep it. And you don't have to make the fucking deal. Your brother's an idiot and he knew what he was getting into. This isn't your mess and it's not your job to bail him out."

"You trying to talk me out of it?" I asked. "Well, you can't. I meant what I said. I'd do anything for Jeff. Anything."

His jaw clenched as he turned, growled and kicked one of the trees so hard it was a miracle he didn't break a toe. Then he marched me back to the trailer.

We went inside to find the other guys sitting around, drinking beer and talking. Jeff lay on his side in the middle of the room, crying silently, the bruises covering what I could see of him getting uglier by the minute. Horse ignored all of them, pushing me into my bedroom and closing the door he'd cracked behind us. He ripped open my closet door, found a backpack and thrust it at me.

"You've got thirty minutes," he said. "Then you're on my bike and we're headed home. Grab anything you want to keep."

"Okay," I replied, hoping he would leave me to pack in peace. Instead he leaned back against my still-cracked door, watching as I dug through my closet. I decided to go light on the clothing. I could always get more stuff to wear, but I wanted my pictures and what few keepsakes I'd managed to take with me from Gary's. It was depressing to realize just how little I had.

I pulled out my shoebox of papers, tossing it on the bed. The box tipped over, spilling out photos. I ignored it, turning back to dig through the closet again. My mom had a pretty nice pair of leather boots in there somewhere, and while I'd never been a boot person, it seemed like wearing something to protect my legs might be important on a bike.

Horse sat on the bed, flipping through the photos. I ignored him, tugging at my cargo capris when they rode down, showing off my thong. Why had I decided to wear it today?

"You wear that shit for him?" Horse asked, his voice like ice. I turned and looked up to find him holding up a wedding picture smeared with dried blood. Me and Gary. So fucking young.

"Wear what?" I asked.

"That butt floss," he snapped. "Why the fuck are you wearing a thong to work at a daycare? Are you seeing him again?"

"No!" I burst out, horrified. "I haven't seen him since he beat the shit out of me, you should know that. He hasn't called me, nothing. When I get all the papers ready, Denise's husband said he'd serve them for me."

"You keeping this?"

"Yeah," I said, studying the picture. I'd had so many hopes and dreams then back then, and I let a man destroy them. "I don't want to forget. At least not yet."

Horse dropped the picture without a word and I kept packing, glancing at my phone periodically to check the time. Finally I surveyed the growing pile on my bed, sad that my entire life took up such a small space. All I had left to grab was bras and panties, which I really didn't want to dig through with him watching me.

I didn't exactly have a choice though.

I stood up and opened my underwear drawer. There wasn't a lot, but if I was going to be Horse's...um...whatever...some pretty panties might come in handy. He came up behind me, reaching down and cupping my hips in his big hands, pulling me back into his body as he leaned over me. He took a deep breath.

"I love how your hair smells," he said gruffly as his hard cock pressed against my butt. I heard Picnic and the others talking in the living room. Jeff was out there, waiting to see if they were going to kill him.

"I have ten minutes left," I murmured, my voice tense. "Please."

Horse let go of my hip, grabbing my hair roughly and twisting my head around to the side. His lips covered mine, taking me hard, tongue thrusting in and out. I moaned, collapsing against him. His other hand reached around to my front, ripping open the buttons on my capris, and I heard one clatter against the floor. His fingers plunged into my panties, sliding roughly along my clit before sinking into me. I moaned, despising myself because it turned me on so much.

He pulled his mouth away from mine, pinning me with his gaze. I couldn't breathe, his eyes were so intense—full of desire and lust and anger, all directed at me.

"This pussy," he said, fingering me. I moaned in response, ashamed at how easily he made me wet. "This pussy is mine. *You* are mine. I'll fuck you when and where I want, and you can either take it or get the fuck out. Are we clear?"

I nodded, shivering. I wanted to hate him but my body disagreed. He kept his hand in my hair, holding me tight as he stroked me repeatedly. My legs weakened and I whimpered, desperate for relief. That's when he took my mouth again.

Now his tongue thrust in time with his fingers. The flesh between my legs tightened, muscles flexing all over my body. Horse stroked harder and I quivered on the edge. He pulled his mouth away from mine, dropping his lips to my neck, licking and sucking as I thrust my hips against him, desperate to come. Then he bit my neck and I moaned.

Loud enough to be heard in the other room, I'm sure.

Horse pulled his hand out of my pants and stepped back. I froze in disbelief, my panting breath loud in the room. When I turned to him, shaky, he gave me a smile that didn't reach his eyes. Then he slowly and deliberately lifted his fingers, licking off my juices.

"Don't care how good you taste, you don't call the shots," he whispered. "We clear?"

"Your rules," I whispered back. "Or I leave. And what happens if I do?"

"To you?" he said. "Nothing. You're with me of your own free will. But the club has to be paid in blood, Marie, not even I control that. Don't forget."

I nodded quickly.

He pushed me gently to the side and opened my lingerie drawer, digging around in it. He pulled out several thongs and a teddy, tossing them on the floor.

"You won't need these," he said. I nodded as he turned back to the drawer, trying not to think of what else he would find in there. I winced as he stopped suddenly, thinking I had the shittiest luck on earth because this wasn't going to be pretty.

He pulled out the bundled black Reapers t-shirt he'd left crumpled on my floor after that disastrous night he'd spent in my bed, hefting it as he glanced toward me with a question in his eyes. I shook my head, blushing fiercely, reaching out to take it.

Horse didn't hand it over. Instead he unrolled it, eyes widening as he found the bright-pink jelly vibrator with the dual heads, one for my clit and one for my G-spot. We both stood there silently, looking at it. Then he rolled it back up and handed it to me, eyes full of satisfaction.

"Pack the shirt and the toy," he said, watching as I stuck it in the bottom of my backpack. I don't think I'd ever been more embarrassed in my life. I didn't meet his eyes as I dumped the rest of my things in, zipped it up and threw it over my shoulder.

"That it?" he asked. "You want anything else from the living room or kitchen? It won't be here if you try to come back."

I shook my head, still unable to speak. *Stupid, stupid, stupid...*

He leaned in close and whispered in my ear.

"Next time you want to play with your pretty pink toy, you do it while I'm watching. If you're a good girl, I'll let you wear the tee. Got it?"

I nodded. We walked out through the living room, past Jeff and the Reapers, and out the front door.

Chapter Five
Aug. 13 – Six weeks earlier

ജ

I didn't expect to see Horse again after the abrupt end I'd called to our lovemaking. Picnic, Max and another guy called Bam Bam had been to visit a couple of times. Jeff seemed happy enough to see them, and they all loved the food I cooked. After they'd leave though, Jeff would always get real quiet and touchy. He'd also started going to the casino more often, which worried me.

He never came home acting like a man who'd won.

But even though I sensed something was wrong, I had come to enjoy their visits. I wasn't sure if I wanted Horse to come back or not. Every time I saw bikes in the driveway, I was terrified I'd see him and disappointed when I didn't. I dreamed about him all the time, and more than once I'd re-lived our incredible morning together with my vibrator.

Apparently he'd forgotten about me though. I wasn't about to ask any of the other guys about him. I couldn't stand pity, and that was about the best I could hope for from them. During this time, Jeff seemed more and more detached, smoking out constantly and barely talking to me or eating. I worried about him, of course, and today I was particularly frustrated because he'd promised me he'd stay sober.

You see, today I planned to go pick up my stuff from my old house.

Yesterday had been my day off, and I'd driven to the Women's Center in Kennewick to try to figure out how to divorce Gary. I couldn't afford a lawyer but I didn't want anything from him, so I figured it would be quick and easy. If I got lucky, I wouldn't even have to see him. I could just send over the papers for him to sign.

But the super-sweet woman who met with me, Ginger, shared some hard truths. For example, when I left, I'd grabbed my purse and a bag full of clothing. But I hadn't gotten my social security card, my birth certificate, the title to my car or my pictures or keepsakes or anything. And she was right when she pointed out that while I might not care about any of that stuff now, I might need it down the line. I certainly shouldn't trust Gary with it.

She made a good point.

She also wanted me to file for a restraining order against him, but I knew Gary. A restraining order would piss him off in a big way. Right now he wasn't messing with me. If I provoked him like that he might find me and hurt me again, so I came up with a plan to go to the house and get my stuff when I knew he'd be gone.

Every Monday he played poker with his buddies. He didn't even skip out when his mom died. If I went on a Monday I'd be safe, unless I ran into Misty, who was not only his new whore, but who'd worked at the grocery store with me for two years. Last time I checked, she had a regular Monday night shift. Even if I ran into her, I figured she'd stay out of my way — it wasn't like I was a threat to her, and I wasn't afraid of her. She might be taller than me, but she was a frighteningly skinny thing who took her manicure way too seriously to get in a cat fight. In fact, the longer I was free from Gary, the more pity I felt for her. I'd already slipped out of the noose, but her?

She'd been stupid enough to take it from me, put it around her own neck and tighten it up.

Still, just in case, I wanted Jeff to make the two-hour drive back home with me to Ellensburg, where I'd lived with Gary for the past three years. I wasn't in any real danger, but I still had nightmares about him hitting me. I felt ashamed and embarrassed too. I hadn't even given notice at Safeway. Even if I didn't see Jeff, what if I ran into my old boss?

I didn't want to face anyone.

When I pulled up to the trailer after work, I found Jeff passed out on the couch with his pipe on the floor next to an empty baggie and four beer bottles. I tried waking him up but he was completely faded. Even if I managed to take him with me, he wouldn't be any help.

So I decided to go by myself.

And yes, I realize now how incredibly stupid that was.

Trust me.

Pulling up to my old house was surreal.

Everything looked the same, but somehow smaller and dirtier. Same ratty lawn, same faded and peeling paint, same battered Mustang up on blocks in the driveway. All in all, it made me feel pretty good about my decision to leave.

Our trailer might be crap, but at least it was in the middle of an orchard. My dad had worked for the owner, John Benson, and part of his compensation included use of the old trailer. When he'd left, John had taken pity on us and let us stay for very low rent, seeing as he didn't really need it for anything else anyway. I think at some point he and my mom had a thing, but I didn't know the details and I didn't want to know them. We did our own repairs, kept a low profile and things worked out okay.

I parked my car in the street, pleased to note Misty's car wasn't there and I couldn't see any lights. None of the neighbors were outside so I didn't have to make awkward small talk with anyone. It wasn't that kind of neighborhood anyway — you know, where people look out for each other or have a neighborhood watch.

I had a moment of worry when the door wouldn't open. I thought maybe he'd changed the locks, but then it popped loose. Everything looked the same inside, but messier. Apparently Misty wasn't much of a house cleaner. I giggled, figuring that had to drive Gary crazy.

Jackass.

I found my papers easily enough, everything except the car title. I kept a shoebox of keepsakes and photos in the closet in our spare bedroom. It hadn't been disturbed, so I carried it out to the car and put it in the hatchback, then gave in to temptation and went back inside. I figured while I was there I might as well see if any of my clothes were around, or if Misty had thrown them out.

Surprisingly, she hadn't. I found them neatly bagged and labeled on the back porch. Convenient. It took four trips to get it all in the car, and then I went in one last time. I wasn't sure what I was looking for... Maybe some kind of closure? He still had our wedding picture up on the wall, right next to the one from our senior prom. I studied myself in them, wishing I could go back in time and give myself some friendly advice, something along the lines of *run away and never, ever look back!*

For some reason I couldn't explain, I pulled the wedding picture off the wall, snapped off the back of the frame and took it out. It wasn't anything special, just a five-by-seven snapshot. We didn't have a real photographer at the wedding.

Still, it was a good picture.

Gary looked young and handsome, and I looked fresh and pretty and full of excitement for the future. I don't know how long I stood there, lost in my thoughts, but I didn't notice when Gary walked into the house, reeking of beer and smoke, until he threw his keys down on the coffee table.

I spun around, jaw dropping. My hands trembled so much I dropped the picture.

"Um, hi, Gary?" I managed to whisper.

"That's the day you fucked me over," he said, tilting his chin toward our wedding picture. His face was bright red and I saw the vein in his forehead start to pulse. He was angry. Really angry. "I could have been anything, but you needed a wedding ring and now I'm stuck in this cow town with nothing. Great fucking plan, Marie. Hope you're proud of yourself."

I watched him warily as he stalked toward me, trying not to give in to panic. The last time I'd seen him was when he backhanded me across our kitchen. I wasn't prepared for the terror and sense of helplessness that hit me at the memory, paralyzing my body. I forced myself to think. Could I make it past him and through the front door? He laughed.

"You here to fuck me over again, cunt?"

The words were slurred. Gary was drunk. Seriously drunk. Maybe even blackout drunk.

I needed to get out of here. Now.

I made a break for it but he lunged at me, tackling me to the floor with the same strength and speed that made him our high school quarterback. My head slammed into the hardwood I'd been so excited to discover last year when we'd pulled out the carpet, pain exploding through me. Gary sat up, straddling me and grabbing the front of my shirt, pulling me up.

Then he started punching me.

Details are fuzzy after that.

I spent a long time on the floor, moaning. Misty walked through the door at some point and started screaming. Gary lay passed out on the couch, oblivious as she helped me get up and walked me into the kitchen. She wanted to call the cops but I begged her not to—I couldn't handle the humiliation of facing them, all the questions and pitying looks.

I also didn't want to like Misty.

I'd felt devastated and betrayed when I learned she was sleeping with my husband—the fight we'd had about her led to him hitting me in the first place. But her touch was soft and gentle, the horror in her eyes genuine. She forced me to take some Tylenol when I refused to go to the emergency room. Then she went and threw everything of hers into three suitcases, crying big, silent tears the entire time. The Tylenol kicked in pretty fast, and while I couldn't help her haul out her things, I held the door for her. We locked it behind us and I watched as she loaded her car. Then she took my arm, walking me over to mine.

"Are you sure you won't let me call the cops?" she asked. "He needs to pay for this. I knew he drank and his temper is kind of crazy, but I had no idea..."

"I just want to go home," I whispered. She took me in her arms, hugging me gently, and a small, detached part of my psyche marveled that my savior turned out to be a woman I'd hated so much. Life is weird.

"Don't come back here," she whispered back. "A man who can do that, he might kill you next time. I'm going to stay with my brother for a while, I think. He's a cop. I'll be safe, but Gary talks about you all the time, how much he hates you, how pissed off he is that you guys got married and he never did anything with his life. Please don't come back."

"I won't be back," I said, and I meant it.

It was after three in the morning when I pulled up to the trailer. I must have the shittiest luck on earth, because there were five bikes parked outside, loaded down with saddlebags and bedrolls. I sat in the car just looking at them, exhausted. Every light in the trailer was turned on and I saw a flickering orange glow around the east corner.

They'd built a bonfire. Apparently Jeff had sobered up enough to light up something besides more weed. I didn't have the energy for this. My body had stiffened during the drive, which made climbing out a challenge. I shuffled over to the door, hoping against hope that they were all out back by the fire so I could sneak in and collapse into bed.

No such luck.

I opened the door and walked in to find Horse, Max, Bam Bam and Jeff. I stood there for a minute, holding on to the frame to keep myself upright.

"Holy fuck," Bam Bam said, and I nodded sagely.

Holy fuck indeed.

Jeff just sat on the couch, opening and shutting his mouth like a fish. I didn't bother talking to him or any of them, just walked painfully toward my bedroom. Then Horse was next to me, very carefully picking me up, kicking open my cracked bedroom door and laying me down on the bed. He turned on the little bedside lamp with a click, washing the room with soft light.

I collapsed back against the pillow, tears of relief welling up in my eyes as I sank into the soft bedding.

Home. I'd made it.

"Who did this?" Horse asked, his voice colder than I'd ever heard it. He sat next to me on the bed, eyes dead and face blank. I didn't want to look at him, couldn't handle the reality of him seeing me like this. I closed my eyes, blocking out his face.

"Gary," I muttered. "My husband. I went to get my stuff. He wasn't supposed to be there."

"You need a doctor," he stated. "You call the cops?"

I shook my head against the pillow.

"No, and I don't want to talk to anyone about it," I muttered. "Nobody. I'm not going to the ER, he didn't break anything. I'm just beat up, nothing serious."

Horse didn't say anything for a minute.

"I gotta ask, babe. Did he rape you?"

Fuck. A harsh, short bark of near-hysterical laughter burst out of my mouth. I hadn't even thought of that—guess it could have been a lot worse. *Thanks for that, Gary. Thanks for not raping me, douchebag.*

"No."

"Babe. Look me in the eyes and answer the question."

I opened my eyes to find him leaning over me, his face filled with terrible tension and a horrible, burning anger I didn't want to think about. I didn't have the energy to manage my own emotions, let alone worry about his.

"No, he didn't rape me," I said shortly, then closed my eyes again, letting myself drift away from the pain. After a time I heard footsteps enter the room, heard the low rumble of Picnic's voice, but I couldn't make out the words at first. He repeated them, coming closer.

"Any witnesses?" Picnic asked. I ignored him.

"Babe, we need to know if there were any witnesses," Horse said, his voice insistent. "Anyone see what he did to you? Have you told anyone at all?"

"Um, Misty," I whispered after a pause. "Misty found me. She helped me get into my car. She wanted to call the cops but I wouldn't let her."

"Who's Misty?" Horse asked.

"Gary's new girlfriend," I replied, reaching up to explore my split lip gingerly. Even talking hurt. "I actually kind of like her. She packed her stuff and took off. Not as stupid as me, got out quick."

"You feel like a ride?" Horse asked Picnic.

"Sounds about right," he replied.

"Let me get her cleaned up, make sure she doesn't need a doctor first."

That worked for me.

I drifted in and out after that. Cool water dabbed my face. Horse stuck some pills in my mouth and then held up a cup of water for me to swallow. Jeff sat next to me, holding my hand as the pain faded completely. Good pills, I mused. Definitely not Tylenol. Bikes roared and then I drifted away. When morning came Jeff called in to work, told them I'd been in an accident and would probably need several days off. He tried to get me to eat some breakfast but I couldn't handle the thought of food. I decided to just lie in bed feeling sorry for myself. Around ten I heard the rumble of bikes again, but this time the whole crew didn't come inside, just Horse. He walked in and sat next to me on the bed without saying anything.

"I'm pretty tired," I said, refusing to look at him. I felt so stupid, so embarrassed. I knew Gary could get violent. They warned me at the Women's Center not to go back by myself, but I'd felt so silly being afraid to visit my own house. "I think you should go."

Horse stroked a finger along my collarbone, one of the only visible places on my body without ugly purple bruises.

"He's not going to hurt you again," he said.

"It's not your problem, Horse," I replied. I didn't want to talk to him. I just wanted to close my eyes and sleep, forget for a little while about what had happened.

"It's not your problem anymore either."

Something in his voice caught my attention, so I forced myself to look up at him. His eyes were bloodshot and the muscles in his unshaven jaw clenched. He lifted my hand and kissed it very softly. That's when I saw his knuckles.

They were completely torn up, crusted over with blood.

He followed my gaze, shaking his head slowly, offering me a strange, sad little smile.

"Don't ask the question unless you want to hear the answer," he said. "I've gotta go, we're on a long run. California. If anyone asks, you were in a car accident, okay? Don't go into it any further than that, as soon as you give out too much information or complicate a lie, it's harder to keep up with it."

I nodded, closing my eyes again.

I didn't even consider asking how he hurt his knuckles.

Chapter Six

ഇ

The Reapers passed through again a week later, heading back home. By then I was up and moving, although I still hadn't gone back to work. Denise had come out to visit me—armed with chicken noodle soup and a basket of fresh veggies, including about twenty pounds of zucchini—and declared that I couldn't watch kids looking like a punching bag. I'd scare them. She promised to hold my job for me though, which I appreciated greatly, and even offered to give me overtime once I was presentable again to make up for the lost income. Her kindness made me cry.

Now I sat outside the trailer in a camp chair, reading an old romance of my mom's and listening to the roar of a bike coming down our driveway.

Horse.

The others weren't with him, and I didn't know what to say as he walked over to me. I still felt stupid and self-conscious. Not only had he seen me at my lowest, but I still looked like hell. Thankfully I'd been right in my initial assessment of the damage—nothing broken, nothing permanent.

"You look like shit," Horse said helpfully as he pulled up a lawn chair next to me. He sounded almost cheerful, which annoyed me. I glared at him and he smirked. "Still got a sweet butt though."

I went from annoyed to pissed.

"Don't call me that," I snapped. "I don't like it."

"I know," he replied. "That's why I do it. You're cute when you're pissed. Kind of like a wet kitten. Gets me hard."

My jaw dropped. Horse leaned back in his chair, running his fingers through his dark, messy hair, grinning at me with that perfect mouth, stubble so long it had turned into a short beard. The man looked extremely pleased with himself.

"Hear from the ex?" he asked.

I shook my head, deciding not address the "gets me hard" comment.

"Glad to hear it, I don't think he'll be bothering you again," he replied. "The guys will be here in a couple hours. They're grabbing some food, we'll camp here tonight before heading home."

"Um, that sounds good," I said. "Does Jeff know?"

He shook his head.

"No, I just wanted to check on you," he said. "Is he around?"

I shook my head.

"He went to the casino with some friends, said he might crash at Krissy's tonight."

Horse's face didn't change, but I felt a distinct chill. Well, fair enough. I didn't like Jeff going to the casino either. He must have work for them he hadn't finished yet. Jeff had been going downhill fast the past few weeks, and I couldn't seem to do anything to halt it or help him.

"Don't let that stop you," I added quickly. "You guys are welcome to stay here, especially if you're bringing your own food."

I meant it too. Even though he'd scared the hell out of me that unforgettable morning, I felt safe around him, especially now. When I'd been hurt, he protected me. I knew he'd done something nasty to Gary. I supposed I should be upset about that, because violence never solves anything. But Gary deserved whatever he got and then some.

"You want anything to drink?" Horse asked, taking in the empty plastic cup sitting next to me on a plastic milk crate. I smiled at him, trying not to wince as it pulled at my split lip.

"Iced tea?"

"You got it," he said, snagging my cup and carrying it inside. He came back out with a second one for himself. We sat companionably for the rest of the afternoon, talking about all kinds of things. I learned he'd grown up in a biker family and his father had been one of the first Reapers. His sister was married to Bam Bam. When I'd first met them, the MC had seemed like a gang of thugs, but the way Horse described it was more like a family. A crazy, loud family that fought a lot and occasionally went to jail, but still a family.

That I could understand—after all, my mama was more than a little crazy and sitting in the county jail as we spoke. I still loved her to pieces.

I told him about the brochures I had in my bedroom from the community college in the Tri-Cities. They had a culinary arts program, and the people at the Women's Center had encouraged me to look into going back to school.

"It's a good idea," he said. "I know you like the daycare, but that's not a long-term thing unless you decide to open a center yourself."

I shook my head, laughing.

"No way," I said. "The kids are fun, but I can't imagine doing that for the rest of my life. Too many diapers."

"So you don't want kids of your own? Had enough diapers?"

I shrugged.

"Well, I don't want to be a single mom, that's for sure," I replied. "My mom's in jail right now for assault with a deadly weapon, which was pretty stupid of her, I admit. But she took good care of us growing up. She worked her ass off before she blew out her back and started drinking. Chronic pain, you know? But she never would have tried to run over that cop if she'd stuck it out in the anger management program. I'm still not sure why she went after the second guy, he's not the one who wrote the parking ticket..."

Horse burst out laughing, biting it back quick.

I shook my head, narrowing my eyes. He wouldn't meet my eye, taking a quick drink of his tea. Then I reached over and poked his side and another laugh escaped, which he tried to hide with a cough. I decided to let him off the hook.

"It's okay," I said with a smile. "Even Mom laughed when she finally calmed down, and thankfully she never came close to actually hitting them. It wasn't her finest moment, that's for sure. She's got another four months ahead of her though, which isn't nearly as funny."

We fell silent for a few minutes. Then he spoke again.

"You didn't answer my question."

"Oh, the kids," I looked up at the clouds. One of them looked kind of like my mom holding a cigarette. I smiled. "Actually, I think I'd like kids. But not by myself and not if I can't stay home with them. Jeff and I had to be on our own way too much, and while I don't blame Mom for that, I want something better for my own family."

I looked over to find him staring at me intently. I blushed, though I couldn't say why.

"What about you?"

"I want kids," he said. "My mom would kill me if I didn't give her at least a couple of grandbabies. Never had an old lady though, not a keeper at least. Kinda hard to have one without the other."

"That's the truth," I replied, feeling more uncomfortable by the minute. "Tell me something. What's with the 'old lady' thing? Seems like a nasty thing to call someone you care about."

"It's a term of respect," he replied. I shrugged, but he reached out and touched my shoulder, getting me to look at him. His expression was intent and focused. "Seriously, a biker's old lady is like his wife. She's his woman, his property, and if anyone fucks with her the entire club will come down on them. Hard."

"Property?" I asked, wrinkling my nose. "That sounds even worse."

"You don't get it," he said, shaking his head. "Things are different in the outside world, but the club is a tribe. If a woman isn't claimed, she's fair game. But when a biker brands her as his property, she's untouchable."

"I still can't imagine being called property," I snapped. He blew out his breath, exasperated.

Before he could reply, we heard the roar of pipes in the distance. For once, his friends had good timing. They pulled into the yard with a rumble, carrying bags full of KFC chicken and biscuits. I don't usually eat stuff like that, but as the sun faded and they laid out their bedrolls, I couldn't imagine anything tastier than the plate of junk food balanced on my knees.

None of them mentioned my bruises, which I appreciated. Picnic brought me a box of chocolate-covered dried cherries. They built a bonfire and we all sat around drinking beer and laughing until my head drooped. When I got up to go to bed, Horse followed me in and it felt natural for him to climb in beside me. He seemed to understand how sore I was and didn't so much as kiss me, although I felt his erection several times during the night. I felt safe in his arms. The next day they took off at first light while I was still half asleep.

That afternoon I got a text from Horse, telling me to look at the "favorites" list on my phone.

He'd programmed himself into it, right at the top.

Aug. 23

Horse: *How's it going?*

Me: *Good. Kid barfed at me at work, but I managed to jump out of the way :)*

Horse: *Sounds like fun. Bike broke down here*

Me: *That sucks. You have a car?*

Horse: *SUV. Good for getting around, esp in snow. Hate feeling caged tho. What you doing?*

Me: *In yard, catching sun.*

Horse: *What you wearing?*

Me: *Nothing. Working on tan all over*

Horse: *!!!! You fucking me????*

Me: *LOL I'm wearing a tee and shorts :->*

Horse: *Too good to be true. Going to try to make it down next week*

Me: *Give me heads up*

Horse: *I will. TTYL*

Aug. 27

Me: *Bored. Hows the bike?*

Horse: *Bored is better than barfed on. Bike up and running again.*

Me: *Congrats! Kind of excited, going out tonight. Friend Cara from HS came to visit from NY. Like old times*

Horse: *Out?*

Me: *Dancing in tri-cities. Some club. Gonna slut up and everything!*

Horse: *Huh. Be careful*

Me: *Always. Excited tho. Haven't gone out since Gary*

Horse: *Looking for new man?*

Me: *Um…not really. Just fun*

Horse: *Watch out and don't dress too slutty. Don't want trouble*

Me: *Had enough trouble, trust me*

Horse: *True. Send me a pic later*

Me: *OK*

Me: *So what you think? Too slutty?*
Horse: *Hot. Definitely too slutty. Go change.*
Me: *Prude :-P*
Horse: *Text me when you get home*

Me: *Night gone to shit*
Horse: *?*
Me: *Jeff is sick, really sick. Asked me to stay home with him. Thought I might have to take him to the hosp but all right now*
Horse: *That sucks. He okay?*
Me: *Think so. Getting checked tomorrow, stomach pain*
Horse: *Sorry*
Me: *Me too. Cara leaving tomorrow, so no party for me...*

Aug. 28

Horse: *Hows Jeff?*
Me: *Fine, like nothing happened. Doc says must have been gas*
Horse: *Heh*
Me: *Bad gas*
Horse: *Sorry about going out. Glad nobody saw you dressed like that*
Me: *Jealous? ;)*
Horse: *What do you think? Gotta go, church in a few*
Me: *Church?!?? Didn't peg you for a church kind of guy*
Horse: *What we call a club meeting. I try to stay away from collection plates*
Me: *Don't get holy water in your beer!*

Sept. 1

Me: *Going to see mom today. Hate jail*

Horse: *Watch out for LEO*

Me: *LEO?*

Horse: *Law enforcement officers. Jail crawling with them*

Me: *LOL. Cause I break so many laws?*

Horse: *No, cause you keep bad company :-> Social visit or something up?*

Me: *Just regular, try to go every week since closer now. Harder when I lived with Gary. Didn't like me seeing her. Calls cost too much $ tho, so visiting important.*

Horse: *I get it. Got brothers inside. Hope visit is good*

Me: *Thanks*

Horse: *Send another pic?*

Me: *Um, not dressed up*

Horse: *Don't care. Send it. Want to see you today*

Me: *Okay :)*

I hate the county jail.

I've spent way too many hours in the waiting room, although I know it's probably better than visiting a real prison. The county guys look at me like I'm trash and occasionally they cop a feel while patting me down.

That's the price of seeing my mom.

They put me in a little room that had a built-in table, sort of like those tables at McDonald's where you can't move the chairs. But here the chairs are just stools and the whole thing is white. After a few minutes the door opened and Mom came in. She was wearing an orange jumpsuit, and even though it had to be the ugliest piece of clothing on earth, Mom looked fantastic. Seriously. My mom is hot, always has been, something that drove me crazy during high school. But from the way she walked, I could tell that her back was hurting worse than usual. She had a bunch of ruptured discs and no health insurance to fix them. The doctors wanted her to have surgery, but the county didn't want to pay for it, so she was stuck in limbo.

I stood and hugged her.

"Hey, Mama," I whispered into her hair, which looked fantastic even though she didn't have any styling stuff or anything. How did her hair look better in jail than mine did after two hours fixing it? Just another part of the mystery that was my crazy, loving, incredibly-difficult-at-times mother.

"Hey, baby," she replied, holding me tight. She smelled a little like cigarettes, which I know a lot of people find disgusting but I find strangely comforting—so long as it's not totally filling our trailer with smoke. It made me think of when she'd come home late at night after work when we were little. She'd walk into the bedroom I shared with Jeff and kiss us both good night. That little hint of smoke was the smell of comfort and safety.

We separated and took seats.

"So how's it going with you?" she asked. I'd put on lots of foundation to cover my bruises but her eyes flickered across them. "Gary?"

"Yeah," I said, flushing. "I was stupid, went back there alone to get some stuff. He was drunk."

Her mouth tightened, eyes filling with tears of anger or frustration, I couldn't tell which.

"I wish I was out of here," she said. "I'd kill that bastard."

"Mom! Don't talk like that, they're probably listening—they'll think you mean it."

She cocked an eyebrow at me and I knew she meant every word. Mom had a temper, no question. That's what got her here in the first place. But I loved the fact that she always protected her chicks, back when we were little and now too. My mom wasn't perfect, but the woman could be an avenging angel when she needed to be, something more than one school bully had learned the hard way.

"He won't be bothering me again," I said quickly. "A friend of mine had some words with him."

"Friend?" she asked.

"Um, actually a friend of Jeff's. He's a biker."

"I see," Mom said. "Since when does Jeff hang out with bikers? Gamers are more his speed, I'd think."

"Ever since I moved back to the trailer," I replied, shrugging. "He's doing some kind of work for them. I don't know the details."

"They good bikers or bad bikers?"

"What do you mean?"

"You know what I mean."

I laughed nervously.

"Um, they're good to me. Kind of rough and they can get scary, but I'm okay with them."

Her eyes narrowed, studying me. I shifted nervously, blushing again. Mom always saw right through me.

"Just 'getting along' or something more?" she asked. I shrugged again and she smirked.

"Well, be careful. Bikers can be great, but the hardcore guys are living in a different world from us."

"Yeah, I picked up on that," I said wryly. "It's nothing serious, mostly just flirting."

She didn't need to know all the details. Does anyone really want to tell their mom about their best orgasm ever?

"I've got news of my own," she replied with a gleam in her eye. Uh-oh, I recognized that gleam.

"What?" I asked, unnerved.

"Well, I've reconnected with someone," she said. "A man. We're getting serious."

That caught my attention.

"How on earth are you doing that from jail?" I exclaimed. "I swear, you're like a magnet, how do you get so many guys after you?"

She giggled, looking years younger than her age.

"Well, I may be getting old but I'm not dead yet," she replied. "He came to see me not too long after I got in here. In fact, he's been visiting me a couple times a week."

"Who?"

"John Benson."

"No way," I muttered, stunned. "John Benson, our landlord?"

"Yeah," she said, looking sheepish. "You may not know this, but he and I had a thing a long time ago..."

"I know," I replied. "I also know he was married."

She had the grace to look embarrassed.

"Well, I've made mistakes. But you should know we both felt guilty. That's why we ended it. His wife never knew. She's been dead for about three years now, car accident. John and I had been avoiding each other for so long it became a habit, but I guess when he read about me in the paper he started thinking about me."

Only my mother would end up finding love by trying to run over two cops. Clearly, John Benson was an idiot.

"He wants me to marry him."

I shook my head, unsure what to say. Finally I managed to speak.

"Well, I guess that's good, Mom. How does he feel about what happened?"

"He knows I have my issues, but I'm sober now, which has helped me sort things out," she said. That was true—she'd joined AA even before her little incident. We'd confronted her about her drinking after Jeff found her passed out outside the trailer in the snow last winter. It was a miracle she survived.

"I've realized now that I need to deal with my emotions or I get…upset."

That was the understatement from hell.

"Aren't you supposed to stay out of relationships your first year of AA?"

"It'll be almost a full year by the time I get out," she replied. "I'd get out a little earlier for good behavior, but they're not cutting me any slack because of the cop thing."

We looked at each other, both thinking back to that day. She sighed.

"I never do anything halfway, do I?"

I shook my head, smiling ruefully.

"That's the truth."

"I'm moving in with him when I get out. That's good news for you and Jeff, I guess. You'll get to keep the trailer all to yourselves."

I shrugged.

"I guess if that's what you want," I replied. "It concerns me a little, but if you're happy, that's good enough for me."

She smiled, the tension on her face easing.

"Thank you, baby," she whispered. "I've been worried about telling you guys. You talk to Jeff for me? He hasn't been to visit in a month and I'm worried. Is everything okay?"

I thought about how to answer her question. I didn't know of anything specifically wrong with Jeff, but there was definitely something going on. How to explain that though?

"He's been kind of edgy," I said finally. "And lost some weight. But he hasn't talked to me about anything and when I asked he blew me off. Wish I could tell you more."

"Thanks for that," she said. "You tell him I love him?"

"I'll tell him."

Sept. 1

Me: *Well that was fun*

Horse: *?*

Me: *Went to see mom. She's good, but crazy news. Getting married*

Horse: *This a good thing?*

Me: *Not sure. He's the guy who owns our trailer. They used to have a thing, but he was married. Wife died couple years ago*

Horse: *Good guy?*

Me: *Cheated on his wife*

Horse: *One-time thing or pattern?*

Me: *Short term accord to mom. Says they both felt awful, ended it. Explains why we get the trailer so cheap*

Horse: *No shit*

Horse: *You like him?*

Me: *I guess. Always been nice to me. She's moving in with him when she gets out.*

Horse: *Then be happy for your mom.*

Me: *Gonna try*

Sept. 3

Horse: *Whens your next day off?*

Me: *Thurs. Why?*

Horse: *Want to visit*

Me: *I'd like that :)*

Sept. 6

I studied my face in the mirror critically, wishing I didn't feel so nervous. The bruises had faded, which was good, and you could hardly see where my lip had been split. There were still a few yellowish splotches but I covered those up with strategically placed makeup. I put on a pretty sundress—

nothing fancy, but bright and cheerful and it made my boobs look fantastic.

All in all, I looked human again.

Horse would arrive any time. The drive was a little over three hours, and he'd texted me when he left at seven that morning. I couldn't define our relationship, but he wanted to visit me, not Jeff, and he was coming by himself. That had to mean something. And I couldn't be just a booty call when he'd never gotten my booty, right?

I heard him pulling up and paused at the door, tugging up the bodice of my dress. Cleavage had seemed like a great idea earlier, but now I felt self-conscious. He knocked on the door.

"You there, sweet butt?" he called. I opened the door and his eyes went straight to my chest.

"Don't call me sweet butt," I snapped at him and he grinned, reaching out a finger to poke my nose.

"Bitchy, aren't we?"

"Rude, aren't we?"

"Always."

We started laughing at the same time and he pulled me into his arms, giving me a welcome kiss that made me forget everything else. While his tongue explored my mouth, his hands roamed down to my rear, cupping my cheeks and pulling me up and into his hips. I felt his cock against my stomach and sparks raced through me. Hard to believe I could make this handsome, intimidating biker so aroused.

Finally the need to breathe got the better of me, and I pulled away from him, taking his hand and drawing him in to the living room to the couch. He looked around, eyes pausing as they took in Jeff's pipe on the coffee table.

"Your brother here?"

"He's still in bed," I said. "Not really a morning person."

He gave a rueful laugh.

"Me neither, got up too early this morning."

A thrill ran through me—he'd been eager enough to see me that he'd gotten up early!

"So you have business down here?" I asked, trying to sound casual. He shook his head.

"Just you, babe."

I grinned at him like an idiot. So much for being cool.

"So what do you want to do?"

He raised an eyebrow.

"Do you really have to ask?"

I laughed nervously. He might be gorgeous, but I couldn't just jump into bed with him, not like this. I needed a little warming up first.

"Um, how about I show you around the area a little, maybe go down to the river or something?"

He gave me a knowing look.

"Chicken."

"Maybe."

"Okay, we'll play this your way. You want to pack a lunch or go out?"

I thought about my bank balance—growing, but still low—and decided a picnic was the way to go.

"Give me ten minutes and I'll have something pulled together."

"You'd better change too."

"Why?"

"Because you can't ride a bike in that dress. Put on some jeans."

"I've never ridden a bike before."

Horse leaned over and gave me a quick kiss on the mouth.

"Lookin' forward to being your first, babe."

Chapter Seven

§9

It took more like half an hour, but I packed a lunch, a blanket to sit on and some condoms (carefully zipped into a pocket in my purse), just in case. Horse handed me a black helmet that looked like what a German army guy would wear—you know, the kind that flares out a little around the edges? I wasn't quite sure how to adjust it, but he put it on my head and fixed the straps carefully, like I was fragile and precious. I loved how that made me feel. Then I got on the bike behind him, which was an experience in and of itself. The Harley was big and wide, and I had to spread my legs around his hips. My naughty bits didn't miss the symbolism there. I wasn't quite sure where to put my arms, but he grabbed my hands and pulled them around to his stomach.

"Hold tight," he said. "Tap my stomach if you need me to stop for some reason and watch out for the pipes. They get hot."

"Okay," I replied nervously.

Then the bike roared to life and we pulled down the driveway.

How do I describe that first ride?

Well, for one thing, the bike vibrates. A lot. I suppose over time it would numb your rear, but for those first few minutes it felt like sitting on the world's biggest sex toy. It didn't hurt that my arms were wrapped tight around a hot, muscular guy who'd made it clear he appreciated my assets. I squeezed him tight as we pulled out onto the highway, holding on for dear life as he opened the throttle.

I'd promised to show him the sights, but he had his own agenda and apparently knew the area well already. After about half an hour, we pulled off the highway and headed up into the hills on a gravel road. This was much slower going and before long it turned to dirt. The next thing I knew, we turned down a narrow track that barely deserved to be called a road. It dead-ended at a turn-around. Horse killed the engine.

I dropped my hands, accidentally grazing his erection. I jerked my hand away, embarrassed, but he grabbed it and pulled it back, rubbing it up and down his length.

"Missed that, babe," he said. I didn't reply, feeling strangely shy, but when he let my hand go I didn't stop touching him. I thought about his dick, how big it was, how hard it'd been the last time I'd seen it, all for me. I shifted on the seat, tilting my hips forward into the hard leather. It felt good to have my legs spread so wide... But I wanted to feel his shaft in my hand. I reached for his fly.

"Shit, babe, not gonna fuck you in the parking lot," he said, laughing. I squawked, jerking my hands away, embarrassed. "Got a better idea. C'mon."

I hopped off the bike, knowing my face must be bright red. Horse grabbed our picnic stuff and one of his saddlebags, holding out his hand. I took it and he pulled me along a trail through the brush.

Now, you have to realize that eastern Washington isn't exactly the garden of Eden. It's mostly desert and scrubland, with low, rolling hills. But as I followed him along a gully between two of those hills, more and more green appeared, along with a little trickle of water. We hiked along the stream for about half an hour until we reached a small, round pond that gave off wisps of steam.

"A hot spring!" I exclaimed with delight. Horse looked smug as I ran to the edge, reaching down to trail my fingers through the water. "How did you know about this? I grew up around here and I've never heard of this place."

"I know all kinds of interesting things you don't," he said, waggling his eyebrows suggestively. I snickered. But I stopped laughing and started running when he dropped the picnic stuff and lunged toward me. I screeched and giggled as he caught me from behind, pulling me back to the ground on top of him and tickling me. He lay on his back, arms around my chest, legs around mine, and held me in place as he reached down for the hem of my tee. He jerked it up and over my head, pausing to tickle me again every few seconds.

Then his hands went down to the fastening of my jeans.

"Don't you dare!" I yelled, but he just laughed and ripped them open. He got them loose and pushed them down over my hips. At that, I bucked hard and he let me go, which pitched me forward. Before I could even think he was on me from behind, jerking my jeans down my legs. He stood up, holding them out of my reach triumphantly.

"You're gonna pay for that!" I yelled, still laughing. I stopped laughing though and started running as he dropped the jeans and lunged toward me again. That worked just about as well as it had the first time, which was not at all. He caught me up and threw me over his shoulder, carrying me over to the spring, giving my butt a little smack, saying, "Quiet, woman."

I screamed "No!" before I hit the water with a splash.

It was like jumping into a hot tub—not too deep, but deep enough I wasn't in any danger. I surfaced, scowling at him and dropping my head back into the water to get the hair out of my face. Then I popped back up to glare at him some more.

Horse doubled over laughing at me.

I splashed him as hard as I could, which made him laugh more, then turned away to pout.

Mistake.

The splash he made jumping in nearly knocked me over, and then his arms came around me, pulling my back into the curve of his body. He'd stripped down to his boxers. His hands slid over me, stroking my curves, and I melted.

"Baby, you're cute when you're wet," he whispered in my ear, sliding a finger down into my panties. He pushed my bra down with the other hand, rolling my nipple between his fingers as he toyed with my clit. I shuddered and arched my back as he flicked his finger faster and faster, playing me like a guitar. I guess I'd been in a constant state of arousal all morning, because I came like a firecracker.

"Holy shit..." I moaned, collapsing against him.

He kissed the back of my neck, then turned me around to face him. I wrapped my legs around his waist and my arms around his neck, kissing him with everything I had. This time it was my tongue taking over his mouth as I dug my fingers through his hair. My bra was pushed down below my breasts, nipples chafing against his chest, and everything between us was all wet and slippery and delicious.

Finally he pulled away, sucking in a deep breath. I used the opportunity to reach down between us and grab his cock. He loosened his arms, making it easier for me to reach, and I pushed the fabric of his boxers down below the length of his erection. I cupped the underside of his penis, drawing the heel of my hand up and down along the edge of the ridge around the head.

"Fuck, baby, that feels good."

Encouraged, I gripped him and started pumping up and down, faster and faster, until his hands tightened on my hips and his breathing grew ragged. I slid my hand down below, cupping his balls, rolling them in his sac, then drew them back up and squeezed him tightly around the base. He shuddered, grabbing my hand in his and jerking it up and down along his cock, way rougher than I would have done on my own.

"Fuck me..." he muttered, resting his forehead against mine. "Like that, babe. Keep going, don't stop."

I pumped him as fast as I could, savoring his little grunts of desire and satisfaction. Then I felt a throbbing deep inside his shaft. His seed shot out between us through the water, and he grunted violently as he came. I caressed him slowly as he softened until he pulled my hand away, drawing it up and around his neck.

"You're so fucking hot," he whispered, lifting me and kissing the below my ear. "I can't believe how hot you are. I hated thinking about you all slutted up and going out without me, letting some other guy hold you."

"Well, I spent the night listening to Jeff moaning and barfing, so that was sort of a bust," I whispered back. "None of them would have come close to you anyway. But I still wish I'd had more time to visit with Cara."

He shrugged.

"Jeff did what he had to do."

His words struck me as odd.

"What do you mean?"

"He needed you at home, so he asked you to stay even though he probably hated keeping you in, that's all."

"Oh," I said. "Yeah, you're probably right. He's been so good to me, it was the least I could do."

I laid my head against his shoulder and we sat there in the hot water, savoring the moment, urgency gone.

Then his stomach grumbled so hard I felt the vibrations.

"Hungry much?" I asked him, smiling.

"I ate breakfast six hours ago," he replied. "Wanted to get here and see you. Would have come last night if I could've."

"I hate to end this, but maybe I should feed you."

"I won't argue. Your cooking's almost as good as your hand jobs."

"Horse!" I sputtered, blushing. I leaned back and splashed his face. He dunked me and we wrestled a little bit before finally climbing out to get some food.

Fortunately it was in the nineties, so even sopping wet we weren't too uncomfortable. It felt sort of strange sitting down to a picnic lunch in my panties and bra, but I figured it wasn't much worse than wearing a bikini. Besides, my undies were pretty—black, with eyelet lace and polka dots, and just a hint of a push-up on top. The panties were boy cut, high in the back across my butt, and I enjoyed feeling Horse's eyes on me as I set everything up.

It wasn't anything fancy—just some chicken sandwiches, veggie sticks and watermelon, with cream-cheese brownies for dessert—but he seemed to appreciate it.

"Jeff's lucky to have you around," he said between bites. "I wish I had someone taking care of me like this."

"You live on your own?" I asked, trying to sound casual. I didn't think he had a girlfriend, but we hadn't actually talked about it. Probably should have asked that before grabbing his dick in the pool.

Oops.

"Been on my own since I got out of the service."

"Army?"

"Marines. Two tours in Afghanistan, that was enough. Came back, bounced around for a while, joined the club."

I wanted to ask how it had been overseas, but it wasn't exactly a question you just blurted out, so I just gave him a questioning look, hoping he'd volunteer something. He caught my eye and smiled, eyes crinkling just a little bit around the edges. Seeing those tiny wrinkles reminded me that I didn't even know how old he was.

Hell, I didn't even know his real name. Double oops.

"What's your name?"

"Horse."

"I mean your real name," I replied, shoving his shoulder playfully. "I don't know you at all, it's weird. Tell me something."

"My real name is Horse, that's what I go by. That's what the people who know me use. But if you want to see my driver's license, have at it." He reached over, snagging his jeans and dragging them toward us. He pulled out the leather wallet attached to his pants with a chain, flipped it open and slid out his license. I took it and giggled when I saw his name.

Marcus Antonius Caesar McDonnell.

"Seriously?"

"Seriously," he replied, grinning. "Mom had me while Dad was serving time. Wasn't a long haul, but damn she was pissed at him for leaving her alone while she was knocked up. She loved history and was reading this whole big series about Rome, so decided fuck it and named me after some Roman general. Worst part? She didn't even get the name right. Marcus Antonius Caesar wasn't a real guy. Dad shit himself, but by the time he got out it was a done deal."

"I can't decide if that name kicks ass or is the scariest thing I've ever seen," I said, giggling.

"It's my name, therefore it kicks ass," he replied gravely. "Seriously, though, I never used it. Dad's the one who named me Horse, first time he saw me."

"Wow, even back then?"

"Even back then," he said, looking smug. "It stuck. Mom hates it."

"So it says here that you're thirty years old and live in Coeur d'Alene, Idaho."

"Correct."

"And that's where the club is based?"

"That's where my charter is. The mother charter is down in Oregon, we've got seventeen overall. Not the biggest, but we're dominant in our territory, which goes a long way. We've got nomads all over the country too, and even some guys overseas fighting. The Reapers were founded by Marines after 'Nam, and that's still where a lot of our prospects come from."

Wow, Horse was suddenly a font of information. I decided to push my luck.

"So what do you do?"

He cocked his head at me.

"I'm in a motorcycle club, babe."

I laughed.

"No, I mean what do you do for a job?"

"I work for the club, mostly. We have different businesses, pretty well established in our area. Got a pawn shop, a bar, a gun shop and a garage. I do the books."

That surprised me. I couldn't see Horse stooped over a ledger, counting money.

"Hey, don't look at me like that," he replied, laughing. "Just 'cause I'm the picture of manly perfection doesn't mean I don't have a brain. I'm actually pretty good at math, took a few classes through the GI Bill and now you see me, a regular fuckin' accountant. Our finances are more complex than you'd think."

"So my brother's doing website design for your businesses?"

The smile on his face died, and he shook his head.

"That's club business, babe, and not the kind we talk about. Enough questions."

With that he reached and caught me behind the neck, pulling me in for a kiss. I dropped my food, but I didn't mind because he draped me across his lap, lips exploring mine slowly. When the kiss ended, I smiled up at him.

"I like how you change the subject."

"Glad I could be of service. Let's get this cleaned up, there's something else I wanna use the blanket for."

Worked for me.

I rolled off his lap to my knees, collecting everything up and putting it back into the bag.

"Hey, why aren't you helping?" I demanded playfully.

"Enjoying the view. Love that sweet ass of yours."

I shook it at him, smirking, and he crawled over to me, cupping my cheeks in his hands, rubbing the inside curves where they met my thighs with the pads of his thumbs.

"Fuckin' hot, babe. Can't wait to get inside."

I shivered, pushing back at him.

"So goddamn sweet," he muttered, dropping his head down to kiss the small of my back.

Sweet.

Sweet ass.

Sweet butt.

"Horse, what does sweet butt mean?" I asked suddenly. He stilled. "I know you said you call me that to piss me off, but it means more. I know it does. Tell me."

"Doesn't matter, babe, you're not one of them."

Uh-oh. I pulled away from him, cooling a little. Didn't like the sound of that at all. I sat down, facing him, knees up to my chest, arms wrapped around them pointedly, and waited.

"Drop it, babe," Horse muttered, sitting back on his heels. "We're in a good place, let's just let this flow like it should. You're thinking too much."

"When a man tells me I shouldn't think, that's a bad sign," I said, narrowing my eyes. "Explain. Now."

Horse ran a hand through his hair and shrugged.

"You don't know much about the Reapers, do you? Or motorcycle clubs in general?"

"I don't know anything about them," I said.

"Well, bikers—bikers like us, part of a club for life—are a different culture," he said after a short pause. "We're not regular citizens, we're more like a tribe that shares territory with citizens but only answers to our own kind. Everyone who's part of the tribe has their place."

"Okay," I replied, wondering where this was going.

"Fuck, this is gonna piss you off and then you aren't gonna let me stick my dick in you," he muttered.

"Do you have to be so crude?" I snapped.

"Have you met me?"

"Who says I'd let you do it anyway?"

"Babe," he replied in a low, rough voice, raising his eyebrow at me. I blushed. Okay, yes, I'd planned on it.

But that could change.

"So tell me."

"Well, there's two kinds of people, those who are in the club and those who aren't," he said. "If you're in the club, you're family, and we've got each other's backs. You got a cut and three patches, you're a member and you vote. We got prospects too, who aren't full members yet, but if they don't punk out, they will be eventually."

"What about women?"

"No women in the club," he said, shaking his head. "Women hang around the club, but they aren't part of it."

"Sounds pretty sexist."

"It is what it is," he replied with a shrug. "Don't have to like it, but that's the reality in the MC world. Remember, we don't live in your world, we live in ours and the rules are different. Some clubs let women ride, ours doesn't. We're old school. Seriously old school. But that doesn't mean women aren't important to us."

I didn't like the direction this was headed.

"A man takes a woman, means to keep her, she becomes his property," Horse continued. "We covered that before—it's a sign of commitment, of respect. It means he'll protect her and everyone else better keep their fucking hands off her or be ready to fight him and all his brothers. You do not want to fuck with a man's old lady."

"Sounds messed up, Horse."

He shook his head, clearly frustrated.

"You're judging it by citizen standards, but we're not like you," he said. "Remember, we're a tribe. We live together, we die together and what's ours is ours. When times are good, we're all good. Bad times, we may eat shit but we eat it together. Most people can't handle that level of commitment. It's like when you're in combat and taking fire—you have to trust that your brothers would rather die than let you down. You feel that kind of brotherhood during war but when you come back home people expect you to sit down and work in an office like it never happened. Men—at least men like me—don't work like that. I turned into something else in Afghanistan and I can't just pretend it didn't happen. In the club, they don't ask me to."

"That's intense," I murmured.

"No shit," he said. "I know this is hard for you, but I want you to understand. This is a different life, and we have our own rules and our own justice, but it's not bad. In fact, it's pretty fuckin' good. I got a nice house, make good money, have a great time almost every fuckin' day of my life. I'm alive, babe. Ninety-nine percent of men are okay with following the rules and doing what they're told. We're the other one percent, so we built our own world with our own rules. You don't fuck with us, we won't fuck with you. But once you fuck us, you will pay."

I shivered, even though the air was warm. I reached over and grabbed my shirt, pulling it over my head. Horse's eyes followed me, holding an expression I couldn't begin to fathom.

"So finish it," I said, breaking the silence. "You're telling me this for a reason, I guess. What does sweet butt mean?"

"Well, not all women attached to the club are old ladies," he said bluntly. "Being an old lady is a big deal, like I said. You don't want to take some skank as your property if you aren't ready to throw down for her. But a man's still gotta get laid. That's what sweet butts are for."

Oh, I didn't like the sound of that.

"Continue," I said, my voice cooling.

"We got women who want to be old ladies," he said. "Or just like hanging around bikers. Maybe they want a place to crash for a while. They come around the club house and if they make themselves friendly enough we let them hang around. They clean up, take care of shit, and we sort of — "

He paused, looking away.

"You're really not gonna like this," he muttered.

"Tell me. Now."

"Well, they're pretty much public pussy," he said. "Man needs a woman, that's what they're for. Entertaining the brothers. Those are the sweet butts."

I saw red.

"You jerk!"

I got up and went for my pants. He reached for me, but I slapped his hand away, yanking up my jeans.

"You think I'm a whore!"

"No. I do *not* think you're a whore. I told you, I like pissing you off sometimes, it's hot. You aren't a sweet butt either. You see any other guys around here? Not exactly lookin' to turn you into Chinese handcuffs, Marie!"

"WHAT?" I didn't even know what that meant, but I knew it wasn't good. I finished getting dressed and grabbed my purse, pulling out my phone. Great. No service.

"Fuck," Horse muttered, pulling on his pants and tee, then grabbing his cut and jerking it on. "You won't even listen to me. You aren't like them, babe. I know that. The guys know that. It doesn't mean anything."

"Then why did you all call me sweet butt the first time we met?" I demanded. "It's not like we had anything between us then, so you didn't do it just to piss me off. Explain that, Mr. Badass Reaper!"

He looked away, rubbing a hand along the stubble on his chin, then turned back to me.

"Because that's what you looked like," he said finally. "You were waiting outside that trailer decked out like a fuckin' wet dream. We knew Jeff didn't have a woman, at least not one in particular. Just assumed, babe."

"Take me home."

"Babe, please."

"Take. Me. Home."

He turned away and kicked a rock, sending it into the hot springs with a splash, running his hands through his hair again. I wished he'd stop doing that, because it just made him look sexier and I didn't need to think about him being sexy right now.

I needed to remember the man was a pig.

"Okay, I'll take you home," he grunted, turning back toward me. "But I want to show you something first."

"By all means!" I declared grandly, throwing my arms wide. "Please, do whatever it takes to get me out of here and away from you."

Horse stalked over to the leather saddlebag he'd brought and opened it. He stood there, staring down inside it for what seemed an eternity, then glanced back at me.

"You need to know that I didn't just bring you here to fuck you, Marie."

I snorted, rolling my eyes.

"Don't give me that shit," he growled. "I can get laid whenever I want, I don't have to drive four hundred miles round trip to get off. Women see the bike, they see the tats and the cut, they're all over that shit. Pussy is just pussy, but you're different. That's why I had this made for you—I wanted to ask you to come back with me, give club life a shot."

He pulled out a black leather vest, much smaller than his, and held it up. On the back were two embroidered patches, reading "Property of Horse, Reapers MC."

Holy shit.

"Are you kidding me?" I demanded.

His face tightened, eyes growing cold.

"Never offered this to anyone else, babe. Not a joke."

"Well, don't offer it to me," I hissed. "I hardly know you, but what I *do* know is that you're a sexist pig and you can go fuck yourself and your stupid club."

"Don't insult the club, Marie."

Something in his tone stopped me mid-rant. All traces of my sweet Horse were gone and the scary biker stood in front of me in full standoff. My anger disappeared, replaced with terrible unease. I'd forgotten how terrifying he could be.

"Let's stop this," I said after a pause. "What we're doing, there's nothing good here. Let's just stop talking and leave before things get worse."

"Works for me. Get your shit."

Funny, but hiking to the spring had taken about thirty minutes. Hiking back felt like ten hours. The ride home was even worse. I worried about falling off the bike the whole time, but I'd be damned if I was going to wrap my arms around him and rest my head on his back like before. I held the sides of his hips, trying to keep my lower body from touching his, which was all but impossible.

When we reached the trailer he didn't even bother getting off his Harley, let alone watch to see if I got in the door all right.

Horse just roared away without looking back.

Chapter Eight

જી

Sept. 7

Me: *Are you there?*

Sept. 9

Me: *Horse, we should talk. I don't want us to hate each other. I think we made a mistake, please call me. I miss you. Let's fix this*

Sept 10

Me: *Are you even getting these? Please, even if you hate me, call me. I need to tell you something*

Sept. 13

Me: *Okay, you win. Bye*

Sept. 15

Things got a little dark after our trip to the hot springs.

Work was okay, but it wasn't like I loved what I was doing. Don't get me wrong, the kids were awesome, but it's tiring to be surrounded by little people constantly when they can't even wipe their own rear ends. And sometimes diapers blow out, which means exactly what you'd think.

Good times.

Life with Jeff wasn't going very well either. It's not like we didn't get along, because we did. We didn't fight or anything. But he'd stopped talking to me, didn't seem to work much and smoked more pot every day. I had my first hint of real trouble coming when he asked me how big my paycheck was. By this time I was buying all the food, which I didn't mind. After all, he'd floated me when I first got here, and when I'd gotten hurt too. But it wasn't like him to mooch, believe it or not. He'd always paid his way and I'm pretty sure he'd carried Mom a time or two.

Things came to a head right after the Reapers visited us again, this time without Horse. Jeff didn't warn me and it was hard to tell whether the visit was planned or not. I'd learned my lesson—don't ask questions unless you want to hear the answers. Honestly, I didn't think there were any good answers to the questions I had about their business relationship.

I came home from work to find bikes in the driveway. Horse's wasn't there. We were totally out of food and beer because I hadn't done my grocery shopping for the week, and I sighed in frustration. I decided to go and buy pizza instead of cooking because I had a little extra cash. I just didn't feel up to whipping something together.

I walked in to find Picnic, Bam Bam, Max and Jeff standing around the kitchen bar in tense silence.

"Um, hi?" I asked, setting down my purse.

"Hey, Marie," Picnic said, and while his voice wasn't friendly, it wasn't cold either. I guess Horse didn't go home and talk too much shit about me. "Just talking some business here."

"Yeah, I see that," I replied. "How 'bout I go and grab some pizzas? Sound good?"

"Sounds great, Marie," Bam Bam said. He reached around to his wallet, pulling out some bills and offering them to me. I was stunned.

"You don't have to do that," I murmured.

"Take the money and don't forget beer," Picnic said, his voice short. Arguing with them didn't seem like a good idea, so I grabbed the bills and retreated. I took my sweet time getting the pizzas. I really, really didn't want to come back home too early, but after hanging out at the takeout place for forty-five minutes I got a text from Jeff telling me all was clear. I grabbed the pies and drove home, hoping Jeff's weirdness lately wasn't connected to the Reapers. I kept hearing Horse's voice in my head.

Fuck with us and we *will* fuck you back.

Jeff wouldn't be that stupid, would he?

When I got back, I had another of those surreal moments that seemed to happen around the Reapers with alarming frequency. Earlier I would have sworn things were ugly between them and Jeff. Now everyone was friendly — practically jolly — and they welcomed me (or rather, the pizzas I carried) with the kind of cheer usually reserved for returning war heroes. I tried to give Bam Bam his change, but he wouldn't take it, telling me to use it for gas.

The evening followed a familiar pattern. We ate together and then they sat around drinking beer while I cleaned up. As the night went on, the jokes got dirtier. I drank several beers. They built a bonfire. Someone suggested tequila shots. I don't usually do shots, but it seemed like a fantastic idea when viewed through my beer goggles. But I'd been up since early that morning and I had to be up again at seven to get ready for work, so eventually I decided to hit the sack.

I couldn't sleep. I kept thinking about the guys outside and how Horse should be with them. Then I thought about how it felt when he held me in those strong arms of his and we slept together, all warm and safe. That made me sad, and this was where things got ugly.

"They" always say you shouldn't drink and text, whoever they are.

I should have listened to them. They're pretty smart.

Me: *Horse, muss yu*

Me: *Why dont anser?*

Me: *Horse like yur name. Horsey. I'd like to rid u horsey, LOL. You sleeping? Or busy with someone?*

Me: *I know yur there. I bet you got a new gurl alredy. Screw you.*

Me: *Screw you and your slut. I hate you. Take yur club and shove it up yur ass I wudn't be yoor old lady for ten milion dollrs.*

To say I was hung over when my alarm went off at seven that morning would be a bit of an understatement. I discovered the messages I'd sent between barf two and barf three, and then that particularly nasty one after barf three. I wanted to crawl under the trailer and die, I was so embarrassed. Through the force of extreme will, I managed to get myself to work on time. Fortunately the head count was low for the day, so the kids weren't too loud and crazy. I kept thinking about those messages, trying to decide whether to call Horse and apologize, text again or what.

I finally decided to text. He probably wouldn't take a call from me anyway, and I couldn't blame him for that. But I couldn't just leave it like that—I wasn't that kind of person. I drove home after work, grabbed a big glass of water and crafted my text carefully.

Me: *I'm really sorry about my messages last night. It's no excuse, but I was drunk and wasn't thinking. I'm sorry I bothered you and I'm sorry for the things I said. I was a bitch, it wasn't called for and I feel like shit. I promise, I won't bother you again.*

I sat, holding my phone, not sure if I wanted him to reply or not. Shit, my head was killing me. Why did I drink the tequila? I couldn't handle tequila, I knew that. The last time I'd done tequila shots I'd stripped off my shirt and danced on the coffee table at a party that had thankfully been very small. Gary'd stuffed dollar bills in my jeans and told me to drink more tequila. His friends had cheered me on and waved around their own money. Gary thought that kicked ass.

Guess I couldn't claim there hadn't been warning signs that the man was a douche...

The door slammed open and I winced.

"Marie, I gotta talk to you," Jeff said, sitting down heavily on the stool next to mine.

"I'm pretty hung over. I don't want to talk," I muttered, closing my eyes.

"It's important. I need money."

"Um, I've got a little in my purse," I replied. "How much do you want?"

"A lot," he replied, not meeting my eyes. "I'm kind of in a bind."

That caught my attention, and I looked at him. Really looked at him. What I saw shocked me. He'd lost at least ten pounds in the past couple weeks, and his hair clearly hadn't been washed in a couple of days. His face was sallow and his eyes dull—not just hangover dull.

"Jeff, are you sick? You don't look good. I want to take your temperature."

"Jesus, Marie!" he burst out, slamming his hand down on the counter so hard I felt the trailer shake. I jumped, startled. "Why are you so damn pushy? I'm not your kid, I'm a grown man."

I froze. Jeff never yelled at me. In fact, Jeff never yelled, period. He'd always been mellow and the pot didn't exactly work to change that.

"I'm sorry," he said, reaching up and rubbing his shoulder, as if he'd been carrying something heavy and his back ached. "I shouldn't yell at you. But I really need some money fast, Marie."

"Why?"

"Capital," he replied, not meeting my eyes. "I've got a business deal in the works, but I need startup cash. In fact, I need a lot of startup cash. Hell of an opportunity, I can't afford to miss it."

I shook my head, wondering if he'd lost his mind.

"Seriously? You know I don't have money like that," I said. "You can have all I've got, but it's about twelve hundred bucks total. That's it."

"What about Gary?"

That stopped me short.

"Gary?"

"It's a community property state, isn't it?" Jeff asked, shifting nervously. "You can call him and make him give you the money. Do it for me, Marie. I really need the cash."

I shook my head slowly, unsure I'd actually heard him correctly.

"Well, for one thing, Gary never has any cash," I said slowly. "He spends it faster than he makes it, and it's not like we owned anything valuable. And for another, did you forget that the last time I saw him *he beat the crap out of me?*"

Jeff leaned toward me, putting his hands on my shoulders, meeting me face-to-face.

"I'm desperate, sis. What about your house? Can you get a line of credit on your house?"

I shook my head again, stunned. Had Jeff lost his mind?

"The house is already mortgaged to the hilt. We're probably upside down on the thing. What's really going on?" I demanded. I didn't buy this "business deal" thing for a minute, and I refused to believe Jeff had forgotten what Gary did to me. I couldn't deny it any longer—something really wrong, really wrong was happening. Something bad enough to make my baby brother desperate.

"Nothing," he said, shaking his head at me, turning away. "I wanted to make this deal happen and thought you might help me. You're right, I shouldn't have asked you. I'm sorry."

With that he turned and walked back out of the trailer. Seconds later his car started and he disappeared for the night. Seems so obvious in retrospect, but honestly—I didn't see what happened next coming.

Not even a little bit.

Chapter Nine
Coeur d'Alene, Idaho
Sept. 16

&

Horse

Horse leaned back against the bed, watching Serena's ass as she rode his cock like a rodeo queen.

Better than looking at her face. Not that Serena wasn't pretty, but she didn't hold a candle to Marie.

Now her… He could look at her face all day.

Most of his brothers wanted him to forget about the bitch. Women like her aren't worth the hassle, just grab some sweet butt to be your house mouse if random hookups aren't working for you. And if she gets on your nerves? Well, there's always another bitch waiting to take her place.

Serena stopped, turning to look at him.

"You paying attention?"

He laughed and shook his head.

"Sorry, babe, lost in my thoughts. Let's keep it up, okay?"

He gave her ass an encouraging smack, and she smiled at him with carefully painted lips. The girl was a pro, no question there. Cunt like a vise, mouth like a vacuum. He'd be crazy to consider giving up hot and cold running pussy like this for an old lady who could be a certified bitch.

But what a bitch…

He never got bored around Marie, and that was the fuckin' truth. And he didn't think he'd get distracted with her on his cock. She might not be a pro like Serena, but she had the sweetest pussy he'd ever tasted. Damn, but he wanted to taste her again. The thought made him even harder.

An hour later, Serena was gone and Horse still hadn't budged from the bed. Time to head over to the clubhouse soon, but he just couldn't stop thinking about Marie. They were going to discuss Jeff-hole's fuckups during church today.

Damn, Marie's fuckwad brother was an idiot.

And it wasn't like they hadn't been patient.

Horse had started finding "mistakes" in the wire transfers almost three months ago. Small ones at first, a thousand here, five hundred there. Then they got bigger. Jeff had all kinds of excuses, from simple typos to running behind on his reports. But in the end, it all pointed in the same direction—Jeff was running a skim. Fuckwit thought he could steal from the Reapers and live to enjoy it.

Just thinking about shit like this made Horse feel old.

Wasn't like Jeff didn't know what he'd gotten into. Hell, *he'd* come to *them*. They'd made it clear from the start that they wouldn't tolerate any bullshit and that the penalty for said bullshit would be high. The worst part would be the collateral damage. Marie. She loved that douche, really loved him.

Horse didn't see a happy ending.

If Marie was his old lady, he might be able to protect her brother a little better. Give him a chance to save his ass. As it stood, the fucker was toast, along with any chance Horse might have with Marie. Best-case scenario she'd never figure out what happened to Jeff, spend the rest of her life wondering and suspecting that the Reapers'd killed him.

Best case.

Worst case?

LEO would show up at her door to tell her that Jeff's body had been found in a shallow grave minus his balls and dick, an "R" for Reapers carved into his damned chest. But Marie didn't want them to "hate each other" for what went down at the hot springs. That was the least of his worries, for chrissake.

Shit.

Horse thought about how hot she looked in the picture she'd texted him, the one where she was all dressed up to go out. Right on schedule his dick stood at attention, begging for a fuck as if Serena hadn't just wrung him dry.

Marie's picture was cute and sexy, just like her. She'd taken it in the bathroom mirror, all dressed up to go party with her friend. Little black dress, showing off way too much of her cleavage. And her legs... He couldn't see all of those legs, but any fucker standing next to her would see them and more if she bent over even a little bit. And those fishnet tights? Fuckin' A.

He reached down and grabbed his cock, sliding his hand up and down the length roughly. He hunted for his phone with the other, wanting to pull up the pic, but it wasn't on the bedside table.

Shit, he'd left it at the clubhouse last night.

Didn't matter, her image was burned in his brain. He'd 'bout lost his mind the night she'd sent it to him. She looked fantastic, no question. But his woman shouldn't be going out dressed like that without him there to protect her. Every man in the place would take one look at those legs and see themselves bending her over a table, shoving their dicks right up her ass.

The thought of her down and spread on a table made Horse gasp, pre-come dripping down his erection. He slid his hand up, smearing the fluid around, and started jacking himself seriously. He could see it already. He'd walk up to her in the club, right behind her where she couldn't see. She'd be talking to her girlfriend, laughing and sipping on some kind of pink girly shit, because Marie was all girl. Her lips would wrap around that straw, sucking down the booze like she'd suck down his come after blowing him.

Horse slid his fingers up, catching more of the pre-come oozing out and circled his head with it. Fuck, that felt good.

What did it say about a man when jacking off to a memory felt better than a hot bitch like Serena doing a reverse cowgirl?

Horse felt a climax building in his swollen balls, a shitload of come just for Marie. She had the hottest mouth, the softest hands and a pussy he'd die for. He couldn't wait to blow all over her tits and make her rub it while she fingered herself.

Why the hell hadn't he managed to fuck her yet?

Time to fix that. He'd walk up behind her, reach around and take the drink out of her hand, setting it on the table. Then he'd grab her around the waist before she could complain, swinging her little body up into his arms and carrying her right into the bathroom.

Ass like hers was too hot to wait until they got home.

She'd probably bitch a little when he bent her over, but he'd shut her up, warning her to brace against the counter. Damn, but his girl could bitch about anything. The thought of Marie's face, all pissed off at him for calling her sweet butt, made his cock jerk, and he had to stop moving for a second.

No good, blowing your wad before the best part.

After about a minute he'd cooled off enough to let the fantasy play out.

He'd push her over and slide his hands under that little dress, pulling it up until he saw the small of her back. Those fishnets would be hooked to a garter belt, with a black thong to match. He'd reach down and push the narrow flap of fabric aside, sliding his finger into her cunt to feel just how hot and tight she was.

She might complain but Marie was always ready for him, no question. Horse let the fantasy take over again. Fuck...

In his mind he unzipped his jeans, pushing them down just enough to pull out his cock and balls, rubbing his cock head against the crease of her ass. She shivered, and he slid off those naughty little panties of hers, dropping them to the floor.

She stepped out of them and set her high heels wide, tilting up her ass and inviting him right on in.

Be rude to turn down an invitation like that.

He reached down, grabbing the tip of his cock, sliding it along the slit of her pussy a couple of times before settling himself. Then he took her hips in his hands, holding her tight, and thrust himself all the way in. She screamed, muscles tightening up around his cock. He should have taken it slower, she'd probably never had a man so big inside before.

"Sorry, baby," he muttered.

"It's okay," she whispered, sucking in deep breaths. He felt her membranes tighten around him, twitching and squeezing him harder than that goddamn masseuse from the spa in downtown Spokane. So fuckin' hot. Horse couldn't wait any longer.

Slowly he pulled out as she gripped him, muscles twitching. He retreated almost all the way, feeling her lips tighten around the rim of his head before slamming back into her.

Things got wild after that.

It took everything he had to stay upright as he fucked Marie. She gasped each time he bottomed out, cunt wrapped around him so tight it almost hurt. Fuck, she felt good. Again and again he forced his way into her small body, until he felt his balls drawing up, ready to blow his load straight into her womb.

Marie was close too. She'd gotten so wet and sloppy that every thrust squelched and she kept begging him for more, to fuck her harder. He leaned over, covering her body with his, bracing himself against the counter with one hand while the other searched for her clit.

There it was.

Horse thrust his finger against it, too far gone to be subtle or gentle. Apparently she didn't mind, because as soon as he touched it she blew up like a fuckin' bomb around him, screaming. It felt incredible, the way her entire body centered on him, gripping him, begging for his come.

He'd give it to her too.

Horse released her clit, leaning both arms against the counter as he started really hammering her. Their grunts mixed as he took her, branding her as his and fucking her so hard she'd feel his cock in the back of her throat.

Marie.

His girl.

His property.

Only his.

Horse blew up, coming so hard he forgot to breathe. He let his hand fall away from his cock, dropping the fantasy. Then he started laughing at himself right there in his bedroom, the sound anything but funny because fucking Marie in his head was better than fucking Serena for real.

Might as well shoot himself, get it over with.

Horse pulled up to the clubhouse, cutting it far too close for church.

One of the prospects stood in the parking lot outside, watching the bikes and keeping an eye on the gate. The Reapers bought the old National Guard armory fifteen years back. With its concrete block construction, walled courtyard and small windows it was perfect, both as a clubhouse and a fortress. Not that they'd come under attack recently. The Reapers were indisputably dominant in the area, with all other clubs operating only with their blessing. That was the subject of the meeting.

Protecting that dominance.

Horse walked into the clubhouse, which was first and foremost a lounge and hangout area. There were rooms upstairs kitted out for overnight visits, of course, and some storage, but they never kept anything too sensitive there. At least nothing where LEO could ever find it. The cops didn't show up often, but the times they'd brought warrants they hadn't found jack shit.

The girls needed to come through and clean the place out, Horse decided, looking around the clubhouse with distaste. Debris from last night's party still littered the tables, couches and the long bar along one wall. Most of them were probably still sleeping it off upstairs, although a dirty blonde wearing a tight jean skirt and halter top was passed out on the couch, legs spread wide. Thank God he didn't live here anymore; now that he had his own place he cringed at what used to seem normal in terms of hygiene.

Yup, getting old.

"You coming, bro?" asked Ruger, a heavily tattooed and pierced man with a short mohawk. He stood by the door with another of their prospects, Painter. "Last one."

"Yeah, sorry," Horse replied. He handed his gun to Painter, who set it carefully on the counter with the others, next to a box full of cell phones.

"You got mine in there already?" he asked. "Think I left it here last night."

"Yeah."

Horse nodded his thanks and walked into church.

Fifteen guys, all but three of their active, full-patch members, already sat around the big, scarred wooden table that had once decorated some fancy-assed conference room. Now it had a thousand nicks and little carvings in it, and a big RFFR painted in the center—Reapers Forever, Forever Reapers.

"Nice you could join us," said Picnic, sitting at the head of the table. "Thought Serena might have sucked you in. Get lost in that snatch of hers?"

"It's five o'clock exactly," Horse said, shrugging as he draped his large frame across an empty chair. "What can I say?

I'm a precisely tuned, high-performance machine, unlike you and that crap-ass bike you ride."

"Fuck off," Picnic said, grinning back. Then his expression grew more serious. "Okay, boys, we got something important to deal with today. I think you all know we've got a thief. Jeff Jensen, computer guy, out of the Yakima Valley. Got back from seeing him this morning, no progress at all."

"He's the guy handling our offshore stuff, right?" asked Ruger.

"Yeah," Horse replied. "Computer genius, knows his shit, our transactions are untraceable. God knows we're paying him for it too. But it's not enough. He's been skimming for months. Been tracking it down for a while now, already gave him opportunities to make it right, so it's not just a matter of him screwing up. Definitely skimming. It's small compared to our total volume, but we can't let shit like this happen. Bad for business."

"We let one do it, they're all gonna try," Picnic said. "We start losing respect, next thing you know the girls at the Line'll be giving drinks and lap dances to another MC."

"So what's the damage?" asked Bam Bam.

"We're right at $50k," Horse answered. "It's been push and pull, he grabs a couple grand, then tries to pay it back. He's gambling, maybe using. I hate to lose him as an asset because we don't have anyone else in the fold to replace him. That's why we've given him so many chances to make things right. But his losses are getting bigger—as of last week he was only into us for $20k total, so it's escalating fast. We let him go much longer and we'll be down serious cash. He might even pull a runner on us."

"We should put him in the ground," Max said, voice firm and cold. Horse glanced at him, surprised to see his face flushed, the little muscle in his jaw flexing with suppressed emotion. Max was still on probation, and it wasn't usual for a guy in his position to talk so much during church. Max's blood tended to run hot though. He was one of the hardest men Horse had ever met, which was saying a lot. "We've done everything but lead this guy to the shitter and wipe his ass. He's always making promises, always got an excuse, but nothing ever changes. You should've seen him last night. He's definitely tweaking. Time to cut our losses."

The words hung heavy in the air.

"How much does he know about club business?" asked Duck, a Vietnam vet who couldn't make the long runs anymore. He spent most of his time in the clubhouse drinking beer and telling the girls stories about back in the day when men were men and women knew their place. Horse didn't much like the man but he'd still trust him with his life.

He'd trust any of the brothers with his life.

"Too much," Horse replied, his voice heavy. "Way too much. He's a liability if we don't take out some kind of insurance."

"What kind insurance is good enough for a guy like that?" asked Max, clearly spoiling for a fight, although damned if Horse could understand why. "He's a liar and a thief. The money we've been feeding him for his work should be enough for anyone. Instead he's livin' in a shithole, smoking weed and waiting for his sister to bring home her fuckin' pathetic little paychecks. What kind of man lives like that? Even if he started playing it straight, we'd never be able to believe him. Probably full of all kinds of crazy lies."

"That's the truth," Picnic murmured. He looked up at Horse, his face grave.

"We in agreement here?"

Horse glanced around the room, seeing Jensen's death written in every face. He couldn't argue with them—the man knew way too much. He needed to be removed.

Fuck.

He thought about Marie, what she looked like when she was pissed at him, spitting fire like a little dragon. Damn, he wanted to get inside that woman. Once wouldn't be close to enough. As usual his dick stood up to salute the idea, but what really pushed him over the edge was the thought of Marie crying over that lame-ass bastard.

He couldn't let that happen.

"What about the sister?" he asked.

"What about her?" Picnic replied, voice carefully neutral.

"She's gonna be my old lady. Some nice insurance there," Horse said, aware of the pointed looks several of the brothers gave each other. "And when it's family, we take care of business different and you know it."

"Last I heard, she wasn't on board with that," Picnic replied slowly. "Girl didn't even ask about you last night, Horse."

"There's precedent. Not all old ladies start out with their priorities in line, but that doesn't mean they can't be claimed if the president approves it and the members agree. It's happened."

"Sure, thirty years ago," snapped Bam Bam. "They did all kinds of shit back then. We're livin' in a modern world, bro, you can't just kidnap some chick and take her home."

Duck snorted and slammed his hand down on the table, startling everyone.

"You pussies talk about the modern world like we give a shit about their rules. Remember who we are," he boomed. "We're men—one percenters. Fucking kings of the MC world. We don't follow the rules, we make our own goddamn rules. My brother Horse wants a woman, wants her bad enough to come to the club and throw down for her. He ever done that before?"

He looked around the room, glaring at each man in turn.

Horse bit back a grin. Duck on a roll, hadn't seen that one coming.

"Our brother has come before this club and let us know his intention to take an old lady," Duck continued. "The situation is complicated. We all know he'll put the club first, so we hear him out and back his play. He may not always be right, but he's always our brother. You little cocksuckers need to think about that, 'fore I show up here one day and find you growing tits in place of your balls."

Duck sat back with a grunt.

"How 'bout you tell us what you really think, Duck," said Ruger, laughing and relaxing back into his chair. "Jesus."

"He's right," Horse said, voice deadly serious. "I may not always be right, but I *am* always your brother—or at least I thought I was. A Reaper takes what he wants. You got my back?"

Picnic sighed.

"You're an idiot, you know that?" he said. "She isn't part of our world, she's got no idea what to expect and she doesn't even want to try. It's not gonna end well."

"That's my problem, now isn't it?"

"It's your problem so long as you keep it controlled and out of club business," Picnic replied. "She's a nice kid, I like her. Good cook, fucking love that potato salad of hers. Puts bacon in it. It'd be nice to have some of that shit with dinner next time we roast a pig. But that still leaves us to deal with her brother. Makes things more complicated."

Horse smiled. He'd won—this was just details.

"So she's our insurance," he answered. "Let the brother know that if he doesn't pay us back, he'll never see her again. Give him a few months, see how things play out."

"You think he'll find a way to pay us back?" asked Picnic.

"No idea," Horse admitted. "The guy practically prints money when he's focused and sober. Enough motivation, he may come through for us."

"Hasn't so far."

"He loves his sister," Bam Bam said quietly. "He's a weasel and a bastard, but he really does care about her. Seen it with my own eyes. I don't think he'll hang her out to dry."

"We make sure he knows—he doesn't pay, she's in big trouble," Horse said. "He pays up, great. He blows this deal, we put him in the ground. Everybody wins."

Except Marie. But Jensen was a big boy and he'd chosen to do business with and then screw over the Reapers MC. If it wasn't for her, fucker'd be dead already.

"And the issue of respect?" asked Ruger. "We have to cover our bases here. Can't look weak."

"That's the truth," Picnic said. "But taking a man's sister, holding her hostage? That's payment in blood, we spread it 'round the right places. It should do."

"You're forgetting one thing," said Max. Horse looked at him, trying to read his mind. Something was up with Max. They all cared about club business, but this was a step beyond. Almost personal.

"The money," Max continued. "It's one thing to let Horse have his little fuck toy, I don't give a shit about that. It's another to just sit back and lose fifty large. You guys may have money stashed somewhere, but I don't. We sure we want to risk that kind of cash on this asshat pulling through for us, on top of the risk of him running to LEO?"

Horse narrowed his eyes at Max, who met them straight on. The man didn't flinch.

"It's a good point," Bam Bam said, his voice mild. "Of course, we take him out now, we never see that money again anyway, Max."

"Well maybe we wouldn't have our asses hanging out so far if Horse'd done a better job watching him."

Picnic sat up.

"Careful, brother," he said, his voice cold. "Horse did his job. It was my call to let this play out, and I had good reason. That little shit made half a million bucks for this club, easy, in the last two years. You don't just throw something like that away if you don't have to. Fucker's got a gift, can't just replace him. That's why I like this idea, maybe we can still save the situation."

"I'm not voting for it," Max said. "We need to put him down."

"Why don't I buy her?" Horse said. Everyone turned to look at him, startled. "I'll buy Marie from the club, and we give Jensen another shot. Fifty grand, outta my pocket and into the club account. We wait and see if Jensen comes up with the money and interest. He does, I get paid back, the club makes a profit. He doesn't, it's on me."

"That's fucked up," muttered Bam Bam. "No cunt worth that."

"She's not a cunt."

"They're all cunts," Max snapped. Horse caught his eye, staring him down.

"Play nice, boys," said Picnic. "I think you're crazy, Horse, but this works for me. That good enough for you, Max?"

Max dipped his head in agreement.

"I'm with Picnic, you're crazy," said Bam Bam. "Should be a hell of a show. She hates you, Horse. Jensen told me."

"Well, I'm pretty pissed at her myself," Horse said. "We gotta work through that. But she's mine and that's the way it is."

Picnic rolled his eyes and Ruger snorted.

"Nice to see youngsters acting like men instead of chorus girls," Duck grunted, looking around the table in approval. "Let's vote. I want beer."

Horse left the meeting feeling pretty good. Paying out the money was gonna hurt, no question. But he'd been thinking about putting up a new shop on the property, so he had the cash. He damned sure wanted Marie more than a shop. He couldn't wait to come home to her after a tough day, the smell of her cooking in the house, the sight of her in an apron and nothing else.

Nice.

Horse grabbed his phone out of the box, thinking he should have called her before now. He'd gotten her sweet little text messages and knew she was hurting. Hell, he'd wanted her to hurt, he could admit it. She'd hurt him, so he let her dangle for a few days...

But now that them being together was a reality? Time to let it go. He stepped out of the clubhouse and into the sunlight, powering up the phone. It pinged repeatedly, letting him know he'd missed a bunch of text messages from the night before.

Marie: *Horse, muss yu*

Marie: *Why dont anser?*

Marie: *Horse like yur name. Horsey. I'd like to rid u horsey, LOL. You sleeping? Or busy with someone?*

Marie: *I know yur there. I bet you got a new gurl alredy. Screw you.*

Marie: *Screw you and your slut. I hate you. Take yur club and shove it up yur ass I wudn't be yoor old lady for ten milion dollrs.*

Fuck.

She'd been drunk, no question. And when people were drunk they said stupid shit, but they also told the truth. Marie might want his body, but she definitely didn't want to be his old lady, despite all her sweet little texts to him trying to mend fences.

"Goddamit!" he yelled, throwing the phone at the concrete block wall of the clubhouse. It hit hard, shattering, as Ruger stepped outside.

"Problem?" he asked, raising a brow and looking from the phone to Horse.

Horse shook his head.

"No problem," he said, tamping down his anger. He'd made his choice, taken a stand in front of the club. He'd play it out. But Marie was damned well going to pay him back that fifty grand one way or another. "Decided it's time to get a new phone, that's all."

"What was wrong with the old one?" Ruger asked, his voice mild.

"It broke."

Sept. 17 – Present Day

Horse looked down at Jeff, feeling detached.

The man knelt in the middle of the floor, hands cuffed behind his back, Picnic standing over him with a gun. Blood ran down his face—they'd given him a decent beating, but not serious enough to need a hospital. Just bad enough to make him really, really uncomfortable and hopefully scare the hell out of Marie.

He'd have a few permanent scars to help him remember not to fuck over the Reapers too.

"I wonder if sissy's gonna bail you out?" Picnic asked Jeff. "You really screwed yourself this time, little man. Do you not know our motto? Fuck with us and we *will* fuck with you."

"I'm sorry," Jeff whispered, eyes wild behind his puffing eyelids. "I'm so sorry, I didn't do it on purpose, you've got to give me another chance."

"How many chances do you need?" Horse demanded. "It's hard to keep a straight face, listening to you talk."

Jeff's phone pinged on the counter, and Ruger picked it up.

"Text from Marie," he said. "She's gonna be home in a few, leaving the store now."

"Text her back," Jeff said quickly. "Please, she doesn't have anything to do with this. Don't let this happen, just tell her not to come home for another hour. Don't let this be her last memory of me."

"Shut up," Picnic said, sounding exasperated.

Jeff shut up.

"You guys said this was a dump, but I didn't realize just how bad," Ruger said, leaning back against the wall, crossing his arms in front of him as he surveyed the room. "Can't believe you let your sister live like this, fuckwad, especially given how much money we've been paying you."

"I'm a shitty brother," Jeff mumbled. "I know that. But don't hurt Marie, she's a sweetheart. Right? Never hurt anyone, doesn't deserve this."

"Oh I'm sure she's *sweet*," Ruger replied, smirking. Horse shot him a dark look, but it didn't shut him up. Ruger grinned at him. "You can't seriously expect us not to fuck with you over this, Horse."

Horse shrugged—he didn't, actually. What a mess. Fifty grand out the door for a woman who didn't even want him. He ran a hand through his hair. At least he'd finally get to fuck her.

For fifty grand her cunt better be lined with gold.

"She's pulling up now," Painter said from his station near the window. "Got an armful of groceries. Should I help her carry them in?"

The men just looked at him, Picnic shaking his head in bemusement.

"Joking, right?" asked Ruger.

"Sorry, guess I didn't think that one through," Painter said. Horse had his doubts about the prospect—still pretty young, and so green. Could take him years to earn his top rocker at this point. The door opened and Marie walked in.

She screamed.

"I'm so sorry, sis," Jeff said, the words muffled and broken. Marie looked around the room frantically, disbelief and shock written all over her face. Horse felt his cock harden and decided he was one sick fuck. The woman was terrified and she didn't want him, yet she still turned him on. Of course, just about everything she did turned him on.

Everything but throwing his offer to take her as property back in his face. Fuckin' bitch and her text messages. He might've paid fifty grand for her, but she claimed a million wouldn't be enough?

She should be grateful to him for saving her brother.

Picnic looked at Marie and winked. That was creepy, even to Horse, and it surprised him that she didn't have a heart attack on the spot. Good, he wanted her afraid.

"Little brother's been a bad boy," Picnic said. "He's been stealing from us. You know anything about that?"

She shook her head, a grocery bag falling, apples rolling on the floor. One hit Horse's foot and it took all his willpower not to kick it at Jensen's head.

"I don't understand," she said, giving her brother a pleading look.

"He's supposed to be working for us," Picnic said. "Pretty good with that little laptop of his, sure you get that. But instead of working he's been playing at the casino with our fucking money. Now he has the balls to tell me that he's lost the money and can't pay us back."

He punctuated the last four words with jabs of his pistol's thick, round barrel into the back of Jeff's neck. Marie looked stunned, blinking rapidly. Horse could almost see the thoughts racing through her pretty little head.

"You got fifty grand on you?" he asked casually.

"He stole fifty thousand dollars?"

"Yup," Horse said. "And if it doesn't get paid back right now, his options are limited."

"I thought you were friends," she whispered, eyes darting between Horse, Jensen and Picnic.

"You're a sweet kid," Picnic replied. "But you don't get who we are. There's the club and everyone else, and this stupid fucker is *not* part of the club. You fuck with us, we will fuck you back. Harder. Always."

Jeff's mouth trembled, tears welling up in his eyes. Horse'd been surprised the guy didn't start bawling earlier, to be honest. Then Jensen pissed his pants.

"Shit," muttered Ruger. "I fucking hate it when they piss themselves."

He looked down at the man and shook his head.

"You don't see your sister pissing herself, do you? What a little bitch," he said, disgusted.

"Are you going to kill us?" Marie asked, starting to tremble. She'd lost the color in her face. Horse looked at Jensen, disgusted. What kind of asshole put his sister through something like this—not just this, here, but living in a dump like this, working all day changing diapers for minimum wage?

"I mean, would you really kill people you shared pictures of your daughters with?" Marie asked, studying Picnic's face. "One of them is about my age, isn't she? Can't we work something out? Maybe we can make payments or something."

Horse snorted and shook his head. Time to move things along.

"You don't get it, sweetie, this isn't just about money. We could give a shit about the money. This is about respect and stealing from the club. We let this pissant fuck get away with it, they'll all start doing it. We don't let stuff like this slide. Ever. He pays with blood."

She closed her eyes for second, and Horse saw the moisture hovering on her lashes. Shit, he hated women crying. No, he hated *bitches* crying, and Marie was just another bitch. He needed to remember that.

"Jeff, why?" she whispered, and the heartbreak and despair in her voice made Painter flinch. Horse grew cold, dark rage building. How dare the little prick look at her like that, pleading with his eyes, and what did he do to deserve her loyalty?

"I wasn't planning to lose it," he replied, his voice full of despair. "I thought I could win it back, make it up somehow. Or that maybe I could hide it in the wire transfers..."

"Shut the fuck up," Picnic said, smacking the side of Jensen's head with his free hand. "You don't talk club business. Even when you're about to die."

"There's another way," Horse said, deciding to lay things out for her. Might as well get it over with and make damned sure she understood her place. He'd offered her better, but she hadn't wanted it. Now she'd take what she got, and she better not complain about it. "Paying in blood can mean different things."

"He doesn't need to die for that to happen," she said quickly. "Maybe you can burn down our trailer!"

She smiled at him like she'd won the cake at a cakewalk.

"Oh, we're gonna do that no matter what," Horse drawled. "But that's not blood. I can think of something that is though."

"What?" Jeff asked, his voice full of desperate hope. "I'll do anything, I swear. If you give me a chance I'll crack so many accounts for you, you won't believe what we can accomplish. I'll stop smoking, that'll clear my head, I'll do a better job..."

His voice trailed off as Horse laughed, and the mohawk guy shook his head and grinned at Picnic.

"You believe this asshole?" he asked. "Seriously, douche, you aren't making a very good case for yourself, telling us just how much you been slacking."

Jeff whimpered, and Horse saw Marie jerk forward, as if she wanted to go to him but thought better of it. That pissed him off even more. He wanted that kind of caring from her and she wasted it on her brother instead. But he was getting too worked up too fast, he needed to keep his cool. He took a second to slow down, stretching his neck from side to side, cracking his knuckles. That cleared his head.

"Let's get a couple of things clear," he said. "We're not going to hurt you, Marie."

"You aren't?" she asked, and the surprise in her eyes stabbed right through him. She thought he'd hurt her, like her asshat ex, Gary. Might as well call him a monster. He forced himself back on track.

"Nope," he said. "You didn't do anything wrong, we aren't pissed at you. This isn't about you. You'll keep your mouth shut if you want to survive, and you're smart enough to know that. That's not why you're here."

"Why am I here?"

"So you can see just how seriously fucked your brother is," he replied. "Because we're going to kill him if he doesn't find a way to pay us back. I think he might be able to pull it off with the proper motivation."

"I will," Jeff babbled. "I'll pay you back, thank you so much—"

"No, you'll pay us back twice as much, fuckwad," Picnic said, kicking him viciously in the side with his heavy leather boot. Jeff pitched to the floor, keening in pain. "That's if we let you live, which is entirely up to your sister."

Now was the moment. Horse wondered if he'd have to argue with her or just throw her in the truck, hands tied behind her back.

"I'll do it," she said.

Well shit. That was a little too easy. Didn't she care about her safety at all? Nope, all she cared about was Jeff-hole. Horse snorted, disgusted, letting his eyes roam across her body. Fuck, she was hot. Even like this, straight from work, scared out of her mind. His Marie was small and curvy, with hair framing her face and tits heaving as she tried to control her fear. He'd bet a thousand dollars she had no idea the top four buttons of her shirt had come undone, showing a hell of a lot of cleavage and the outline of her black bra.

His dick approved. It wanted to squeeze between those boobs and shoot out a pretty pearl necklace for her to wear. Horse took a deep breath, this wasn't over yet. He could fuck her tits later. Might be the first thing on his list.

"Don't you want to ask what it is first?" he asked.

"Um, sure," she said. "What do I have to do?"

"It seems Horse here wants a house mouse," Picnic said. She looked blank. Picnic sighed and looked at Horse. "She's clueless, you sure about this? Seems like work to me."

Horse glared at him, wondering if he could hit him without fucking up his plan. Probably not. He turned back to Marie, forcing himself to stay calm, collected.

"This is your option," he said, voice clipped. "You want to keep dumbass alive, pack a bag and climb on my bike when we leave. You do what I tell you, when I tell you, no questions and no bitching."

"Why?" she asked, so cute and confused and blank it pissed him off even more. Didn't she have any survival skills at all?

"So you can cook dessert for me," he snapped.

Her mouth dropped open. Seriously, she didn't get what was happening here? He shook his head, frustrated.

"Why the hell do you think?" he said, the words grating and harsh. "So I can fuck you."

Chapter Ten

ഌ

"You're threatening to kill my brother just so you can sleep with me?" Marie asked, her face stricken.

Ruger walked over to Horse, draping his arm around his shoulders.

"She's cute, but not real smart. Why don't you let me take her for a ride, get her trained up for you."

Ruger pumped his hips lewdly toward Marie. Horse turned and punched him in the stomach, the prick. He'd had too much of this shit, time to move along. He wanted Marie alone, naked, riding his cock. Enough with the pleasantries.

Grabbing her arm, he dragged her out of the trailer and into the orchard, pushing her back against one of the trees. She was breathing hard, making her boobs rise and fall, taunting him. He was pissed at Jeff, pissed at Ruger and pissed at Marie for being so damned perfect that she'd pushed him to this after he should have cut her loose. He'd offered her everything and she'd thrown it back in his face, yet she was perfectly willing to pimp herself out for that fuckface of a brother.

"I don't want to *sleep* with you," he told her grimly. "I want to *fuck* you. Sleeping, cuddling, all that other shit is for girlfriends and old ladies, and you've made it pretty fucking clear you aren't interested in any of that," he said, thinking about the leathers he'd gotten for her. What a joke. "I'm threatening your brother because he stole from the club, which had nothing to do with you. You steal from the club, you pay in blood. You're his blood. We take you, he pays. Fucking you is just a bonus."

"So you're taking me to show that people shouldn't steal from the club?" she asked, and he thought he saw a glint of understanding in her eyes. Finally.

"It's a fuckin' miracle, she gets it," he muttered to no one, throwing up his hands. "Your brother's lucky, because I wanna stick my dick in you more than I wanna kill him. Otherwise this wouldn't be worth the trouble. If Jeff-hole gets his shit together and pays back the club I might let you go — when I'm done with you. If he doesn't, then I'll find some other use for you. Got it?"

Let her go? Not likely. Still, he had to play out the game. At some point she'd talk to her brother again, and when she did, dickwad needed to hear the right message.

"No games, no bullshit," he said. He stepped away, trying to calm down, then turned back toward her. She looked terrified, clutching her hands together, tears streaming down her face. Suddenly he felt like an asshole. "You do this, it's your choice. I'm not raping you. You're making a decision to pay for your brother's mistake on your back. You get me?"

She stared at him, eyes full of condemnation. That shamed him, and he didn't like the feeling. Anger felt better.

"I'm serious," Horse said, glaring at her, daring her to defy him. Fighting would be better than just watching her silently sucking it up for her brother. Hell, he *liked* fighting with her. Made his dick stand up and take notice. "You call it off any time you want. I'm not gonna lock you up and watch you every minute. You make this deal, it's up to you to keep it. And you don't have to make the fucking deal. Your brother's an idiot and he knew what he was getting into. This isn't your mess and it's not your job to bail him out."

"You trying to talk me out of it?" she asked with quiet dignity. "Well, you can't. I meant what I said. I'd do anything for Jeff. Anything."

Horse clenched his jaw and spun away from her, needing some kind of outlet for his anger and frustration before he did

117

something really stupid. He kicked one of the trees and the throbbing pain in his foot helped him focus.

What exactly did he want from her, anyway? He needed her in his bed, in his house. She'd made it clear she wouldn't end up there on her own. Was it his fault her brother was the biggest idiot on earth? Horse was offering them a lifeline, yet she judged him for it. Again. Just like she'd judged him for offering her a place as his old lady.

Stupid woman didn't have the first clue what she needed but he'd give it to her anyway.

Hopefully ten times a day.

Horse watched as Marie dug through her closet. The room felt too small, he couldn't breathe. It didn't help that every time she leaned over, her shirt rode up and her pants pulled down, exposing the black line of a thong he wanted to rip off her body with his teeth.

His cock had gone from hard to painfully swollen. He adjusted it, trying to find a comfortable position, but the only place it wanted to be was pumping between her legs. Determined to drive him crazy, her ass wiggled at him every few seconds until he started to seriously wonder if he'd come in his pants. Marie pulled out a shoebox and tossed it on the bed. It spilled open and he sat down and flipped through the photos, desperate for a distraction. He saw shots of her when she was a teen, her and Jeff decked out in swimsuits as kids, arms around each other. There was a picture of her at a school dance… And there was her wedding picture.

Shit.

He pulled it out, noting the streaks of dried blood staining it. So this was Gary. The guy looked like every played-out, high school jock-turned-bully on earth. Big and meaty, he probably ran to fat now that he didn't have a coach to kick his butt. He looked like an asshole, holding the sweet and delicate Marie in his hands like some kind of county fair prize. Marie was gorgeous, but way the fuck too young. She wore a simple white dress and held a bouquet of daffodils. Douchebag wasn't even wearing a suit. Everything screamed cheap-wedding-between-kids-way-too-young, but Horse still felt a powerful wave of jealousy.

Gary had taken that pretty girl in the picture home, pulled off her dress and fucked her.

Should've killed the man when he had the chance.

Horse glanced over at Marie, who was still digging through the closet. Her thong teased him and he realized that she'd probably bought the damned thing for Gary—and she still had the picture of them together. The wave of jealousy turned tsunami, and Horse had a sudden vision of her meeting up with Gary, of him trying to change her mind about leaving. Women got back together with losers all the time.

"You wear that shit for him?" he asked, holding up the wedding picture. She looked blank.

"That butt floss," he snapped. "Why the fuck are you wearing a thong to work at a daycare? Are you seeing him again?"

"No!" she said, eyes wide. "I haven't seen him since that last time, you should know that. He hasn't called me, nothing. When I get all the papers ready, Denise's husband said he'd serve them for me."

Horse grunted, trying not to lose it. Of course she hadn't seen him again, the man beat the shit out of her. Marie wasn't stupid. *And what about the asshole who's kidnapping her?* Horse wondered. *What does she think of me?* He pushed the thought away, focusing on the thong again—once they got home, he'd take her to Victoria's Secret, get her all new shit. None of Gary's sloppy seconds in his house.

"You keeping this?" he asked, looking at the picture.

"Yes," she replied. "I don't want to forget, at least not yet."

He dropped the picture, disgusted, watching as she moved to her dresser. Every time she reached up, he caught flashes of her tiny little waist, swelling down into hips built to cradle his. Her figure was the ideal combination of small and curvy, every part adding up to perfection.

Horse wasn't sure how much longer he could take this. He needed a taste, just a taste. Now. He got up and stood behind her, taking her hips and pulling them back into his. Horse rubbed his cock against her butt, so aroused it caused him physical pain. He leaned into her, smelling her hair. Impossibly, his dick got harder.

This woman was going to kill him.

"I love how your hair smells," he muttered. He wondered what it would feel like trailing across his chest or wrapped around his cock. Better put that one on the list too.

Marie tensed.

"I have ten minutes left," she said, her voice full of strain. "Please."

That pissed him off, spinning him out of control. How much more of this did he have to take? She belonged to him now, he'd paid *fifty fucking thousand dollars* for her. Hell, he'd even gone to the mat to save her worthless brother from the club. He'd offered her everything he had and she'd thrown it back in his face.

Horse let go of her hip, reaching up to grab that hair and twisting her head around to the side. He covered it with his mouth, thrusting his tongue into her mouth like he wanted to thrust his cock down into her cunt—hard and fast, without mercy. She moaned, collapsing against him, and he slid his other hand down her stomach to her pants, ripping them open. Then his fingers plunged into her pussy. He pulled back, wanting to see her face, watching as her breath came faster and she flushed with desire and need. The sight gave him savage satisfaction.

Marie was his property now.

"This pussy," Horse said, fingering her roughly. "This pussy is mine. You are mine. I'll fuck you when and where I want, and you can either take it or get the fuck out. Are we clear?"

"Yes," Marie whispered, shivering as her eyes dilated. He felt how close she was to release, the flesh between her legs tightening. He took her mouth one more time, punishing her with his tongue and his fingers, dancing right on the edge. She thrust her hips at him and he ended the kiss, dropping his lips to her neck, licking and sucking, wanting to mark her for everyone to see.

He bit her and she moaned. Loud.

Gloating, Horse pulled his hand out of her pants and stepped back. His cock was like a pillar of granite and his heart beat so hard he could feel it pounding in his forehead, but he'd sent her a message about who was in charge. He lifted his fingers, slowly licking off her sweet juices.

"Don't care how good you taste, you don't call the shots," he whispered. "We clear?"

She nodded, flushed and needy, still quivering.

"Your rules," she whispered back. "Or I leave. And what happens if I do?"

He forced his features to stay smooth.

"To you? Nothing," he said, but he knew better. If she left him, he'd hunt her down and drag her back home by the hair if he had to. "You're with me of your own free will. But the club has to be paid in blood, Marie, not even I control that. Don't forget."

"Okay."

He pushed her gently out of the way as he reached into the lingerie drawer, pulling out panties, bras and a teddy. He thought about Gary's hands on her, stripping these scraps of lace off her perfect body, and wanted to rip them apart with his bare hands. Instead he tossed them on the floor.

"You won't need these."

He saw something tucked in the back, black fabric with Reaper colors. *What the hell?* He reached in, grabbing it. It was his t-shirt, he realized, with something wrapped inside it. She'd kept it. He pulled the bundle out and turned to Marie.

She blushed, holding out a hand.

Horse shook his head slowly and started unrolling. What he saw nearly sent his cock punching through his jeans. It was a vibrator, and a beast at that. Not too long, but it split into two parts, one clearly designed to go inside and stimulate a woman's G-spot, the other for her clit.

Marie kept her toy wrapped in his *t-shirt.*

Oh yeah. He owned her now.

"Pack the shit and the toy," he said, barely able to get the words out. What would she look like, using that thing on herself? He couldn't wait to find out.

She threw everything into her backpack and zipped it shut, throwing it over her shoulder.

"That it?" he asked. "You want anything else from the living room or kitchen? It won't be here if you try to come back." *It'll be burned to a crisp, along with any evidence your brother might have hidden here.*

Marie shook her head, blushing fiercely. He leaned in close, whispering in her ear, "Next time you want to play with your pretty pink toy, you do it while I'm watching. If you're a good girl, I'll let you wear the tee. Got it?"

Marie nodded. Horse took her arm and pulled her through the living room, past Jeff and his brother Reapers, out to his bike.

Chapter Eleven

❦

Marie

The ride to Coeur d'Alene surprised me.

For one, it seemed to take forever because riding on the bike was work. I had to hold on and pay attention the whole way and given all I'd gone through that day, it wiped me out.

On the positive side, I didn't have to talk to Horse.

We stopped twice at rest areas so I could pee and Horse could make phone calls. I watched him, feeling naked without my phone. They'd taken it from me, along with my car keys, and I didn't get the impression I'd be getting it back. Horse didn't tell me what the calls were about and I didn't ask. I also didn't know where the other Reapers were or how my brother was doing. All I cared about was staying upright on the bike.

By the time we pulled off the freeway in Coeur d'Alene it was dark. I didn't pay attention to where we went or our route. I did notice that we drove through several populated neighborhoods near a very big lake before turning off on a narrow road through the woods. Buildings grew sparse. Horse pulled up to an old farmhouse, complete with quaint-looking outbuildings and a big red barn.

So not what I expected from a biker.

Horse cut the engine and I got off stiffly, trying to stretch.

"Is this your place?"

"Bought it three years ago," he replied, walking past me toward the wide, covered porch, which had a swing, for God's sake. Like something on a country postcard. It wasn't fancy or big, but it was very well cared for and I suspected it had been painted within the last year or so.

I grabbed my backpack and followed him through the front door. I found myself in a living room furnished in what could only be called "man cave". Big flat-screen, giant comfy L-shaped couch, four different remotes on the coffee table and a poster on the wall of a naked woman straddling a motorcycle backward, flat on her stomach and cheek resting on the back seat.

I hadn't known bikes and human women could have sexual intercourse, but that was the clear implication. Lovely.

There was a hallway going straight back to what I assumed was the kitchen. A flight of stairs hugged the left wall of the house, which is where Horse headed. I really, really didn't want to follow him.

"Get your ass up here."

All-righty then.

I trailed him up the wooden stairs, which were covered in the center with a runner so old you couldn't even tell what the original pattern had been. Horse flipped on the light and stood on a landing big enough to run the full width of the house, waiting for me. A person could've put some chairs and a little table in there, but he just had boxes piled around. Three doors led to other rooms, two toward the back of the house and one toward the front. He pointed toward the front room.

"That's mine. Stay the fuck out of it unless you're invited."

"Okay."

"This one's the bathroom, here's your bedroom. There's another bathroom downstairs if you need it, next to the kitchen. Don't flush the toilet if someone's in the shower, the pipes are old. Go put your shit away and meet me downstairs. I'm hungry."

I had a vision of him showering and me deliberately flushing, suddenly burning him. Maybe I'm a bad person but it made me smile. Horse narrowed his eyes at me, suspicious. I ignored him and went into my room. It was small and plain, with aged and scuffed wood floors, cream-colored walls with old-fashioned trim and two sash windows. A queen-sized bed took up most of the space, covered with very modern bedding—you know the type, one of those bed-in-a-bag things with a giant fluffy comforter that you can get for cheap at Walmart. There was a small dresser against the wall opposite the door with a mirror. A small closet stood open on the right.

The place was lifeless, which I appreciated in a way. It would be easy to put my stamp on it, even given how little I owned. I liked the idea of having my own space, separate from Horse and all the confused feelings of anger and lust that came to life whenever I saw him.

I unpacked quickly because I was hungry too, and the last thing I wanted was for him to come looking for me in the bedroom. I still wasn't sure what his expectations were for the night. Probably not good to give him more ideas than he already had.

When I went downstairs, I found the TV on to some sports network but no sign of Horse, so I wandered back toward the kitchen. Sure enough, a door on the left led to a small bathroom under the stairwell. Double pocket doors defined the dining room opposite, which held a full-sized pool table instead of a dining room table, complete with a light hanging over it with beer logos. Definitely man cave.

That's why the kitchen startled me so much.

I reached the end of the hallway to find what had to be the cutest kitchen I'd ever seen—like something out of a country-style magazine. Serious reality disconnect... Horse stood in front of the fridge, pulling things out and putting them on a large, wooden butcher's block in the center. A wrought iron rack dangling pots and pans hung high above it and there were stools all around.

In a normal kitchen that would have taken up a ton of space, but this one was so huge you hardly even noticed. Horse had an old-fashioned farm kitchen, practically a living room in and of itself. Off the back I could see a door leading through a mud room. The walls were bright yellow with cutesy, chicken-themed wallpaper edging near the ceiling. The curtains over the windows were sunny, gingham-checked ruffles edged with lace.

"Who helped you set up the kitchen?"

"My mom," he said, not looking at me. "She wanted to do the whole house, but once I saw this I made her stop."

"Why? It's a lovely room, Horse," I said, heroically holding off a laugh. It felt good to tease him—it eased the tension just a bit. Horse turned and looked at me, all badass biker in his boots, jeans and leather Reapers' cut, face black with stubble and hair tossed by the wind.

"I made her stop because I don't have a pussy and I didn't want to start growing one," he replied, voice testy.

Fair enough. I couldn't keep the smirk off my face though.

"Make me some food, I'm gonna go take a shower," he ordered. My mouth opened automatically to protest his tone, but I caught myself and snapped it shut. Horse held the power in this relationship, not me. It would be easy to forget that—I'd gotten too comfortable around him.

I searched through the fridge and cupboards, finding enough food for sandwiches. I would need to hit the grocery store soon if we didn't want to starve. By the time he finished his shower I had everything ready and had spent several minutes debating whether or not to start eating without him. Fortunately Horse came back down before I could make the decision, hair all wet and slicked back. Without a ponytail it just brushed the tops of his shoulders. He wore a faded pair of sweats low on his hips and nothing else.

Damn.

I don't know how long I stared at him, just taking in the tattooed, muscular glory that was Horse almost naked. He broke the spell.

"Glad you like it."

"What?" I asked, confused.

"My body," he replied, smirking. "It's the only one you get to look at or fuck, so it's good the package works for you."

I blushed fiercely, turning away to grab the plates and put them on the block. He took a seat and grabbed his sandwich. I did the same, trying my hardest not make eye contact with him. That was more difficult than it looked because he sat right across from me. He was big and bare-chested and I really, really wanted to take a closer look at those tattoos. I'd seen them before, but not enough to satisfy my curiosity.

"You want a beer?" he asked, standing and walking over to the fridge.

"That sounds good," I replied, giving myself permission to check out his ass. Nice. He caught me looking as he turned around, but just handed me the bottle and we ate in companionable silence. I drank a second beer and started to feel a lot more relaxed. After we finished eating, he helped me load the dishwasher, perfectly civilized. Sometimes it felt like Horse was two different people—a badass biker jerk who gave lots of orders and a sweet, sexy man who made my body feel things Gary couldn't even imagine, let alone spark.

Which guy was real?

"You want a shower?" Horse asked.

"Yeah, I think so," I replied. "Been a long day."

"Use the bathroom upstairs, it's nicer than the one down here."

I nodded and left the kitchen, where Horse wiped up the table and counter like a perfectly normal person. So weird.

Just my luck—no lock on the bathroom door.

On the bright side, the bathroom had clearly been upgraded at some point in the recent past. In fact, looking around I was pretty sure it had been another bedroom at one point, that's how big it was. All the fixtures matched the house perfectly—big, claw foot tub, and old dresser/vanity that had been converted by putting in a sink basin surrounded by a marble top. There was a sash window on one side, and the fact that it didn't have real shades bothered me until I realized there wasn't a chance of anyone ever seeing me in here. Just too far up and in the middle of nowhere.

In addition to the tub was a giant, modern shower stall with jets on both sides and a long bench. It should have been out of place, but somehow it all fit together. The best part? A big skylight that would illuminate the entire room beautifully when the sun was out. I couldn't help but wonder how a bathroom like this wound up in an old farmhouse.

Horse's laundry still sat in a pile on the floor, so I picked it up and threw it in the hamper. I figured I would probably be doing the laundry and wondered if he had a washer and dryer. I hadn't seen any, but I hadn't seen the mud room yet. All in all, the house might be a little rough in places but it was definitely comfortable. Certainly better than the trailer, and with a lot more potential than the place I'd shared with Gary.

Go figure.

So, the lack of lock was a problem, and as much as I wanted to give that tub a test run, I didn't feel comfortable with it. Instead I stripped down and hopped in the shower, where I was pleased to find shampoo, conditioner and body wash. They weren't my usual, but they'd do until I could get to the store. Thankfully the shower had lots of hot water, although it took awhile to reach the second floor. I soaped up my hair and rinsed it, then followed with conditioner.

The door opened and Horse stepped in as I started with the body wash. I should have seen it coming, I mean how predictable? I'd been worried about the tub but honestly didn't see the shower thing coming. I guess I'm too pragmatic—he'd already showered, why would he want to shower again?

Duh.

Anyway, I shrieked when I saw him, a shriek he shut down quickly enough by grabbing me and lifting me up into his body. I wrapped my legs and arms around him instinctively as he pushed me against the shower wall. Then he took my mouth and I no longer had any doubts how this evening would end.

How to describe that kiss?

Well, it was rough and deep. His tongue thrust into me over and over, and I felt his penis gliding across my slit as he restlessly pumped his hips in time with his tongue. I'd love to say I didn't enjoy it, that I was a poor little victim of the Big Bad Biker, but that straight up isn't the truth. I caught fire and would have rubbed myself against Horse like a cat in heat if he weren't holding me tight. As it was, I dug my hands in his hair and I tilted my head to take him deeper.

One of his hands slid down my back, moving along the crack of my ass. He grazed over my rear entrance and I jumped, but he kept moving down. Then his fingers entered me, and I gotta be honest here, it kicked ass. Horse's cock slid back and forth along my clit from the front and his fingers delved deep inside from the back. He went after my G-spot first, sending me into shuddering convulsions just short of coming. Then he pulled his mouth away from mine and pinned me with his eyes as his fingers fucked me. That's when the torture began.

He worked me just to the point of orgasm over and over. I whimpered and moaned, desperate for him to give me more, but he just watched my face with that cold expression of his. I hated that look but there was something about it that turned me on too. He controlled every touch, every bit of stimulation taking over my body, and he wasn't merciful. Finally he pulled his fingers away from me, hoisting my body higher until my hips were halfway up his chest. His mouth took my nipple right as his finger pushed into my ass and I moaned, stiffening against his invasion.

He ignored me, focusing on my nipple, sucking it deep into his mouth as his finger explored my rear, something entirely new to me. I always thought it would hurt to be touched there, but however rough he was with my breast—

and he was rough, make no mistake, alternating between sucking, licking and little tiny bites — he kept his finger in my back passage gentle. I was so turned-on now that I couldn't begin to process everything I felt. Pressure built in me and I felt my orgasm coming. I stiffened, bracing myself and tensing tight around his finger.

That's when he pulled away and set me down without warning.

I swayed on my feet until I found my balance while he steadied me. Every nerve in my body was strung tight, jangling and overstimulated. I whimpered in protest, but he just gave me a smile that could have frozen lava.

"Payback's a bitch, ain't it?" he whispered, pulling away from me to sit down on the bench, legs spread wide. Bastard. If I'd had any doubts about his arousal before now, the sight of him now destroyed them. His cock was long and hard, his balls drawn up tight, showing just how close he was to the edge.

"On your knees," he ordered, his voice harsh.

I knelt slowly before him, feeling like a slave wench servicing her conqueror, which I guess wasn't too far off. I took his cock in both hands, smoothing up and down it as I looked up at him. I licked the little notch on the underside of the head, flicking my tongue rapidly.

"Fuck me…" he groaned, and I couldn't tell if it was an order or just an expression of how good it felt. He reached down and tangled his fingers in my hair, urging me to wrap my mouth around his cock. Sounded good to me. I opened my mouth, sucking him in as deep as I could, which wasn't very far because he was so large. Still, what I could take I worked with my tongue, bobbing up and down on him as my hands got into the action. I used my right to jerk him off in time with my mouth. The left I dropped down to his balls, alternately rolling and gripping them. His cock got harder and he started jerking his hips toward me a little with each stroke, holding my hair so tightly it hurt.

Horse leaned back, head turned to the side, eyes closed and an expression of infinite need on his face—that's when I realized just how much power I held over him. He couldn't take that from me. So long as he wanted my body, I had my own kind of control.

Holy shit, that turned me on.

I let go of his balls, reaching down between my legs to finger myself. Faster and faster I worked, until I heard him giving little grunts of encouragement and I felt little pulsing twitches start at the base of his cock. My legs quivered as I hovered right on the edge of my own explosion.

Then Horse came in my mouth, something I'd been fantasizing about for months. He didn't do it halfway, just like everything else in his life. I've only ever given a blowjob to one other man—Gary—and it was nothing like this. After he finished, I kept sucking on him as I rubbed my own clit hard. He didn't soften completely, although the urgency was gone. Unfortunately, that's when he noticed what I was doing with my hand.

"Stop it," he ordered, reaching down to grab my arm, pulling me to my feet in front of him.

"Horse, please," I begged.

"Do you realize how much time I've spent jacking myself off, thinking of you?" he asked, still sitting. I shook my head, startled by the question. "Any idea what it felt like that time you pulled away from me? Blue balls don't come close to what you did to me, babe. Enjoying watching it happen to you for a change."

"I'm sorry," I said. "But I couldn't make love with you when there was an audience. I just couldn't."

"*Make love*? Don't fool yourself, this is about fucking, Marie," he said. That hurt, hurt way more than I could have expected. Then he made it worse. "And get used to the idea of an audience, because I'm not gonna let you off easy just because you're squeamish."

"What do you mean?" I asked, stiffening.

"In my world we don't follow the rules, babe," he said. "There's nothing about me my brothers don't know. Remember what I told you while you were packing your shit?"

"Yeah," I whispered, mesmerized as he leaned forward, nuzzling between my legs, flicking his tongue over my clit twice, which was almost enough to sent me over.

But not quite.

I shifted restlessly, wishing I could bring my legs together, squeeze them just enough to finish the job, but he wouldn't let me.

"This is my pussy," Horse said, reaching up inside me with two fingers, rubbing against my inside wall purposefully. I shivered. "I'll fuck it when I want and how I want. We party with the club and I get horny, you spread for me and you don't bitch about it. That means against a wall, on the floor, in the middle of the fucking grocery store, you give it to me when I want or this deal is off. Get it?"

I nodded, torn between anger at his words and desperation for his touch. Fortunately he stopped talking and sucked on my clit. I blew about ten seconds later, my moans echoing in the shower as I came. It took everything I had to stay on my feet, and even then I gripped his shoulders hard enough to leave marks.

He left me to finish washing, which consisted mostly of getting the conditioner out of my hair and my heart rate down to normal. I wrapped my hair in a towel and pulled on sweats and a ratty t-shirt to go back to my room. The door to Horse's room was closed and the house was silent. That surprised me somehow. I guess I expected to see him again, that he'd want more from me. I knew he liked sleeping together, we'd done it twice and he'd held me all night both times. That's when it really sank in.

Horse didn't want me in his room because I wasn't his woman. He'd offered me that and I said no—now my job was to service him and stay out of his way. Suddenly having my own room wasn't looking so good. I actually felt lonely for the jerk, wishing he'd spend the night with me. But Horse had made himself clear—cuddling was for girlfriends and old ladies.

Now I was just a quick fuck, and it was my own damned fault.

Chapter Twelve

ઈ૭

A hand slid into my sweatpants sometime during the night, fingers grazing my clit as a mouth claimed my breast. I moaned, sleepy and unsure if this was a dream or not. Then the hand left me to pull down my sweats. I opened my eyes, awake now, trying to figure out what was happening. A man was on top of me. *Gary?* I opened my mouth to scream and a hand covered it even as he spoke.

"No more sleeping in shit like this," Horse murmured as he pushed his leg between mine. "You sleep naked or in something sexy, no excuses." Then he kissed me gently below my left ear, nuzzling my neck. He pulled his hand from my mouth and I punched his shoulder.

He laughed.

"Don't cover my mouth!" I hissed.

"Didn't want you screaming and rupturing my eardrum, babe," he replied, his voice low and sexy. He pressed his hips into the cradle of mine and I shuddered. How could he piss me off so much and turn me on at the same time? It wasn't fair. "You gonna behave or should I tie you up?"

"Are you serious?"

"Fuck, yeah, I'm serious," Horse replied, reaching down to find my clit. I arched up and moaned, because no matter how angry he made me, my inner slut wanted him. Bad. "I'm the boss. You remember that or I'll teach you."

He caught my hands and pulled them roughly over my head, holding them prisoner with one hand while his other worked me like he'd done in the bathroom. My body was starved for this, still wound up from earlier. I'd been too paranoid to touch myself after the shower, nervous he'd come into my bedroom and discover me. I don't know why keeping that part of myself from him seemed so important, but it was.

In less than a minute, he had me primed and ready. He pulled away and I heard the crinkle of a condom wrapper tearing. Horse muttered a curse in the darkness before coming back, catching my hands and pinning them on either side of my head as he lined up his cock with my opening.

Horse had a big dick—I knew this. But I didn't truly grasp the implications until he started pushing into me, slow and steady, no hesitation and no stopping. I squirmed against the bed as he filled me, the satisfaction of feeling full tempered with little twinges of pain as he stretched me wide. I could just make out his features in the faint moonlight streaming through the window—a mask of determination and desire that overwhelmed me. Then he hit bottom, balls-deep in my body. My muscles twitched around him, little tremors running through me as I struggled to hold him.

"Gotta get used to me, babe," he murmured, dropping kisses across my face before taking my mouth again for the first time without urgency. "I'll take it slow."

And he did. Gradually I felt myself relax around him, and when he started stroking, that big cock of his rubbed against me in places I hadn't even realized existed. Gradually he moved faster and I started lifting my hips to meet his, body eager for more. Usually I don't come from vaginal sex alone—I need more stimulation for my clit. Horse was different though, because his body was big enough to spread me wide open, exposing my center to the delicious slide of his erection as he pumped in and out of my body. Having my arms pinned wide added to the experience because I couldn't do anything to stop him. I had to take what he gave me, no arguments, and that was weirdly liberating—utterly guilt-free sex.

I don't think even a minute went by before I came, arching my back up from the bed, every muscle in my body squeezing hard enough to hurt.

That's when he let go and started fucking me for real.

Horse went from gentle lover to biker thug, rising on his knees as he released my arms. He grabbed my waist, lifting and tilting my pelvis to provide a better angle as he literally fucked himself with my body. I have no idea how much time passed, but I know at one point I reached down and rubbed my clit, chasing a second orgasm. When it hit and I clenched around him again, he fell over the edge, exploding inside me. He dropped me back down on the bed, covering me as his cock bucked and shuddered his release.

Holy shit.

We both stilled, panting as we recovered. Then Horse rolled off me, stood up and pulled off the condom, tossing it in the little trash can next to the dresser. He walked out of the room without a word, leaving me in the darkness.

I've never felt more alone in my life.

I woke up to bright sunlight and silence.

Rolling out of bed, I winced at the soreness between my legs, although I couldn't say I regretted it. I'd never come like that before, not even with my vibrator. I pulled on a tank with a shelf bra and jeans without panties. I hadn't thought to rinse my others out last night, and I certainly wasn't going to put them back on dirty. Horse may have declared my privates a panty-free zone, but we needed to have words about that. No way I wanted to go commando permanently.

I hit the bathroom and then walked downstairs, listening for sounds of life.

"Horse, you here?" I called. He didn't answer, but I heard the clicking sound of a dog's toenails on the wooden floor. I wasn't entirely comfortable with dogs, and this one sounded big to me.

Horse wouldn't leave me alone with a violent animal, I told myself firmly. He might be a jerk but he didn't want me dead. I peeked over the banister, poised to run back up to my room if it turned out to be a monster. Instead I found a mid-sized dog with long silver-black hair broken by white streaks looking up at me hopefully. Its mouth hung open in a wide puppy grin, tongue flopped to the side.

Not exactly a killer.

"Hey there," I said softly, working my way down the stairs. The dog watched me intently, mouth closing as it took on the fixed look of a herd dog at work, ready for anything. I reached the bottom of the steps and held my hand out low. The dog approached me, sniffed my hand and then started butting against it for a scratch. I obliged as the dog melted to the floor, writhing in ecstasy.

"You're not much more than a puppy," I murmured. "I'll bet you fly when you jump—do you like chasing sticks?"

"Be careful what you say to him," Horse said. "You start making promises, he'll hold you to them. Takes a hell of a long time to tire him out too."

"I didn't think you were here," I muttered.

"Not all of us make noise constantly," he replied. "You sounded like a herd of moose up there."

I scowled.

"I did not sound like a moose," I said. "It's not my fault the floors are old and creaky."

"I didn't say you sounded like a moose," he replied, an almost friendly expression on his face. "I said you sounded like a *herd* of moose. There's a big difference."

I rolled my eyes at him.

"I made breakfast," he said, jerking his chin toward the kitchen. "It's not much. I want you to take over the cooking and shit, but I was hungry and you weren't moving."

I blushed, thinking about why I'd been tired, and he gave a low, satisfied chuckle.

"That's Ariel, by the way," he added, jerking his chin toward the dog. "But I call him Ari."

I stared at him.

"You have a boy dog named Ariel?" I asked, not quite sure I'd heard him right.

"My niece named him," Horse replied, shrugging. "Would break her heart to change it and I figure the dog doesn't give a shit. I can live with Ari."

I nodded, biting the side of my cheek. Once again, the badass biker was a mystery. He issued threats, carried a gun that I was pretty sure he knew how to use, and he let his little niece name his dog after a mermaid.

Split personality, no question.

Breakfast wasn't fancy but it was surprisingly good. He'd made French toast with some ham on the side and wedges of ripe, juicy cantaloupe. The meal followed the same pattern as the night before, except this time he told me to put together a shopping list after we finished. Then he disappeared, taking the dog with him.

I spent about an hour working my way through the kitchen, making notes of what he had and what he needed, surprised to find that while he didn't have a ton of fancy gadgets, what he did have was solid and high quality. Same with the pots and utensils. By the time he came back I had a list long enough to fill both sides of the paper. He looked at it, raising an eyebrow, but didn't complain.

"Rig's out front," he said, starting toward the door. I followed him hastily, wishing I had my purse but not entirely sure he'd wait for me if I went to find it. Ari danced between us and tried to jump up into the dark-green Tahoe parked next to the house.

"No fucking way," Horse said to Ari, and the dog barked at him, clearly pleading.

"No," he repeated, voice firm.

Ari slunk away, looking pitiful.

"You don't tie him up or anything?" I asked as we started down the driveway.

"No need," Horse said. "I'm far enough out that I don't need to worry about kids or strangers hurting him. He knows where his house is and I guess if he decides to run off that's his choice. So far he seems happy to stay put."

Kind of like me, I realized. I could leave at any time, but I wouldn't and Horse knew it.

He surprised me by pulling onto the freeway after we hit Coeur d'Alene, driving across the border into Washington. After about twenty minutes he exited near a giant mall, pulling around and parking without a word.

"I thought we were getting groceries," I said, confused.

"We are," Horse replied. "Gotta get some other stuff first."

I followed him into the mall and couldn't help but notice how much attention he got—most of it from women. I got that, because Horse was a hell of a sight. Tall, tattooed, hair back in a ponytail and wearing his cut over a shirt so faded you couldn't tell what the original design had been. Jeans showcased his exceptionally fine ass, and the chain dangling across his hip attached to his wallet completed the picture perfectly. Men noticed him too. Most of them got out of his way, even the young toughs wearing gang colors and pretending to be badasses. I couldn't decide if it felt more like walking with a superhero or a super villain—either way, people cleared out of path fast.

I tagged along without question until we stopped in front of Victoria's Secret. Then I crossed my arms and shook my head.

"Oh hell no. I'm not going in there with you. We can hit a Walmart or something."

"Don't want you wearing shit that you wore for Gary," Horse replied, draping an arm around my neck, pulling me into his body. He leaned over and spoke directly in my ear, voice husky. "I don't give a damn if you never wear panties again, but I know women are weird about that. Here's the compromise. I'm gonna buy you new shit, but only shit I like. You're gonna wear it until I pull it off to fuck you. Everyone wins."

I opened my mouth to protest, then snapped it closed. I needed panties and bras, and I didn't have my own transportation. I'd been smart enough to shove my cash and debit card into the backpack last night, but that money had to last until I got another job.

Shit, I'd forgotten about work.

"I need to call my boss," I said.

"You scheduled to work today?" he asked, sliding his hand up to tangle it in my hair. I shook my head.

"No, not until tomorrow."

"So you call her when we get home."

"What am I going to tell her?" I fretted. "She's been so good to me, she doesn't deserve to have me just disappear on her without notice…"

"Tell her you got kidnapped by a biker and now you're a prisoner in the mountains," he said, leaning over and catching my mouth with his in a long, slow kiss that left me shaky. Before I could collect my thoughts, he grabbed my hand and tugged me into the store. I pulled back, still not too happy about the idea. He turned toward me, put both his hands on my shoulders and leaned in to me, face to face.

"Babe, I can't wait to see you in some of this shit," he said. "Your old job is not my priority here. I don't give a fuck what you tell her so long as she doesn't file a missing persons report and make my life a pain in the ass. She does, things aren't gonna go well. We clear?"

"Okay," I said, biting my lip. His eyes caught on my mouth and grew dark, so I quickly pulled away and wandered toward a rack of panties—simple ones. Pretty but not slutty, plain cotton hip-huggers. Horse followed me, watching as I picked out a couple and shook his head.

"Get a few of those, you'll want 'em when you're on the rag," he muttered, fingering one distastefully. "But the rest of the time I want you in something sexier."

His tone didn't leave any room for negotiation, so I didn't bother arguing when he turned me bodily and pushed me toward the racks of higher-end stuff. A saleswoman came up to us, all fluttering lashes and smiles for Horse. Before I knew it, I was in a changing room with her, she had measured me and there was a pile of stuff for me to try on. Horse wanted to come in too, but I held my ground, so he waited outside and I called him in to look at each set once I had it on. I don't know what the store policy was on couples in the rooms alone, but apparently it didn't apply to giant bikers.

Unfortunately, this meant that he made the final decision on both what I tried on and what he planned to buy. In the end, I had six new pairs of sexy panties with matching bras, in addition to six pairs of plain cotton ones. Some of them were thongs, some were boy cut high across my ass, but all of them showed off my figure in a way that even I had to admit was hot. Then he started picking out corsets and nighties. Some of them looked like something from a bordello, all black lace, cutouts and bright red satin. Others were more tasteful, including a long, lacy nightgown and matching silk robe that looked almost virginal. My favorite piece was an ivory corset and bustier trimmed with faintly pink ribbons shaped like tiny roses. There were matching panties, and the look on Horse's face when he saw them turned me liquid.

We ended up spending more than a thousand bucks. I almost had a heart attack, but Horse just ignored me as he paid the girl in cash. I don't know whose eyes were wider when he pulled out that wad of bills, hers or mine. Then he handed me a black pushup bra and matching thong, saying, "Go put them on."

I did what he said.

I figured that was the end of our shopping, but when we got back in the car he drove me to a motorcycle dealership.

There he bought me a couple of Harley-Davidson tank tops that were way, way tighter than anything I'd ever worn in public before and a lightweight leather jacket. Next we stopped at a place called the Line—a strip club with an attached store full of women's clothing. Apparently it belonged to the Reapers, and while the place wasn't open yet for the day, the staff had arrived and were busy getting ready.

"I don't like this place," I told him as I followed him through the club toward a door in the far wall. Everywhere I looked were girls wearing almost nothing, some of them naked except for thongs and high heels while others wore silky robes. A few of them took his arm, pressing against his side. Some looked at me speculatively. One reached down and slid her hand over his fly, squeezing as she kissed his neck.

"Back off," Horse said, clearly annoyed. She pouted and turned, glaring at me. "Fuckin' bitches," he murmured, unlocking a door leading into the store next door.

It wasn't open for the day and I was thankful for that. This place made Vicky's Secret look like a burkha warehouse. Edible panties, stripper heels, leather and lace and sex toys everywhere, including a few that made Horse's equipment look small, which kind of frightened me. I literally couldn't find a safe place to put my eyes, so I watched Horse instead as he picked out an outfit best described as "post-modern slut". It included a dark-brown leather corset/bustier that stopped mid-stomach, exposing my bellybutton and the curves of my waist. He threw in a skirt so short I seriously wondered if I'd get arrested if we went out in public.

"I can't wear this," I told him, shaking my head as I looked at myself in the mirror. He stood by the counter, ignoring me. "I can't, Horse. I'll die."

"You'll wear it," he replied, obviously preoccupied as he wrote something in a ledger.

"No."

He looked up at me, taking in my belligerent stance. His eyes narrowed and we stood frozen for nearly a minute, neither of us blinking or giving an inch.

"We gotta go over the rules again?" he asked finally. "Because the way I remember things, you were begging to do whatever it took to save your pansy-ass brother, despite the fact that he came to us, asked us to back him and then screwed us over. In my world, that's a prepaid funeral. You changing your mind about our deal? Door's right over there, babe."

"I don't understand you," I said, voice low and unsteady. "You can be so nice sometimes. Why do you do this?" I asked, gesturing to the horrible outfit he'd picked. "Do you really hate me so much? I don't think I deserve this, Horse."

He shook his head, reaching up and gripping the bridge of his nose between a thumb and forefinger.

"I don't hate you, babe," he said. "You piss me off, but I can live with that. Hell, fuckin' turns me on most of the time. But you just don't understand all that's happening here and I can't tell you without fucking things up. If this bothers you I'm sorry, but there's a good reason for it. You'll just have to trust me."

He turned back to the ledger, ignoring me for another minute. I watched him, seriously considering whether or not to back out of our deal, but I couldn't do that to Jeff. He needed me.

"Shit, I forgot," Horse said suddenly. "You need some shoes too. Go pick something out. Doesn't matter which ones, any of 'em will do."

Happy for a distraction, I wandered over to the wall of shoes, thankful that for once I could pick for myself. Then I realized why he didn't bother telling me what to get, because each and every pair were clearly designed for stripping and nothing else. I settled on a pair of patent leather Mary Janes that would have looked almost demure if they didn't have a four-inch spike heel.

Amazingly, almost every other shoe had even higher heels, some of them on platforms so tall I doubted I'd be able to take a single step wearing them. I grabbed the shoes and gave them to Horse, who didn't say anything. His eyes darkened though, and he reached down to adjust his pants. I felt a little thrill of desire and power roar to life, which bugged the crap out of me. Why couldn't I decide whether I liked him or hated him? How could I go from being angry to horny so incredibly fast? It wasn't fair. I changed back out of my clothes and he bagged them, along with some teeny tank tops and baby doll t-shirts that read "Support your local Reapers Motorcycle Club".

At least the trip to the grocery store wasn't bad. It took us about an hour to get everything on the list. Once again, people took care to stay out of his way, which worked just fine for me. We didn't even have to wait in line to check out, everyone just waved us ahead of them.

"Is it always like this?" I asked him as we loaded up the groceries.

"Usually," he replied. "We're not the biggest club, but we're definitely in charge around here. So long as they give us respect, it's all good. Not many citizens up for taking on a Reaper, that's for damned sure."

"What happens if they do?" I asked. He gave me a sharp look.

"What do you think?"

Stupid question.

When we got home Horse insisted on unloading the groceries, telling me to go upstairs and put away my new things. While just thinking about the stripper skirt gave me hives, I had to admit that the shoes made me feel sort of sexy. I couldn't resist trying on the bustier again, which wasn't so bad with my hip-hugging jeans. I couldn't see my whole body in the mirror on the top of the dresser, but I saw enough to know I looked good.

Really good.

Once I finished pulling off tags and putting things away I wandered downstairs. Horse was gone, but I found a note on the table.

Got shit to do – hang out and make yourself comfortable. I'll be back around seven. Have dinner ready. We're going out tonight.

Not exactly the master of conveying information.

I grabbed Horse's cordless house phone and a book, then settled myself on the front porch to call Denise and let her know I wouldn't be back to work. I felt like a complete ass when I told her I couldn't give any notice. She didn't buy my excuse for a minute.

"What's going on?" she demanded. "Don't bullshit me, Marie. Your trailer burned down last night and now you tell me you're living with some man you barely know? What's really happening? Tell me why I shouldn't call the cops."

It was hard to do, but I tried to put just the right amount of concern about the trailer burning into my voice while still sounding happy about my new circumstances.

"Jeff called me last night and told me about the trailer," I said, trying to sound earnest and sad. "He said he started it, I guess he left his pipe on the floor before going on a beer run. I'm bummed that it burned down but I'm lucky because I already had all my stuff packed up and moved out. Jeff told me he's crashing with a friend. He doesn't want me to come back, says it's his problem and he doesn't have a place for me to stay anyway."

"I see," Denise said, although clearly she didn't. "I don't think that's the whole story, but I guess it matches the newspaper story. Marie, I hate to say this, but I'm not going to be able to give you a reference."

"I understand," I replied, feeling depressed. She sighed heavily.

"You call me if you need me. I'll respect your decision but things go bad fast sometimes. I'll drive up and get you any time."

"Thanks, Denise," I said, eyes watering up. I didn't deserve her kindness, yet she offered it without strings. As I put the phone down, I decided that sometimes kindness hurts more than getting hit physically.

Go figure.

True to his word, Horse disappeared until a little before seven. I spent my time alone reading and exploring the property. There were several outbuildings, including an old barn and a bunkhouse. The barn had been cleared out and converted into a shop where Horse seemed to be rebuilding a couple of different bikes. I found a fridge out there with some beer in it, which made me think of Picnic, Max and Bam Bam visiting me and Jeff in better times. Horse also had a big fire pit out back, surrounded by stumps that appeared to do double duty as seats and chopping blocks as needed. There were four picnic tables too, obviously hand-crafted.

I guess Horse was good with his hands in more than one way.

I fixed chicken and dumplings for dinner, one of my favorites because it always filled the house with a welcoming and comfortable smell, perfect for day's end. I heard Harley pipes outside and then Horse walked in through the mud room.

"Smells great in here," he said, wrapping his arms around me. I leaned back into him, enjoying the feel of his body against mine. Apparently nice Horse would be joining me for dinner instead of his evil twin. "After we eat, we're going out. I want you to wear the clothes we picked up at the Line."

I stiffened, pulling away from him. So much for nice Horse. He sighed but didn't pull me back. Instead he walked over to the stove and peeked into the simmering pot. I glared at him, deciding he could serve his own damned food. He shrugged, taking a bowl and filling it before he put some salad on a plate. He carried it all to the table, sitting down and tucking in.

"You gonna eat?" he asked after a couple of minutes.

I wanted to tell him to go to hell with his strippers and their lurid, nasty clothing, but my stomach picked that moment to growl, totally ruining the moment. I grabbed food and sat down across from him.

"This place we're going tonight," he said. "It's another MC's clubhouse, Silver Bastards, outside of Callup."

"Where's Callup?"

"Silver Valley, between here and Montana. Middle of nowhere, really. They're a Reaper support club, run the valley for us."

That led to about a hundred questions, all of which I suspected would fall under the category of "club business". I decided to focus on logistics instead.

"How am I getting there?"

"Back of my bike," he replied, like the answer was obvious.

"In that skirt and those heels? Not a good plan, Horse."

"Not the most comfortable," he agreed. "But we need to do it."

"Why?"

"Gotta make the right impression," he replied. "Enough questions. Listen up—when we get there, you stick with me, and I mean all the time unless I tell you otherwise. You got no property patch, you're not an old lady. Every biker in the place'll tag you in the first five minutes. That means open season, and wearing clothes like that will attract a lot of attention."

"Then don't make me wear them."

"Just do what you're told. Don't take a drink unless I okay it. Don't dance with anyone. You gotta pee, you tell me and I'll walk you back to do it. Some bitch gets in your face while you're in the bathroom, you scream loud so I can hear you. Got it?"

I agreed, not liking the sound of this at all.

"Go upstairs and get ready now. Your hair's gonna be blown to shit on the bike, so don't worry too much about it. I want to see a lot of makeup though. And don't bother bringing a bag, just your ID. I'll carry it for you."

I grimaced. Of course he'd carry it for me. Stupid stripper clothes didn't exactly come with pockets.

This was gonna suck.

Chapter Thirteen

ઠ૭

I don't know quite what I expected from the Silver Bastards' clubhouse. Some dark pit full of bikers and sluts screwing on tables maybe, or drugs changing hands in the street out front while armed guards with machine guns patrolled restlessly.

Not so much.

We pulled up around ten at a low, squat building that looked like every other small-town bar on earth. It sat outside the thriving metropolis of Callup, Idaho, located just six short miles from Bumfuck, Egypt. I saw a faded sign reading "Silver Bastards" over the door, and there had to be at least thirty bikes parked out front. A couple of guys hung outside, watching over the bikes, and when Horse pulled up they exchanged friendly grunts.

"Prospects," he murmured, putting his arm around my neck possessively and pulling me tight into his side as we walked through the door. His body heat felt good. Even with my jacket (left with the bike, of course—wouldn't want to risk covering up that classy corset!) the ride had been chilly. "See how they only have a bottom rocker, not three patches? That's how you tell. They watch the bikes, run errands, shit like that. They'll keep an eye on my bike even though they aren't Reapers because this is a support club."

I wasn't too sure what all that meant, but remembering his warnings about club business, I didn't ask. Inside, the mountain-side watering hole motif continued. Scuffed wood floors, a long bar on one wall with a hallway beyond, presumably leading to rest rooms. Lots of high tables with stools stood in the center of the room, with couches lining the walls and arranged in groups for conversation. The music was loud but not too loud, and several women dressed remarkably similar to me were dancing in an open area toward the back. A guy stood behind the bar, and when he turned away I saw he was another prospect.

Men stood up as we walked in, all rough-looking, all wearing cuts. A girl in a bikini top and Daisy Dukes asked us if we wanted anything to drink. The guys didn't speak to Horse unless he spoke first, which was weird, because clearly they were eager to talk to him. I decided Horse must be the biker equivalent of visiting royalty. He did say this was a support club, so the attitude of respect and deference must be part of that. Strange that a whole different world of bikers, complete with their own bars and laws and leaders, could exist without regular people like me even knowing about it—yet here we were, smack-dab in the middle of that world.

I stayed close to Horse as he exchanged back-thumps and manly hugs with some of the other guys. Then he grabbed my hand and pulled me behind him toward a couch against the back wall, which magically cleared for us. I nearly fell over trying to keep up in my ridiculous heels. He took a spot on one end, spreading out and relaxing as he pulled me down onto his lap sideways, my back against the arm rest, legs dangling down over his. His left arm cradled me and he dropped his right hand down to my leg, fingers sliding up the inside of my thigh. This pushed my skirt high enough that the big, burly man who sat down on the other side of the couch had to see my bright-red thong-style panties. Not cool.

I leaned over and whispered in Horse's ear, "Why don't you just pee on me and get it over with?"

"Don't flip me any shit, Marie," he replied softly. "You wanna fight with me, do it in private. It makes me hard when you run that mouth of yours. Right now I'm picturing it wrapped around my cock. That's between you and me. But tonight, in public, you do what I say or things will get ugly.

Nobody insults a Reaper in front of an audience, not without consequences, and they are always extreme."

He squeezed my thigh for emphasis, brushing a fingertip against the front of my panties to make his point. His cock grew under my ass and I shivered. Horse talking tough turned me on in a way that my brain insisted was flat-out wrong. My body remembered exactly how good it felt to take him inside though, and it wouldn't be happy until he filled me up again. At least I wasn't the only one suffering. I wiggled a little more to get back at him, enjoying the sharp intake of his breath as my butt teased his dick.

"Kelly, get your ass over here with a drink for the man," the guy next to us bellowed. He was probably ten years older than Horse, with just a hint of gray in his hair. A lot of the bikers seemed to wear beards, but his face was clean-shaven, and he wasn't shy about checking me out. I didn't get the impression that his appraisal was personal though. More like he was sizing me up, trying to judge me on some level I couldn't understand.

Bikini girl showed up with a tray full of beers and shots, which she unloaded on a little table in front of us. The guy next to us handed a beer to Horse, who reached around me to take it in his left hand. The man offered me a beer next. I wasn't sure what to do, so I looked to Horse.

"Have at it," he told me.

"Damn, that didn't take long," said the other man, laughing. "Mousie knows her place, I take it?"

I stiffened, and Horse's hand squeezed my thigh again in warning.

"She's learning," he said. "Gonna be interesting. You heard the news?"

"I heard something. This is her, I take it?" the man replied, glancing toward me. I chugged down almost half my beer, more than ready for a little liquid courage.

"Collateral," Horse replied and his friend grunted. They ignored me as they started talking about people I didn't know, so I let my eyes wander around the room, starting with the guy sitting next to us. He had tousled, deep-brown hair and greenish eyes. His cut had "President" written on it, along with a one-percenter patch and a few others I didn't recognize. Picnic had a president patch too, but I'd never seen anything identifying Horse as an officer. The Reapers must be pretty powerful if a regular guy like Horse got this much respect from the president of another club. I took another long chug of my beer, surprised to discover I'd finished it. That seemed funny to me, and I had to catch myself before I burped.

What can I say? I've always been a lightweight.

I looked longingly toward the remaining beers on the table, thinking another would really hit the spot. Bikini girl reappeared, winding her way toward the couch. She leaned down low to take my empty, boobs hanging right in Horse's line of sight, ass pointed at the other guy. That sort of pissed me off, but when I tried to glare at her she just offered a friendly wink and handed me another beer.

Not such a bad sort, I decided.

I glanced at Horse, catching his eye before I started drinking again. He nodded absently, fingers starting a slow slide back and forth across my thigh as the conversation continued. The guys ignored me for the most part as they shot the shit, talking bikes and business, using words that had to be code because the conversation didn't make any sense to me at all. Occasionally other men walked up and took a chair for a while, then they'd drift away. Certain words and phrases jumped out at me as being potentially important, but I couldn't put it all together. Respect. Something about a charity run for toys (which seemed totally out of sync with the criminal-biker-vibe hanging in the air). Meeting up with the Mexicans, whoever they were. Border patrol and "fucking homeland security".

I tuned them out because there were far more interesting things to do. Drinking a third beer, for one. Watching the crowd. There had to be fifty or sixty people in the room. Most of the men wore Silver Bastards cuts, with big patches on the back that had a stylized picture of a man with a pickaxe, flames shooting out behind him. There were lots of women around too. Most of the women were dressed like me—slutty as hell—and they circulated through the crowd, handing out drinks, picking up empties and occasionally settling in to make out with one of the Silver Bastards. There was a lot of groping, and not limited to individual couples. The guys seemed to have a real thing for being double-teamed. I saw several girls disappear down the back hallway, giggling as men dragged them away.

Then the front door opened and a tall blonde woman with tasteful makeup and an air of authority walked in. She looked around for a minute, spotted us and cut straight through the crowd. She was different from the other women, anyone could see it. For one thing, she wore jeans that were tight enough to show her figure, but not painted on. She had on a black tank top with a Silver Bastards' emblem on it, which displayed her rather well-developed cleavage perfectly. Her hair had been highlighted by a professional who knew his shit and she wore a black leather vest.

Most of the women circulating seemed to get their asses grabbed regularly, but nobody tried it on the blonde. Men moved out of her way, several of them calling out a welcome, but I didn't catch a single one checking out her boobs or ass.

The president-guy sitting next to us stood up as she walked our way, a look coming over his face that could only be described as deep satisfaction. She ignored everyone else as she reached him. He pulled her close, one hand tangled in her hair and the other on her butt as he gave her a long kiss so intimate I felt embarrassed to watch them. He reached down with both hands now, urging her to wrap her legs around him as he lifted her high and nuzzled between her breasts. She laughed and smacked him. As he turned and set her back down I made out the patches on the back of her vest.

"Property of Boonie, Silver Bastards MC".

Horse's hand tightened on my thigh again, and I didn't dare look at him. For the first time, I almost got what he'd been trying to tell me. This woman, Boonie's property, fell into a whole different category from the rest of us girls, and it showed. Her man clearly thought she was the shit, and he wasn't afraid to let everyone know it—even I could see the invisible aura of untouchability surrounding her.

So that's what Horse had offered me...

His hand fell away from my thigh and he urged me to my feet. He stood and waited until the president and his blonde stopped making out, turning to face us.

"Darcy, this is Marie," Horse said. She looked me up and down, eyes questioning.

"Hey, Marie," she replied. "You're new around here, I'm thinking."

I glanced at Horse, unsure if I should be talking to her or not.

"Go with Darcy," he told me. "She'll take good care of you. Boonie and I need some privacy."

I must have looked a little panicked, because he leaned over and whispered in my ear. "She's Boonie's old lady, she won't let anything happen to you. You stick to her like shit on a blanket. Tell her why you're with me, about your brother and the money. Got me?"

I agreed. Darcy offered me a soft smile, then leaned up for one more kiss from Boonie before gesturing me to follow her. Horse smacked my butt as I walked away, making me jump. I felt immediately exposed, men's eyes falling on me speculatively as Darcy led me down the back hallway. We passed some bathrooms and seeing them made me aware of my full bladder.

"Can we make a pit stop?" I asked.

"Sure," she replied, pushing open the door for me. I don't know what I expected, some kind of setup with stalls and a couple of sinks. Instead I found a single, dingy room with a toilet and sink. She followed me in, which surprised me. I must've had a funny look on my face because she laughed softly. Of course, I usually hit the bathroom with my friends when we went out, but I didn't even know this chick.

"Oh, sugar, we got no secrets here and privacy's hard to find. What's a girl like you doing with Horse?"

I stood there, uncertain whether to answer or pee first. I decided to multitask, pulling down my panties.

"I'm with him because my brother owes the club a lot of money," I said, going as quickly as I could. I pulled up my panties and found her staring at me.

"You're with him because your brother owes money?" she asked very carefully, crossing her arms over her chest. "Explain. Now."

"Um, I guess my brother was working with the Reapers on something, I don't know what," I said, feeling incredibly uncomfortable. "They found out he was stealing from them. They decided to kill him, but Horse wanted to fuck me and so they gave him another shot to pay the money back. I'm the collateral. Something about paying in blood."

She just looked at me for a minute, eyebrows raised, and I shuffled nervously, wondering if I'd said too much. Then her face softened.

"Oh you poor baby," she said, reaching out and pulling me into her arms. I started telling her everything about me and Horse in a disjointed tumble of words. I didn't know this woman, but it felt so good to talk about it. At some point I cried, and she just held on and rubbed my back, making soothing noises until I settled down into snuffles and hiccups. A woman's voice called through the door, demanding that we get our asses out. *Now.* Darcy yelled back, "Go pee outside, you fucking skank!"

That startled me out of my little pity party. I pulled away, wiping my eyes, fingers dark with mascara. I'd piled on the makeup just like Horse'd asked. Wasn't going to be easy to fix that.

"Um, how did you know she was a skank?" I asked, voice wavering. Darcy smiled at me encouragingly, holding my shoulders and looking down into my face with a grin.

"Darlin', they're all skanks," she replied, smiling. "You and I are the only females in the entire place that aren't human petri dishes. Old ladies aren't into bullshit parties like this, and despite what the boys might pretend in public, a man who fucks around on his old lady at one is gonna discover just how cold things can get at home. We don't tell them what to do. We just tell them what we're gonna do and let them figure it out for themselves. The system works."

I giggled a little bit at that, feeling better than I had since arriving.

"What I don't get is why he brought you here," she said, grabbing some paper towels and dabbing at my face. I turned toward the mirror, but she stopped me. "Trust me, babe, you don't wanna see what you look like right now."

"Thanks," I said. "I don't know why I'm here either. And I really don't know what's going on with me and Horse. For a while things were great. Well, great on and off."

"So why are you 'off' at the moment?" she asked, biting her lip as she carefully wiped below my eye."

"Well, I think I hurt his feelings," I said. She stopped, giving me a look of patent disbelief.

"You hurt his feelings?"

"I told him I wouldn't be his old lady for a million bucks. By text."

"Shit. That's a big deal, kid."

I nodded.

"He told me it was, but I blew him off when he tried to explain. He stopped talking to me and I got drunk and sent him a bunch of texts and that's when things really fell apart. Then I found the Reapers holding a gun to my brother's head and Horse told me they'd give Jeff another chance if I came with him, so I did."

Amazingly, Darcy didn't accuse me of making it all up or some other normal, reasonable reaction to my crazy story.

"Okay, you can look now," she said. I was impressed with what she'd accomplished. My eyes were smudged from the mascara but she'd blended it so they looked more smoky than scary. Darcy put her hands on my shoulders, meeting my gaze in the mirror as she stood behind me.

"Horse is a good man," she said, and I didn't doubt her sincerity. "But he's clearly fucked in the head. This is not good shit."

"Tell me about it," I replied. "He told me that if I didn't want to be an old lady he wouldn't treat me like one. I apologized for the texts I sent but I don't think it mattered."

She gave a little laugh then shook her head.

"Sounds like you're right—you bruised his precious little man feelings. But he can't just acknowledge that, they never do."

I smiled back at her, but it died as I thought about Jeff.

"What about my brother?" I asked. "Got any insight into that one?"

She sobered and shook her head.

"He's in deep shit. Wish I could tell you something else, but the Reapers don't fuck around when it comes to their rep. They lose that, we're all at war. Lotta clubs just waiting to step in and take over this territory."

"That's what Horse said."

"Here's a piece of advice, whether you want it or not. Your brother's a dead man unless he makes things right with the club. Horse can't change that and you can't either. Sounds like you're buying him some time, but don't think for a minute that they won't follow through if he doesn't pay them. So remember—it's not your fault if things don't go well for him."

"But it is," I replied. "I'm the only reason he's still alive. Horse told me I can leave any time, but if I do, that's it for Jeff."

"So don't leave," she replied. "But don't fool yourself either. This isn't about you. Now we're going back out, so put on your game face. Horse brought you for a reason, probably to scare the crap out of every guy here who's got a sister. They see you, they won't think Jeff is getting off easy. I know Horse well enough to know this isn't his usual thing. I doubt you'll get dragged out like this again unless your brother tries to make trouble. Think he will?"

"He's a smart guy, but he wasn't smart enough not to steal from the Reapers," I said, shrugging. "I guess it could go either way. Something's gone really wrong with him."

Someone pounded on the door again. Darcy walked over, opened it wide and glared at the drunken girl standing outside. She leaned over and vomited on the floor.

"Fuckin' hate parties like this," Darcy muttered, grabbing my arm and carefully stepping over the puddle. I hopped along with her as she dragged me down the length of the hall into a room with a giant table. Horse and Boonie sat studying some papers.

"You boys need more time?"

Horse leaned back, eyeing me as Boonie broke into a sly smile.

"Nope," he said, standing and walking toward Darcy. "Missed you, babe. I hate it when you're out of town. Next time make your mom go by herself, okay?"

Darcy murmured some reply I couldn't make out and they fell into another clinch even more intense than the first. Boonie lifted her and set her butt on the table. That appeared to be our cue to leave, because Horse came over and took my hand, drawing me back out into the hallway.

Chapter Fourteen

ଚ

Talking with Darcy made me feel both better and worse. What she had with Boonie looked pretty good. They seemed to keep focused on each other despite the chaos around them. Horse had offered me the same deal and I'd thrown it back at him, with prejudice. Still didn't excuse kidnapping me. As we left Darcy and Boonie behind, a woman stumbled over to the wall across from us, bracing against it as she threw up noisily.

"You wanna go outside for some air, or back into the bar?" Horse asked, arm hooked around my neck, casually dominating me without even trying. He didn't seem to notice the barfing.

"Some air might be good."

He led me down the hall to a propped-open door. Beyond it was a cleared area, surrounded by a six-foot chain link fence. A huge bonfire lit up the place and I saw a lot of people smoking. My nose told me it wasn't all tobacco. That made me think of Jeff rather wistfully. He was so smart — why did he get himself into this situation? He could do anything if he put his mind to it.

Horse pulled me over toward the back of the fenced area, still part of the party but outside the ring of light from the bonfire. He sat down in the grass, leaned back against the fence and tugged me down to sit between his legs. He wrapped his arms around me, pulling me back against his chest. It felt good. Of course it always felt good when he held me, even when he was being a total asshole.

"You and Darcy have a good chat?"

"Yeah," I replied. "Very educational."

"You give her the whole sob story?"

"Uh-huh."

"Good," he said. "She'll pass it on to the right people. Word'll get out where it needs to go."

We fell into silence for a while. I watched a couple of guys drag out some big speakers, fiddling with the wires until classic rock burst out. Zeppelin, that kind of thing. Made me think of my mom. Not my favorite but it fit the night somehow. Girls started dancing around the fire, stumbling drunkenly into men who swung them up and around before dragging them off into the darkness. Horse's hand slid down to my breast, reaching in to pop it out the top of the corset. I would've been utterly humiliated but I didn't think anyone could see us so far out of the light and I had the start of a good buzz going. I knew there were other couples around us but I couldn't see them, so we were probably safe from the audience.

That's why I didn't protest as his other hand pushed up my skirt and slid aside my panties to tickle my clit. I just leaned back into him, closing my eyes and focusing on the sensation as he coaxed me to life. Then I heard a shrieking noise and opened my eyes. A couple pulled away from the fire, close enough to us that we could see and hear them, but not so close that they noticed us.

The woman knelt in front of the man, unzipping his pants and pulling his cock free. He grunted as she started sucking him off expertly, bobbing her head up and down while working his cock with both hands.

Live porn, right in front of me.

I couldn't tear my eyes away. I'd fallen into a strange and terrible world where people didn't follow the rules, and instead of being horrified at what I saw, I felt myself getting wetter under Horse's fingers. It affected him too—he was hard as a pike behind me. I knew he wanted me, not those girls around the fire, because it was all too clear he could have any of them whenever he wanted. A second man joined the couple in front of us and I perked up, fascinated. The first dropped down to his knees, the girl still working him, although with just her mouth now because she'd fallen to her hands and knees. The position pushed her ass into the air and the second man dropped down behind.

They formed the perfect silhouette of debauchery. The man in back pushed aside the flouncy little skirt she wore, gripping her panties and actually tearing them apart. I stiffened as Horse's finger hooked into me and he whispered in my ear.

"You like that, baby?"

I shook my head, but I couldn't seem to say anything. If I kept quiet, I could pretend this was all some dream where I didn't have to take responsibility for my actions. The woman took the man's cock deeper into her throat, his hands coming up to hold her head as he started moving his hips. The second man's cock came out of his pants, and while he wasn't as big as Horse, he was plenty big. He grabbed her hips, centering on her opening and thrusting in with one powerful motion. Her entire body stiffened but she didn't cry out.

Probably because her mouth was too full.

The men slid in and out, creating a kind of weird rhythm, alternately filling her at both ends. I felt myself stiffening, tingles racing through my body as Horse popped out my other breast to twist and pinch the nipple while he drew his fingertip over and across my clit repeatedly. My hips lifted, encouraging him to do more. Clearly he got what I wanted, because he sped up to match the trio giving the show. The bikers fucked her hard now and I wondered how she took it without feeling pain. She obviously didn't mind, because she didn't struggle at all—not even when the guy behind her pulled out and centered his cock on her rear entrance, rubbing the tip around to lube her with her own fluids. She pulled her mouth free, dropping her head low, and groaned.

"Shit," I muttered. Horse laughed in my ear as the man pushed slowly into her. His friend took her by the shoulders, bracing her as his buddy conquered her ass, inch by inch.

Horse reached down with both hands, grabbing my thighs from the inside, pulling me up and onto his lap so my ass cradled his jeans-covered cock. The girl gave a startled grunt as the man bottomed out. I watched as she twisted, pinned by his cock, arms and legs quivering from the strain of taking him, but she didn't protest or fight back. To my amazement, she opened her mouth and caught the other man in her mouth again.

As they started moving this time, I saw her stiffening a bit each time the cock in her ass hit bottom. The man reaming her stroked her back almost tenderly as he fucked her deep. The guy in front jerked and came, hips bucking. He pulled free and she collapsed forward onto the grass, face down, ass still in air. By this point I felt so wound up I knew it wasn't a matter of if I'd come, but when—now or after the little show in front of us ended. Horse must have sensed the same thing, because he slowed and stopped as the man in the back abruptly shoved the girl flat into the ground, covering her as he went to town on her ass. Over and over he pounded her—so hard I worried he'd hurt her. But she didn't complain or protest, and she definitely could've. This was no rape.

"You wanted to know what a sweet butt is?" Horse whispered in my ear, pausing a second to trail his tongue along the shell of my ear. I shivered, twitching around his fingers deep inside. "That's a sweet butt. She's here to take cock and clean up after the party. Anyone who wants her can have her. Do you think for one minute that I see you like that? That I ever could?"

I shook my head, almost afraid to ask the one question burning through me.

"What is it?" he asked, starting to move his fingers again. I shuddered against him, muscles deep inside clenching as I wound tightly toward orgasm.

"Are you going to do that to me?"

He gave a low chuckle.

"Gotta be specific, babe. You mean fuck you in the ass or share you with another guy?"

"Either," I whispered, wiggling my hips as my butt rubbed his penis, the layers of fabric keeping his skin too far from mine. "I don't want you to share me, Horse."

He didn't answer, just rubbed my clit harder. I squirmed against him as he caught a nipple and rolled it between his fingers. In front of me the man stiffened, thrusting one last time. He grunted as he came. Then he rolled off her to the side. She caught his arm, reaching over to kiss him. He pushed her away, laughing, and stumbled to his feet.

"I can't do that, Horse," I said, shivering with a mixture of physical need and fear. "Please, don't give me to them. I couldn't handle it."

"I'm not gonna share you, Marie," he whispered, digging his fingers deeper, grinding against my clit with the heel of his hand. Pleasure pulsed, hovering just out of reach.

"I told you before, this is *my* pussy," he continued, softly but with a hint of threat too. "I fuck you, nobody else does. Which hole I fuck is up for negotiation."

At his words I tipped over the edge, moaning as stars exploded through me, grinding his cock with my ass. I collapsed against him, panting. He lifted me, laying me down in the grass flat on my back. Now the panties getting ripped were mine as he covered me, pulling out his cock and slamming it into my well-lubed center without a word. I moaned achingly. I had no idea if anyone could hear me but I didn't care at all. I just wrapped my arms and legs around him as he pumped furiously into my body. That dick of his was huge, but it felt good and I'd loosened up a lot because taking him didn't hurt at all. It felt great, and I loved the way his girth pushed me open, stimulating my clit like nothing I'd ever felt before. It didn't take long for me to shoot over the edge again, and he followed right after. I felt his hot seed spurting deep inside and moaned as my body slowly recovered.

That's when I realized he hadn't used a condom.

I pushed him off, sitting up and trying to pull my skirt down so that I didn't give the entire party a crotch shot. He leaned up on one arm to stare at me speculatively.

"What's the problem now?" he asked. I narrowed my eyes, wondering if he'd "forgotten" on purpose. Apparently Horse liked riding bareback. "I know something's crawled up your ass, so spill it."

"You didn't put on a condom!" I hissed. "I haven't been tested yet, I'm not even on the Pill, what—"

He reached out, wrapping his hand around the back of my neck and pulling me to him for a kiss, ending the conversation. He didn't stop kissing me for a long time. Then he let me go and smiled.

"Calm down," he said. "It's not that big a deal. We'll get you to a doc tomorrow, get you tested, make sure you're clean."

"I'm not on birth control, Horse," I said through gritted teeth. "What if I got pregnant? I'm not having an abortion, you can't make me. I won't do it."

He looked me right in the eye.

"Babe, the odds you get pregnant this one time are pretty damn low. But if it happens, we'll deal with it, okay? I like kids. I could do worse. Tomorrow we get you fixed, then we move forward. Not a lot of sense in freaking out because we can't exactly go back in time and slap that condom on, now can we?"

I studied his face, calm and reassuring, incredibly handsome in the firelight. He smiled, encouraging me. I smiled back at him, forcing myself to breathe.

"Okay," I said.

"Okay," he repeated. "Marie, I swear, you're crazy sometimes, but once I get my dick in you I couldn't care less. Just calm down and relax, sweetheart."

He rolled off me, rising to his knees to tuck himself away and close up his pants. Then he leaned back against the fence. I pulled down my skirt as far as it would go, sitting back between his legs carefully, keeping my own shut tight. We sat like that for a long time, listening to the music and watching the fire. Couples disappeared and reappeared, their soft laughter filling the occasional lulls in the music.

Apparently we weren't completely hidden from view, because one of the prospects stopped by every once in a while to see if we wanted more to drink. Horse nursed a beer slowly, but I ended up downing two more, bringing my total up to five. By the time I'd grabbed a sixth, I'd stopped worrying so much about someone seeing up my skirt. As I started a seventh, I sat forward and started singing and moving my body to the music. Horse laughed, but he stood and pulled me to my feet, apparently enjoying the show as I spun in the firelight. Everything was great and I was starting to think about a pee run when I heard a loud bang and the ground next to me exploded with a crack like thunder.

Gunfire.

Horse tackled me, rolling us away from the area as a second shot rang out, apparently hitting the speakers because the music stopped. Yet another shot went off. Men shouted, women screamed and I sobered right the hell up. Horse pushed me behind a big rock and then he was up and running, tackling a guy standing near the fire. The gun flew out of the shooter's hand and another man grabbed it, popping out the magazine and clearing the slide with a loud click.

I peeked up and over the bench to see Horse dragging the shooter to his feet by the front of his shirt before punching him hard in the face. I heard panting nearby, and a girl I hadn't even realized was crouched next to me gave a squeak of fear. It was Miss Double Penetration, and she wore a streak of dirt across her cheek and a look of total shock on her face.

I imagined my own held a similar expression.

I reached out and took her hand. She squeezed it back as Horse methodically beat the shit out of the shooter, yelling at him between blows.

"You don't fucking shoot a gun at my woman!" he shouted, taking a final shot at the guy's gut as the man collapsed in the dirt. Horse stood over him, panting, furious, and I had another of those eye-opening realizations that seemed to happen so often lately.

Horse was capable of violence. Terrible violence. I wasn't sure if this guy was going to survive. I'd known it intellectually, seen him with a gun, but this was different. This was right in front of me, real and visceral and scarier than anything I'd ever seen. The girl next to me started crying shocked tears. I felt them running down my face too. The guy was definitely down, but Horse rolled him over and kicked him again in the nuts with enough force to dent metal. The horrific scream he gave tore through my soul.

Horse stood back, chest heaving, glancing around in disgust. Everyone seemed frozen.

"This cocksucker missed my girl by about six inches," he announced, looking around at the crowd. "I should put him in the ground, but it's not worth my fucking time. Next time I won't be so forgiving, you got me?"

Around him men nodded, murmuring their agreement. I heard someone throwing up off to the right, back in the darkness. I hugged the girl next to me and she hugged me right back, all differences between us forgotten. Horse left the circle of firelight, reaching out to take the now-unloaded gun from the man who'd grabbed it before. Then Horse grabbed the clip, slammed it back into the gun and pulled back the slide with purpose. He turned and carefully aimed the gun at the man's head.

"Not so fucking fun now, is it?" he snarled. The man gibbered, whimpering and shaking. Lightning fast, Horse tilted the gun to one side of the man's head and pulled the trigger. Dirt exploded next to his face.

"Marie, get your ass over here."

I didn't want to move, but I *really* didn't want to piss Horse off even more. I gave the girl a quick hug and stood shakily. I realized about a second later that the stripper heels just weren't going to work, so I kicked them off and scuttled over to Horse. He tucked the gun into the back of his pants, grabbed my hand and dragged me back through the clubhouse. Boonie caught up to us, but Horse just snarled at him when he tried to talk. Darcy followed behind, eyes darting between us.

Horse pulled out the gun again when we reached his bike, letting the magazine drop and clearing the slide. Then the entire thing went into one of his saddlebags. We climbed on the Harley and took off into the night.

I didn't notice the cold at all on the ride home. Go figure.

We got back to the house way too fast. I wasn't ready to deal with Horse or what I'd witnessed. That guy had to be hurt, bad. I hoped to hell they got him to a hospital, although that might make things worse for us—the cops would come after Horse. Where would that leave me?

Safe, a little voice whispered deep down inside.

We pulled up to the house and he killed the bike. Silence fell between us and I had no idea what to do or say. Wasn't the first time I'd felt this way either. We seemed to be following a pattern. Outstanding sex. Violent outburst. Cold war.

At least I wasn't the one who'd pissed him off this time.

Horse didn't say a thing to me as we walked into the house. But when the door shut behind us and he slid the bolt home he turned to me, eyes burning with something dark and terrible. I froze, pinned by that gaze, understanding what it must feel to be a deer at the moment the hunter pulls the trigger. He shook his head and pulled me into his arms.

"I can't fucking believe he almost shot you," he muttered, gripping me so tight it hurt. Then he picked me up and carried me over to the couch, falling back on it and draping me over his body. I collapsed against him, a rush of tears bursting out of me. I don't know what it was, relief maybe? Horse rubbed my back, making little soothing noises, and eventually I stopped crying. Then I realized my skirt had ridden up and my bare ass was hanging out. I tried to pull away from him but he wouldn't let me. Instead he took my face in both his hands, forcing me to meet his eyes.

"I'm so sorry, babe," he said. "I can't believe that fuckwad. Boonie should be ashamed of himself, letting that shit happen in his house. He wasn't even a member of the club. You almost got shot by a goddamned hangaround."

"But I didn't," I whispered. "I'm fine, Horse. Really. It scared me but I'm okay."

He shook his head.

"I scared you too," he said. "I'm sorry, babe. But it had to be done. I couldn't let that guy get away with that any more than I can let your brother off the hook. This is my reality and it's ugly sometimes. Dragging you into this, I should be sorry. But I'm not. I'm not gonna let you go, Marie. I'm keeping you and I don't care if I go to hell for doing it. I don't care about anything but fucking you."

With that, he pulled my mouth down to his, kissing me hard, tongue thrusting in and taking command. He sat up slowly, swinging his legs off the side of the couch so that I had to straddle him. He thrust his lower body up at me, hands holding my hips as he rubbed the ridge of his jeans-covered cock against my bare clit. In all the excitement I'd forgotten I was naked under my skirt. Now his fingers reached between us, dipping into my wet opening and sliding around. Suddenly he pushed me up and lifted his hips. I grabbed his shoulders to steady myself as he slid his jeans down, freeing his cock. He took it and rubbed the tip through my wetness, then lined it up with my slit.

"I meant what I said," Horse told me, his face tight and cold. "You belong to me. Nobody else gets in this pussy. You got that?"

I nodded quickly, biting my lip.

"Give me the words."

"I belong to you," I whispered as he took my hips, gripping them firmly.

"All of them."

"Nobody gets in this pussy but you, Horse."

He held my eyes as he pressed my hips down, forcing his cock deep as I cried out. Even though he'd fucked me once that night, this new angle hit me deeper than he'd ever gone. I screamed when the tip of his cock hit my cervix and spasmed around him. I don't know if it was pleasure or pain or what, but as he slid me up and then down again, hard, I exploded around him with a cry.

"Put your hands on my shoulders and ride me," he grunted as I recovered. I did what he said, taking over the rhythm as his hands bit deep into my ass. Every stroke slammed my clit into his pelvic bone, every thrust hit my cervix, and almost immediately I spiraled up again toward another orgasm. His hand dug down between the cheeks of my ass and then his finger went inside me from behind. He thrust it deep, controlling how I rode him as I moved faster and faster. Suddenly he groaned and stopped me, grabbing my hips and standing up to turn me toward the couch, pulling me off his cock and setting me down.

"Kneel, facing away from me," he said, voice icy. I shivered, but the look on his face was full of an intensity I'd never seen. Slowly I did as he asked, kneeling on the couch and leaning forward to brace my arms against the back. Once again his cock entered me, sliding in and out slowly several times. Then he pulled it free and slid it higher, pressing it against my anus.

I froze as he nudged me, trying to breach my opening. I quivered as he absently rubbed one hand up and under the skirt I still wore, as if to soothe me. He started to work the head in and it hurt. A lot. I shivered, thinking of Jeff, telling myself I had to go through with it if I wanted my brother to live. But everything Horse had done to me so far—at least everything sexually—I'd wanted.

This felt like rape.

"Please don't," I whispered, knowing I couldn't stop him. "I don't think I can handle it if you do this to me. Please."

Horse stilled and I stopped breathing. I felt the tip of his cock nudge my opening again and he groaned. Then he dropped it down and plunged back into my pussy. It's a good thing he grabbed my hips and held me as he started thrusting because I think I would have collapsed in relief. Then his clever fingers found my clit and I forgot to be upset with him. My arousal returned with a rush and I gasped, dropping my head down against the back of the couch as need spiraled up into me fast and hard.

I came with a desperate cry as Horse joined me, hot seed shooting deep inside my body. We stayed that way, joined, panting. Finally he pulled out and dropped back down on the couch next to me. He grabbed my arm and pulled me across his lap, taking my chin and kissing me one last time. When it ended, I opened my mouth to say something and realized I didn't know exactly what to say. *Thank you for not raping me because my brother owes you money?* Um, no.

"Let's sleep," he said, lying back and pulling me over his body. He reached up and grabbed the blanket draped across the back of the couch, managing to cover both of us with it. Then his hand wrapped about my ass, sliding between my cheeks, rubbing across my rear opening absently.

"Someday," he whispered softly in my ear. "I don't want to hurt you. Not until you're ready for me… But someday I'm going to own all of you, Marie. You're all mine, babe. Knew it the first time I saw you. Couldn't give you up if I tried."

I pretended not to hear him. It took me a long, long time to fall asleep.

Chapter Fifteen

ɞ

A loud, pounding noise woke me abruptly. I had no idea where I was or what was happening. Horse groaned and I did too. My head hurt like hell. Too much beer...

Oh shit. The party. The sex. Horse beating a man almost to death. This couldn't be good.

"Horse," I whispered. More banging. Someone was outside the front door. His eyes opened, taking me in all rumpled and sleepy. He smiled and his hand squeezed my ass as I felt the evidence of his appreciation grow under my stomach.

"Shut the fuck up!" he yelled toward the door, making me flinch. The pounding got louder. Horse rolled me to one side so he could get up and started toward the door, tucking his morning erection into his pants with some effort. Clearly he planned to make the noise go away.

"Horse!" I hissed. He glanced back at me, his expression questioning. "It's probably the cops. They're here to arrest you. Should you just open the door like that? Shouldn't you go out the back or something while I delay them?"

That made him smile and he shook his head, bemused.

"Marie, babe, we're not on TV," he said, a hint of laughter in his voice. "What happened last night was club business. No cop's ever gonna hear anything about it."

"You almost killed that guy," I replied, eyes wide. "People tend to notice stuff like that, club business or not."

"Not a problem," he said, shaking his head again. "We handle things like this our own way. If I'd roughed him up for no reason, it would start a shit storm like you can't imagine.

But a fucking hangaround shooting at a Reaper's woman? Drunk and out of control? He's lucky I got to him before Boonie. Fucking insult to the Silver Bastards, as much as me. Hell, for all I know, Boonie finished the job after I left. Now run upstairs and put on some clothes. I love that look on you, but your pussy's flashing me and I don't feel like sharing. Think we covered that already."

I blushed and jumped up, having totally forgotten my lack of panties, or even a real skirt. As I ran up the stairs, I heard Horse laughing out loud as he opened the door, and then the clomping of boots as people walked in. I pulled on some jeans and one of my new Harley Davidson tank tops, which actually looked pretty cute and not nearly as slutty as I thought it would. Then I gave my teeth a quick brush and washed my face. The rest of me needed washing too, but I didn't want to miss anything downstairs so I twisted my hair on top of my head and walked back down.

The living room was empty but I heard voices in the kitchen so I followed them. Horse was pouring freshly brewed coffee for Max and Picnic. All three men looked up as I walked in. Picnic grinned at me. Max stared at me intently, like I was some puzzle he couldn't quite solve. I nodded, uncertain of my position but wanting to hear any news they might have.

"Hear you had some fun last night," Picnic said, leaning back against the counter. He wore his gray t-shirt, black leather boots and cut casually, but as always, his looks struck me. That grin didn't help. I couldn't quite reconcile the man who stood before me casually drinking coffee with the biker who'd held a gun to my brother's head two days ago.

"Horse tells me you're worried about him getting in trouble," Picnic said, smirking. "Thought we might be the cops."

I nodded, unsure what to say.

"No worries, darlin'. Horse did the right thing, Boonie already called, explained everything," Picnic said, grimacing. "Damn, this coffee tastes like ass, Horse. So Marie—for what it's worth, Boonie feels like shit about what happened. And knowing Darcy, he's gonna catch more shit about it for a long time. Apparently she's taken a liking to you, wanted to be sure and let you know you can call her any time. Bitch woke me up at seven in the fucking morning to give me the message."

He shook his head, looking annoyed. Apparently Picnic liked his sleep.

"Don't let Boonie hear you call his woman a bitch," Horse said dryly. "Man's whipped, might take offense. Remember last time?"

The guys all laughed and I felt completely out of my depth.

"I don't have her number," I said, deciding to focus on little details—like Darcy's phone number—rather than the fact that we were calmly discussing Horse almost killing a man with his bare hands last night.

"It's in your new phone," Picnic responded, grabbing a large, padded envelope from the counter and tossing it to me. I managed to catch it, awkwardly, and opened it to find my car keys, a cell phone and a section of newspaper folded open and highlighted. I pulled out the paper first. It only took about four short sentences to describe the total destruction of our trailer by fire. Resident Jeff Jensen was uninjured, had been found outside, inebriated. No official cause yet, but the fire appeared to be the result of a pipe left burning on the carpet.

My hands shook as I put it back in the envelope.

"Sorry, sweetheart," said Picnic, and he actually sounded like he meant it. "But we had to get rid of any evidence. Also part of the message to other clubs. Either your trailer or your brother."

I agreed, remembering how I'd suggested burning the place myself. Anything to protect Jeff. The trailer was just a place to live, and not much of one to be honest.

"I'd like to visit my mom at some point," I said to Horse. "Can I do that? She'll be really worried and she doesn't have a way to get hold of me."

"You can write her," he said. "Give her your new phone number if you like, she can call collect after that."

I pulled out the phone. It wasn't fancy, but it wasn't crap either. I turned it on and touched the address book icon. It already had several entries. Horse, Picnic, Darcy and "armory", whatever that was.

"What about my old phone?" I asked. "Why a new one?"

"You needed a new account for your own protection," Picnic said. "We aren't the only people your brother pissed off. Hearing new rumors all the time. This is safer, you should cut contact for a while. Horse will fill you in after we give him the details."

"Am I allowed to call anyone I want?"

"Depends on whether you want them to stay alive," Picnic said, shrugging. "Far as I'm concerned, make that first call to your brother. Educational experience for both of you."

I powered down the phone and stuck it in my pocket quickly.

"Car's outside," Picnic added, like this was just some normal social visit. "Painter drove it up here the other day. Piece of shit, broke down on him twice so I had the guys at the shop fix it up for you."

I pulled out the keys and felt better immediately. Now I had a way to leave. I liked that idea a lot.

"Thanks."

"No worries," said Picnic, shrugging. "Don't do anything stupid, Marie. Got me?"

"Okay."

"Got that stuff in the barn for you to pick up," Horse said to Picnic, watching me with speculative eyes. "We'll talk when I get back," he told me. "Won't be long."

The three men headed outside without another word. I clutched the car keys and ran my fingers over the bump the phone made in my pants. I had my car, I had a phone and I had a little bit of money in the bank. I could call Jeff if I wanted, or just send him a text to make sure he was all right.

I could just drive away and never look back.

Instead I fixed breakfast, finishing up just as Horse walked back into the house. Ari followed him in from outside, looking at the food-filled counter hopefully.

"Good timing," I said. "Food's ready. You hungry?"

"Yep," he said, but he didn't sit at the table. He came over and wrapped a hand around my neck, pulling me in for a long, slow kiss that tasted like coffee and sex. Every time he touched me I melted. It wasn't fair. I wrapped my arms around him and Horse reached down, lifting my butt and setting me on the counter. I opened my legs and he nestled up between them.

Unfortunately, he stopped kissing me, pulling away to cradle my face between his hands, examining my face.

"You okay?" he asked.

I nodded. He closed his eyes and then shook his head before opening them again.

"This sucks. Last night was crazy and I scared you, and now I have to tell you something bad," he said. I stopped breathing. What more could be wrong? I was overloaded already.

"Your brother's stupider than we thought. He's got other shit in play, shit we didn't know about until this morning. You call him, it's *really* not gonna help. If he's smart he's already ditched his phone and gone off the grid, but I don't have a lot of faith in his intellect at the moment."

I opened my mouth to protest, to say something. Horse pressed his finger against my lips, silencing me.

"Not done yet, babe. Believe me when I say talking to him isn't a good idea for either of you. These guys he's pissed off, they aren't gonna give him a second chance if they catch him, and he's sure as fuck used up his second chance with us. Whole damn cartel's after him. You want to keep him safe, you don't reach out to him."

"Bad shit?" I whispered. He nodded, face sober. "Like, a drug cartel?"

"Very bad shit with an exceptionally nasty drug cartel. Shit that's gonna get him dead very soon. Shit worse than anything he's got with us, which comes as a huge fuckin' surprise to me, considering how fucked he was already. These guys…" He shook his head slowly, swallowing hard before continuing. "These guys are not the good guys. You aren't safe if you're anywhere near him, and you aren't safe if they think they can use you to find him. You use that phone to call him, they track it… Let's just say they won't be offering him a chance to make things right."

"If I can't call Jeff, why did you give it to me?"

"Because believe it or not, keeping you hostage and completely out of communication with the rest of the world isn't exactly a long-term plan," he replied, smoothing my hair behind my ears. "Might work for a while, but sooner or later it'll blow up in my face. I know it's hard to believe because I'm such a giant asshole, but I don't want you to be unhappy. So it's up to you to protect him by not drawing him out. It's up to me to protect you, which includes educating you on just how bad things are for him. And I gotta tell you, he pulls shit that comes down on you, time's up. He'll be in the ground up there in those mountains and nobody will *ever* find his body. You got me?"

"Do I get a vote in how we handle this?"

"Nope."

"You just expect me to do what you say?"

"Yep."

I wanted to argue with him some more, but I couldn't think of a damn thing to say. I didn't like him being in charge, but that was the nature of our arrangement. And I didn't know whether to believe him about Jeff or not. If he was lying, I didn't get to talk to my brother and that sucked.

But if he told the truth and I called, Jeff might die.

"I won't contact Jeff," I said. "But at some point I really want to go see my mom. It's important."

"You write your mom that letter, I'll see that she gets it. Just don't write anything about your brother. You with me?"

"Yeah." He looked down at my mouth like he wanted to kiss me, but I turned my head away.

"Breakfast is ready," I said, pushing at him. He stepped back and I hopped down, grabbing plates. We sat and ate together and I didn't say anything. I was too busy rolling the situation over in my head and trying to make sense of it. Things had looked simple when Picnic held a gun to Jeff's head.

Go with Horse, save Jeff.

Now Jeff was in even bigger trouble—assuming Horse wasn't lying to me. I was his collateral, except sometimes he treated me like a hostage and sometimes he gave me fantastic orgasms. We had our own separate rooms but we'd slept downstairs together. Oh, and he almost killed a guy who almost shot me after definitely having public sex with me at a party. Sex I enjoyed.

Nope, nothing weird going on here at all.

"How would you feel about me going to town for a while, by myself, today?" I asked, tracing the grain in the wooden block with my finger. Might as well test this arrangement a little, see if I actually had the choices he said I did. If I could really leave.

"I guess that depends on what your plans are," he replied slowly. "I have to go by the armory today. You can ride in with me if you'd like."

"I'd rather go on my own," I said, stealing a quick glance at him. He sat back, relaxed, thoughtful. The silence stretched between us and I couldn't take it any longer. Too much quiet, too much weirdness. "I want to start looking for a job as soon as possible."

"What do you need a job for?"

"To earn money?" I said. He stared at me. "You know, green stuff to exchange for goods and services?"

"All this shit going down around you and the thing you're gonna focus on is finding a job?" he asked, raising his brows.

"It's better than sitting around and thinking about all this shit going down around me," I snapped. I suddenly wanted something normal, something that I controlled. Wanted to be alone and think somewhere that I wasn't surrounded by him, his sexy smell or his things.

"You need money, let me know and I'll give it to you," he replied. "You need shit to do, take care of the house and cook. No job."

"Is that because of my brother or because you don't want me working or what?" I demanded, the words tumbling out so fast he didn't have a shot at answering before I hit him again. "I thought you said this is all my choice. What are the limits of this little arrangement? You gave me a phone and my car, so why can't I get a job? How long will this go on? How will I support myself when it's over? Everything is up in the air and I can't call Jeff and my mom doesn't know where I am and—"

Horse stood up and reached across the butcher block and pulled me over to him. He kissed me, hard, shutting me up. A dish fell to the floor and shattered, but he just maintained his assault on my mouth, falling back into his chair, pulling me down onto his lap and arranging my legs on either side of his hips. He kept kissing me as he rubbed his hands up and down my back, soothing me. Finally he stopped, and I stared into his eyes, emotionally exhausted.

"You can't do this," he said.

"What?" I whispered.

"Freak out over stuff you can't control."

"So I'm just supposed to do nothing and wait for my brother to get killed by these really bad guys? That's assuming you don't kill him first, right?"

"No, you're supposed to take care of yourself and keep safe, so that if your brother pulls his shit together he'll have a sister alive to celebrate with," he replied, his voice serious. "And in the meantime you can keep busy taking care of me. Cook, clean, all that crap. I'll watch your back and maybe we'll get through this without everything blowing up in our faces, okay?"

"Cook and clean. Are you serious?"

He sighed, shaking his head, sighing.

"Fuck if I know what women do all day," he said, shrugging. "Figure it out, keep yourself busy doing something else then. You can start by hitting up the clinic today, get on the Pill, get tested. Only a couple of rules. Don't call your brother, don't disappear on me, and keep wearing tank tops like this one, because I really like what they do for your boobs."

He leaned forward, kissing me at the base of my throat, then sliding his nose down the front of that tank, nuzzling my cleavage. I softened against him, hating how easily he could distract me, but my body didn't care one bit. It liked the idea of going for a ride. He was right, I needed to get on some birth control asap — not to mention get tested for STDs. *Thanks again, Gary.* If I did have something, I guess Horse'd be out of luck, because we'd swapped a hell of a lot of fluids in the past forty-eight hours.

"Most women work all day, Horse," I murmured as his hand grabbed my butt, tilting my pelvis into the always-impressive erection he seemed to have permanently installed in his jeans. Was the man even human? "They have jobs or take care of kids, which is a job all by itself. I'd go crazy stuck here alone, and I get the impression that sooner or later you're going to have to do some work yourself."

"Today," he murmured, reaching up and pulling down my tank and bra, freeing my breast. His warm breath teased my nipple and I squirmed, trying to think.

"What?"

"Today. I need to get back to work today," he said right before he sucked my nipple deep into his mouth. Oh damn, that felt good. Every tug of his lips shot fire through my body, tightening things between my legs. I felt my hips start to rock against his, thinking there was far too much clothing between us. I wanted to forget about this whole situation—an orgasm or two would go a long way toward making that happen. The world lurched as Horse picked me up, walking me into the living room. Then I was on the couch, sliding out of my pants. About two seconds later he had his cock out, grabbed my hips and lined the head up with my slit before shoving it straight into me without a word.

Holy fuck I needed that, even though I was sore and swollen.

The weight of his lower body pressed me back into the couch as his arms braced on either side of me. He took long, slow strokes, steady and relentless. I wrapped my legs around his waist, wondering if I'd gone crazy. So many things happening, yet he only had to touch me and I lost myself in him again and again. This wasn't like any sex we'd had before. It wasn't fast, it wasn't hard and it wasn't urgent. It was relentless, however. Every time he hit bottom, every time he stretched me open, sliding his cock along my clit, I had to bite my lip to keep from screaming. I wanted him to go faster, pound me hard so I'd fall over the edge and get the relief my body needed. Fuck out my frustration in general.

I reached down, urging him to go faster. He ignored me, pumping at his own speed, the corner of his mouth turning up as I glared at him.

"You still pissed at me for last night, babe?" Horse asked. "You wanna fight about it? Now's a great time. I'm in a pretty good mood, probably agree with anything you say."

"You're insane," I muttered, straining up toward him. Dammit, I needed to come. He must too. If he was any harder he'd start popping blood vessels, the bastard, yet he just smirked at me and went even slower.

"Maybe," he replied, grinning openly at me now. "But I'm the bastard fucking you and pretty much your only hope of getting off, so you might want to stop trying to kill me with those eyes of yours."

"Jerk."

"Hot piece of ass."

"Don't call me that!"

"I was referring to myself," he replied, thrusting deep before stopping. He grabbed one of my hands, then the other, pinning them on either side of my head as I squirmed.

"Just do it!" I demanded. He dropped his mouth down, taking mine in a long, slow kiss. I tried to thrust my tongue into his mouth, wiggling against him. I wanted more and I wanted it now. He pulled back, and now his face wore a definite smirk.

"Do what?"

"You know," I gritted.

"I'm confused," he replied. "I think you need to explain to me. Otherwise I might just give up and go away."

I closed my mouth and squeezed my inner muscles around his dick as tight as I could, gloating when he stiffened and groaned. I let go and then started squeezing him in a slow and steady rhythm. Two could play this game.

"Fuck, Marie," he moaned, then pushed my hands down deep into the couch as he lifted himself, finally thrusting into me like I needed. I still couldn't move much, but that didn't matter because the games were over. Now he hit me with deep strokes, each one more forceful than the last. I felt my muscles growing tight as I lifted my hips to meet his. Oh damn... I was close — so incredibly close. He pushed my hands together over my head, imprisoning them as he hammered home. I hovered right at the edge then slipped over, screaming out my orgasm.

I have no idea how long it was before Horse came, because I was floating in my own little world. He collapsed on top of me, managing to keep enough of his weight to one side that he didn't crush me. Our breathing slowed. Then he leaned up on one elbow, sliding me so we lay face-to-face.

If I'd spent a million years trying to guess his next move, I still wouldn't have seen it coming.

"Why don't you go down to the community college and pick up an application," he said. That broke right through my post-coital haze.

"Why would I do that?"

"You're here. You're not going anywhere any time soon, and you need something to do. You told me you want to go to school, so look into going to school."

"It's not that simple," I said, shaking my head. Horse's reality and mine were two very different things. Why were we even having this conversation, let alone right now? "I can't just go to college."

"Why not?"

"Well it costs a lot of money, for one thing," I snapped. "And right now I'm worth a total of eleven hundred bucks if I'm lucky. You have to do tests, you have to apply and get accepted and even then you have to... I don't know, you have to do all kinds of stuff. And my brother's in big trouble, I don't have time for school..." I ran out of steam at that point, so I glared at him instead. He kept changing things on me and I couldn't keep up.

"You can't do anything about Jeff," he said firmly. "But the rest? You gotta do that shit to get into school, start doing it. Go down there, see what it takes. Get the papers and fill them out. It's not gonna happen if you sit around listing all the reasons it can't."

"What part of 'I don't have any money' did you not get?"

"What part of 'I'll give you money if you need it' did you not get?"

"Horse, that's crazy."

He sighed and shook his head.

"You're here, Marie, and I know you like to earn your own way. But—and don't get pissed when I say this—you don't have the skills to make good money, which means any job you get is going to be minimum wage, despite the fact that you're smart and hardworking and could do just about anything if you had the chance. But you won't have a chance without some education, so you might as well start now."

He trailed his hand down along my body as he spoke, fingers tracing my curves, pulling my hips closer into his. I shook my head, wondering if I'd lost my mind. Jeff might get killed, I'd just had mind-blowing couch sex with his potential killer and now I was supposed to apply for college.

Just like that.

"You're serious? You want me to go to school?"

"Why not?" he challenged. "So long as you take care of shit around here, I'm fine with it. Might want to move on that whole divorce thing too while you're at it. Club's got a lawyer, I'll set up an appointment for you. I can pretty much guarantee your ex won't put up a fight."

He smiled when he said it—not a nice smile.

"Okay, I'll go check it out," I said slowly. "This is weird, you get that? You kidnapping me, holding me hostage and then sending me to school? This isn't how things like this usually work."

Horse grinned at me, eyes lazy and satisfied.

"Just roll with it," he whispered. "And keep doing whatever exercises you do to make your cunt squeeze like that. They got a college degree for that?"

"You're a pig," I whispered back. "You know that, right?"

"So far bein' a pig works for me, babe," he said. "Gotta go now. Check out the college. Hit the clinic and get some pills. Don't call your brother. Cook something fuckin' great for dinner and don't wear any panties. That's all I ask."

With that he pushed himself up off the couch. I watched him pull up his pants, stunned and bemused. He walked out the front door. I heard his bike roar to life and then I was on my own.

That whole cooking dinner/no panties thing didn't quite work out.

My trip to Coeur d'Alene was great. I didn't really know my way around, but it wasn't hard to find downtown. It was right next to the great big giant lake that gave the place its name, sort of a "once you drive into the water you've gone too far" kind of situation. I stopped off and bought a cup of coffee and a bagel at a little coffee shop right down on Sherman Avenue, the main strip through town. The waitress there helped me find the college campus—surprisingly, just a few blocks away, also on the lake. I ended up walking there along a broad, paved trail that had a beach on one side and a really pretty park on the other. Everywhere I looked there were kids running around and having a good time, punctuated by painstakingly casual groups of teens in tiny swimsuits trolling with their friends. Just offshore, a seaplane took off from the water. Farther along I saw someone parasailing.

The trail took me into a residential neighborhood and then I started seeing college buildings. From there it was easy to find the admissions office. I talked with a lady for close to an hour and left with a handful of brochures.

On the walk back I saw a bank, so I went and checked my balance on their ATM. Exactly $1,146.24 total. Seeing my balance felt good, and I got out $200 in cash, just in case. Horse said he'd give me money, but I hadn't given up on finding a way to earn my own. It might be okay to play house with him for a while, but I wasn't stupid enough to think I should count on him. I couldn't define what we had, and I couldn't afford to fool myself about my situation. I was a still-married woman held as collateral by a motorcycle club for her brother's debt.

I might have to leave town in a hurry at some point.

I finished up by visiting the women's clinic and got a prescription, reminding myself I was way too early in my cycle to seriously worry about a pregnancy. That seemed like enough for one day, so I headed home to start dinner. Horse hadn't said what time he'd be back but I didn't want to call and ask. That would be a little too real or something. Playing house scared me.

There were two strange cars in the driveway when I pulled up—a small, red convertible and a classic Mustang, beautifully restored. I parked my little car next to them, wondering who I would be dealing with now. No sign of Horse's bike, and he hadn't mentioned someone coming to visit either. I pushed through the front door to find four strange women sitting in the living room, laughing and drinking beer. All of them had that biker chick vibe going on—not slutty, but definitely not shy about showing some skin. They smiled and started coming toward me. Thankfully, Darcy walked in from the back of the house, carrying a tray with a bowl of chips and some dip on it.

"Marie! I'm so glad you're back, we weren't sure how long you'd be!" she said, setting down the tray on the coffee table and pulling me into her arms. It was a little overwhelming but it felt good too. Then she let me go and turned me toward the other women, who'd collected around us.

"Girls, this is Marie," Darcy said, wrapping an arm around my shoulders. "She's Horse's property now, think I filled you in on that. Marie, this is Cookie, Maggs, Dancer and Em."

I smiled uncertainly at the women as they crowded forward, most of them hugging me and kissing my cheek. They ranged in age from Em, a young girl who looked strangely familiar to me and had to be in her early twenties, to Darcy and Maggs, both of whom were probably in their forties.

"Come on," said Cookie, taking my arm and pulling me toward the couch. Dancer grabbed my purse and hung it on a hook by the door. Maggs handed me a beer and they settled like a flock of birds, watching me. Awkward... I couldn't even remember all their names, let alone think of anything to say.

"I'm Dancer," said a tall, black-haired woman with chocolate-brown skin. Her features were sharp and she wore her hair long and straight down her back. She looked Indian to me, and I wondered if she was part of the Coeur d'Alene tribe. I'd seen several historic markers around town, and a lot of them seemed to be sponsored by the local tribal casino. "I'm Bam Bam's old lady."

That startled me—Horse was pretty darn pale to be this woman's brother, but he'd said his sister was married to Bam Bam.

"You're Horse's sister?" I asked. Then I blushed, realizing how rude I must sound. She laughed.

"Half-sister," she said. "I'm Coeur d'Alene, he's not, but it works. Bam and I have been together forever, got three beautiful little babies to prove it. I'm really happy to meet you, honey."

I smiled a little uncertainly.

"I don't know how much you know," I started to say, thinking I should probably clear things up pretty quick here before they got the wrong impression.

"We know it all," said Maggs. She was petite with shaggy blonde hair, bright eyes and a great big smile. She reminded me of Goldie Hawn. "I hope you don't mind, but Darcy told us. I mean, some of it's club business and we don't have those details, but she told us everything you told her."

I frowned. I guess I hadn't exactly sworn Darcy to secrecy, but I hadn't expected her to make all the details public either. Maggs reached forward and took my hand, rubbing it between hers with a look of concern.

"Oh honey, don't worry," she said quickly. "We're all family here. If you're with Horse, you're with us and trust me, these boys cause enough trouble that they need all of us to keep them straight. It's a group effort."

The others murmured agreement.

"Old ladies have to stick together," Darcy said. "Things can get rough, but no matter what we have each other. This is your family now, and we're here to welcome you."

I shook my head.

"I'm not Horse's old lady," I said. "I don't know what I am, but we've only been together for a couple of days."

"Bam says Horse is crazy for you," Dancer said. That caught my attention in a big way. "Never seen him this way. You may not get this, but my brother doesn't exactly have trouble finding women. He doesn't need to drive across the state to get laid, Marie. And this collateral bullshit? The club doesn't work that way, this is a special situation. He's never brought anyone home before. Never."

"Really?" I asked, still uncertain.

"Never," she replied. "It's a rule of his, actually. 'No bitches in the house.' Drives me crazy, he's such a dumbass, sexist pig about it. Been that way since high school."

"Wow."

"Wow is right," chimed in Em, a tall, slender girl with a shy smile. "I never thought Horse would hook up with someone. We're excited to have you here. I'm Picnic's daughter."

"I saw your pictures!" I said, placing her now. I could see Picnic's features in her face, although softened and feminine. "He showed them to me once when they came to visit. He's really proud of you."

"Thanks," she replied, blushing. "It's good to have you here. Dancer's right, the club is like a family and sometimes it feels like we've got a lot more brothers than sisters. We're excited to get to know you."

"No kidding!" chimed in Cookie, a bouncy, petite girl who had bright red curls, green eyes and lots of freckles. "I'm Bagger's old lady. You haven't met him, he's over in Afghanistan right now. We girls have to stick together, for sure. I don't know what I'd do if I didn't have Maggs and Dancer and the others to keep me sane."

"I guess that means it's my turn," Maggs said. "I'm with Bolt, you haven't met him yet either. He's down in Kuna, at the prison."

That caught my attention. Why was her man in prison? I felt for her, thinking about visiting Mom in jail. Prison had to be so much worse, and for longer too. I knew for myself that good people could do stupid, stupid things.

"My mom's in jail right now," I told her, taking her hand. "She's going to get out in a few months though. Have you been on your own for long?"

"About two years now," she replied, looking momentarily tired. "But we're working on an appeal. I know everyone says this, but Bolt honestly didn't do what he went down for, and we can prove it. It's actually been kind of a big case. Every time there's a hearing we have reporters come around like a bunch of fucking scavengers—there's a big scandal about prosecutorial misconduct and mishandling DNA evidence. At least I don't have to deal with it alone though."

"Exactly," said Darcy. "None of us are alone. And this isn't all the girls either. This is just the posse I managed to round up on short notice. Between the Reapers and the Silver Bastards there are about fifteen old ladies, and we stick together."

"What about those girls at the party last night?"

Em made a gagging sound.

"They're definitely *not* family," she said, rolling her eyes. "Bunch of sluts and losers."

"Some of them are nice girls," Cookie protested. "I met Bagger at a club party."

"That was a real party," said Em. "Not one of those drunken fuckfests my dad likes to pretend I don't know about."

"Whoever they are, they aren't old ladies," said Dancer firmly. "They aren't like us, and you aren't like them," she added, catching my eye.

"And that's why we're here," said Cookie. "We decided you probably need a break, so it's ladies' night. We're going to take you out and show you just how much fun your new sisters can be."

I sat up straight, shaking my head and leaning forward to set down my untouched beer. They might not understand my situation, but I certainly did. Going out to party was not on the agenda. Horse left me with orders and I intended to follow them.

"I don't think Horse would like that," I said. "He told me to make dinner, I think he was planning something…"

I trailed off as Dancer walked over to my purse, pulled out my phone and scrolled through the numbers, hitting one and putting it on speaker. It rang and then I heard Horse's voice.

"Babe, what's up?"

"This is your sister," Dancer announced, flashing an evil grin. "We're kidnapping Marie and taking her out tonight. You'll just have to jack off if you get horny. She'll be busy."

There was a pause from the phone.

"Give the phone to Marie," he said. "I need to talk to her."

I lunged for it, but Dancer tossed it to Cookie, who jumped up on the couch to hold it out of my reach. "Too bad! I've got a cooler full of jello shots and a flask, so we're gonna have fun fun fun! You might as well camp out at the armory tonight, stud."

The girls all laughed, but I felt a little sick. I couldn't afford to piss Horse off. They might think I was part of the "family" now, but I knew better.

"Put Marie on the fucking phone," Horse said again, and the tone of his voice was not amused one little bit.

"This is Dancer again," said his sister, grabbing the phone from Cookie and taking it off speaker. "You might as well give up, Horse. We're going to take her, she needs a break and you're a dick if you won't let her have one. I heard what you did last night. Poor girl probably needs therapy after that. I promise I'll take good care of her and drive sober. Find something to do that doesn't involve shooting anyone, okay?"

Then she hung up the phone.

I stared at her, stunned.

"You can do that?" I asked.

"What?"

"Hang up on Horse."

Dancer burst out laughing.

"Oh, he'll be pissed. He and Bam'll probably bitch to each other all night. But we're just going out for a little fun and he'll look like a pussy-whipped baby if he makes too big a deal out of it. And our boys may *be* pussy-whipped, but they sure as fuck don't want to *look* like they are. It's all good."

I wasn't too sure about that.

"Time for shots," said Cookie, hopping off the couch and walking toward the kitchen. The others pulled me to my feet and dragged me down the hallway, my phone left behind. Then the music started and things got a little crazy.

Chapter Sixteen

ॐ

"Seriously, you would not believe how big it is," I slurred, leaning forward and holding out my hands for scale.

"That's disgusting," yelled Dancer, slapping at me, and I burst into giggles, almost falling out of my chair. "That's my brother you're talking about. Stop it before I puke!"

I held my hands farther apart, opening my mouth wide and flicking my tongue at her like a snake. We all exploded into fresh gales and I nearly peed my pants. Potty break time.

"I'm gonna pee. Anyone?"

Em stood up and we stumbled toward the bathroom together. Seriously, I loved each and every one of those girls. I couldn't imagine why I'd been worried about Horse. Horse kicked ass. In fact, when I saw Horse tonight I was going to rip off all his clothes and give him the best blowjob he'd ever had in his life. And Jeff was going to be fine too, because despite what everyone thought, he really wasn't totally stupid. I knew that for a fact, just like I knew that I really, really needed just one more shot to make the evening perfect.

Old ladies kicked ass.

A couple of guys met us on the way to the bathroom, one of them holding out a hand to steady me as I lurched into him.

"Can we buy you girls a drink?" he asked, smiling at me. I smiled back. He was kind of cute in a college-freshman way. Horse would eat him for breakfast, I mused.

"Not gonna happen," came a low voice behind us. I turned to see Painter, one of the Reapers' prospects, standing behind us looking mean. With his honed muscles, sneer and white-blond hair all spiked up, he was pretty hot. Yum. Oops, too much booze... I couldn't check out Painter, that was just weird. "You need to step the fuck away from them right now."

Painter might not have had his top rocker but he was still a scary biker guy. He'd showed up at Horse's house about twenty minutes after Dancer hung up on Horse and had been following us around ever since. The guys backed away instantly, mumbling apologies. Em turned and smacked Painter's chest. He grunted and narrowed his eyes at her, but he didn't say anything. I watched the exchange with wide eyes. Em grabbed my arm and pulled me away toward the bathroom. She slammed the door open, banging it against the wall as she dragged me in.

"I cannot believe him," she muttered, walking over to the stall, which was just an open toilet separated from the rest of the room with a wooden partition. "How am I supposed to meet anyone like this? I am never going to find a real boyfriend. Never."

I swayed, trying to follow her words.

"I don't get it."

"Imagine being the oldest daughter of the president of the Reapers MC," she said. "How many guys do you think asked me out in high school? I had to go to my prom with a *prospect*. A prospect who *wasn't allowed to dance with me.*"

Oh. Now I got it.

"That sucks," I said, feeling very sage. "But it's probably better than having some guy take advantage of you."

My own prom was an excellent example—Gary had been like an octopus on Viagra and I'd been stupid enough to find it flattering.

"I want a guy to take advantage of me!" Em snapped, pulling up her jeans. "You have no idea how many guys've ditched me once they learned about my dad. I tried to get away. I even went to college in Seattle. Picnic had his friends over there checking on me. For about three months it was great, and then the rumors started that they'd kill anyone who touched me. You'd think I have two heads or something. I'm a virgin, despite my very best efforts to give it away, and at this rate I'll be dead before I find a penis to put in my vagina."

I took her place, pulling down my own jeans and peeing. She made a good point. I decided to tell her that.

"You make a good point," I said, standing back up. I swayed again, and she laughed, catching me.

"Wow, I think you ate too much jello."

She helped me over to the sink. I washed my hands and we both took a few minutes to check out our hair and makeup. I thought we looked pretty good—no wonder those guys wanted to buy us drinks. I'd buy us drinks if I was a guy.

"So who *would* your dad let you date?"

"I don't know," she said, shaking her head. "I'm not sure anyone is good enough. He'd like me to be with someone in the club though. That way I'll never move away from him."

"Aw, that's kind of sweet," I said. "I mean, at least your dad cares about you. I hardly even remember mine."

She shrugged.

"Yeah, I guess you're right," she said. "I guess I wouldn't trade him. Mom was pretty great too. I miss her."

"What happened to her?" I asked, and then bit my lip. The booze had apparently dissolved the filter between my brain and my mouth.

"Breast cancer," she said, clearly not wanting to talk about it. "Long time ago. Let's get shots."

"Sounds good," I replied, following her out the door. Painter stood outside, leaning against the wall with his arms crossed, looking bored. I grabbed Em's arm and pulled her into me.

"Why does he have to be here?" I stage-whispered. "Are they afraid I'll run away or something?"

"Oh it's not personal. They send someone with us every time we go out," she said, shrugging. "Usually a prospect, but every once in a while Ruger tags along. He's fun. They don't want anyone bothering us. That way we can party and they know we're safe. It's no big deal, at least not for you because you already have a man. For me, it sucks."

"So all old ladies get watched all the time?" I asked. "Isn't that creepy?"

She laughed and shrugged.

"Mostly just when we go out at night," she said. "It's a security thing. There are a lot of clubs and not all of them are friends to the Reapers. This is their way of making sure nobody hassles us. Knowing we have a sober ride home. It's great, unless you're looking to lose your virginity."

I giggled and she glared at me, which made me giggle more as we headed back out onto the main floor. Then I stopped, because a tall man wearing Reaper leathers suddenly blocked my path. I looked up, trying to focus. Max.

"Hey, Max," said Em. "What are you doing here?"

"Just felt like getting a drink," he said, looking us over with a gleam of approval in his expression. We looked good and Max noticed. *Nice.* "Talked to Painter, heard you ladies were here. Thought I'd offer to buy a round. You look great tonight."

"You're too sweet," she replied, smiling up at him flirtatiously. He smiled back, and I wondered if there might be a little more going on with Max and Em than I realized. Painter came up next to us, standing tall as he and Max shared a look. Then Painter shook his head and stepped back, and he didn't look happy about it.

That was interesting.

Max followed us back to the table, where Maggs put him in his place, telling him to buy us drinks and stay out of our way, "because it's laaadddieess niiighhttt!" Everyone howled with approval as he grinned and took orders, bringing back a round of shots. Despite my earlier conviction that I needed more booze, looking at the little cup of vodka made me feel sick so I pulled out my phone to see what time it was. Almost two. Horse had texted about four hours ago.

Going to the Line with the guys. Don't wait up.

The Line. Why did that sound familiar? My brain was all fogged up.

"What's the Line?" I asked Cookie, who sat next to me. She'd put on a leather vest before coming into the bar, and her patches said "Property of Bagger, Reapers MC". The whole property thing still made me uncomfortable but she seemed happy enough wearing it. And Cookie wasn't exactly oppressed. I'd figured that out by chatting between the jello shots she poured down my throat. She was way too busy running her coffee shop and taking care of her and Bagger's three-year-old daughter to be oppressed.

"Oh that's the club's titty bar," she said. "Makes a fortune, although those strippers can be such sluts. But some of them are okay. I always tell Bagger I'm gonna start working there while he's deployed and it pisses him off. I love doing that," she laughed.

"What are you talking about?" yelled Darcy from across the table.

"The Line!" Cookie yelled back. Darcy got a huge grin on her face.

"We should go there!"

"What?" I asked, startled. Cookie clapped her hands.

"Oh that's a great idea!" she said. "We can play on one of the poles. I need pictures for Bagger!"

"Are you serious? Why would we go there?" I demanded, mystified.

"Well, for one thing, if the guys are at the Line, it's fun to show up without warning," said Darcy, winking at me. "Scare 'em straight, you know? Plus it's kind of interesting to watch the dancers. Some of them are really good, I've learned some excellent tricks from them. Boonie can testify to that."

She leaned over and gave Maggs a high five for emphasis.

"Not to mention that if your man is gonna spend the night around naked bitches that aren't you, it's not a bad thing to make sure he brings his hard-on back home, you know?" added Maggs. That was a good point. I didn't like the idea of Horse with another woman, I didn't like it at all. I scowled down at the phone and the offending text.

"And the shop has support merchandise," she added. "I need to pick up a new tank top. Gonna go see Bolt this week, want to give him something to look forward to."

"Oh I hate that place," whined Em. "And if Dad's there I'll have to watch some stripper rub all over him and it's gross. No girl should have to watch her dad screw so many different women, especially when he won't let me date anyone at all! I'd rather go home."

"Have Painter give you a ride," said Max, coming up behind me and leaning against the back of my chair. He was kind of in my space, but nobody else seemed to notice so I just scooted forward, frowning. "It's almost last call anyway. I'll take everyone else to the Line, give him a break."

Dancer smiled at him.

"That's sweet, Max," she said. "Let's do it."

Ten minutes later I was crammed in the back of her car with the others, Max following us on his bike. I expected Em to complain about catching a ride home with Painter, but she seemed happy enough with the situation. That surprised me because I thought I'd caught a hint of something between her and Max earlier. Apparently I'd imagined it.

It was almost two-thirty in the morning when we pulled up to the strip club. We stumbled and giggled our way across the parking lot, which was mostly empty. Then the sign flickered and turned off.

"It's closed," I said, stopping in my tracks. "We can't go in."

"Oh that's the best part," Darcy said, grinning at me. "It's closed to the public, but we aren't the public, babe. We can party as long as we want."

"What about the dancers?" I asked dumbly. Max laughed behind me, putting a hand on the small of my back and pushing me forward.

"Don't worry about them," he said. "They're not old ladies. They won't get in your way."

"Last time we were here, Dancer got up on stage and showed us her moves," said Cookie, giggling. "It kicked ass. Well, it kicked ass for everyone but Horse. He looked kinda sick to his stomach."

"I'm sober this time," Dancer replied. "It's your turn tonight."

"You know, I think I will," said Cookie with a grin. "I could do a little show in one of the private rooms. You film it for me and I'll send it to Bagger on the computer. He's always asking me to send him pictures. This'll blow his mind!"

"He'll definitely blow something," Maggs replied, cackling.

A big black guy stood guard by the bar's main entrance. He let us in without a word. I'd been inside with Horse the day before, but things were different tonight. For one, the lights were dim, which gave the whole place a completely different feel. Sort of murky and dirty. There were a few waitresses bussing tables and two bartenders restocking and cleaning up. A man wearing a Reapers' cut sat in a booth counting money. Music still played and the center stage held one dancer working the pole. Below her sat several of the guys nursing beers, including Picnic, Ruger, Bam Bam, Boonie and a couple of others. I didn't see Horse.

"Hey, baby," yelled Darcy, sauntering down toward them. Just like the night before, Boonie's face lit up when he saw her and he stood, turning his back on the naked chick slithering around the pole. He wrapped his arms around

Darcy and they fell into another of those all-consuming kisses, oblivious to the world. Dancer and Bam Bam were a little more subdued with their greeting, but they disappeared off into a darkened booth without a backward glance.

"Fuck, I miss that," muttered Cookie, and I glanced over to see tears in her eyes.

"Buck up, bitch," said Maggs, giving her a little punch on the shoulder. "You wanna make a porno for your boy, you can't be crying in it. That's not his kink—unless you've been holding out on us?"

Cookie laughed, shaking off her melancholy with a visible force of will. These were strong women, I decided. *Really* strong women. I could learn from them.

"You know I draw the line at soft-core, no fetish stuff," Cookie replied, waggling her eyebrows suggestively. "I'm gonna get drinks. Maggs, show the newbie where the VIP rooms are, will ya? And make sure it's wiped down before I strut my stuff. My man likes his girls clean and tight, no sloppy seconds!"

She gave a little shimmy and we whooped, clapping. Maggs pointed me across the floor to a long, dark hallway.

"Rooms are over there, sugar," she said. "I left my phone in the car, and I'm definitely gonna need my own personal copy of this for blackmail purposes. See you in a few."

She pushed me toward the rooms. I crossed the floor to the hallway, feeling awkward as all get out. Dark doors lined the both sides of the hall, all of them closed. I had no idea what I'd find inside and exploring on my own felt weird. I decided to wait for Maggs. Then Max strolled up, offering me that same friendly smile he'd worn at the bar.

"You lost?" he asked. I shook my head.

"Not so much lost as a little out of my depth," I admitted. "I guess Cookie's gonna have us film her dancing for Bagger. She said to find a room, but I'm afraid to just start opening doors."

"No prob," he said, shrugging casually, although his eyes held a pleased gleam. "Follow me."

Something felt off. My instincts said I shouldn't follow him, but I couldn't think of a reason not to and I was still pretty drunk. My drunken instincts weren't so hot—Gary'd asked me to marry him after I'd just killed a six-pack.

When Max pointed me toward the last door on the right side of the hall, which had a little green light glowing above it, I hesitantly walked over and pushed it open. It took a second for my eyes to adjust to the darkness and soft red light. Then I saw Horse sitting on a black leather couch against the wall, arms stretched out along the back. His shirt was off and an almost-naked, bleached-blonde woman straddled him. Her hips writhed against his and when she turned to look at us, I saw she had giant, obviously fake boobs. She wore a blue, sparkly G-string and nothing else.

Horse met my wide, frozen eyes and glared.

"What the fuck are you doing here? Thought this was ladies' night."

"Nothing," I whispered, stepping back and very carefully shutting the door. I felt brittle, fragile, like I was going to break apart into a thousand pieces. I don't know why. It wasn't like we had a real relationship. I didn't own him. But seeing him with another woman—that hurt me deep down inside. I bumped into Max, who caught my arms and steadied me. I looked up at him, devastated, and he wore an expression I couldn't begin to describe.

"Did you know he was in there?" I asked.

"Yeah," Max replied. His easy response, completely unapologetic, threw me.

"You set me up?" I whispered. "Why?"

"Because you're living in a fucking dream world and the girls were filling your head with shit. I can be a dick, but not as big a dick as he's being. Thought you had a right to know."

I tried to think. Unfortunately, everything was spinning around me.

"I didn't do it to hurt you, Marie," Max said, pulling me in for a rough hug. I stiffened, then relaxed into him, needing the comfort. He rubbed my hair, combing it with his fingers.

"You're a sweet kid and you're in a really fucked-up situation," he said, not unkindly. "You need to keep your head straight. Horse is not your old man, you're not going to live happily ever after with him and your brother isn't going to come through for you. The faster you figure that out, the better your life is going to be. That's the truth."

I pulled away from Max and glanced back at the door, willing Horse to open it, to come out and explain that this was all just some sort of mistake. He didn't. The green light taunted me.

"You want a ride home?" Max asked.

"Yeah," I said.

"Okay."

He took my arm and went to the fire door, quickly punching a code into a keypad on the side. A tiny red light blinked green and he pushed through the door. I followed him across the parking lot to his bike. My phone started vibrating and I looked down to see Horse's name on the screen.

I turned it off.

The ride seemed to last forever, and I was pretty much sober by the time we reached the house. Ariel ran out to greet us, smiling his big puppy grin, but I didn't pet him so he whined and crawled under the porch. Max surprised me when he left his bike and followed me into the house. I guess I expected him to just drop me off or something. It felt strange and awkward with him there, and I wished I could be alone.

"You want a drink?" I asked, hoping he'd say no.

"Yeah, grab me a beer," he replied, pulling out his phone. I left him fiddling with it while I found a beer for him and a glass of water for myself. As I came back down the hall he met me halfway, taking the drinks and walking into the dining room. He set them on the pool table and cocked his head to the side, studying me again.

"Why do you do that?" I asked.

"Do what?"

"Look at me like that?"

"Trying to decide what the fuck Horse is thinking," he replied. "You don't need to be with him, Marie. This is fucked up. You should let me help you."

"Help me how?"

Instead of answering, he leaned down and threw me over his shoulder. I shrieked, hitting him on the back and kicking. Max ignored my struggles, carrying me back into the living room and throwing me down on to the couch. I hit hard and lost my breath. Before I could recover he was on me, thrusting a knee between my legs, covering my mouth with his. I struggled against him, but I shouldn't have bothered. Way too strong for me. His legs pinned me, pelvis grinding into mine as his arms wrestled my own into the couch. His kiss wasn't sensual, just a brutal attack. No tongue, no seduction. Just a crushing of his lips against my mouth. I seriously couldn't breathe and my vision started going dark.

"Oh no fucking way. You're a dead man."

I heard Horse's angry voice and felt a surge of hope. Then Max flew off me so hard I almost rolled off the couch. Horse threw him across the room into the wall, missing the TV by about six inches. I screamed as Horse leapt after him, hammering him with his fists. Max writhed under the onslaught, but he started laughing, the sound horrible and dark and oddly punctuated by the blows slamming his body. A loud, clicking noise cut through his laughter and I looked up to find Picnic aiming a gun at the two men.

Horse didn't pause.

"Horse!" Picnic said. "Drop him or I'll shoot you."

Horse gave Max one last, vicious punch to the gut before he stepped back, chest heaving. Max rose to his feet unsteadily, grinning at Horse in a way that was truly unbalanced. Now I got the whole "Mad Max" thing…

"You got a problem, *brother*?" Max asked as he wiped the blood streaming from his nose with the back of his hand. "Your bitch didn't seem to think so. Practically jumped into my arms at the Line. I'll admit she's a sweet cunt, but is she really worth fighting over?"

"Shut your mouth," Picnic said, stepping forward. "You don't talk to a brother that way. And you don't fuck around with a fellow Reaper's woman. We'll deal with this at the armory tomorrow. You got that?"

Max laughed again. Then he turned to me and stuck two of his fingers in a "v" in front of his mouth, flicking his tongue between them at me.

"You asshole!" I yelled, filled with sudden rage. "You *fucking asshole*, you get out of here! Get the fuck out of here and don't fucking come back or *I'll fucking shoot you myself!*"

All three guys froze, looking at me in surprise.

I sneered back at them, disgusted.

"What, surprised that the bone you're fighting over can talk? Well fuck all of you!"

With that I turned and stomped up the stairs to my room, slamming the door behind me. Moments later bikes roared to life outside. I paced my room for a minute, furious and full of energy, then threw my door open and headed back downstairs.

I had a few more things I wanted to get off my chest.

I found Horse standing in the center of the living room, running a hand through his hair, scowling at the splatters of blood staining his floor. He turned toward me, and we glared at each other across the room, neither of us giving an inch. I was still a little drunk, but I'd had it. Time to lay things out with Horse. I opened my mouth to let him have it, but he started in first.

"Who the fuck you do think you are, showing up at the Line like that?" he demanded. "And why did Max have his tongue down your throat?"

Oh, that *really* pissed me off.

"You don't get to talk about tongues down throats, asshole," I hissed. "And for your information, I was at the Line because *your sister* took me there. I guess it didn't occur to her that you'd be screwing some slut in the back room!"

"I wasn't screwing anyone. It was a lap dance. No big deal," he said, eyes narrowing on me.

"So sorry I interrupted you before you got to the happy ending!" I yelled. I didn't think I'd ever been this angry before in my life. The edges of my vision actually turned red. I felt like throwing things at him, and I glanced around, trying to find something with a good heft. Horse stalked over, looming over me as he yelled in my face, backing me toward the wall.

"Why the fuck *shouldn't* I have a happy ending? It's not like I have an old lady to worry about! No, not me!" he declared, throwing his arms wide, speaking to the room at large. "I don't have an old lady, now do I? Nope, because you're too fucking good to wear my patch, now aren't you? What haven't I done for you, Marie? I kept your brother alive. Didn't come cheap, babe, you got no clue how pricey your ass is. And tonight? It's not like you were around to take care of me, was it? We had plans and you blew me off. You can't have it both ways, Marie. Either we're together or we're not, but if we're not don't expect me to sit around with my thumb up my ass while you're out partying. And this bullshit with Max? In my own home? I should throw your ass out and call the hit on your brother myself. You can go fuck yourself, Marie. Seriously. I'm done with you."

I snarled at him. How dare he play victim?

"Max was trying to rape me," I said, the words cold and hard. "And the only reason I caught a ride home with him was because you were too busy letting some whore grind her skanky crotch against you to notice. I go out one night without you and you can't keep it in your pants?"

"Why should I?" he demanded. He shifted his weight forward as he caught my hands, twisting them behind my back and forcing me against him. A sexual thrill ran through me, all mixed up with my anger and the crazy rush of adrenaline making my heart race. I felt his cock, hard and ready, and smelled the mixture of sweat and motor oil that always seemed to follow him. My pussy was a swollen, hot well of need and my panties were sopping. I wanted to bite him and lick him and kick him in the nuts all at the same time.

"Cookie hasn't seen her man in months, but when *she* goes out, she wears his patch," Horse snarled. "She's *proud* to be his old lady. You want me to keep it in my pants, you wear my patch."

Horse thrust his hips against me for emphasis and I laughed at him. Then I lunged forward and caught his lip in my teeth, biting, and not a little love nip. He dropped me with a shout and I took off up the stairs. He tore after me, catching the back of my shirt as I reached the top, pulling me down three steps and trapping me under his body on my stomach. One hand tangled in my hair, holding my head tight as the other ripped open my fly and jerked my jeans down around my knees, pinning them together. I moaned as he fumbled to free his cock, pushing my ass back at him, feeling my juices run down my leg because I wanted him inside me so badly.

Horse's dick ripped through me and I screamed.

What happened next was not gentle and nice and sweet and romantic. Horse tore into me, fucking me so hard I'm surprised nobody got hurt. His hand in my hair hurt, but his cock filled me exactly how I needed it. I don't know how long it lasted. I'm not even sure how many times I came. I just know that every orgasm I took felt like a victory over him, and when

207

he finally blew into me—hot seed shooting deep into my womb—he shouted and pulled my hair and that turned me on like nothing I've ever experienced before in my life.

Shit...

I collapsed down on the stairs, cradling my face in my arms as Horse's cock slowly softened inside me. His harsh, panting breaths echoed in my ears. Then he pulled out, turning and sitting down on the steps below me. I rolled over and looked up at the ceiling.

"This is really fucked up," he said, sounded stunned. I knew the feeling. "Did I hurt you?"

"No," I replied, running a hand through my hair. I needed to pull up my pants, but it took everything I had not to melt into an exhausted puddle. "I'm fine. I know this is sick, but that was incredible. I've never felt anything like it."

"Yeah."

We sat there for I don't know how long. My heart rate slowed and I started to notice things, like the rough texture of the carpet under my ass and the risers cutting into my back. And how wet I was. Ewww...

"I think I'm dripping on the rug," I murmured. Horse gave a short bark of laughter. I looked at him and the complete and utter absurdity of our situation hit me. I couldn't help myself, a little hysterical giggle started deep down in my chest. I twisted my mouth, trying to keep it in, but it broke free. I laughed harder and harder, my body shaking as Horse watched me like I'd lost my mind. Maybe I had.

"I'm so sorry," I said, tears building up in my eyes. "But this is beyond crazy. What's wrong with us? Where do we go from here?"

Horse shook his head, shrugging.

"Fuck if I know," he admitted, and for once he didn't bother putting on a front. "This is a whole new level of dysfunction for me, and that's saying something. I don't want to figure this out tonight. I just want to go to bed and I want you with me. Is that okay? Just for tonight? Can I hold you?"

I nodded.

"Yeah. Let's finish fighting tomorrow. I'm exhausted."

We stumbled up the stairs and he took my hand, pulling me into his room for the first time. I was too tired to look around. I just pulled off my clothes and fell into the bed. Horse stripped down and climbed in next to me, tucking me into his side. Like always, it made me feel safe.

How fucked up is that?

I woke up to find Horse lying next to me, watching as he traced his fingers across my face. He looked thoughtful and tired.

"I'm not sure ladies' night was such a hot idea," I whispered.

"I'm a dick," he replied, closing his eyes, face pained. "I'm an asshole and a dick and I shouldn't have been in that room at the Line. I did it because I was pissed you went out and I wanted to get back at you, which was bullshit. I'm sorry."

I looked away, trying not to think of him half naked with that girl, big boobs rubbing all over him. I hated the idea of them together but I also had to be honest with myself. I'd refused an exclusive relationship with him when he offered, and then I insulted him on top of it. Sure, he'd kidnapped me in return...and then offered to pay for my college.

Did that make us even or just exceptionally fucked up?

I really shouldn't have skipped biker babe orientation, I mused. Next time I'd definitely attend. A little laugh sneaked out and Horse flopped back, groaning.

"I'm fucked," he said.

"Let's talk this through," I said, rolling over. Now it was my turn to lean up and look down at him. "We're not in an exclusive relationship, or at least not one we agreed to together. I'm not even sure we're in a relationship at all. I don't know if I have the right to be so pissed at you, but I hated seeing you with that bitch. You have no idea how much I hated it. I didn't expect that. And I am definitely pissed off about it. And I'm pissed off about Max too."

"Do you want the right to be pissed at me, seeing as you're so good at it?" he asked, mouth quirking. The humor didn't quite reach his eyes. He took a deep breath, as if bracing himself. "What if we started over? Do you think you could give me another chance?"

"Do you actually think we could?" I replied. There were so many things between us, so many complicated feelings that I didn't know how to even begin dealing with them. "Or is it too late? There's a lot of baggage here. I mean, even if we let all the things between us go, there's still Jeff."

"I don't want to be your enemy," he said firmly. "I want to be your man. You make me feel crazy things, Marie, and I don't want to lose you. I don't want trouble for Jeff either, but I've done everything I can to help him. I can't do any more, it's up to him now. I hope you believe that."

He dropped his hand down along the length of my body, catching my leg and pulling it up and over his hip. His cock brushed my center and I shivered, like always. His gaze caught mine, full of intensity. "I want you to be my old lady, babe. That's all I have to offer. I'm a Reaper, and this is my world. You wear my patch, you be my woman and I'll be your man. We take the good times together and fight through the bad times. No games. That's everything I've got and it's all yours if you'll take it."

I sighed, trying to think. I wanted it—I wanted him. I still didn't like the whole property thing. But I'd seen Darcy and Dancer and Cookie in action—they weren't helpless victims and what they had with their men might be different, but it was good. Much better than I'd had with Gary—and that was another whole load of baggage. Horse would be taking on a woman who was still married to another man, a woman with no assets and no skills.

I guess it just came down to a leap of faith.

"I want to try," I said slowly, holding his gaze. "If we do it, I think we need to give each other a fresh start. Only look forward, leave all the past behind us. Let go of the anger. Otherwise we could spend the next year fighting over things we can't change."

"That works for me," he replied, face still grave. "But I need to know — are you ready to wear my patch? That's how it works in the club, babe, and there's no leaving the club. If you can't live with that, I'll find another place for you to stay until this shit with your brother resolves. It'll kill me, but I'll do it. I'm ready to let you go if that's what you need. No strings."

"I want to be with you," I said, reaching down to run my fingers along the length of his rapidly hardening cock. I moved my mouth toward his, letting my lips hover over his. "I'll be your old lady and I'll wear your patch. But if you ever let some bitch shove her tits in your face again, I'll shoot you myself."

At that, I wrapped my fingers around his dick and squeezed a little too tight for comfort.

"Noted," Horse said, smiling against my mouth. "You got a gun?"

I laughed, shaking my head, brushing my lips against his.

"Okay, we'll take care of that today," he said, nuzzling my mouth. "Gonna fuck you first though. Honest to God, you wouldn't believe the checklist I've got in my head for us to work through."

Horse wasn't kidding about the checklist. We got a good start on it, but after a couple hours I needed a break for food. We ate breakfast together and cleaned up, basking in each other's presence.

Then he took me out to the barn and I learned Horse wasn't kidding about the gun either.

"Okay, hold it straight like I showed you. Left hand down low to brace your right. Keep your finger off the trigger until you line up the sights. Good. Now put your finger on the trigger and pull back until it just stops. Double-check your aim and fire."

I shot the little semi-automatic .22 pistol at the target pinned against a hay bale three times, then pulled my finger off the trigger like he'd taught me and pointed the gun at the ground.

"You like it?" Horse asked, looking pleased with himself. He'd presented me with the pistol like it was a diamond ring or something. Probably best not to think about that too much.

"It kicks ass," I said, because it did. Firing it made me feel sort of powerful and tough. "But are you sure it's big enough? Those are really tiny little bullets, Horse. If I'm gonna be a badass biker chick, shouldn't I have a bigger gun?"

"A .22 was big enough to kill Bobby Kennedy," he replied, and I stopped smiling and raised my brows.

"Damn."

"No shit. Honestly, it's about accuracy, not size, babe."

"Did I seriously just hear you, Marcus "Horse" McDonnell, tell me it's not about size?"

"Yeah," he said, ignoring my little jab. "It's true it doesn't have the stopping power that a bigger gun does, but I'd be more afraid of a woman with a .22 who really knows how to shoot than a man with a .45 he bought because his dick's too small. It's not like the movies, Marie. A handgun isn't gonna stop someone in his tracks unless you hit something important, not even a big handgun. You need a shotgun for that. It's just physics."

"So even this little thing could kill someone," I asked, looking at the pistol with new respect. I handed it to him very carefully. "It just looks like a TV prop or something, you know?"

"No shit," he replied. "I want you to practice with it, really get used to it. We'll do it every day. Just remember, you ever point this at a person, you shoot it right at his heart and you shoot to kill. Never point a gun unless you're ready to end a life. And don't fool yourself that you can shoot them in the foot or some such shit. If it's bad enough to shoot, it's bad enough to kill. And nobody's that good a shot anyway."

"What about that night at the party?" I asked, my voice soft.

"What about it?" he asked, grabbing another, larger pistol out of his bag and sliding in the magazine with a click.

"You pointed a gun at that man. You didn't kill him, you shot next to him. But you could have killed him."

"Yep, I could've," he said. "I got real lucky that night because when he shot near you, he didn't hit you. Then he got lucky, because I put him in the same situation and he didn't get hit either. The difference is, he chose to pull his gun on a bunch of innocent women at a party. Then he chose to pull the trigger three times. No excuse for that. He deserved more than he got."

"You're scary sometimes, you understand that, right?"

Horse grinned at me, leaning over to kiss my nose.

"Try the .38, little Miss I-don't-know-if-my-gun-is-big-enough. It's what I like to carry, big enough to do some damage but small enough to be discreet."

I picked it up. This one was heavier and my hand shook just a little as I aimed it. I lined up the sights, braced my body with one foot back and pulled the trigger. The pistol bucked and while I didn't lose control, I didn't like how it felt either. The gun seemed kind of wild to me, and I decided an even larger one would probably knock me on my ass.

"I see what you mean," I said. "That one's harder to hold."

"Yup," he said. "And they have more kick as you go up. I'd rather see you with a gun that feels comfortable. Otherwise you might hesitate to use it when you need it. It's your choice and if I don't have what you want, we'll go find it."

"I want to try the .38 one more time," I said. He nodded, and I took my stance. This time when I shot, the shell casing flew back and hit my face, bouncing down my neck and into my cleavage.

"Holy shit!" I yelled, dropping the gun and jumping round, trying to shake the hot metal out of my clothing. It slid around, burning me until I managed to pull my bra away from my body and the shell casing fell to the ground.

"Jesus, Marie!" Horse said, picking up the gun. "You drop a gun like that it might go off. You could've killed yourself!"

I stood and looked at him, breathing hard.

"The casing burned me," I said, my voice faint.

"Honey, that sucks, but it'll hurt a lot more if you shoot yourself. Or me. If you're gonna shoot me, I want to do something to earn it first. Seems only fair."

"I think I'll stick with the .22," I said, biting my lip. He set down the gun and then shook his head, smiling at me.

"You're not boring, you know that?"

"But you like that about me, right?" I asked hopefully.

"Yeah, I like it," he replied, leaning down to kiss me. "Now practice loading your gun so you can shoot it some more. If you ever need it, I want it to be more than a paperweight."

"Do you seriously think I'll need a gun? Is life as an old lady really that rough?"

He shook his head.

"Probably not," he replied. "No more than life is rough for any woman, depending on her circumstances. It's an ugly world. But if you know how to use one, and you take it seriously, it's not going to hurt you. You don't and you need it? I couldn't live with that, Marie. Shit, you needed it last night."

That sobered me.

"What about Max?" I asked. "What happens with him?"

"That's club business," he replied. "You don't ask—you trust me to take care of it. He'll be punished and he definitely won't bother you again. If he does, I'll kill him."

"You're serious, aren't you?" I whispered. "You'd really kill him?"

"He fucks with you, he's dead. That's the way it is. Enough questions—now show me how you load your gun, babe. We're gonna practice every day until you're comfortable with it, can do it without thinking. This gun is part of you now. You got me?"

"I got you."

"Oh baby, you have no idea," he replied ruefully, brushing back my hair and tucking it behind my ear. "No idea at all. Now let me watch you shoot. Chicks with guns are hot."

Chapter Seventeen

December 10 – Three months later

છ

I'd love to say that things got easy after that. That every day was a new, perfect adventure and life with Horse was like living in a Disney movie with motorcycles instead of carriages.

That would be a big fat lie.

Horse had been by himself for a long time and he was in need of the occasional attitude adjustment. I'd already lived with one asshole and I wasn't in the market for another one. He claimed I could be a raging bitch myself. I can't say he was wrong about that.

But it was never boring.

For every bad time we had there were ten good ones, and they were very, very good. Horse and I had been working through his list of fantasies and I could attest to the fact that using the pink vibrator with him was a lot more fun than using it on my own. Gary had been a slam-bam-thank-you-ma'am kind of guy. Horse was creative and the only thing he liked more than fucking me was making me come.

This worked for me.

I didn't learn what happened to Max. I knew he wasn't around for all of October and most of November, although he reappeared at the Thanksgiving party, slinking around the armory like a half-drowned cat, all grumpy and defensive. The rest of the club seemed to ignore it, so I did too. It was okay. Not quite as good as castrating him with a dull spoon would have been, but life is all about compromises, right?

Especially life in the Reapers MC.

That was another thing I had to get used to. I hadn't just moved in with Horse at his house. I'd moved into the club, which was as much a family as he'd said, albeit a really weird family. The heart of the club was the armory, a place I kept hearing about but couldn't quite wrap my head around until I saw it the first time. Maggs called one morning to let me know we were having an impromptu barbeque. I was supposed to make a "shitload of that fuckin' great potato salad" (a direct quote from Picnic) and be ready at four when she'd come and get me.

The armory, as I discovered when we arrived, was an actual National Guard armory that had been purchased by the Reapers fifteen years earlier. It was just outside of town, three stories high and built like a fortress for obvious reasons. It had a large, walled courtyard in the back and by large, I mean big enough to park lots of cars and trucks and bikes. There were several sheds and outbuildings too. Most of it was paved, but it also had a grassy area with picnic tables, a giant fire pit and a swing set complete with children running around screaming and laughing.

Not exactly what I expected. Neither was the party that followed. It was wild and crazy, but not nasty like the one I'd gone to with the Silver Bastards. This was a family gathering, and I saw for the first time just how tight everyone was. We laughed and danced and took stupid pictures and ate way too much food. That night Horse brought me up onto the roof, laid out a blanket and taught me just how much nicer drunken Reaper sex could be when it didn't end with a shooting. The kids were long gone by then and I could hear other couples in the darkness. It should have felt uncomfortable but it actually kicked ass. Go figure.

Now it was three months later and things were really good between me and Horse. I'd be starting school in January. My divorce was still working its way through the system, but Gary—as predicted—wasn't causing any trouble. I'd been to see my mom a few times and she seemed happy enough for me, although she wanted to come and check out Horse and the club for herself when she got out.

The only thing missing in my life was Jeff. Apparently he was in touch with the Reapers sporadically and had even paid them some of the money he owed. Not much though. I still hadn't talked to him, but I'd gotten a couple of emails from an anonymous address. They said to lay low and hold on, that he'd take care of things soon. I broke down and replied, telling him I was fine and to worry about himself, not me. I also set up a new, anonymous secret webmail account and gave him the address. I trusted Horse, but my brother's life was on the line and to say my man had a conflict of interest was an understatement from hell. I needed to be able to communicate with Jeff privately. He sent me a couple of notes after that, but they didn't really say much.

On the bright side, Horse and I were getting ready for our first Christmas together, which was pretty exciting. I'd decided to go shopping with the girls at the Spokane Valley Mall that day. Cookie and Maggs were the leaders of our little group, probably because they needed the support of their sisters even more than the rest of us. The Reapers looked out for them, of course, but being away from your husband long-term had to suck, especially for Cookie. Her little girl, Silvie, cried for Bagger almost every night.

That would be ending soon. We'd just gotten word that Bagger would be home right after New Year's. He'd been out of touch a lot lately, and Cookie was pretty close to the end of her rope when we got the news. That's why we'd hit the mall—to find the perfect welcome-home ensemble at Victoria's Secret.

"I want to look hot, but not slutty," Cookie said, digging through the nighties. "You know what I mean?"

Maggs laughed.

"Babe, he's not gonna care what you wear. Remember what he said after you sent that video?"

Cookie blushed and I burst out laughing. Bagger had liked the striptease quite a bit...after he knew for sure none of the other guys had seen it. I'd "met" him on Skype a couple of times now, and it was clear the man worshiped Cookie and his daughter, and he didn't like the idea of sharing her at all.

"I still can't believe I let you talk me into that," Cookie said finally, wiping away tears of laughter. "I can just see it now. Silvie will be fifteen years old and she'll find it on my computer. How am I going to convince her to wait for sex when she sees me doing something like that?"

"Silvie and Em, perpetual virgins!" I said, shaking my head. "Ah, the horror of life as a Reaper's daughter. The poor darlings are screwed, no question. No pun intended, of course."

That set us off laughing again.

"Screwed is what I'm looking for," said Cookie, sighing. "Screwed, fucked, pleasured and reamed, you name it. I've worn out three vibrators on this deployment, I swear. I cannot *wait* to see my man again."

After an hour we finally found the perfect welcome-home outfit. Several of them, actually. Maggs grabbed a few things too, but I didn't like spending Horse's money. He kept saying not to worry about it, but I felt weird buying things for myself. We still argued about me getting a job sometimes, but to be honest I was keeping myself pretty busy. I helped Cookie at her shop, which led to me watching Silvie three days a week. Cookie told me she could teach anyone to make coffee, but finding a sitter she could trust was a lot harder. This was perfect, because I was helping out and also earning a few extra bucks each week. I'd have done it for free, but she insisted. I also ran errands for the guys and started cleaning the pawn shop when their cleaning lady flaked. The Reapers really did have a lot of stuff going on, and Horse had come to appreciate my willingness to kick in whenever help was needed. The other guys noticed too, and they seemed to enjoy having me around.

My phone dinged. I pulled it out to find a text from Horse.

Come by the armory? Need to talk to you.

That sounded ominous.

Everything okay?

Complicated. I'll explain when you get here. No detours, okay?

Maggs and Cookie wanted to keep shopping, so I said goodbye and left. Fortunately I had my own car with me so I drove straight to the armory. I pulled up and parked in the front lot. Painter met me outside, taking my arm and guiding me through the gate and the courtyard to the back entrance, which seemed weird. He said Horse would be out in a minute so Painter and I stood and waited.

This sucked, because Coeur d'Alene might only be two hundred miles from my hometown, but it was way, way colder here in the winter. I shivered and rubbed my arms, noticing there were a lot more bikes than usual in the courtyard, along with some big trucks and SUVs I didn't recognize. Then Horse pushed through the back door, holding it for Painter, who ducked back inside. Just seeing Horse warmed me a little. He wore a black jacket over his cut and a dark, knitted cap on his head. He'd let his beard fill in a little with the cold weather and I had to say, it looked hot. The look on his face wasn't hot though. It was so cold I wondered if I'd forgotten something really important.

"We got a problem, babe," he said without greeting me.

"What's the problem?"

"Your brother's made a deal with another club. Somehow he's getting information about our business and he's feeding it to them. In return, they're supposed to snatch you and hand you over to him. These are bad guys and this is going to blow up in his face, which sucks for him, but I'm not letting it spill over on you. We're locking you down, only way to keep you safe until it's worked out."

I stared at him, gaping.

"He's trying to save you," Horse said, shaking his head. "I swear, he's either the stupidest fuck who ever lived or has the worst luck of any human being I've ever met. He reached out to the Devil's Jacks, who in addition to being our enemies are quite possibly the least trustworthy group of bastards ever born. They've been looking for a way to fuck us up for a long time and now they have it. Could be a war, we don't get this under control. The first step is to lock your shit up tight until we find Jeff."

"I don't get it," I said. "What could he possibly be giving them? How did he go from laying low to plotting a war to get me back? You said he was against the wall—where is he getting this leverage?"

"No fucking idea where it's coming from," Horse said, his face grim. "I swear, if he'd put half this much effort into doing his job in the first place we'd all be fuckin' millionaires. Instead he's playing us like his personal chess game, which would be pretty impressive if it wasn't for the fact that all the chess pieces have guns. The guys are all worked up, pissed as hell, and it's a damn good thing everyone likes you because this is not a good scene. You're gonna be moving into the armory for a while, into one of the apartments upstairs."

"How long?" I asked, feeling a little panicky. Horse shrugged.

"Long as it takes, babe. The Jacks manage to take you, the club goes to war," Horse replied. "Jeff's set them on you, and for now he's got enough info to make the effort worth their while. You stay inside and lay low. Tonight you don't even leave the apartment. We've got guys from other charters coming in, a lot of them already here, could get a little wild. You stay in your room, you keep your mouth shut and you do not do or say anything to draw attention to yourself."

"Okay," I said, feeling a little sick. "Is that all?"

He gave a short, abrupt laugh that had nothing to do with humor.

"No," he said, rubbing his chin. "Another change of plans. It's time for you to try to get hold of your brother. Email him, call him, call anyone who knows him. We need him to end this, for your safety and for the club. Then he needs to disappear. Permanently. He can make that happen or we will. I'm telling you this because I love you, babe. You want your brother to live, you get him to cooperate with us. That's his only shot."

I grew very still.

"Are you planning to kill him for this? That's two strikes now," I said, feeling lightheaded. "You already threatened to kill him over the money. Now he does this. I won't lure him in for you to kill."

"Not gonna lie, babe," Horse said, looking me right in the eye. "He has one shot here. He starts a war, he ain't gonna make it. He's hired our enemies to take one of our women. This shit will not stand. He has to make things right without sucking you in. You got me?"

I nodded, feeling like I might throw up. Why did Jeff keep doing this crazy stuff? I shouldn't have listened to Horse, I should have called Jeff a long time ago and worked with him to figure something out—or at least stayed in close enough touch for him to really believe I wasn't in danger. I'd followed Horse's directions because I thought it was safest for Jeff. At least, that's what I'd used as the excuse to ignore my brother while I built a new life.

Had I been lying to myself?

"Let's go to the apartment now," Horse said. "Remember, lay low. You need something, call my cell. Don't come looking for me or anyone else. I already talked to Em, she's packing up some clothes and shit for you."

He took my arm, opening the back door and leading through the hallways to the stairs. I saw a few new faces, male and female, and the palpable air of tension everywhere sickened me. Nobody said hi or even looked me in the eye. We climbed the stairs to the third floor, where they had remodeled the original offices to make studio apartments. I got the smallest, all the way at the end. There were bars on the windows and Horse told me to keep the shades drawn.

I sat down on the queen-sized bed, alone.

I pulled out my phone and sent an urgent email to Jeff's anonymous account. Then I started making phone calls to as many of his friends as I could find numbers for. I had to reach him, although I wasn't sure what I would tell him. Could I really trust the Reapers if he came in?

I wasn't so sure about that.

Horse

Church was standing room only. Picnic presided, the visiting presidents from Portland and LeGrande flanking him. Horse leaned against the wall, eyeing Max across the room. He hadn't forgotten what he'd done, but he'd paid his price and was back in the fold. He might not like the guy but he was still a brother—and if war came, they needed every man.

"We've lost three shipments so far," said Deke, the Portland president. Horse had spent a lot of time visiting that charter, and he knew Deke didn't fuck around when it came to security. If someone was hijacking their product, things had gotten bad. "Couldn't figure out how they were getting their information. Devil's Jacks aren't exactly the brightest assholes in the bunch, but it's like they're reading our minds or something. This last time we caught one. He didn't talk much, but we searched his cell and found some contacts. That's how we learned about your boy."

"What'd you do with the guy you caught?" Picnic.

"Got him at a safe house," Deke replied, giving a feral smile. "Holding on to him for now. Figured it might be useful to have him, goddamn bastards are loyal, if nothing else. That's more than I can say for this Jensen guy. Business is out of hand, Pic. Why didn't you take him out?"

"That's my fault," Horse said. "His sister's my old lady. The man's got incredible skills, really thought we'd be able to turn the situation around and keep using him. Obviously I made a serious error in judgment."

"Whole club made that decision," Duck said. "Mistake? Maybe. But you go around putting talented people down all the time, eventually you run out of talent. In this case we fucked up. Could've gone the other way just as easy. And we all know the Jacks have been looking for a way to move in on us for years. We'd be facing this sooner or later no matter what."

There were grunts of agreement all around the table.

"So how's he getting his information?" asked Deke. "That's the real question here. You know him. What are we missing?"

"I have no idea," Horse said, shaking his head. "Hacking? Only explanation I can think of, although it's a long shot. We aren't stupid, not like this shit is on a spreadsheet or something. The other explanation is a rat."

The room grew quiet. Then Deke spoke.

"We do business online all the time, banking, transfers, you name it. Money's gotta move somehow, can't do it all in cash. That's the reality. Someone could be giving out clues without even realizing it."

"Maybe texts or personal emails?" Ruger piped up. "We all got burners for business, but we've got personal phones too. Email. All that shit. Can't get by without it and I'm thinkin' someone's gotten sloppy. Could even be a kid or a woman, no idea what they're doing. We need to lock information down, take it from there and see what happens."

"Marie's upstairs trying to get in touch with him," Horse said. "I gave it to her straight. She knows this is serious. If she finds him, she'll let me know."

"Can we trust her?" asked Picnic, scratching his chin. He looked tired. "You know I like her, but shit like this would fuck with anyone and she's new to the club. She might tip him off."

"Even if she tips him off, that's better than letting things stand," said Max, surprising Horse. "She tells him he's putting her in danger, he might back down. He's doing this because he's scared and he's trying to help her. Must not've been able to pull the money together so he's playing a new game. I'll bet he has no idea the shit storm he's creating."

"I'm keeping her here until this is handled," Horse said. "She's up in the back apartment. Anyone have a problem with that?"

Picnic rolled his eyes, and Ruger shook his head. Deke laughed and pulled out a knife, picking at his fingernail with it.

"Got no problem with that, brother," he said. "She's club property. We don't share with anyone, don't care how or why they want her. It's about all of us now."

Horse felt the tension in his chest loosen. He knew Jeff wouldn't harm her, but the Jacks? He'd seen what they could do to a woman.

"We still owe those cocksuckers for Gracie," Deke added, his face grim. "I know we took action, but I still say it wasn't enough. We need to show them who owns this land, throw their asses so far out of our territory that the fall back to earth kills 'em. We stop Jensen, great. But I think we should consider taking the fight to them, finish what we started ten years ago. I don't give a shit about this guy, I want to take them down."

"Fuck yeah," muttered one of the Portland guys. Horse nodded, understanding. The Oregon charters had suffered over the years and a threat to one of the club's women would hit them harder than most. He didn't want war, but if it came he wouldn't be holding back. They owed the Jacks for a lot of things.

"So here's how I'm seeing it," Picnic said. "We reach out to all the charters, in person. Tell them to get ready. Make sure their information is locked up tight. New phones, new codes. Women and children taking safety precautions. Marie may be the one with the bounty on her head, but they're all vulnerable. Might wanna consider bringing them in for the duration, especially you guys down south. You think Marie can make contact with him?"

"Yeah," Horse replied. "She's got an email. He's a smart little fuck, he'll be waiting for her to reach out. Might be able to use him to feed the Jacks information, offer him a way out. We have a shipment we can afford to give up for an ambush?"

"We got something coming through in a couple of weeks," said Grenade, the LeGrande charter's VP. "You leak it, we can set things up. Might not be bad to hit them back at the same time. Send some boys down to Cali, raid 'em while we ambush up here."

"Not a bad idea," Picnic mused. "Guys from Roseburg could do it. Thoughts?"

"I like the idea of turning him," Deke replied. "Take it from there. I don't want to send men down unless we're sure we'll catch the Jacks off guard. Could be a bloodbath otherwise."

"That settles it then," Picnic said. "We need a vote? Any opposed?"

Nobody spoke.

"All in favor."

Assorted "ayes" echoed around the room.

"That's settled then," said Picnic. "You guys staying tonight? Got the girls pulling together food and shit already."

"Sounds good," Deke said, grinning. "Eat and drink while you can, boys. Got work to do tomorrow. Fuck with us and we will fuck you back!"

"Hell yeah!" someone yelled.

Church was over. Time to party.

Horse didn't plan on getting drunk, but it felt good to kick back with his brothers. Em'd brought shit for Marie, which he took upstairs after church. He'd grabbed her some pizza and a couple of beers too, and spent half an hour sitting with her. But she didn't look at him, didn't kiss him back when he'd tried to get close, so he figured she needed some space. Hell of a lot to process, he got that.

Downstairs things were getting crazy—always the case when charters got together, particularly when blood was in the air. Didn't get much bloodier than the Devil's Jacks. Tonight wasn't a family party either, something Picnic made clear when he sent Em packing after she dropped off Marie's things. Horse grinned, thinking of her. Poor kid, at this rate she'd be fifty before she found a man.

As he sauntered into the main lounge, a girl wearing a miniskirt and thigh-high fishnets, along with a bikini top so small it defied physics, brought him a beer, reaching around his waist and rubbing her boobs against his arm. Some chick from the Line, he couldn't remember her name. He gave her a pat on the ass, then shrugged her off. Sweet butts and strippers, place was crawling with them, hospitality for the visiting brothers. Horse chugged the beer and handed the cup to another girl as she walked by. He wanted a word with Ruger before things got too crazy.

The man wasn't in the main lounge or the meeting room, so Horse headed back toward the office. They kept their records there, at least the official ones, and Horse stored the legitimate business accounts there too. It was convenient and would make things efficient if they ever got served with a warrant. Just for fun, he'd filled a couple lockboxes with shady-looking paperwork and decoy overseas account numbers—he liked the idea of some cop blowing his wad if he found them, then spending months trying to put it all together. Horse opened the door to find Picnic pounding into a woman face down on the desk, his pants around his ankles, her hair pulled back like reins.

"Getting an early start?" Horse asked, smirking. "No wonder you wanted Em the hell out of here. You're a perv, you know that?"

"Get the fuck out unless someone's shooting at us," Picnic grumbled and Horse laughed, closing the door and heading back toward the shop. Ruger was a hell of a gunsmith and he did his most sensitive work back there, away from any curious eyes at the gun shop. If the visiting boys needed hardware, that's where they'd find it. Horse threw open the door and saw Ruger at his bench, holding up a fully automated assault rifle, one of his specialties. Several of the brothers stood around, talking shit, while one of the Portland men reached for the gun.

"It's a thing of beauty, but not exactly practical," he said, laughing as he hefted it. "Can't see this in my saddlebags. Like something out of Thunderdome."

"Yeah, I know," Ruger replied. "But these dumb-fuck militia dicks can't get enough of 'em. Think they're all Rambo or something. 'Master race', my ass, I make a fortune off those idiots."

"Ruger, got a minute?" Horse asked. Ruger ambled on over.

"What's up?"

"Marie's upstairs, and I'm thinking about security for the next few days," Horse said. "You got any thoughts on that? I know manpower's limited, and I'm wondering if we wanted to rig up any extra precautions."

"Already ahead of you," Ruger said, flashing a smile. He flicked his lip ring with his tongue as he grabbed a laptop from the bench, popping it open. The guy looked scary as hell with his tats, mohawk, chains and piercings, but around technology he was more like a little kid at Christmas. Ruger popped open the security control panel for the clubhouse on the laptop, and he clicked on a multicolored layout of the armory and surrounding property. "See here? We've got the cams and basic motion sensors, of course, but I'm planning on putting in some new stuff around the perimeter, right here. We need detection, but I'm also worried about manpower. I want to rig some traps that we can trigger by computer or phone if we need to. I know we can't count on the electronics a hundred percent, but we can only spread ourselves so thin. This gives us more options."

"Can we put something outside her room?" Horse. "I know it's not a top priority, but I'd like to keep an eye on her. Just in case they buy off one of the girls or something. This probably won't come down to a frontal assault."

Ruger scratched his head, considering.

"I can rig something up for you," he said. "Won't be until tomorrow. After I fix the guys up back here I'm ready for some pussy. Speaking of, you sure about yours?"

"You sayin' I have a pussy?" Horse asked, crossing his arms and cocking an eyebrow.

"Don't be an asshole, you know I meant your girl upstairs. I get that you're into her. But she knows his life is at stake and we might be the ones to kill him. You might want to consider the possibility that she's working with Jensen on this. She's only human, Horse."

Horse shook his head.

"Marie can't lie for shit," he replied, pinching the bridge of his nose, feeling tired. "And even if she was, she doesn't know a damn thing. Couldn't be his source of information."

"If they're talking, she wouldn't have to be his only source," Ruger replied, his tone reasonable. "He might be using her. I don't think she's screwing you on purpose—"

"Oh, she's definitely screwing me on purpose," Horse replied, deadpan.

"Fuck you," Ruger replied, grinning. "You know what I mean. She's the victim in this situation and she believes in her brother. She tells him about your day-to-day life, he puts that together with a couple other sources, could add up. You don't tell her about club business, but she sure as shit knows when we're on a long run. All the women do. Fuck, for all we know he's on Facebook with them or something, pretending to be some chick they know. You get enough old ladies talking about their men being gone, it adds up."

"Shit," muttered Horse, shaking his head. "Never thought of that. This is a pain in the ass, you know that?"

"Ya think?" Ruger asked, rubbing a hand across his tattooed scalp and the short buzz of his mohawk. "So you want cameras on her. Sure you don't want something inside the room too?"

"Nope, don't want your sick ass watching us fuck," Horse replied. "But I do want to check on her, make sure nobody's lingering, trying to get to her. You know what I mean? Oh, and a GPS on her car. Want to be able to find her. Make sure she doesn't see you, want to keep her safe, not freak her out more."

"I'll do it tomorrow. Right now I need someone sucking my dick, and unless you're planning to share your old lady, I got higher priorities than this conversation."

Ruger grinned and Horse laughed, putting a hand on his shoulder and squeezing it hard enough to leave marks.

"Touch Marie and I'll cut off your balls."

"Yeah, right," Ruger replied. "So much for taking care of your brothers, you cock-blocking bastard. Talk to me tomorrow and I'll set it up to feed to your phone, along with the computers."

"Thanks, man," Horse said.

The party was raging back in the main lounge. Two girls were bumping and grinding each other up on one end of the bar, and a third served up body shots in the middle. Duck, the filthy old pervert, sat back on a couch with a barely legal redhead eating out his mouth with her hand thrust down between them, working furiously. Picnic caught Horse's eye across the room, apparently finished with his important business in the office. The man gave a chin jerk, inviting Horse to join the Portland and LeGrande officers at his table.

"Interesting times," Picnic said as Horse grabbed a seat. "Deke tells me the Portland boys are itching for this."

"Glad for the excuse," Deke said. "Jacks've always been trouble, we all know that, but they've been working up on us for a while. Nothing too overt, always just this side of what's acceptable behavior. Wearing their cuts on our territory, dicking with support clubs, that kind of thing. There's a group of them that's set up near Brooklyn Park. They're just camping in some shitty rental and doing their thing like they think they're citizens or something. I know two of them are going to school at PSU, if you can believe it, and they aren't doing anything for us to call them on, besides existing and being general assholes. No respect."

"They're up to something," Horse replied as yet another half-naked girl set a beer down in front of him. "They always are. Shit, if it was us, we'd be up to something."

They all laughed, knowing he was right.

"My thoughts exactly," Deke replied. "And since we're the ones losing shipments, I'm thinking there's a good chance the leak is close to home. But no matter how much we check on the local guys, we haven't caught them doing shit. I wanted to ask you about this Jensen guy. How good with computers is he? Do you really think he could hack in, pull stuff from our home computers, that kind of thing?"

"Yeah, he's good," Horse said. "Guys like him are why I do the books on a laptop without a wireless card. Lock it in a safe, back it up once a week and keep that backup in a different safe. That's the only kind of computer security we can really trust."

"That's what I thought," Deke replied. He tugged on his short, black goatee, shaking his head. The Portland president was a big guy with long, black hair he kept in a ponytail. His arms were covered in full-sleeve tattoos, and the rumor was he operated as national's unofficial hit man. Horse didn't doubt it for a minute. "We find him, we have to get rid of him unless he hands us the Jacks. Even then, might have to get rid of him."

Horse nodded, knowing the truth of it. Fuck, this was gonna kill Marie.

"If it comes down to that, can you make it an accident? Maybe in a couple of months?"

"I can," Deke replied, glancing over at Picnic, who shrugged. "Gotta tell you, I'm a little concerned about your commitment on this one, Horse. You seem more worried about your girl's feelings than someone fucking with the club. We got a problem?"

Horse shook his head.

"No problem," he replied. "This is my life, I know that and she knows it too. Just hoping to walk out alive and still keep my old lady. We all make sacrifices. Hoping mine isn't bigger than it needs to be."

"Good to hear," Deke said. "I'll keep that in mind. Make our lives easier if the Jacks killed him anyway."

"That's the truth," Picnic said. "But don't count on it— they've never done anything to help us before, doubt they'll start now. Wish we had better control over the timing, but it'll be good to take them down, especially given your situation, Deke. But that's enough business. I know you boys had a long ride today. Time for some hospitality."

Picnic glanced around, spotting a couple of girls standing not too far away. He whistled, calling them over.

"Take care of Deke and Grenade for me, will you?"

They smiled and obediently moved toward the visiting charter officers. Picnic looked at Horse and cocked an eyebrow.

"You planning to partake tonight?"

Horse shook his head.

"Got something better waiting for me upstairs," he said. "Giving her some time to settle in, get used to what's happening. That's all."

"Some men say a brother who's afraid to enjoy pussy at a party is a pussy himself," Picnic replied. "Who's in charge, you or the old lady?"

Horse laughed.

"You're full of shit," he replied. "When your old lady was alive, you were a monk. I saw how it was."

Picnic looked thoughtful and took a long pull of his beer. Then he looked up and held Horse's gaze.

"Caught a lot of shit for that," he said. "But I'm telling you, I'd give every piece of ass I've had in my life for another day with that woman. This," he continued, gesturing toward the party. "This is good fun. But it's not the real thing. We'll do our best to protect your girl. And if we take out Jensen, we'll do it quiet. Want you to know that."

"Thanks," Horse said. "You're a good brother."

"That's what it's all about," Picnic replied. He smiled. "What I said aside, my old lady may not be here, but remembering her makes me horny as fuck. Girl in the office only took the edge off. Think I'll do something about that."

Picnic got up, moving toward another group of giggling women. Hands came around Horse's head from behind, covering his eyes as a warm body pressed into his back.

"Hey sexy," said a woman's voice. He recognized it instantly and smiled broadly. Serena. He pulled her hands off and stood to hug her.

"Haven't seen you in a while," he said, stepping back to take her in. "Fantastic like always. Haven't been around at all lately, what's up with that?"

She offered a knowing smile.

"I've got a new man, I think. Guy from California, comes up here on his private jet, that kind of thing. Been seeing him for a while, but his divorce is final now, so he's got a little more freedom. We've been hanging out. I'm thinking about heading south with him, unless there's a better reason for me to stay around here..."

Horse caught the unasked question and shook his head ruefully.

"I'm taken, babe."

She nodded, looking a little wistful but not unhappy or surprised. That was Serena—always a realist, and a good friend too. He'd been hooking up with her on and off since high school, and she was one of the few women he'd slept with that he actually liked and trusted.

"I heard rumors," she replied. "Kind of scary rumors, to be honest. Answer me one question and I'll leave you alone. She a prisoner?"

Horse shrugged.

"I told her she can leave, but her brother's under a sentence. It's way beyond her now, he's on his own at this point."

Serena studied his face, then shook her head.

"You're tricky," she replied. "You 'told' her she can leave? Does she know you lied?"

"We're not having this conversation," Horse said, his voice firm. Serena laughed.

"Okay, big boy. Just asking. I always thought the two of us might make something of it, that kind of thing. But I'm happy for you, Horse, I really am. You're one of the good ones. Buy a lady a drink, for old times' sake?"

He offered her his arm as they headed toward the bar. Just one girl danced on top now, and she'd lost her clothes. The other was down on a couch, one of the brothers from LeGrande eating her out while she gave a blowjob to another. It didn't interest him much, which made Horse feel sort of old and jaded. He might be taken, but a man could still look. But honestly, it just seemed so boring.

He snagged a couple of beers for them from the bar and looked around for a spot quiet enough to talk, but it wasn't happening.

"Let's go upstairs to the game room."

Nearly half of the armory's the second floor was a large, open room where they'd set up pool tables, an air hockey table and a bunch of old couches. There was a big-screen TV up against one wall hooked to the satellite and about six different kinds of video consoles. Later on people might bed down in here, but for now it was quiet. Down the hallway was a series of rooms they used for all kinds of things, from storing extra inventory for the businesses to privacy for a quickie. He escorted Serena to the couch in front of the TV. She looked around, eyes lingering on the hallway.

"The room in use tonight?"

Horse grimaced and shrugged.

"Who knows," he said. "Nobody makes 'em do it. You starting to judge?"

She shook her head and laughed, leaning toward him to brush her hand along his cut.

"Babe, I've spent a night or two in there myself," she replied, winking. "I think you were off with the Marines or something."

"You mean you were with someone else while I was gone?" he asked, clutching a hand to his heart, pretending to be offended. She burst out laughing.

"You know me. I'll stand by my man so long as he's in the room and has a pile of cash."

Horse laughed with her, loving her honesty. Being with Serena was comfortable, no question. A part of him wished he could care about her the way he did about Marie. They would've been a good pair, and she sure as shit knew her way around the club. Intimately. Yeah, that wouldn't work, he decided. Someone took her as property the other old ladies would probably kill her.

Or she'd kill them, he decided, eyeing the long, red talons she called fingernails.

"What's the look for?" she asked, arching a brow.

"Just wondering who'd win if you got into it with the old ladies," he answered. "I'm not sure."

She burst out laughing so hard that she snorted beer out her nose, which made her laugh more. That's what he loved about Serena—whatever she did, she did it openly and without any pretense. He took the glass from her, looking around to find something to help her clean up. There was an old sweatshirt tucked into the end of the couch, so he snagged it and leaned toward her, helping to wipe off her chest and lap. Serena didn't help, giggling and slapping at him.

"You're just trying to cop a feel, you dirty bastard!" she exclaimed. He grinned at her.

"Yeah, you know me. Always looking for my next lay."

Then a voice cut through his laughter and it was his turn to choke.

"I can see why you t-t-t-told me to wait upst-t-t-tairs."

Horse turned his head to see Marie standing behind the couch, wrapped in a blanket, face pale and teeth chattering.

"Well, shit," he muttered. Serena looked between them, eyes wide.

"I take it this is the old lady?"

Chapter Eighteen

Marie

I couldn't get the window closed.

It was stupid to open it but I've got a bit of a claustrophobia thing. To be fair, I was stuck in a room alone all by myself, and it wasn't a particularly big room. I heard the noise of the party below and I knew that Horse would be up eventually. But the bars on the window and the fact that I couldn't make contact with Jeff *and* I couldn't leave made me feel a little panicky.

So I decided to open the window for some fresh air.

Of course it was stuck, so I worked at it, rocking the old wooden sash back and forth until I got my fingers underneath. Then I braced against the floor and pushed up with all I had. Because I have shitty luck, it held for a second then burst free, sliding all the way up and getting stuck again, this time open. It took about ten minutes before I realized this might be a serious problem. The place was heated with one of those big old freestanding radiators that didn't have separate controls for individual rooms, so I couldn't turn it up. It hadn't been too warm in here to begin with. Outside the night was cold and clear and perfect, the evergreens on the hillsides surrounding us dusted with a hint of frost like something out of a Christmas card.

Now it was becoming cold and clear but not-so-perfect in the room.

I tried to get it closed of course. And I put on my coat, but it was just my leather jacket and not particularly warm. I'd been looking for a winter coat but they all cost so much and I didn't like spending money, so I'd been hunting in consignment shops for just the right thing. I started pacing, trying to decide what to do next. I dug in my purse, pushing aside my gun to find my phone. Not that I carried the gun all the time, but Horse wanted it with me until they dealt with the Jacks.

No voicemails or texts, but I decided I might as well check my email. There was a new message from Jeff on the webmail account. I start reading, a sinking sensation filling my stomach.

Sis, I'm glad they haven't hurt you. You need to play along and do what they ask, don't give them any reason not to treat you well. I'm sending a decoy message to your main account too, telling you that I'm thinking about getting in touch with them. But you need to know the Reapers are bad guys and they won't hesitate to kill you. Neither will the Devil's Jacks, but I've got things worked out with them so that you and I should be okay.

Couple of things you need to know. You say it's good between you and Horse, and that scares me. He's stringing you along, you can't trust this guy at all. I've learned a lot about him. Did you know he was special forces in Afghanistan? His specialty was recon, which means they'd send him out ahead to get information and do their dirty work. He killed a lot of people and he got investigated for murdering civilians. Women and children, sis. They were going to court martial him, but then the witnesses either wouldn't talk or disappeared. It was a cover-up, that's the only explanation. They couldn't even give him a dishonorable discharge, that's how sneaky he was. Here are some links to articles about the massacre. I found other records too, but I can't send them to you, it's too dangerous.

Your boyfriend is a killer and if he finds out you know the truth, he'll probably kill you too. Do what he says and play the good girl. Write to me on the other email account and I'll pretend to cooperate. Play dumb and be ready. I'll contact you again later this week when I have things set up. Remember, it's not enough for you to just hop in your car and drive away. They may look like a club, but they're like the mafia. We need an escape plan for all of us, you, me and Mom, and I'm working on it. Just hold on a little longer.

I love you and I'm sorry I got you into this. You'll never know how sorry I am.

Jeff

I followed the link to a news story from eight years ago. A bunch of Afghani families were murdered in their houses, located in a region under the control of US allies, but heavily infiltrated by Taliban forces as well. A Marine recon team was under investigation for war crimes. Included was a picture of a much younger Horse, in one of those standard military mug shots you see all the time.

I barely made it to the bathroom before I threw up.

Afterward I lay down on the bed, wrapping the covers around me and listening to the noise of the party below. An hour passed before I realized that no matter how depressed I felt, I couldn't just stay in the bed. The room was bitter cold now, and the blankets nowhere near thick enough to protect me. I tried texting Picnic with numb fingers. No response. I thought about calling one of the girls, but with the party going on below I knew that was a bad idea. Jeff said to keep the Reapers happy. I ran a hundred different ideas through my head and then texted Horse. Nothing. Then I called him. No answer.

That's when I ventured out of my room into the hallway. I knew there were other rooms up here, it's where they put up guests or members when they needed a place to land. I could go to one of those and warm up while I waited. The doors were all locked, though. Now my teeth were chattering and I fumbled to hold the blanket around me. No getting around it—I needed to go downstairs and find Horse.

The third floor of the building was only about half as wide as the first two, just one long hallway running the length of the building with a single row of rooms on either side. There were stairwells on each end. The main stairs, which I'd come up with Horse, intersected the game room and the main lounge. But the back stairwell bypassed the game room entirely and let out down by the offices. I figured I'd attract less attention there, so that's where I went. Unfortunately, the door was locked on the main level, which left me to go back up or out into the cold of the courtyard. Easy call. I climbed back up to the second floor, pushing through the door from the stairwell as quietly as possible. I heard voices and grunting and shouts coming from an open door on my left. I walked toward it slowly, hoping I'd find Horse in there.

What I saw shocked me.

There were five men standing around the room, none of them guys I recognized but all wearing Reapers' cuts. They stood around a bed with one woman on it, and she was getting fucked—seriously fucked—by a man standing at the edge of the bed, pants just pushed down, hands holding her tight around the hips.

"Harder, baby!" she yelled, giving a little howl and arching her back.

"Jesus, can't believe this bitch," muttered one of the guys, and I recognized his voice. Max. I saw him now. He'd been turned away from me before. I couldn't move. I just stood watching as the man at the foot of the bed finished with a grunt, then pulled out and stepped aside. Max stepped forward to take his place.

Oh my god, she was doing all of them. I studied her face, wondering why she wasn't screaming for them to get off her, but if anything she looked satisfied. Not so much sexually satisfied but triumphant. I shook my head, backing away and shuffling down the hallway, feeling disgusted and sick. Horse might not have been in there, but this was his clubhouse and his club. Did he know about stuff like this? Did it happen often? I couldn't wrap my head around it, didn't want to wrap my head around it. I just wanted to run down to my car and get in and drive as far and as fast as I could.

But I remembered Jeff's email. I couldn't do that. They might find me, or they might find him. They could even go after Mom. She was stuck in jail, and God only knew what kind of connections guys like this had in jail. I'd watched *Oz* on Netflix last winter, I'd seen how prisons worked. Were jails the same way? I didn't think so, but could I bet Mama's life on that? *You can do this,* I chanted under my breath. *You can do this, you're strong and smart and you're going to figure everything out. Just put on your big-girl panties and get on with it.*

I continued down the hall, taking deep breaths and forcing myself to stay calm. It was a lot warmer on the second floor, which felt incredible. I was still freezing and shivering in my jacket and blanket, but I'd survive. I'd already survived losing my dad, not to mention Gary. I walked into the game room to see a couple sitting on the couch, very close to each other. Their posture was intimate, like people who'd known each other for years and were comfortable together. The woman was laughing.

It was Horse and some girl I didn't recognize.

"Just wondering who'd win if you got into it with the old ladies," Horse was saying to her. "I'm not sure."

She burst out laughing even harder, snorting and spilling her beer. Horse chuckled, grabbing the beer and fumbling around on the couch. I saw him lean into her, rubbing her chest, his hands disappearing lower. The woman giggled and slapped at him.

"You're just trying to cop a feel, you dirty bastard!" she exclaimed. He grinned at her.

"Yeah, you know me. Always looking for my next lay."

Wow. The cold in my body was nothing compared to the ice filling my heart. Jeff was right. I didn't know this man and I certainly couldn't trust him. He'd promised. I'd been an idiot and now I had to stay with him and do what he said and pretend not to know he might have murdered women and children in some remote village in Afghanistan. I felt myself starting to panic, so I clamped down on my emotions, withdrawing deep inside where I'd be safe. I couldn't even run away and hide—I had nowhere to go. Then I spoke.

"I can see why you t-t-t-told me to wait upst-t-t-tairs," I said, startled by how much my teeth chattered when I spoke. Horse turned and looked at me, his face hardening, eyes full of guilt. I wondered why he bothered.

"Well, shit," he muttered. The woman next to him looked rapidly between us, eyebrows raised.

"I take it this is the old lady?" she asked.

"Fuck," said Horse, pushing up from the couch so hard it slid back a foot across the old wooden floor, stalking toward me. I thought maybe I should run but I couldn't seem to move. He grabbed my shoulders and shook them, punctuating his words. "I told you to stay in your room. What are you doing down here? You realize what could happen to you at a party like this? Jesus!"

I didn't reply, just let him shake me and mused at how truly insane my life had become.

"What's wrong with you?" he said finally, anger disappearing as he reached out and felt my face. "Shit, you're freezing! What the fuck? Talk to me, Marie."

"M-m-my wind-d-dow is st-tuck," I managed to say. "I t-tried to c-c-call you."

He dug into his pocket, pulling out his phone, punching it on and finding the notifications. He winced.

"Shit," he said, pulling me into his arms, rubbing my back hard. "I couldn't hear it. I'm so sorry, I can't believe how cold you are. You need to get warmed up. Serena, run to the office and grab the apartment keys. Meet me upstairs."

He swung me up into his arms and carried me back to the third floor. Thankfully we didn't go back down the long hallway, past the crazy woman and the group of men taking turns screwing her. I don't think I could've handled that. The woman—Serena—was fast, because she came rushing up with the keys right behind us. Horse stopped by a room on the other end of the hallway from my original one, waiting impatiently as she fumbled the door open. He set me down on the bed and stripped me methodically, ignoring my protests. Then I was totally naked and under the covers.

"Go down to the room on the far end and get her stuff," he said to Serena. "All of it, bring it down here and then lock up. We'll deal with the window situation tomorrow."

Serena disappeared and I wanted to protest. I didn't want Horse's whore touching my things. I bit my lip, remembering Jeff's email. Horse killed people. Maybe women like me. Children. I thought about his guns, how easily he handled them, how he'd made me practice for hours with my little .22. I remembered our first night together, when we'd watched the Johnny Depp flick and he'd talked about how the hand-to-hand combat was all wrong.

I guess he'd know.

Horse crawled into bed beside me, buck-naked, spooning me and wrapping around my body like a big, warm blanket. My body craved his heat, soaking it up even as my mind stayed cool and detached. The more I warmed up the harder I shivered until my jaw hurt from clenching my teeth and I ached. Serena bustled in with my things at some point, then closed the door and disappeared. The entire time Horse made soothing noises and rubbed me softly, and for once he didn't try to touch my breasts or reach between my legs. Finally I stopped shivering and I drowsed.

"Babe," he whispered, kissing the top of my head softly. "Babe," he said again, shaking me gently. I stirred against him, and he rolled me over and onto my back, rising over me on his elbows. "Why was the window open? What happened?"

He sounded so worried, so loving. Would a murderer be able to fake that kind of emotion? But how many times had I looked at Horse and thought he was more like two different men—good and bad—stuck in one body? I couldn't explore that right now, I couldn't let him know what I'd found out.

"I just needed some fresh air," I said, deliberately keeping my voice soft and weak. It wasn't much of a stretch. "It got stuck and I couldn't get it closed again. The room got colder and colder and I waited too long before I left to get help. It's okay, I'm fine, Horse. Honestly."

"Why are you always saying that to me?" he asked, although it seemed like he was talking to himself. "You're so strong, always strong. You shouldn't have to be that way. I should've been there for you. I'm so sorry, babe."

I shook my head, closing my eyes and turning away from him. His body felt good on mine, strong and safe like always. I felt his penis harden and his hips flexed, almost involuntarily. The achingly familiar chemistry between us came to life and my nipples tightened as my legs shifted restlessly. He started kissing me near my ear, sucking and licking his way down my neck toward my breast, sending tendrils of sensation racing through me. When he sucked my nipple into his mouth I cried out, then reached down and grabbed his hair, pulling him away.

"I can't do this right now," I whispered. He sighed and rolled over next to me.

"It's not what you think," he said, his voice firm. I looked over at him, panicked. In addition to everything else, could he read my mind or something? How did he know what I'd found out? Was he monitoring my phone?

"Serena is an old friend," he said. "I've known her for years. We've slept together, I won't lie to you about that, but nothing was happening between us tonight. We were just joking around."

My eyes opened wider as I processed what he'd said. Serena. The woman on the couch. I felt hysterical laughter bubbling up in my throat and I swallowed it down painfully. This was a good thing, I realized. I could use this as an excuse to be angry with him. He expected it, he deserved it, and he wouldn't have to know that my mind was way too full of visions of him killing Afghani children to give a flying fuck about him and Serena.

"You promised," I said, letting the tears I'd been holding back well up in my eyes. Might as well let them out while I had an excuse. They started falling and I gulped. "You promised that you wouldn't be with those other women, the night we decided to give this a shot. You lied to me."

"I haven't been with any other women," Horse said, his voice a mixture of frustration and something else I couldn't identify. "I was talking to an old friend. She's got someone else in her life and I've got you. I was just killing time, waiting until it got late enough for me to leave and come back up to you."

"Can we not talk about this right now?" I asked, trying to roll away from him. He held me, taking my chin and making me look at him.

"Fight with me all you want, babe," he said. "But you don't turn away from me. Let's talk about this."

"I don't want to talk," I whispered, feeling panic rise again. He searched my face, mouth hardening.

"Is there something else?" he asked. "Have you heard from your brother? Tell me. I'm here for you, Marie."

Shit.

"Let me check my email," I said quickly. I pulled away from him and started to get up, but he stopped me, getting up and digging my phone out of my jeans pocket himself.

"Here," he said, handing it to me. I turned it on and clicked on the email app—the one linked to my main account. There it was, the fake message Jeff had promised.

"He wrote," I said.

"Read it to me."

"He says, 'So sorry about all this, sis. I got your message about coming in and talking to the Reapers. I'm not sure I can do that. No offense, but I'm pretty sure they're planning to kill me. Talk to them, find out if they're willing to make a deal and get back to me. I love you. Jeff' That's all of it."

"About what I expected," Horse said slowly, climbing back into bed. "I'm not surprised he doesn't trust us. He's scared and he should be. Odds are good he's not gonna survive this. But there's a huge difference between staying in bed with the Jacks or trying to make peace with us. He needs to wrap his head around that."

"What's the difference?" I asked, afraid to hear the answer.

Horse rolled onto his side and propped his head up on one elbow looking down at me.

"You," he said.

"Me?"

"We're not going to hurt you," Horse said, reaching over and tracing the curve of my cheek. "The Jacks will. No question of it. He should know that."

"You said they were trying to take me back to him," I said softly. "He's trying to save me."

"The Jacks will get you if they can, but their record with women isn't too good. Three years ago Deke had a niece, Gracie, get in trouble with them. His old lady's sister's kid. No connection to the club, other than that. She decided to go to school down in California and turns out she wasn't far from a Jacks charter. Started dating a guy who seemed nice enough, but he was one of their hangarounds. Apparently she mentioned her uncle was in the Reapers at some point. She went to a party with him and they raped her. All of them. One big fucking train, nearly killed her. They finished her off by carving 'DJ' on her forehead. Dumped her by the side of the road. Sent Deke a picture afterward taken with her own phone."

I swallowed, feeling sick. Then I thought about the woman on the second floor, and wondered if she'd finished with those men yet. What if she wanted to stop halfway through? Would they let her?

"What about downstairs?" I asked, mouth getting away from my brain. "What makes that any different?"

Horse cocked his head.

"What are you talking about?"

"There's a woman downstairs, I saw her in a room with a bunch of guys on the second floor. They were taking turns..."

"Fuck..." Horse muttered, dropping onto his back and running his hands through his hair. "What else is gonna fall to shit tonight? I'm sorry you saw that, babe. I didn't think about that at all. Shit."

"You didn't answer my question. Are they going to hurt her?"

"No!" he said, sitting up and looking down at me. "Shit, no, I can't believe you have to ask that. We're not a bunch of rapists, Marie. Shit. If she's in there, she chose to be there. Fuck if I know why, but women do it all the time. It's a thing with some of the sweet butts, like counting coup or something. I can't exactly defend it as upstanding behavior, but that's nothing like what they did to Gracie. They tore her up so bad, I can't even explain it. She'll never have kids. She tried to kill herself twice before they got her into some kind of psychiatric facility. Damn."

He looked so genuinely upset that I believed him.

"How often does it happen?" I asked softly. "What else goes on at your parties?"

"All kinds of shit happens at parties," Horse said, sighing heavily. "But that's really none of your business. It's wilder tonight because there's blood in the air, that's all. Nobody's getting hurt and nobody's here against their will. That's all you need to know."

"Have you done it?"

He shook his head, although whether he was denying it or just making it clear I couldn't expect an answer, I couldn't tell.

"Are we really gonna do this?" he asked.

"Do what?"

"Dig up everything either of us has ever done? I thought we were over that. I'm not a saint, babe, and I've never pretended to be. But I promised you that I wouldn't cheat on you and I haven't. I won't. I trust that you won't either. Isn't that good enough?"

I nodded, wondering if killing children fell under the category of "not being a saint".

"You need to write back to Jeff," he said abruptly. "The faster we work through this the better."

I nodded and grabbed my phone. It took about three minutes to type out the message, which he read over before hitting send. It was simple enough—I asked Jeff to call me and told him I was safe with the Reapers but that the Jacks were dangerous. I was afraid of them.

I set the phone down on the little bedside table. Horse reached over, pulling me to him, kissing me as his fingers reached between my legs. I resisted at first, turning my head away, tensing. He just rubbed up and down, slowly and steadily, as he leaned over and started on my breasts. He licked at them, sucking my nipples in and then flicking his tongue until I twisted against him, wanting more even though I despised myself for it.

Jeff claimed the man was a murderer. Yet when Horse hooked two of his fingers deep inside me I crumbled, spreading my legs and mewling for more, pumping my hips against his fingers. He slid farther down the bed, taking my knees and pushing them up and over his shoulders as his mouth covered my clit. Horse had the tongue of a devil, sliding around my little nub, alternating between teasing it and fluttering, then moving to suck just strong enough to almost hurt me but not quite. The entire time he worked me over inside until I twisted and moaned against him, hovering on the edge of climax.

That's when he stuck his finger in my ass.

He'd been doing this more and more and while I found it startling, I also enjoyed it. In fact, he'd been sticking in two and even three fingers, stretching me and shaping me, usually while he played my clit. Other times he'd put me on my hands and knees, thrusting into me from behind with his cock in my pussy and his fingers in my ass. I knew he wanted anal sex. Sometimes he rubbed the head of his cock against my opening, pressing lightly. He'd always been incredibly careful, but I hadn't let him stick it in me. To be honest, our sex life was so great I didn't think it needed much in the way of improvement, and his size scared me a little.

But there was something different that night. Looking back, I wonder if he sensed just how wrong things were, despite my attempts to reassure him. He worked me over hard with his tongue, making me come three times, leaving me limp and quivering, every muscle in my body loose and pliant. I wasn't thinking about Jeff or the party or anything other than the sense of completion and sensual satisfaction he gave me. That's when Horse rolled me onto my stomach, then lifted my hips and pushed a pillow under them. I stayed limp as his hands spread my cheeks, and he pressed lightly against my opening with his finger. It slipped in easily.

"I want this," he said softly, leaning over and kissing me between the shoulder blades. "I need to own you. All of you. Make you scream and realize that you belong to me and I belong to you and nothing else matters. I can't let you slip away from me, babe."

A second finger joined the first and I wiggled my hips a little, feeling the stretch and the pressure. He guided his penis into my vagina, sliding in and out, the position perfect for reaching the spongy spot on my inner front wall. His fingers mirrored his penis, rubbing me and stretching me from behind. Then he pulled his fingers out and something cool and wet dripped into my opening. His fingers rubbed the lube in deep, warming it, and then he pulled his cock free from my body. He fumbled for a minute and I heard the tear of a condom wrapper.

I stiffened as he placed the head against my rear. I was afraid it would hurt, but he shushed me softly and rubbed the small of my back until I relaxed again. Then he started pushing in very, very slowly. It stretched and pinched, but not nearly as much as I'd imagined it would. It was more pressure than anything else, a strange kind of fullness I'd caught hints of from his fingers. Every few seconds he'd stop, giving me time to grow used to the feeling of him deep inside me. Then he'd push a little more.

He had to be about halfway in when his hand reached down under the pillow to find my clit. After all he'd done to me, I was incredibly sensitive and he seemed to know that, because he used a light touch to rub it in circles, pushing deeper into my ass until I felt the muscles of his stomach against my bottom. I flexed, trying to accustom myself to this new intruder, and he groaned sharply. I felt him jerk inside me, and I squeezed again.

"Holy shit," Horse muttered, starting to rub my clit more quickly. "You're gonna kill me, babe."

I sighed and then moaned as he started pulling out, which caused a whole new flood of feeling. That started the slow glide of his cock in and out of my ass. It hurt at first, but it didn't hurt badly and that little bit of pain was all mixed up with the incredible sensations building in my lower body. He was rock-hard inside me and every time I squeezed him he took his revenge by dragging his rough finger across the swollen tip of my clit.

The torture was mutual.

After an eternity of easing the way, he started moving more quickly in me. Not fast, mind you. He still took care, but this was definitely pumping action, not a slow glide. I found myself twisting under him, seeking my own relief as his fingers played me expertly. My need wound tighter and tighter and I thrust my butt back at him, ready and waiting to go over the edge a final time. Sensing this, he pressed my clit down hard as he seated himself deep within. That tipped me over the edge and shivers swept through me, along with sweet, shuddering relief. He groaned hard and leaned down, biting my shoulder as his cock surged deep inside, held captive by my clenching ass. That's when he blew, gasping and panting against my back.

He lay on top of me for several minutes, cock slowly shrinking down, which was a very strange feeling. Then he pulled out and went into the bathroom. I heard the sink running and the toilet flush before he came out and climbed back into the bed. He pulled me into his arms and I lay against him like a limp doll, spent and sore and completely satisfied.

"That was incredible, Marie," he whispered, kissing me deeply. I hardly had the energy to kiss him back and he pulled away, chuckling softly. "Sleep, babe."

I tucked into him, body exhausted, thought processes long shut down. Sleep was instant and dreamless.

A phone rang in the early morning darkness. I grunted, pushing at Horse. It kept ringing and finally he moved, reaching over and grabbing it. I whimpered because he'd pulled the covers off me, letting in tendrils of hateful cold.

"Yeah?" he answered, voice rough and gravelly. He listened for a moment, and then I felt the air in the room change.

"Are you sure?" he asked, alert now, his voice utterly devoid of emotion. "No, I hear you. Is someone with Cookie?"

That didn't sound good. It really didn't sound good. I sat up in bed, pulling the covers across my breasts. Horse ignored me, utterly focused on the phone call. I felt a twinge in my ass but I ignored it. Last night felt like some surreal dream—a dream I wasn't ready to remember just yet.

"Thanks," Horse said finally. He dropped the phone down, then rolled away from me and stood up, reaching for his pants. Tension roiled off him, along with waves of anger so powerful it scared me.

Last night's lover had left the building.

"What happened?" I asked, keeping my voice low and calm. He didn't look at me as he spoke.

"Bagger's dead," he said, reaching down for his long-sleeved thermal shirt. Then he grabbed his cut. "Died two days ago, took them awhile to locate his body for confirmation. Cookie's at the hospital, she collapsed when they told her last night. I've got to go. You can call the other girls but don't leave the armory. We're still on watch against the Jacks. You got it?"

He glanced at me, waiting for me to acknowledge his orders. I nodded and he left without another word.

Chapter Nineteen

ൟ

I've never felt so helpless in my life.

I didn't even know Bagger, aside from saying hi to him on Skype a couple of times. I didn't have a right to mourn him, not like everyone else. But I mourned for Cookie and Silvie, his little girl who cried for her daddy at night and begged to perform for him in front of their webcam with her little stuffed dog. I wanted to do something to help, even if it was something stupid like cleaning her house or cooking. Instead I sat alone in my room and watched a stunning sunrise while everyone I'd come to know and love in Coeur d'Alene suffered.

Around nine Horse called me and told me I should go downstairs, find some food. He warned me that the place was a mess and told me that if any of the women gave me shit I could to throw their asses out. Um, right. I needed to stay in the building, other than that I'd be okay. I walked down the stairs cautiously, expecting to see wreckage and evidence of some kind of giant orgy. Instead I found subdued men drinking coffee and a bunch of tired, hungover-looking women. A few of them huddled in a corner, crying. One of them was Serena, the woman I'd seen last night sitting next to Horse. She approached me cautiously, like she expected me to go crazy on her. I didn't have the energy and it just didn't seem very important anymore.

"You hungry?" she asked, taking my shoulders and looking at me, clearly checking me over for I don't know what...injury from Horse's giant penis? She would know, I thought, feeling morose.

"Not really, but I should probably eat," I answered.

"I know what you mean. C'mon, we got donuts over here." She led me over to a table on the far side of the room, littered with donuts and a couple boxes of coffee to-go from Starbucks.

"Starbucks? Seriously?" I asked. She shook her head and grimaced.

"I knew the boys would need something," she said, shrugging. "It's what was easy. Eat something, hon. It's gonna be a long day."

"Do you know Cookie?" I asked. I'd tried to call Em a while ago, but she hadn't answered and I didn't want to bother anyone. The last thing they needed was to be worrying about me. But I really wanted to know how she was holding up. I couldn't begin to imagine what she was going through. Serena shrugged.

"Yeah, although not well," she said. "I'm not really the girl they parade in public, you know?"

"Does that bother you?" I asked. Then I bit my tongue, realizing how insensitive that was. "I'm sorry. I shouldn't have asked that. Please forgive me."

"Don't worry about it," she replied, giving me a small, weak smile. "I don't want to be one of their old ladies, and despite what you might think, I've had more than one opportunity. I like my freedom. I've got my place and it's worked for me. I'm moving on to something new now anyway. But this... This throws me. They always seem so strong, you don't think of anything being able to kill them, you know?"

I nodded, knowing exactly what she meant. When I'd first met him, I'd half wondered if Horse was a Terminator.

"Did you know Bagger?" I asked. She nodded, pouring herself a cup of coffee.

"Yeah," she said without elaborating. "He was crazy about Cookie, you know. He didn't cheat on her. Horse isn't a cheater either. Last night, that wasn't anything, what you saw with us. We were just talking. I hope you believe that."

I shrugged, not sure what to believe. Cookie's life was in ruins and I supposed that at some point I should check my email to see what fresh games Jeff was playing. Things kept hitting so hard and fast I couldn't keep up.

"Hey," she said, shaking my shoulder a little. "Wake up, look at me. This is important."

"What?" I asked, trying to make myself focus.

"He loves you," she said, holding my gaze with hers. "I know all about what happened, everyone does. They spread it around, wanted to be sure people know they didn't give your brother a pass. You're collateral for him, and all that shit. But the reason you're really here is that Horse loves you. Do you get that?"

"I honestly don't know what to think about any of this," I replied. "All I know is that Cookie is in hell and I can't do anything for her."

"You can help me get this shithole whipped into shape," Serena replied sharply. "There's going to be a funeral, and they'll have tons of people coming in from out of town. Three states worth of bikers will be here to show their respects. We have to get ready. It's something you can do for Cookie, she knows Bagger would want a hell of a wake. This is where it'll happen. We have to get it cleaned up and ready, you up for that?"

I looked around. She was right. The place needed cleaning in a big way. And we'd need food too. Lots of it. I knew there was a kitchen somewhere on the ground floor, but I wasn't sure how good it was. Could it handle that many people?

"That's better," she said, smiling at me. "Nice to have you join us this morning. I knew there was a reason Horse shelled out so much for you."

"What's that supposed to mean?" I asked, caught off guard.

She tilted her head at me, eyes speculative.

"Horse paid a shitload of money for you, girl," she said softly. "Didn't you know that? Maybe not, that's not part of the public story..."

"I have no idea what you're talking about," I said, eyeing her suspiciously. I wasn't sure I could handle another shock, I really wasn't. But I needed to know what she meant by that comment.

"Horse paid the club $50,000 out of his own pocket to give your brother another chance," she said bluntly. "They were going to kill him outright, but Horse wanted you for his old lady and he knew how much your brother means to you. He paid the club to give your brother another chance. How do you not know this?"

I shook my head, feeling dizzy.

Horse paid the club to save my brother. Horse was a murderer who killed women and children. Horse offered to send me to college, knew how to fight hand to hand and taught me to shoot. Multiple personalities? Two certainly weren't enough... But I'm a practical girl. I'd spent a good chunk of the past day feeling dazed and confused, but now I had a job.

"Okay," I said, pushing all that away. I'd think about it later, like so many other things piling up. "So how do we want to do this?"

"Let's get the girls together in the game room," she said. "We'll figure out who's just party leftovers and who's willing to pitch in and help."

Eventually we rounded up about twenty women in various states of undress, a few of the guys watching in interest without interfering. Serena stood up and introduced me as Horse's old lady, which made all of them sit up a little straighter. Then she looked over toward me, obviously waiting for me to speak. That was a surprise, I thought she'd take the lead but apparently not. Clearly, as the only old lady in the room, I was supposed to be in charge.

"Okay, so it sounds like most of you heard the news," I said. "Bagger is dead, he died in Afghanistan. I didn't know Bagger, but I know his wife and daughter. Obviously this is a big deal, and if you want to do something to help, I need to get the clubhouse clean and ready for company. I don't know how much time you have or how much work you can do, but anything is a help. Who can stay and clean?"

A few raised their hands, but most of them looked away, unwilling to meet my eyes. One, definitely not a girl but a woman, walked over to me.

"I'll be in charge of getting the guest rooms and studios ready," she said. She was a tall brunette who looked to be in her early thirties, with tight jeans and a lot of swagger. Unlike the others, she looked sexy but not slutty, which was impressive considering how many were sporting giant raccoon hangover eyes. "A lot of them are full right now, but we'll need to find room for more people to camp out. Some'll get hotel rooms, but a lot will stay here. What's your name? Aside from Horse's old lady?"

She offered me a genuine, if sad, smile, and I decided I liked her. This sweet butt situation was more complicated than I'd realized, because obviously they weren't all brainless sluts.

"I'm Marie. What's yours?"

"I'm Claire," she replied, holding out her hand for me to shake. Her grip was firm and reassuring. "I've been a friend of the club since high school but I'm not with any of the guys. Just came by last night to see some friends from out of town, you know how that is."

I shrugged, not quite sure what she meant and not too worried about it. Her obvious respect surprised me, although I was starting to realize it shouldn't have. There seemed to be a hierarchy of Reaper women, with old ladies at the top, but right now I didn't care what their status was if they'd help me get the armory ready for Bagger's funeral.

"I'm glad to meet you," she said, genuine kindness in her eyes, tempered with a fatigue that had nothing to do with being hung over. "We'll get this done, don't worry. Don't take shit from anyone, okay? You're an old lady, and not one of these girls has a right to tell you a damn thing. Not even me," she added ruefully. "But if you don't mind, I think some asses could use a little kicking and that's one of my favorite things to do. You mind?"

I glanced at Serena.

"Works for me," she said. "She takes the upstairs, I'll take the main floor and you can coordinate food. Sound like a plan?"

"Sounds great," I said, feeling grateful.

Claire turned the group and clapped her hands for attention.

"You heard Marie," she said loudly. "She's nice and polite, but I'm not. Get off your asses and get working, or get the hell out."

Nobody moved for a minute, and she put her hands on her hips and glared around the room.

"I'm serious, bitches!" she yelled, and I believed her. "If you're a friend of the club, now's the time to show it. Otherwise get the fuck out and don't come back. You won't be welcome. Got me?"

About four girls got up and left quickly, but the rest seemed to break out of their stupor, sorting themselves out quickly enough and breaking into teams. Within minutes half had followed Claire upstairs and most of the others followed Serena downstairs. I found myself alone with a woman I recognized with horror—she'd been the one on the second floor, screwing an entire room full of men.

"Hey, I'm Candace," she said quietly. "I'm a caterer. Can I help you get the food situation figured out? I know my way around the kitchen and have a pretty good idea what to expect."

She smiled at me like a perfectly normal person, rather than a woman who'd had sex with five men in a row the night before. How could she even walk? I shook my head, and she gave me a quizzical look. Of course, she didn't realize I'd seen her.

"Yeah, that sounds good," I said, and we started downstairs. She led me through the lounge to the far end of the building, where double doors opened to reveal a dining room with a serving bar separating it from a kitchen. Not a full-on, modern industrial one, more like the kind you'd find in a church. Several big fridges, big dishwasher, that kind of thing. Empty platters and bags of chips littered the counters, debris from the night before, I assumed.

"I've done a lot of parties for them," she said, flipping on lights and going to the fridges, opening them and checking out the contents. "I give them a deal, they take good care of me. A few years ago my ex decided to use me as a punching bag. I knew one of the girls who likes to party here and she passed the word along to Ruger. He and a couple others offered to take care of the problem for me in exchange for some help in the armory kitchen and things grew from there."

"Horse beat up my ex," I said, feeling a sudden sense of sisterhood with her.

"It's a relief when it stops, isn't it?" she replied, with a sad little smile. She started grabbing food wrappers and tossing them in a big plastic garbage can. "He's a real good guy. You're lucky to have him."

I nodded, not sure I wanted to go there. Everyone seemed to think he was so great—did they know the real man? Did I? I felt my phone vibrate and I pulled it out to find a text from Em. *Cookie is home again. They gave her some drugs to help her sleep. Maggs asked if you can stay on top of things at the armory, some of us will be over in a couple hours to help. ((Hugs))*

Already on it, I sent back, relieved I could tell her something positive, no matter how small. Candace and I finished cleaning up and sat down to plan food for the day. Then I sent her to the grocery store with my debit card, which still had about five hundred dollars on it and another hundred in cash. I was torn about that—if I had to get away, I'd need the money. But I wanted to help, and the realization that Horse had already spent fifty grand on me still floated around in the back of my head, waiting to be processed.

It seemed like the least I could do.

By the time Horse took my hand and pulled me upstairs to bed that night I was exhausted. The day had been endless, a blur of people crying, yelling and worst of all, just sitting in silence and staring into nothing.

Candace had been amazing. She'd gone from gangbang hoochie to kitchen goddess apparently without need for transition. Around noon she came back with a ton of food, so much I couldn't imagine we'd go through it all yet it disappeared almost entirely by the end of the day. The party girls worked hard to clean the armory before melting away when the old ladies started showing up—a club dynamic I still couldn't wrap my head around. Surprisingly, Serena and Candace stayed. They kept to themselves back in the kitchen, but every time I turned around they were quietly serving people, bringing them drinks or food, helping the few remaining guests find a place to sleep.

Most of the visiting charter members left, although I got the impression they'd be returning for the funeral. At one point Horse cornered me and told me that the situation with the Jacks was under control, but that I'd still need to stay in the armory.

We waited for news on Bagger's body.

Cookie stayed at her house, but Maggs brought Silvie over after her nap. I took her up to the game room and we played for a couple of hours and ate dinner together. I gave her a bath in our room and dressed her in jammies before Maggs took her back home. The poor girl didn't have a clue what was really going on but she obviously felt the tension in the air.

Now Horse and I were finally alone in our room and I wasn't sure what to say. Some of the guys had been visibly broken up, while others were stoic. Horse was just blank. Nothing. No concern, no sorrow, nada. He'd found me a few times during the day, asking if I'd heard from Jeff. I hadn't, from either email account, which made things easier. I wasn't sure if I could pull off a lie tonight. I watched as he stripped down to his boxers mechanically, then sat down on the side of the bed. He leaned forward, elbows on knees, just looking toward the window. I went to use the bathroom and get ready for bed. When I got back he hadn't moved. I wasn't sure what to do.

"It's bad over there," he said softly. I went and stood in front of him, reaching down to run my fingers through his soft, silky hair. I didn't know where this was going, but I wanted to be close to him, absorb some of his pain. "You have no idea, nobody does. They're crazy, they kill little kids and women and entire families. Every day, Marie. At one point my team set up shop in some town and there were these two boys who liked to come and play with us. Probably about ten years old. They were cute and we liked them, would kick a soccer ball around with them, give them candy, that kind of shit. It was my buddy's ball, but we let the kids take it home, figured they'd enjoy it more than us. Just a ball. One day only one of them came back, threw the ball at us and he took off running. We found out later his friend and his mom were shot in the street for being friends with the Americans. It was just a ball, babe, and he died for it and because we gave him candy. That's so fucked up. And shit like that happened all the time. You wouldn't believe how many civilians are dying over there."

I massaged his scalp, feeling the tension tying him in knots with every touch. I wanted to ask him about the article but I couldn't do it. Words seemed so incredibly trite compared to the pain that radiated off him.

"Another time we found an entire village massacred," he said, voice rough. "Whole damn place shot to hell. Kids. Women. Men. Fucking donkeys. Goats. All of them dead, houses burning, you name it. You know what's totally fucked up? We go in there and find this, call it in, but the next day *we're* the bastards under investigation. Apparently there's all kinds of people saying we did it. You know how fucked that is? You go to a country, you try to help the people there and they spend all their time and energy either trying to kill you or set you up."

I stilled, wondering if I could believe him. Horse had no reason to tell me about this. Not unless he'd found my email account. But I'd been careful, really careful, clearing out my phone's cache and cookies and browsing history. I'd never put the address into my email app, I only checked it on the website. Could he trace that?

"Do you know how insane this is? Bagger just died for this country in a war that's gone on for *ten fucking years*, and people around here think they're *suffering* if they can't afford a new iPhone," he said, looking up at me for the first time. The stark grief written all over his face tore through me and that's when I knew. It wasn't fake. Not this. Jeff was wrong about him. Horse might be many things, but he didn't kill those people. The article said Marines were under investigation, but it didn't say how the investigation ended. Even Jeff acknowledged Horse had an honorable discharge.

Horse didn't kill those people. I knew it in my bones.

I felt such incredible relief that I trembled with it, but I didn't say anything. Whatever else happened, I would protect Jeff. But that didn't mean I'd give up on what I had with Horse. There had to be a way to walk the line between the two men I loved. I just had to find it. Horse leaned forward, pressing his head into my stomach, shuddering. His arms wrapped around my hips and he pulled me forward between his legs. I have no idea how long we sat there but it seemed like forever. He didn't talk, just held me, shaking, as his grief poured out.

Finally the shudders eased and he pulled back. I looked down at him, running my fingers across the lines of his face, feeling the softness of his lips with my thumb. He reached up and caught my hand, tugging it to his mouth, kissing my palm. Heat flared in his eyes and he fell back on the bed, drawing me down to him.

We'd made love so many different ways in our time together. Urgent, slow, angry and laughing—but never like this. He held me like his life depended on it, hands digging into my hips and spreading my legs across his body as his hips ground up into mine urgently. I took his head between my hands and kissed him, long and deep, full of pain for his suffering and relief so intense I thought my heart might explode. I couldn't believe I'd doubted him. I knew he was a violent man living a violent life. But what he'd told me, the way he suffered—that wasn't a lie.

His cock pressed into me, long and hard as I rubbed myself across it. I wore a tee and panties and all he had on were boxers, but that was way too much. I wanted to be naked so I could take him deep into my body, give him my love until the sadness in his eyes changed to something else. Instead we ground against each other, too desperate for sensation to stop long enough to pull off our clothes. I let his lips go, put my hands on either side of his head and arched my head back, maximizing the pressure between us.

"You're going to kill me," he gasped, hands digging into my ass so hard it hurt. "It's worth it. I'll take whatever you have. I never want it to stop."

I ignored him, focusing now on the pressure and need growing between my legs. Everything in my body wound tight and I realized I might come dry humping him like a teenager in the back of a car—that's how much his body called to mine. I ground harder, feeling it just beyond me, and then it burst and I moaned, shuddering over him.

I rolled off, reaching down to slide off my panties. Horse shoved down his boxers just enough to free his cock, which sprang up long and hard between us. He reached toward me, obviously planning to pull me on top of him, but I stopped him. Instead I leaned over his lower body, wrapping my lips around his erection and sucking him in deep.

He shuddered, wrapping the fingers of one hand in my hair as I swirled my tongue around his head and started stroking him with my hand down below. I couldn't fix anything for him. I couldn't bring back Bagger or change what had gone down overseas. But I could make him forget for a little while and I didn't plan to do it halfway.

I sucked him and licked him, pulling away every once in a while to attack his balls with my mouth, drawing them in and rolling them around my tongue. Then I got creative, sliding one of my fingers up into his ass as I suctioned hard, squeezing and stroking him with my fingers until he groaned and twisted underneath me, captured and desperate for release. He tugged at my hair, trying to pull me away, but I wouldn't let him. Instead I held him captive with my fingers and mouth, swallowing triumphantly when he exploded into me, hips jerking and trembling.

When he finished I pulled away and sat up, wiping my mouth off with the back of my hand. He smiled up at me, and while he still looked sad, his terrible tension had eased.

"Thanks," he said softly, reaching up and tracing the line of my lips.

"No problem," I whispered. "I'm going to brush my teeth. No offense, okay?"

He gave a low chuckle and nodded. When I came back to bed I found him naked. He pulled me close into the crook of his arm, bringing my leg up and over his. I felt peace. Nothing could undo what had happened, either to him or Bagger, but for tonight he could sleep.

I felt like a very, very good old lady.

Chapter Twenty

ഇ

The morning of the funeral was cold. I wondered how much of it was the temperature and how much was the cloud of wrongness and grief hanging over all of us. Bagger hadn't been a religious man but Cookie had asked a biker chaplain from Spokane to come over and do a graveside service. It would start with a viewing at the funeral home, followed by a procession to the cemetery for the interment.

Maggs and Darcy took charge of making arrangements because Cookie couldn't handle the details. Her in-laws, who didn't live locally, were elderly and utterly devastated. They were pathetically grateful for the support, unable to think of anything but their lost son. That's why the night before the service, the women of the club held a strategy session at the armory. Apparently Cookie was particularly worried about Silvie coming to the cemetery. It would be cold and she'd started acting out, probably from all the tension and grief in the air. She still didn't understand what had happened to her daddy, and would carry the laptop to any adult she could find so she could talk to him online.

Cookie asked me—as Silvie's favorite babysitter—if I'd help watch her at the service. If Silvie couldn't handle things, she wanted me to take her back to the armory rather than subject her daughter to something she couldn't possibly comprehend. Of course I said yes, so the morning of the funeral Maggs parked my car around the back side of the cemetery. That way if Silvie needed me, I could take her and leave quickly and unobtrusively. Horse didn't like the idea but even he had to admit that the Devil's Jacks wouldn't dare disrupt the funeral. Not with a hundred Reapers watching, not to mention half the veterans in north Idaho.

I hadn't left the clubhouse all week but Em had been my lifeline. She even bought me a black dress to wear, and that morning I rode to the funeral home with her. The men followed us on their bikes, which had to be incredibly uncomfortable in the bitter cold. Nobody complained.

Driving motorcycles in a winter funeral procession didn't seem that sensible to me, but apparently that's the way things were done at a biker's funeral. Maggs had warned me, but I was still stunned to see hundreds of motorcycles parked outside the funeral home. Not only Reapers, but the Silver Bastards and a bunch of other clubs I'd never heard of. There were men who weren't part of any club too, and vets flying MIA/POW flags off the backs of their Harleys. Even more of the riders had American flags. There was no way this many people could fit inside the funeral home for the viewing but nobody seemed to mind. Maggs took me inside and I watched as more people arrived, waiting patiently in the cold, talking to each other quietly in small clumps. Some of them stuck what looked like bumper stickers on the casket, which freaked me out at first. Then I realized they were Reapers support badges and nobody seemed to have a problem with it. I saw Cookie and managed to go up to her to offer my respects. She smiled at me but I don't think she even recognized me. Silvie did, though, and I picked her up and carried her around. She loved it and I lavished attention on her.

Then it was time to pile into the cars for the procession. I walked Silvie over to Cookie, who seemed completely disconnected from reality. Couldn't blame her for that. When her mother-in-law tried to take her granddaughter from me, the little girl started crying and clung to me, kicking.

"Come with us," Cookie said suddenly, as if she'd been startled awake. "Whatever makes her happy. Please take care of her for me, I need your help."

That's how I wound up riding in the limo with the family, right behind the hearse. It felt so wrong, so presumptuous, but it made Silvie happy and Cookie certainly wasn't up to handling her. We drove slowly through town and I was astounded at the show of support and respect. I guess I'd been cut off from events out at the armory, but I honestly hadn't realized just how big Bagger's funeral procession would be. This wasn't just the club, or even a group of clubs. The whole town was stepping up to honor Bagger for his sacrifice.

It started with six police cars, driving two abreast with their lights flashing. The Reapers weren't big cop fans, but Bagger's dad had wanted to accept their offer of an escort so no one complained. Then came the hearse and the family in three limos, followed by the indescribable roar of hundreds of bikes. We drove right down Sherman Avenue and instead of having us avoid the main roads like a typical funeral procession, they closed off the streets in his honor. People lined the curbs to pay their respects, standing at attention as we drove by. Many held American flags and handmade signs saying things like "Thank You" and "We Will Not Forget".

Cookie watched them with dead eyes while Silvie pressed her little face to the glass, fascinated. When we finally arrived at the cemetery, the limo stopped and we got out. The Reapers came behind us, more of them than I'd ever seen. It seemed like hundreds, although I learned later there were about a hundred and twenty-five. Behind them rode other clubs and veterans' groups, followed by an endless line of cars. There were also active-duty servicemen in dress uniforms and even the local high school marching band, wearing poorly fitted black suits instead of their usual flamboyant regalia. It took nearly an hour before everyone could park, so we made Cookie get back into the car to wait. I climbed into another limo with Silvie and let her play on my phone.

Finally everyone had arrived and we congregated around the gravesite. Once again, I felt like I was far too close to the front for a woman who'd never met Bagger. So many people had known and loved him. But Silvie wanted me so I stood to one side of Cookie's chair, bouncing her in my arms. The service was a strange mix of military formality and biker tradition. Instead of the Marine honor guard serving as pallbearers, Cookie had requested Horse, Ruger, Picnic, Duck and Bam Bam. They carefully carried the flag-draped coffin from the hearse to the grave. There were three on one side and only two on the other, something I'd never seen at a funeral before.

"Cookie wanted them to leave a spot open for Bolt," Maggs whispered next to me, choking up a little. I felt my own eyes tear up, amazed that even in the depths of her grief, Bagger's wife would remember Bolt and honor his friendship with her husband. Once the coffin was settled, the preacher spoke and so did some of the guys from the club. The band played the Star Spangled Banner.

Then the military honors began.

A group of ten young Marines in full dress uniform had been standing patiently off to the side during the service. Their commander called them to attention and gave out a series of orders. Then seven of them raised rifles and shot three perfectly timed volleys in unison. The sound split the air like thunder, so loud it rattled off the hills. Cookie shuddered at every shot like they were firing right through her. Silvie squealed as I covered her little ears.

One of the remaining Marines raised a bugle to his lips and played Taps, the haunting song echoing through the eerie silence of the cemetery. Silvie squirmed in my arms and started to fuss. The commander and remaining man walked carefully over to the coffin and lifted the flag, stepping to the side and away from the casket, folding it carefully into a star-spangled, blue triangle.

Finally, when it was perfect, the commander walked forward to Cookie and leaned forward to present her with the flag, voice carrying in the cold, still air.

"On behalf of the president of the United States, the commandant of the Marine Corps and a grateful nation, please accept this flag as a symbol of our appreciation for your loved one's service to country and corps."

Cookie took the flag and cradled it against her chest, utterly silent, as Bagger's mother sobbed loudly. Silvie crumpled up her face and started crying too, and I decided she'd had enough. I made my way to the back of the crowd and walked across the frosted grass quickly, which seemed to distract the little girl. I put her in the car seat now permanently installed in my vehicle and sat down to turn on the engine and get the heater going. A knock on the window startled me and I gave a little scream, which made Silvie burst into tears again.

Max stood outside.

I wanted to hit the gas and run him over. Instead I lowered the window a crack and glared at him.

"I need to get Silvie out of here," I said, filling my tone with ice.

"I know," he said. "Look, I'm really sorry about what happened. What I did to you was out of line, so out of line, and there's nothing I can do or say to make up for that. But I'm worried about you leaving by yourself. I just got a text from a friend who says he saw four of the Devil's Jacks eating at Zip's. There's only one reason they're in town and I don't think you'll be safe if you leave by yourself. Let me make sure you and Silvie get back to the armory okay."

"You're the last person I'd trust," I said, shaking my head.

"I know," he replied, face full of remorse that seemed real, but who could tell? "I deserve that. But Horse shouldn't have to leave right now. If he had any idea the Jacks are already in town he'd be with you right now. But think about this — with the way everyone's on edge, things could get pretty ugly if there's a confrontation. Horse isn't in a good place."

He made a good point.

I didn't want Horse to wind up in jail. I didn't want any of them in jail and I definitely didn't want Bagger's funeral to turn into a debacle.

"Let me drive home with you," he said. "I'll keep my hands to myself and my mouth shut. Email Horse right now, so if I pull something he'll know we're together. Then text him as soon as we get there, once the service is over. That should make you feel safer. Please, if you won't do it for yourself, do it for Silvie. If they spot you, they'll move in and they'll take her too. I can't let that happen to Bagger's kid. It's one last thing I can do for him."

That convinced me. Max was right—whatever was between us, Silvie needed to be safe and I really didn't want to pull Horse away from the funeral. I might loathe Max, but he was loyal to the club. Horse hated him too, but he'd told me time and again that he'd trust any of the Reapers with his life. Max was still one of his brothers, and the only thing that scared me more than the thought of the Jacks catching me was the thought of them hurting Silvie. Even Max at his worst would be better than that.

"Get in the car," I said, sighing. "Don't talk to me or touch me."

He nodded and walked around to the passenger's side, sliding in as I sent Horse a quick email. The fact that he didn't reach for the car keys impressed me—Horse never let me drive, and based on what the other girls said it was a common bone of contention. Reapers liked to be in control. I turned on the radio and drove straight to the armory. Max kept his word. No talking, no touching, nothing until I turned the car off.

"I'll walk you in and make sure the prospects are on top of things," he said. "Then I'm going back to talk with Picnic and the guys, give them a heads-up. Nobody will want to leave the reception or party but we need to be aware. Don't go outside, okay?"

I nodded, still feeling nervous when he looked at me. I'd never feel safe around that man. We walked inside to find Painter and a couple other prospects from different charters hanging around. Painter didn't look too thrilled when he glanced from me to Max, but I caught his eye and flashed him a quick thumbs-up. Then I took Silvie into the kitchen for a sandwich. While she tucked in her food, I texted Horse and let him know where I was and that Max had escorted me without incident. He didn't respond, which wasn't a surprise. I took Silvie up to my room and laid her down for a nap, thankful that I'd been able to help and bemused that Max had proven capable of decency.

Dancer came and took Silvie to a family friend's house around seven that evening. People had been pouring into the armory for hours by then. Cookie pulled herself together enough to eat dinner with her daughter and read her stories before Silvie left. I went to find Horse and see how he was holding up.

I found him outside around yet another bonfire, with a mixed group of Reapers, Silver Bastards and family members. Like most wakes, it started off somber enough but was growing louder as people shared beer and stories. I came up behind him and wrapped my arms around his stomach, resting my face against his back. After a while he pulled me around to his front, draping his arms over my shoulder and leaning down to whisper in my ear.

"Thanks for everything today, babe," he said. "I'm sorry you had to ride with Max. You made the right call though. We've spotted the Jacks a couple of times, they're definitely planning something. It'll be good to finish this out."

I leaned back against him, drinking in his warmth and thinking about going back home together. I was tired of the armory. I just hoped they managed to get rid of the Jacks without hurting Jeff…

"Will it be dangerous?" I asked.

"Not if we do it right," he said. "We're not stupid and this isn't the first time we've had to protect what's ours. Don't worry about it, babe. Tonight's about Bagger."

After a while I got cold, so I went inside to find Maggs and a bunch of women I didn't know standing around the kitchen's center island, passing a bottle of Jack Daniels. I didn't feel much like drinking, but I joined the circle when Maggs waved me over. I was learning that the sisterhood of biker babes was bigger than I'd grasped. I saw respect and welcome in their eyes when she introduced me as Horse's property, and for the first time the word didn't bother me. It just meant something different to us than it did in the civilian world.

Us.

I was part of "us" now, I realized. These were my sisters, Horse was my man, and I could trust all the guys to keep an eye out for me, even Max. I still loathed him and he made my skin crawl, but he'd been watching out for me and Silvie in his own weird way today. It'd always been me and Mama and Jeff against the world — it felt good to have more.

An air horn sounded at nine, calling everyone outside to the bonfire. I followed the girls and found Horse again, tucking myself into his arms to keep warm as Picnic stepped out in front of everyone, solemn. Cookie stood not far away, flanked by Maggs and Dancer. She looked unsteady but determined. She still wore her black dress, but she'd put her "property" vest on over it, trading her heels for black leather boots.

"Tonight we say goodbye to a brother and a friend," Picnic said, his voice hoarse. "He truly understood that brotherhood is forever and that no matter what happens in this life, a real man never walks away before the fight is finished. No matter what, we stand together. He gave his life standing with his brothers in Afghanistan and we'll respect him for the rest of our lives.

"Bagger wore the Reapers' patch for ten years and always brought it honor. When he left for his last deployment, he gave his colors to me to keep safe. He's Freebird chapter now and he doesn't need his patches anymore. It's time to send them back to him. We won't forget. Reapers forever, forever Reapers."

A lot of the guys, including Horse, echoed his words like a mantra. Then everyone grew silent and the opening strains of Lynyrd Skynyrd's *Free Bird* started playing. Picnic stepped forward, holding up Bagger's cut for all of us to see. He'd almost reached the fire when Cookie cried out.

"Wait!" she said, pulling away from Maggs. "Wait for me. Mine's going with his. They belong together."

I watched as she shrugged out of her "Property of Bagger, Reapers MC" vest and draped it over Bagger's cut.

"They go together," she said again, voice breaking. Picnic shook his head and Maggs came up to her, taking her arm.

"You'll want it," she said. "You aren't thinking straight tonight. Bagger would want you to keep it."

"It belongs with his," Cookie replied, her voice fierce. She and Picnic stared each other down for a minute as the song played, then he jerked his head once in acquiescence. Cookie sighed in relief and let Maggs pull her away, unsteady on her feet again, as if she'd used up all her energy on this final chore. The song soared around us as Picnic threw the two sets of patched leathers into the fire. All around me I heard women sniffling. Men blinked quickly, their eyes suspiciously moist. All too soon the song ended and the leather cuts were lost in the flame.

It was official. Bagger had left the Reapers behind.

I stood in the bathroom off the game room an hour later, fiddling with my hair and wishing I could leave. Horse needed space and wanted to be with his brothers. The women were friendly but I didn't know most of them and I didn't want to intrude on their grief. The toilet flushed behind me and Cookie stepped out of the stall.

"Hey," I said, not sure what to say. I didn't want to ask her how she felt or offer some empty platitude.

"Hey," she murmured, washing her hands. She looked in the mirror and then glanced at the door. She took a deep breath and touched my arm.

"I need to get out of here," she said, her voice matter-of-fact. "Can you take me home? Everyone's drunk and I can't find anyone to drive me. Are you sober? You look sober."

"Yeah," I said, startled. "You really want to leave? Everyone's here for you—"

"No, I need to go right now," she said, shaking her head with unnatural composure. "I'm holding on by a thread and if I have to listen to his name or any more stories I'm going to fall apart and I don't want an audience. Not only that, they all say I shouldn't be alone tonight and probably won't let me leave. That's not working for me. I'm not going to do anything stupid, but I can't handle listening to a party when all I can think about is my husband lying cold and dead in the ground a mile from my house. Will you take me home?"

There was only one answer to a statement like that.

"Let me get my purse. I'll meet you out front."

I ran upstairs and grabbed my things, trying to decide whether I should tell Horse. The Jacks were out, I knew that. But Horse needed his mourning time and I didn't want to take it away from him. Maybe I could find a prospect to go with us. Painter stood outside with a few other guys, but when I went up and asked him to drive home with me and Cookie, he said he needed to check with Picnic. Cookie paced nervously by my car and I could see her starting to visibly fall apart. What if Picnic didn't want her to leave? Then Max walked around the corner and I made a snap decision.

"Are you sober?" I asked him. He stopped, obviously startled.

"Um, yeah, I am," he replied. "Wanted to be alert if the Jacks showed up. Why?"

"Cookie needs to go home and I'm taking her," I said, putting my cards on the table. "I asked Painter to ride with us but he said he had to check with Picnic first, and Picnic might not let her leave. We have to get out of here now. Will you come with us?"

"Sure," he said, and we all got into the car, Cookie taking the backseat. During the drive my phone started ringing, Horse and Picnic both, so I let it go to voicemail. I'd deal with the fallout after I got Cookie home. None of us spoke on the way to her house and when we pulled up, she paused only long enough to thank us before heading inside.

"You think she'll be safe?" I asked Max. "I mean, from the Jacks?"

"They won't bother her," he replied. "Not a war widow, not with this many guys in town. They go after her, even their own support clubs could turn on them. She's untouchable. You aren't though. We should get back."

My phone rang and I grabbed it, wanting to reassure Horse.

"Hey, babe, I'm sorry—"

"Marie, it's Jeff."

I stilled, eyes darting toward Max.

"Um, yeah," I replied, keeping my tone friendly and casual. "Just a sec."

I stepped out of the car and closed the door, strolling a few feet down the street in front so Max could see me without hearing me.

"What are you doing calling me?" I demanded. "You were supposed to email. What if someone else had answered? It's after midnight, what if I'd been in bed with Horse?"

"You're not," Jeff replied. "I know there's a wake at the armory. Are you there?"

"No, I had to give someone a ride home," I said quickly. "How did you find out about the wake?"

"I know everything they do," he said. "I've got things all set up now, it's time for us to go. I want you to meet me out at Horse's place. I'm in the barn."

"What? How is that even possible?"

"I don't have time for this," he said sharply. "You need to get your ass out here so we can go. We'll talk while we drive."

"I'm not alone. Max is with me."

"Lose him," Jeff snapped.

"I don't think I can," I replied. "They're worried about the Jacks. He isn't going to just hop out of the car. Jeff, you need to know I'm not going with you. I'm with Horse and I'm going to stay with him."

He sighed.

"You're brainwashed," he said. "But I told you, Horse isn't who you think he is. I have proof, I'll show you. Everyone's busy, they won't have a clue until it's too late. At least come and see what I've found. If you still want to stay after that I'll call off the Jacks and leave you alone."

"Max, remember?"

"Bring him," Jeff said. "Tell him you need something in the house, ask him to come with you. I've got a gun. We can tie him up while we talk, lock him in the tack room. He'll be fine."

I felt my stomach sink.

"This is a really bad idea, Jeff," I said softly. "Think it through. What if it doesn't work? He could kill you. You need to stop doing crazy things and deal with this situation in a way that doesn't make it worse."

"You're so damned naive," he muttered, frustration clear in his voice. "Max is a violent criminal, all the Reapers are. You need to stop protecting them and think about your family. Now get your ass out here."

He hung up on me. I turned back to the car, pasting a fake smile on my face for Max's benefit. No way I would be bringing him out to Horse's place. Jeff had lost his mind. But I still wanted to talk to him and see if we could figure something less crazy out together. I also wanted to look at this proof he kept talking about. There had to be an explanation.

"That was Maggs," I said, climbing back into the car. "She wants us to stop by the grocery store and pick up some garbage bags. I guess they've run out and things are getting ugly. Let's swing into Safeway, okay?"

"Sure," he said and I kept my eyes forward, counting every breath as I drove to the store. As we pulled into the parking lot I chose my spot carefully, then stopped the car. Max got out and as soon as he shut the door I clicked the locks and hit the gas.

My phone rang at least fifteen times during my drive to the farm. I had no doubt that Max had called Horse within seconds of my little stunt, and Horse was mighty pissed.

I'd deal with that later.

Still, I didn't want him to worry about me more than he needed to, so after I pulled up I sent him a quick text saying that things were all right but that my brother had called and I needed some privacy to call him back. Then I silenced the phone, planning to ignore his response.

The fallout from this was gonna suck, no question.

I grabbed my purse and walked toward the barn. No sign of Jeff. No sign of Ariel either, which made me really nervous. I pushed through the open door, noting the broken lock. Horse wasn't going to like that either, I thought, biting back a hysterical giggle. Poor man would have a heart attack before the night was over at this rate. Jeff grabbed me as soon as I walked into the barn, pulling me to the side of the door with one hand and waving a gun around in the other. All of Horse's training must have sunk in, because I hit the ground automatically as the barrel swung toward me.

"Don't point that at me!" I hissed, and Jeff glanced down at the gun, startled.

"Oh shit, I'm sorry," he said. "Did you come by yourself?"

"Yes," I replied, standing up and dusting off my knees. "But they were lighting up my phone on the drive out here. We don't have a lot of time. What's the proof you were talking about?"

Jeff walked over to a work bench and pulled out a folder. I flipped it open and saw several articles about the massacre from different news outlets. None of them had any information I hadn't seen already.

"Keep looking," Jeff said. I flipped further, finding a copy of Horse's discharge papers. Honorable. I found a memo stating that his unit was being cleared of charges based on a lack of evidence. Another newspaper article followed, this one stating that the killers had never been found and now several key witnesses had disappeared. That was it.

"You see?" Jeff asked. "It's right there. Now do you understand?"

I looked at him, confused.

"This doesn't say he did anything," I replied softly. "It just says they never figured out who did it. Sometimes that happens during war, Jeff, especially in areas with competing guerrilla groups. This doesn't prove anything."

He shook his head, clearly frustrated.

"It's a conspiracy, you have to read between the lines," he said. "The witnesses disappeared. Why do you think that happened?"

"Probably because they were afraid they'd get murdered if they collaborated," I replied, shaking my head. "Jeff, forget about this. You need call off the Jacks and stop working with them. Then you need to disappear. Otherwise I'm afraid the Reapers will kill you. I love you so much—I can't lose you."

Jeff's face softened, and I saw a trace of the laid-back, loving brother he'd been most of my life. He pulled me into his arms but he didn't feel right to me. His heart raced, he'd gotten far too thin and I felt and smelled clammy sweat coming off him. I pulled back and looked into his face, feeling indescribably sad.

"Jeff, what are you doing to yourself?" I asked. His features hardened and he jerked away.

"I'm trying to take care of my family," he snapped. Outside I heard the roar of bikes and I froze.

"Oh shit, they're gonna kill you," I said, panicking. I started looking around, trying to find somewhere to hide him, which was ludicrous. The barn door flew open and banged against the wall. It was Horse and Max, holding guns. They froze as Jeff grabbed me and held his own weapon to my head.

"Don't worry, sis," he whispered in my ear. "I would never hurt you. I just need to get out of this so we can start over somewhere else. It's going to be great, you won't have to worry about anything."

Oh fuck.

Chapter Twenty-One

≈

Horse

Horse saw red when he saw the gun at Marie's head. Jensen stood next to her, trembling so hard he thought it might be enough to pull the trigger. The man was obviously tweaking hard on something, probably meth. Very bad news. Might even be hallucinating. It took everything he had not to charge Jensen and kill him with his bare hands, but he had to be smart.

"Hey," Max said, sounding a little too casual. Horse glanced over at him and caught his play. "We're just here to make sure Marie's all right. We were afraid the Jacks got her. We know you love her and would never hurt her so let's talk this through. Win/win, right?"

Jeff laughed, the tone high-pitched and more than a little crazed.

"I showed her the evidence," he said. "She knows all about what you did in Afghanistan to those kids. And now you're going to die for what you did to her."

Horse ignored his words, focusing on reading his tone and body language. No clear shot, obviously. How could he get to her? He'd been in tighter situations but never with so much at stake.

"I'm going to put down my gun," he said, setting the gun very slowly and carefully on the floor. Then he held his hands up, showing Jeff they were empty. "Max will do the same. Then you can take the gun away from her head. I don't want any accidents. We'll let you get in her car and go, sound good?"

Jensen laughed again, something new and ugly on his face...honest glee, with a hint of gloating.

"I want you out in the center of the floor," he said. "No tricks."

Horse stepped forward, hands up. The gun trembled in Jensen's hand as he pulled Marie backward, deeper into the barn's open central floor. *Fuck.*

"That's good," Jeff said. "Your turn," he added, looking at Max now. Horse heard Max shuffle behind him and then Marie's eyes went wide. She opened her mouth and screamed at him as a bullet tore through his back, pain exploding as his vision started going dark.

He hit the floor, seeing his blood flowing out onto the ground next to him. He couldn't move but he could feel, the pain beyond anything he could have imagined. *This is how Bagger went,* he realized. *Alone in a pool of blood, knowing that he failed his woman.* Then he stopped thinking and everything stopped.

Marie

Horse hit the floor and my world ended. I think some part of me had doubted whether our love was real. Not anymore. I hardly noticed as Jeff let me go, I just ran over to Horse and felt his neck for a pulse. It was there, and while the blood was pooling beneath him it wasn't spurting out.

I still had a chance.

I stood to see Max and Jeff greeting each other, guns lowered. *Holy shit.*

"This was a setup," I said. Jeff glanced over at me.

"Max is my inside source. He knew I'd be here tonight and planned to deliver you, but it made things a lot easier when you gave Cookie a ride home."

"Too much talk," Max said, narrowing his eyes at Jeff. "We can't trust her."

Jeff nodded, looking sad.

"Yeah, you're right," he said. "Marie, I know this is hard for you but you'll get through it. You've only known him a few months and it was all fake anyway. You'll see."

"Everything ready?" Max asked. Jeff nodded.

"All set up," he said. "Haven't pulled the money from the accounts yet, didn't want to do that and tip them off until we got her out. Marie, grab your purse, we gotta go."

He picked it up and tossed it toward me, then pulled Max away, talking with him quietly. Both men seemed extremely excited and agitated as they pored through papers on one of the work benches. I didn't care about that—I needed to find something to stop the bleeding. I saw a pile of rags that looked pretty dirty, but figured we'd worry about infection if he managed to survive. It wouldn't matter if I kept the wound clean if he bled out.

Once I had the rags on him and started applying pressure, I tried to think of the next step. I definitely wasn't going anywhere with Max and Jeff. I'd finally grasped the reality— I'd already lost Jeff. There was something really, really wrong with him and I'd never be able to fix it. Even if I did, I didn't want him in my life anymore. Not after he killed Horse. *Tried* to kill Horse.

He wasn't dead yet. *Gotta keep the thoughts positive.*

Max and Jeff were engrossed in whatever they were studying—apparently I wasn't a threat to them. I could use that. I glanced down at my purse and realized I had two very powerful tools in there. My phone and my gun. I couldn't call and say anything though, because they'd hear me. I guess I could've called 9-1-1 in the hope they'd find me, but considering it was a cell phone that wouldn't happen very fast.

I'd call Picnic and hope to hell he answered. Maybe he'd hear something useful.

I scooted around Horse's body, turning my back to them. That felt wrong, but I needed some cover to dig through my purse. I also needed to keep up the pressure on his wound, so I leaned down and across him, holding down the rags with the weight of my body as I searched quickly through the bag. I found the phone first, turning down the sound and hitting Picnic's number. It rang forever. Nothing. Shit. I heard their conversation shift and realized I was running out of time. I hit Maggs' number and set the phone on the floor behind Horse's arm, hoping she'd answer and hear something. I couldn't do more than that, not right now.

Now for the gun.

Horse had given me a really cute leather purse that had a little compartment in it designed especially for a handgun — crazy, right? I was damned thankful for it at the moment though, because my .22 slipped right out when I pressed the latch. Now all I had to do was cock it. I got ready and then coughed loudly as I chambered a round, sliding it under his arm.

"You should leave him," Jeff said behind me. "He's going to die, no way you can change that. Grab your shit and let's go."

I lifted my chest and pressed against Horse again with both hands. Then I scooted around to find Jeff standing over me.

"I'm not going with you," I said, meeting his eyes. "You guys should get out while you can. Leave us. I won't even tell them who did it, I just want you gone."

Max laughed and came up behind Jeff, holding up a paper. He smiled and shook his head, studying whatever it said.

"I can't believe it's this simple," Max said, shaking his head. Jeff turned back to grin at him, the maniacal gleam coming back into his eyes. "You're a genius. We'll be set, even after we pay off the cartel."

"It's only simple because I spent so much time setting it up," Jeff said, looking pleased, although I noticed his hand had started twitching again. Of course, he kept his finger on the trigger. Just what I needed.

"You did a hell of a job," Max said, shaking his head ruefully. "It's a thing of beauty, man."

Jeff grinned at the compliment.

"I'm really glad they didn't listen to me back in September," Max continued. He looked at me and smiled almost fondly. "Gotta thank your old man for that, Marie. I wanted to kill you months ago, Jeff. Figured you might expose me on the skim. Never figured on a payoff like this. Damn. I'm actually sorry I have to do this. It's not personal, okay?"

Jeff looked at Max, puzzled. He never saw the biker's hand lift and for the second time in ten minutes I found myself screaming a warning too late for someone I loved. Jeff's head exploded. Literally exploded, chunks flying off. One of them hit me in the face, which I didn't notice at the time because in the instant Max shot him, Jeff's hand spasmed and pulled the trigger on his own gun. A second shot rang out almost instantly and I felt a line of fire across my arm. I ignored it because my brother was dead, my lover was almost dead and I had a really, really bad feeling that I'd be dead, soon too.

Max looked down at me, tapping his gun against the side of his leg. He wore the same puzzled look he'd had the night he'd attacked me.

"He's going to die," Max said, looking down at Horse thoughtfully. "Your brother was right about that. You might as well let him go, because his blood is getting all over your clothes."

"What's wrong with you?" I whispered. "Why would you do this?"

He shrugged.

"Money, what else? Get out of the way unless you want me to shoot you too. I want to fuck you first. Your call."

My eyes widened as he raised his gun and pointed it right at Horse's head. This was it. Horse was out of time. I needed a distraction, just for a second.

"Oh my god, I'm covered in blood!" I squealed suddenly, pulling my hands away from Horse to tear off my shirt and bra. Max's eyes went straight to my tits right as my hand grabbed my gun. A thousand memories flashed through my mind in an instant, but the one that stayed with me was the sound of Horse's voice, that first day he taught me to shoot.

Just remember, you ever point this at a person, you shoot it right at his heart and you shoot to kill. Never point a gun unless you're ready to end a life.

I lifted my gun and pointed it straight at Max's heart like I'd practiced hundreds of time. I didn't even think as I pulled the trigger over and over and over until I ran out of bullets. Like Jeff, Max'd pulled his trigger as he died but his arm had dropped just enough to miss us. I crawled over to his body and grabbed his gun, taking it back with me as I climbed onto Horse, sitting on the rags as I grabbed my phone.

"Maggs, are you there?" I asked, my voice.

"What happened?" she demanded, her voice steady and calm. Apparently Maggs took gunfire in stride. "The guys are on their way, they'll be there in two minutes, tops. They had GPS on your car. Are you okay?"

"Horse needs an ambulance," I said, my voice shaky. "I think he's still alive. Max and Jeff are dead. Please save us, Maggs. I'm really, really scared."

The barn door burst open in front of me and I dropped the phone, bringing Max's gun up and pointing it at Picnic, Bam Bam, Duck, Ruger and a couple other guys I'd seen at the armory, guys from another charter.

"I want cops and an ambulance," I said, and my voice might have been weak but my hands were steady.

Picnic surveyed the scene, his face calmer than seemed reasonable.

"Max tried to kill Horse," I told him. "He killed Jeff. I don't trust any of you. I want an ambulance for Horse and I want you out of here."

"Babe, I have no idea what went down here," Picnic said slowly. "But you have to let us help Horse. Put down the gun."

"*No fucking way*," I replied. "Max shot him in the back. I'll shoot any one of you fucking Reapers who try to touch him. Ambulance. Now."

"There's one on the way," Picnic said. "Bam's called it in. But if you're sitting there holding a gun on us when the cops get here, that's going to make it a lot harder for them to take care of Horse. He's our brother, we aren't going to hurt him."

"Max was his brother too."

"A bad thing happened here," Duck said, stepping forward. Something about his voice mesmerized me, and his eyes looked soft and sad. I watched as he crossed the floor and sat in front of me, about three feet from the gun. "Don't make it worse. We can still control the situation, but not if you get in a shootout with the cops."

That startled me.

"I don't want to shoot the cops, I just want to protect Horse," I said.

"How are they going to know that?" he asked reasonably. I heard sirens in the distance. "You're running out of time, let us help you through this, okay?"

I wanted to agree and had opened my mouth to tell him when something tackled me from behind. Duck's hand darted forward at the same instant, wrenching the gun out of my grasp as Ruger rolled me away from Horse's body. He held me down, hand over my mouth, and leaned his face in close to mine. His expression was intense, almost feral. In the corners of my eyes I saw the guys spring into action, throwing things into a bag, which Bam Bam grabbed before he took off running out the back door of the barn.

"All hell's gonna break loose when they come in here," Ruger told me, his tone urgent. "They're probably going to arrest you, maybe all of us. Keep your mouth shut. I don't care what happened here and I don't care who did the shooting. You keep your mouth shut and the only time you open it is to ask for a lawyer. Keep asking for a lawyer 'til you get one, we'll send him to you. Do *not* talk, you got me?"

He pulled his hand away from my mouth and I nodded, eyes wide. A single cop came flying through the door and stopped abruptly, obviously shocked at the scene.

"Holy shit!" he yelled, reaching up to grab his radio. "We need backup now. Everyone, hands up where I can see them. Get off that girl, let her go."

Ruger rolled off me and stood, backing away with his hands raised high. The others followed suit and then I joined them. The lone cop watched us anxiously as EMTs rushed over to Horse, bundling him onto a stretcher and hauling him out the door. More cops arrived, which was the start of a very, very long night.

I asked for a lawyer and eventually I got one, but he couldn't answer the one question I cared about.

Was Horse still alive?

Horse

He felt detached from his body, almost floating. Pain roared through him. Voices echoed in the background, along with sirens. Then the world went black again.

More voices. Pain, but muted. Horse opened his eyes slowly, taking in a blurry room and a bright white light. A woman stood over him, asking him questions. He tried to answer, telling her his name, but he was so damned tired. He needed to sleep.

"Wake up, asshole. You're late for church. No excuses."

Shit. Had he slept in?

Horse opened his eyes, blinking rapidly, trying to focus. Not his room...hospital. Had to be a hospital. It came back to him in a rush—he'd been with Marie and then somebody shot him.

"Did they get Marie?" he demanded, but it came out in a whisper. Fucking pussy, he couldn't even talk. He hated feeling weak.

"Marie is safe," Picnic said, stepping into Horse's line of sight. Horse studied his face to make sure the man wasn't lying to him. "She's in jail right now. Our guy's arranging bail. He says that if the ballistics match her story, they probably won't charge her with anything. She'd be out already but they're pissed that she's stonewalling about why her brother and Max were fighting."

"Jail?" he asked, confused.

"Marie shot Max," Picnic said, his face grim. Horse wrinkled his forehead. "Ruger's in there too. Hands covered in blood so they arrested him. He had to tackle your girl to get the gun away from her. She'd gone all *Pulp Fiction* on us, ready to defend you by killing all of us if she had to. Crouched over your body like Wonder Woman. Gives me a boner just thinking about it."

"You're the asshole. Why would she shoot Max?" Horse asked, every word grating against his sore throat. Had the bullet hit his mouth, for fuck's sake? Why couldn't he talk right?

"Max shot you in the back," Picnic said shortly. "And then he shot Jensen. Marie was probably next—she told our guy that Max was getting ready to finish you off when she took him out. Kid is like a fucking commando, never saw that coming. Shot him seven times."

"Fuck," Horse muttered, feeling himself smile. "Damn, that's amazing. My girl's a one-woman army."

"No shit," Picnic said, shaking his head. "Took care of business, no question about that. Hey, gotta ask you something important."

"What's that?"

Picnic leaned over and spoke softly.

"Cops found all kinds of papers," he said. "No idea what was in them, but Marie told the lawyer they were talking about money transfers. Jensen said it was all set up. Could we be in trouble?"

Horse wrinkled his forehead, trying to think.

"I changed everything after we found out about Jensen," he said. "New accounts, the whole thing, a lot more than just passwords and shit like that. Shouldn't have been traceable."

"Wonder what he was talking about?"

Horse searched his memory, which was way too hard. Must be on drugs, he realized. Something hovered just out of reach, something he knew was important. Then it came to him.

"We're good," he said, smiling.

"How's that?"

"Max was in the office the last time I printed out a list of the overseas account numbers and contact information," he said. "Told him I was making dupes for the lockbox. Probably left to take a piss or something and he copied them. Bet he thought he'd hit the jackpot."

"Tell me that isn't as bad as it sounds, bro."

Horse tried to shake his head, but it didn't work.

"They were dummies," he replied, savoring the moment. "You know I like to fuck with the cops. Couple times a year I update my fake accounts and ledgers, make 'em realistic enough that if we ever get raided they'll be chasing their tails for months. I never told Jensen, and Max sure as fuck wouldn't know. Max gave him accounts with about five grand in them. Just enough to trick someone trying to do a test transfer, you know? Little game I like to play, extra insurance...guess it worked out."

"Jesus Christ... Thank fuck for that," Picnic said.

"Nope, not Jesus, just a man," Horse whispered. "Although when women see my dick for the first time, they've been known to fall down on their knees and worship me."

Picnic laughed.

"Yeah, you're gonna live," he said. "Ego's too big to die. Cops'll want to talk to you at some point. Tell 'em you can't remember anything beyond being at the party, lawyer says a traumatic head injury can make you forget the hours right before it happened. Yours hit the ground when he shot you. That'll get you off the hook and drive 'em crazy at the same time. I'm gonna call the nurse now, let them know you're awake."

"Wait," Horse said. "Tell me about the Jacks. I miss anything?"

"Nothing yet," Picnic replied. "We'll keep an eye on them, this is just getting started. War's coming. Doubt your girl'll be their target though. Not worth their time to range this far out of their territory if they aren't getting paid."

Horse heard the room door open, and the sounds of a busy hallway behind it.

"Hey, Picnic, I just went down to grab a drink," Dancer said as she walked in. Horse managed to open his eyes again and look at her. She froze, eyes wide, then her face exploded in a huge smile as she rushed over to him. She leaned over to give him a hug, pulling back at the last minute with a grimace. Thank god for that, a hug right now and he'd probably need another gallon of whatever painkiller they'd given him. "Horse! I'm sorry I wasn't here when you woke up. How do you feel? Can he talk?"

"You look like shit," Horse said. "What's wrong with you?"

"My brother got shot, you douche," she said. "I thought you were going to die. Marie saved your life, did he tell you that?"

"Yeah," Horse said, closing his eyes again. Damn he was tired.

"Fuckin' pansy," Picnic said, and Horse heard him laugh, as if from a distance. "Damn woman had to protect him, lazy asshole wouldn't even get up off the ground. Dripping blood, making a mess…"

Horse opened his mouth to tell him to fuck off, but before the words came he was out again.

Epilogue
Yakima Valley, eastern Washington
Five months later

ɞ

Marie

I drove past our old elementary school on the way to the church. Jeff and I loved that playground — in the summer Mom would drop us off there before heading in to work a block away. We'd check in with her every couple of hours, feeling very mature. The familiar ache of sorrow and loss hit me, a stealth attack.

I missed him.

Jeff'd been messed up, way more messed up than I'd realized, but that didn't change that he was my brother or that I'd watched him die right in front of my eyes. At least the nightmares were getting better. For the first few weeks I'd been terrified to sleep because he'd visit me at night, accusing me of killing him while his brains dribbled out his mouth. Thankfully, I hadn't had one of those nightmares for two months now and most days I didn't even think of him.

Today wasn't like other days though.

I pulled into the parking lot and grabbed my dress bag. Mom was going to be pissed — I was supposed to be there almost forty-five minutes ago but I'd been delayed. The church coordinator glared at me as I walked in, grabbing my arm and rushing me downstairs to the bathroom. There I found my mother looking like a dream in an elegant, Grecian-style, peach-colored wedding dress.

"Oh Mama," I said, feeling tears spring to my eyes. "You look so beautiful. John's gonna die when he sees you."

293

Her face crumpled at the word "die" and I swore under my breath. Mom was fragile these days and I still wasn't sure how to deal with that. I was used to her being the strong one, because she'd suffered so much and always survived. Now I'd become the strong survivor.

"You need to get dressed," she said, forcing herself to smile again. Joanie, her longtime beautician, clucked at Mom to sit down so she could finish up her makeup. Her hair was already done, swept up in keeping with the Grecian style, little ribbons woven through it along with fresh flowers.

An hour later we waited in the back of the church. The last of the guests were inside and then John came out to stand at the altar. The music started and I reached over to take Mama's hand, squeezing it. John's daughter Carla walked ahead of us carrying white lilies. She was hard to read and I still wasn't quite sure how she felt about our families being joined. I guess it didn't matter, because she wanted her dad to be happy and that was enough to make her overlook our oddities. The wedding march started and I took Mama's hand to give her away.

It should have been Jeff's job.

I wondered if he could see us from wherever people go after they die. I hoped he knew Mama was finally happy. Then I stopped thinking about Jeff because the stunned, almost worshipful look on John's face as we came down the aisle filled my heart. I put their hands together, popping up on my toes to kiss first his cheek and then hers. I liked him. I liked him a lot, actually. He adored my mother and the feeling was mutual.

I stepped back and took my spot next to her as maid of honor. The minister started talking and that's when I let myself look over at Horse for the first time. He stood strong and tall next to John's grown son, Paulson. They wore matching tuxes, which I'd never imagined Horse would be willing to tolerate. He'd done it with grace though, telling me I'd find a way to pay him back.

I blushed, because that's why I'd been late. He'd already started collecting.

They held the reception in the old Eagles lodge, where John was a lifelong member. Their first dance together was beautiful, and somehow Mama resisted the urge to smash cake on John's face. She hadn't been married to my father, so this was her first wedding. That seemed to please John in some weird way. I guess he liked the idea of being her only husband. Horse held my hand all through dinner, stealing little glances at me when he thought I wasn't paying attention. It made me a little nervous—I knew him well enough to realize he was up to something. That could be very good. Once when he'd gotten that look, he'd taken me up to Canada for a surprise weekend at a gorgeous bed-and-breakfast.

Of course, last week I'd seen that look on his face the instant before Maggs dumped a bucket of water on me from the second floor of the armory.

I stood talking to Denise next to the dance floor when he struck, throwing me over his shoulder and carrying me out of the room to cheers and whistles. My mom's voice was the loudest, something we'd be having words about later. I squawked as he hauled me up the stairs and out onto the roof. Then he set me down and I saw a blanket covered with red rose petals.

My eyebrows raised.

"I get that this is probably some romantic gesture, but what have you done with my old man?" I demanded, looking at him with narrowed eyes. "This isn't your style, babe."

Horse grinned, looking almost sheepish. Wow. Didn't know Reapers could do sheepish.

"Your mom's idea," he said. "She said I couldn't be trusted not to fuck things up. This is the price I paid to keep her from following us up here. C'mon."

He took my hand and led me over to the blanket, standing in front of me and kissing my lips very softly. Then to my utter shock he lowered himself to one knee and took my hand.

"I feel like an asshole because this is so corny," he said, shaking his head. He started to get back up and I grabbed his shoulders, pushing them down hard.

"Ouch," he said, glaring at me.

"Just say it," I burst out, glaring back at him. "Don't make me get my gun."

"Fuck, am I ever going to live that down?" he asked, shaking his head. "You know they're calling me your bitch at the armory now, does that make you happy?"

"I'm aware. Not my fault I had to save your big, bad, biker ass. You know what they say with guys who—"

"Shut the fuck up, Marie," Horse said, rolling his eyes. "You gonna let me do this or what?"

"Okay," I replied, feeling a little giddy. Sure it was corny, but it also kicked ass.

"Marie Caroline Jensen, will you do me the honor of being my permanent bitch?"

I smacked him on the side of his head as he burst out laughing, then aimed my foot for his nuts. He grabbed me, shoving me down onto the blanket and covering me with his body, still shaking with laughter.

"You're going to ruin my dress."

"I guess your mom was right—I am fucking this up."

"Do it right or I'll say no."

"Marie Caroline Jensen, will you marry me?" he asked suddenly, looking right into my eyes. I bit my lip, trying to decide how long to drag it out. Maybe a little longer…he'd used the "b" word, I should probably make him suffer. I looked away, refusing to meet his eyes as he stopped laughing and grew still.

"Marie?" he asked, his voice suddenly strained. "Oh fuck, don't do this to me, please. I—"

296

"Yes," I said, catching his eye and smirking. "I'll marry your big, dumb ass but only because you said the magic word."

"Fuck? You're right, that is a magic word. Let's test it out."

I burst out laughing, which only lasted for a few seconds before his mouth took mine, kissing me deeply. I felt the length of his erection between my legs and realized that whatever damage he'd already done to my outfit was probably just the beginning.

He stopped kissing me long enough to lift himself and pull up my dress. That's when he discovered I'd left my panties off. He growled in approval as I giggled, covering his face with kisses while he fumbled with his fly. Then his cock was out and pressing into me, sliding into my wet depths with a singular focus that drove me crazy.

Horse thrust into me over and over, touching me deeper than I'd imagined possible before him. I wrapped my legs up and around his waist, holding him to me and tilting my pelvis just the right way to make the most of his hard length.

"Can't believe you're stupid enough to marry me," Horse muttered, sitting up and lifting my hips, one of my favorite positions because now every stroke drew the round lip of his cock head across my G-spot with a force that drove me insane. He knew it too, and he grinned at me as I flew over the edge, moaning and arching my back. Two more strokes and he followed, spurting deep inside.

We came down together, panting under the stars, the faint sound of Mom's reception floating up from the open windows below. After what seemed like forever, Horse sat up and I joined him, pulling down my dress as demurely as possible considering I'd just been fucked senseless on a roof. I brought my knees to my chest and wrapped my arms around them, looking out over the lights of the valley.

"No second thoughts, right?" he asked.

"No second thoughts," I said, feeling warm and happy all over. Then I held up my left hand. "Did you forget something?"

Horse smiled at me, looking very pleased with himself again.

"Yeah, I brought it for you." He stood up and walked over to one of the rooftop air conditioning units. He grabbed a small, black bag and brought it back to me, dropping down onto the blanket. Then he reached in and pulled out a box.

A too-big box.

I narrowed my eyes and took it from him to discover that—in addition to being too big for a ring—it was way too heavy. I opened it and found a large, semi-automatic black pistol.

"It's a .38," he said proudly. "I know you're a .22 girl, but it's time for us to take the next step in our relationship. I think if you start practicing you'll get used to the feel of it. This is a great piece because—"

"I swear if you say one more word I'm shooting you," I growled, thoroughly disgusted. Of course he'd buy me an engagement gun.

Stupid biker.

"At least take it out of the box and see how it feels in your hand."

I shrugged and picked it up, wondering how many anniversaries we'd have before I needed my own private bunker to store my weapons. But as I pulled it out, a beautiful, sparkling silver engagement ring came with it, tied to the trigger with a short thread. It was gorgeous, not so big that it was tasteless but still absolutely stunning. It held a large blue sapphire with small diamonds on either side. I loved it instantly. Horse pulled it loose and I held out my hand for him to put it on. Then he took my chin and looked right in my eyes.

"Love you, babe. Are you still planning to shoot me?"

"Love you too," I replied, grinning at him. "I haven't decided yet about shooting you though. I'll get back to you on that."

"So you want to stay up here a little longer, just the two of us? Or do you want to go downstairs and show your mom your new bling?"

I laughed at him, leaning against his side as he wrapped an arm around me.

"Does it make me a horrible, shallow person that I want to go flash this thing around to everyone?"

"I'm fine with that," he replied, kissing the top of my head. "Then you need to call Maggs and Em—it took everything I had to keep them from crashing the reception. They're having a party for us when we get back to Coeur d'Alene. Picnic wants you to make potato salad. I told him no fucking way you're cooking for your own engagement party."

"Really?" I asked. He shook his head.

"Naw, I told him I'd do whatever it took. Love that shit. It's the bacon that really sets it apart."

"Baby!" my mom squealed, rushing out onto the roof. John followed her, along with Denise. "I'm sorry, but I couldn't wait. Tell me all about it! Did he screw it up?"

"Go on, go to your mom," Horse said, rolling his eyes. He stood and took my hand, lifting me to my feet. Then he smacked my ass, pushing me toward my mom and her new husband. "But when she's done with you I'm taking you home to celebrate."

I lifted to my toes to kiss him and then ran over to show Mama my new ring. I decided to leave the gun with Horse.

At least for now.

Also by Joanna Wylde

ଌ

About Joanna Wylde

ഔ

Joanna Wylde is a freelance writer and a voracious reader.

ഔ

The author welcomes comments from readers. You can find her website and email address on her author bio page at www.ellorascave.com.

Tell Us What You Think

We appreciate hearing reader opinions about our books. You can email us at Service@ellorascave.com (when contacting Customer Service, be sure to state the book title and author).

Why an electronic book?

We live in the Information Age — an exciting time in the history of human civilization, in which technology rules supreme and continues to progress in leaps and bounds every minute of every day. For a multitude of reasons, more and more avid literary fans are opting to purchase e-books instead of paper books. The question from those not yet initiated into the world of electronic reading is simply: *Why?*

1. *Price.* An electronic title at Ellora's Cave Publishing runs anywhere from 40% to 75% less than the cover price of the exact same title in paperback format. Why? Basic mathematics and cost. It is less expensive to publish an e-book (no paper and printing, no warehousing and shipping) than it is to publish a paperback, so the savings are passed along to the consumer.

2. *Space.* Running out of room in your house for your books? That is one worry you will never have with electronic books. For a low one-time cost, you can purchase a handheld device specifically designed for e-reading. Many e-readers have large, convenient screens for viewing. Better yet, hundreds of titles can be stored within your new library — on a single microchip. There are a variety of e-readers from different manufacturers. You can also read e-books on your PC or laptop computer. (Please note that Ellora's Cave does not endorse any specific brands.

You can check our website at www.ellorascave.com for information we make available to new consumers.)

3. *Mobility.* Because your new e-library consists of only a microchip within a small, easily transportable e-reader, your entire cache of books can be taken with you wherever you go.

4. *Personal Viewing Preferences.* Are the words you are currently reading too small? Too large? Too… ANNOYING? Paperback books cannot be modified according to personal preferences, but e-books can.

5. *Instant Gratification.* Is it the middle of the night and all the bookstores near you are closed? Are you tired of waiting days, sometimes weeks, for bookstores to ship the novels you bought? Ellora's Cave Publishing sells instantaneous downloads twenty-four hours a day, seven days a week, every day of the year. Our webstore is never closed. Our e-book delivery system is 100% automated, meaning your order is filled as soon as you pay for it.

Those are a few of the top reasons why electronic books are replacing paperbacks for many avid readers.

As always, Ellora's Cave welcomes your questions and comments. We invite you to email us at Service@ellorascave.com or write to us directly at Ellora's Cave Publishing Inc., 1056 Home Avenue, Akron, OH 44310-3502.

Make each day more *EXCITING* With our

Ellora's
Cavemen
Calendar

www.EllorasCave.com

ELLORA'S CAVE
Romanticon

Annual convention
for women who
refuse to behave

www.ECRomanticon.com
For additional info contact: conventions@ellorascave.com

2-14

CPSIA information can be obtained at www.ICGtesting.com
Printed in the USA
LVOW11s1543100214

373092LV00002B/428/P

9 781419 970290